The V...

3 MAY 20..

Jean Plaidy, one of the pre-e... ... of historical fiction for most of the twentieth cen... is the pen name of the prolific English author Eleanor Hibbert, also known as Victoria Holt. Jean Plaidy's novels had sold more than 14 million copies worldwide by the time of her death in 1993.

For further information about our Jean Plaidy reissues and mailing list, please visit
www.randomhouse.co.uk/minisites/jeanplaidy

Praise for Jean Plaidy

'Plaidy excels at blending history with romance and drama'
New York Times

'Outstanding'
Vanity Fair

'Full-blooded, dramatic, exciting'
Observer

'Plaidy has brought the past to life'
Times Literary Supplement

'One of our best historical novelists'
News Chronicle

Further titles available in Arrow by Jean Plaidy

The Tudors
Uneasy Lies the Head
Katharine, the Virgin
Widow
The Shadow of the
Pomegranate
The King's Secret Matter
Murder Most Royal
St Thomas's Eve
The Sixth Wife
The Thistle and the Rose
Mary Queen of France
Lord Robert
Royal Road to Fotheringay
The Captive Queen of Scots

The Medici Trilogy
Madame Serpent
The Italian Woman
Queen Jezebel

The Plantagenets
The Plantagenet Prelude
The Revolt of the Eaglets
The Heart of the Lion
The Prince of Darkness

The Battle of the Queens
The Queen from Provence
The Hammer of the Scots
The Follies of the King
The Vow on the Heron
Passage to Pontefract
The Star of Lancaster

The French Revolution
Louis the Well-Beloved
The Road to Compiègne
Flaunting, Extravagant
Queen

**The Isabella and
Ferdinand Trilogy**
Castile for Isabella
Spain for the Sovereigns
Daughters of Spain

The Victorians
The Captive of Kensington
Palace
The Queen and Lord M
The Queen's Husband
The Widow of Windsor

The Vow on the Heron

JEAN PLAIDY

arrow books

Published by Arrow Books 2009

6 8 10 9 7 5

Copyright © Jean Plaidy, 1980

Initial lettering copyright © Stephen Raw, 2008

The Estate of Eleanor Hibbert has asserted its right
to have Jean Plaidy identified as the author of this work.

First published in Great Britain in 1980 by Robert Hale and Company

The Random House Group Limited
20 Vauxhall Bridge Road, London, SW1V 2SA

www.rbooks.co.uk

Addresses for companies within The Random House Group Limited can be found at:
www.randomhouse.co.uk/offices.htm

The Random House Group Limited Reg. No. 954009

A CIP catalogue record for this book is available from the British Library

ISBN 9780099533061

The Random House Group Limited supports The Forest Stewardship
Council® (FSC®), the leading international forest-certification organisation.
Our books carrying the FSC label are printed on FSC®-certified paper.
FSC is the only forest-certification scheme supported by the leading
environmental organisations, including Greenpeace. Our
paper procurement policy can be found at
www.randomhouse.co.uk/environment

MIX
Paper from
responsible sources
FSC® C016897

Typeset by SX Composing DTP, Rayleigh, Essex
Printed and bound in Great Britain by Clays Ltd, St Ives PLC

❀ Contents ❀

I	The Haunted Queen	1
II	The Scottish Adventure	5
III	The King's Bride	33
IV	Treachery at Corfe Castle	62
V	The End of Mortimer	95
VI	The Marriage of Eleanor	111
VII	The Exiles of Château Gaillard	136
VIII	The King and the Heron	172
IX	Joanna's Betrothal	189
X	Trouble at the Tower	225
XI	The King Falls in Love	243
XII	The Joust at Windsor	272
XIII	Crécy	290
XIV	Neville's Cross	307
XV	Jilted	321
XVI	The Burghers of Calais	333
XVII	The Black Death	344
XVIII	The Pride of Isabella	367
XIX	Poitiers	380
XX	Murder in Melrose	403
XXI	The Marriage of the Black Prince	419
XXII	Isabella and De Coucy	436
XXIII	The Passing of Philippa	442
XXIV	The Lady of the Sun and the Old Man	449
	Bibliography	469

THE PLANTAGENETS

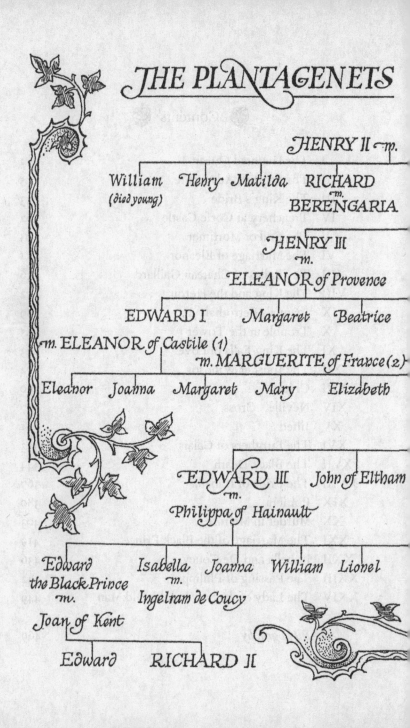

HENRY II *m.*

William (died young)　Henry　Matilda　RICHARD *m.* BERENGARIA

HENRY III *m.* ELEANOR of Provence

EDWARD I *m.* ELEANOR of Castile (1) *m.* MARGUERITE of France (2)　Margaret　Beatrice

Eleanor　Joanna　Margaret　Mary　Elizabeth

EDWARD III *m.* Philippa of Hainault　John of Eltham

Edward the Black Prince *m.* Joan of Kent　Isabella *m.* Ingelram de Coucy　Joanna　William　Lionel

Edward　RICHARD II

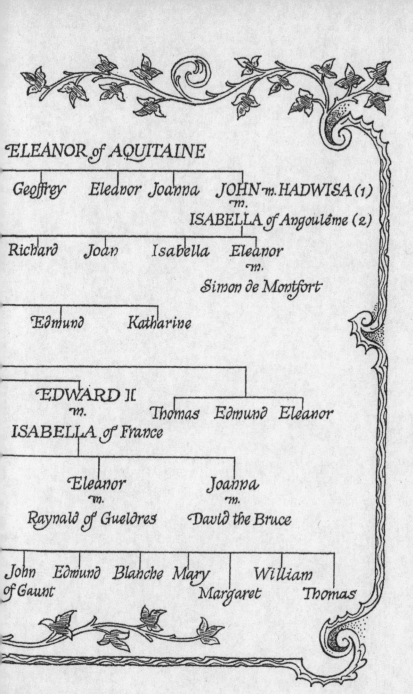

ELEANOR of AQUITAINE

Geoffrey   Eleanor   Joanna   JOHN m. HADWISA (1)
                                    m.
                              ISABELLA of Angoulême (2)

Richard   Joan   Isabella   Eleanor
                                    m.
                              Simon de Montfort

        Edmund   Katharine

        EDWARD II
            m.   Thomas Edmund Eleanor
    ISABELLA of France

            Eleanor   Joanna
                m.   m.
    Raynald of Gueldres   David the Bruce

John   Edmund   Blanche Mary   William
of Gaunt   Margaret   Thomas

Chapter I

THE HAUNTED QUEEN

In the ancient castle of York, Queen Isabella lay sleepless beside her lover. There was nothing to fear, he assured her. This castle of York, this great fortress which was said to have been built by the Conqueror, with its deep moat, its drawbridge and its palisades, was invulnerable. The watch from the top of Clifford's Tower would warn them of the approach of any enemy; none could break through the massive stone walls, and those circular turrets. But it was not an invading army Isabella feared; it was the ghost of her murdered husband.

Since they had brought her the news of that night when his agonised screams had been heard, so she was told, even by those outside the walls of Berkeley Castle this terrible unease had settled upon her. Sometimes she would awake and fancy she saw a tall shape in the room. He had been a tall man and she would picture his face in the darkness distorted by an expression of hideous anguish. Sometimes she dreamed that his lips moved and that he uttered curses on those who had condemned him to such a brutal death. In the sighing of the wind she heard his voice.

'Isabella, you are the guilty one . . . you . . . with your lover Mortimer. I know he was your paramour. I know you live with him in blatant sin, you, the She Wolf of France. How long did you deceive me? How long did you plan my murder?'

How long? she thought. As soon as it had become necessary. You blame me. Have you forgotten the way you treated *me* . . . how you humiliated me and passed me over, when I was ready to love you, ignored me to be with your pretty boys? You deserved what came to you.

No, not that. No one could deserve such a death. Why did they have to do it in such a way?

She pictured the sly face of Ogle. 'But, my lady, it was on your orders . . . yours and my lord's. No marks on his body. None must know that he had died by any but a natural death.'

It was but a settle she saw in the darkness. It took on its own shape as her eyes grew accustomed to the gloom. Only briefly had she thought it had the shape of a man and was Edward come forth from the grave to mock her. But because he lived on in her mind, he would not let her forget him and he came unbidden . . . in the dead of night.

'Mortimer,' she whispered, 'are you awake? Gentle Mortimer, wake up for me.'

Gentle Mortimer sighing turned his big body to face her. 'What is it, my love?' he murmured sleepily. 'More dreams?'

'Dreams,' she answered. 'Always dreams.'

'They are of no substance then.'

'I cannot sleep,' said the Queen. 'I think of him there . . . on his bed. They placed a table over him so that he could not move. It was an iron spit red hot in a case of horn to leave no mark . . . and with it they burned his entrails.'

'Death would come quickly,' soothed Mortimer.

2

'And agonisingly,' she answered. 'They say his screams penetrated the walls of Berkeley Castle.'

''Tis nonsense. Remember Berkeley . . . built like a fortress.'

'I would I could forget Berkeley. Mortimer, listen. In the castle they talk. The servants . . . they whisper together.'

'There will always be rumours when a man dies and if he is a king these rumours go on for a while. Give them time. They will pass away.'

'What if they should reach the King's ears?'

'He would never believe them. We could deal with that. Has he not always listened to you? He is but a child.'

'But he will grow up.'

'By then your husband will be forgotten. Your son will have heard of his father's death by now.'

'Messengers were sent to him and they will surely have reached him. He will be told that his father died peacefully in Berkeley Castle, and that he had been ailing for some time.'

'By God, how he clung to life!'

'Making it necessary to remove him, I know, but the means . . .'

'Now Isabella, my queen, you must not dwell on this. It would have been swift, I know. Young Edward will accept what he is told. He has his own wounds to nurse just now. The peace with Scotland will occupy him. This little exercise should humble him a little, should show him how much he depends upon us. I believe he thought he was marching north to glory.'

'There is something about the boy, Mortimer. Something his father never had.'

'God be praised for that.'

3

'I have heard it said that he has a look of his grandfather.'

'I doubt the First Edward would have made much of a ruler at the age of fourteen.'

'He is growing up fast.'

'But he has a lot of growing to do yet. Isabella, my love, stop plaguing yourself. All is well. Think of the plans we made. Think of our victories. Here we are . . . rulers of this realm. They did not make us regents, did they, but we outwitted them. The King is ours to guide and that is how we wanted it to be. Come, take heart. We shall never be troubled by your husband. He is dead. Forget him. He is no longer of importance. Rumour. There are always rumours. But we are strong enough to quell them. He was a danger to us. He had to die. It was better for the sake of the country that he did so. Now we have our third Edward, your promising son, who has much to learn and I promise you this, he will return from his Scottish enterprise considerably chastened and he will turn to us and we shall continue to guide him. That is how it will be, my Queen. Leave it to your gentle Mortimer.'

'Oh gentle Mortimer, you comfort me as always. Soothe me now to sleep and all my fears will be gone by morning.'

But it was not so, for very soon the ghost of her murdered husband was back to haunt her.

🌹 Chapter II 🌹

THE SCOTTISH ADVENTURE

When young Edward, a few weeks after his coronation, had ridden out at the head of his army to meet the Scots his father had been alive, and Edward believed comfortably lodged in Kenilworth Castle as the guest of his cousin, the Earl of Lancaster.

It was somewhat disconcerting to find oneself a king at the age of fourteen, but Edward had always been aware of his destiny and was determined to show them that he could be his grandfather all over again. Throughout his life he had been compared with his grandfather. 'He grows more like Great Edward every day.' How often had he heard that whispered. It was never 'How like his father.' And he had learned that that would not have been a compliment, for he had realised that all was not well with his father.

He had never really felt at ease with the tall fair-haired handsome man who had always been kind to him, though often absent-minded as though, much as he delighted in his son, he was not really interested in him. Hugh le Despenser was constantly with him and it seemed to the boy that they shared private jokes and that anyone who came near them was intruding.

When he had joined his mother in France he had been ready to believe that his father was not a good man and to accept the fact that she could no longer love him. There had been so many to convince him that she was right. Roger de Mortimer, Earl of Wigmore and now the Earl of March, was one of them and, although there was something about Mortimer which he did not like, the Earl was a powerful man with a convincing way with him and his mother said that he was their most faithful friend.

Sir John of Hainault was another and he was a great soldier. Then there were his uncles, the Dukes of Kent and Norfolk. They had come to help her; and with so many supporters and the people of England acclaiming her, he was certain that she had done right when she came to England with an army and his father was forced to give up the crown.

Then had come the moment when he had had to make his decision and something had told him that he must not take that which was his father's unless his father first gave his consent; and it was not until they came to him with his father's agreement that he had allowed himself to be crowned. It was his first act of defiance and it had surprised them a little. It had taken a certain firmness to insist on that but being about to become a king he was determined to act like one.

Almost immediately he was setting out on the Scottish campaign for Robert the Bruce had agreed to meet him to discuss peace terms. Robert the Bruce was a man he had heard mentioned throughout his childhood and he knew that there was a leader to be reckoned with in spite of the fact that, according to rumour, he was dying of leprosy, which was probably the reason why he wanted a permanent peace. He was a bold man and it was soon realised that in spite of his desire for peace he was determined to have it on his own terms and if he could not achieve this then he would invade England. For this purpose he had gathered together a large army and there must only be one reply to this. Edward must march at the head of *his* army and be ready for action if the talks should fail.

Newly crowned and with the knowledge that his father was the guest of his cousin the Earl of Lancaster in Kenilworth he had set out for the North. With him and his army came his mother and Mortimer, his eleven-year-old brother John, and his two sisters, nine-year-old Eleanor and six-year-old Joanna. They would not of course go into battle with the army but remain in York while the troops, with Edward at their head, marched up to the Border and into Scotland.

They had been joined by Sir John of Hainault, a rather exuberant romantic-minded knight, brother of the Count of Hainault, who had taken pity on Queen Isabella when she was exiled from her brother's country of France and needed help to begin the invasion of England. Sir John was so overcome with admiration that he had persuaded his brother to provide the money for Isabella and Mortimer to raise an army.

That was not entirely the truth. There had been an understanding between Isabella and the Count of Hainault and it concerned Edward's marriage. They had bargained in secret and strangely enough Edward had felt no resentment and this for a very special reason. When he had arrived at the Court of Hainault, after having somewhat humiliatingly left the French Court where they had become unwelcome guests, Edward had enjoyed one of the most pleasant weeks of his life. This was due to the happy time he had spent with the Count's four charming daughters, and there was one of these daughters who had become his special friend. That was Philippa. He had found her elder sister Margaret charming and her two younger sisters Jeanne and

Isabella pleasing; but it was Philippa who had affected him most deeply. She was a tall girl, brown-haired, brown-eyed and with a dazzling pink-and-white complexion, and he had been struck by a certain simplicity lacking in the girls of her age he had met at the Court of France. Not that she was by any means stupid, far from it. She was lively and laughed easily and was so frankly honest that he could not help being charmed by her. Perhaps too his delight in her company was enhanced by her admiration for him. When he had left Hainault she had astonished everyone by bursting into tears because she had to say goodbye to him; and she did this before her parents and their entourage who had gathered together to wish him, his mother and their followers well.

So the fact that his mother had contrived to get the means to raise an army from the Count of Hainault on the condition that her son should marry one of his daughters, and the money supplied was in truth the dowry of that daughter, did not greatly perturb Edward.

One thing he would insist on was that when one of the Hainault girls was chosen for him that girl would have to be Philippa.

When he thought of Philippa and his marriage which must take place soon he felt a rising exultation. It was true he was not yet fifteen but his age would be no deterrent. Philippa was some months younger than he was but when they had ridden out together and he had come to know her he had seen that she was as ready for marriage as he was. It would be gratifying to offer her the crown of England, and he wanted to return from Scotland a conqueror. When he thought of these matters he could easily suppress uneasy thoughts about his father. Had he not given up the crown of his own free will? He preferred a life of ease at Kenilworth in the company of his cousin Lancaster to ruling a country. There was no need to wonder or worry about him. He had always been rather strange, different from other men; and the Queen had assured him that all had been done for the best.

He could believe that, and when Philippa came to him it would be wonderful to have her crowned as his Queen.

Once this Scottish matter was over he would insist on marriage and that his bride must be Philippa of Hainault.

He welcomed Sir John to York. He was delighted to see him not only because he was Philippa's uncle but because he came with a great army.

His mother greeted Sir John with great affection. She would never forget what he had done for her and she constantly told him so. Sir John was in love with the Queen which made the situation charmingly romantic.

Edward found his mother in her private chamber. Roger de Mortimer was with her. It was becoming more and more impossible to see his mother without Mortimer's being there too.

'My dearest son,' said the Queen embracing him, 'is it not good to see these men of Hainault in the town?'

'I welcome them,' replied Edward.

'They have been good friends to us,' commented Mortimer. He was a little forward, Edward thought. He behaved as though he were a member of the family. Mortimer's manner often irritated him, but his mother did not seem to notice that there was anything wrong and Edward felt too unsure of himself to show he was aware of it.

'Indeed, it is so,' said Edward with a certain hauteur. 'The Count of Hainault proved himself most hospitable to us.'

'At a time we most needed it,' went on the Queen. 'Now I would show similar hospitality to Sir John. I am arranging a banquet to welcome them to York.'

9

Young Edward inclined his head. Perhaps they should have asked his permission first. Not his own mother surely! He was of course the King but he had to be guided by them in most things. It was not so bad when it came from his mother, but he was not sure that he liked to see Mortimer there all the time nodding as though he himself had been the main judge in what should be done. He wondered whether he should speak to his mother about Mortimer. Whenever she mentioned the man there would be a very special note in her voice. What was it? Respect? Admiration? Affection? Well perhaps Mortimer *had* stood by her when she most needed friends.

'Sir John will be lodged in an abbey belonging to the White Monks,' said Mortimer. 'His men will be close by in quarters allotted to them. It is well not to have them too close to our English troops.'

Edward looked puzzled.

'There has been a certain amount of friction,' explained the Queen. 'The Flemings do certain things differently from the English and it seems that people are inclined to sneer at those who are not exactly like themselves. A strange trait of human nature . . . but one commonly found I believe.'

'How stupid,' said Edward.

Mortimer smiled his slow rather patronising smile. ' 'Tis so, my lord, but so many things in life are.'

As though, thought the King, reminding me that I have much to learn.

'Where is the banquet to take place?'

'In the house of the Friars Minor,' his mother told him. 'It seemed suitable – both the Earl of March and I were of the opinion that it was the best place.'

The Earl of March! Roger de Mortimer. He was nothing but

a Marcher Baron until he made his escape from the Tower – where he was being held a prisoner – and was joined by the Queen in France. Then they had gone to Hainault and found help there and come to England, as a result of which his father was a guest at Kenilworth Castle and he was a king.

'Sir John has been invited?' he asked coolly.

'Yes,' replied his mother. 'And he is delighted.'

'Perhaps it would have been proper for the invitation to have come from me.'

'My lord,' cried Mortimer with mock consternation, 'but of course it was given in your name.'

'Without my knowledge!'

'Such a trivial matter seemed far beneath the notice of the King, my lord.'

Mortimer was smiling that rather sly smile. His mother laid a hand on his arm. 'You have no objection to this banquet, Edward?' she asked anxiously.

'Oh no, no. It is merely that . . .'

He looked from one to the other. They managed to assume expressions of concern. He was unsure. Oh how he wished he were not fourteen years old. He had the feeling though that Mortimer was laughing at him.

He said quietly: 'I shall be glad to welcome Sir John and his men to the House of the Friars Minor.'

There was a certain tension in the hall of the House of Friars Minor. In the centre of the table on the dais sat the King and on one side of him was Sir John, on the other his mother. Beside his mother was Roger de Mortimer and men of rank made up the rest of the table.

From the tables in the main body of the hall it soon became obvious that the men of Hainault did not mix with the English. It was almost as though two enemies had met for a banquet rather than two allies, for it was impossible not to be aware of the contemptuous looks they bestowed on each other and Edward heard a few insults flung from one side of the hall to the other.

The Queen did not appear to notice. She was chatting amiably with Mortimer, but Sir John was alert.

He whispered to the King that his men were getting restive. They had been away from home too long.

'After this campaign,' he added, 'they must be disbanded. They need to go home to their families.'

'We should not be long in Scotland,' said Edward. 'They say Robert the Bruce is a sick man.'

'A sick man,' agreed Sir John, and added: 'but a shrewd one. Let us not delude ourselves into thinking this will be an easy victory.'

'I am determined to win back all that my grandfather won.'

'Yes, my lord, you will be another such as he was. It was a pity so much won with blood and toil should have been so quickly lost.'

It was another reproach to his father, Edward knew; and he was not displeased because it was a further justification of what had happened. It was good that he was the King. He was going to be all that his grandfather had been . . . and perhaps . . . Yes, it was a dream of his that he might even surpass him.

At that moment two men who were playing dice at one of the tables stood up and faced each other. Suddenly a stool went flying through the air. It hit one of the men and he fell. That was the signal. For a few seconds Edward watched dismayed.

Sir John, the Queen and Mortimer were equally and silently disturbed.

Mortimer cried out in a loud voice: 'Stop that. By God, any man who brings his quarrels before the King condemns himself as a traitor.'

That should have sobered them. The traitor's death of hanging, drawing and quartering was the most dreaded end which could befall any man. But it had no effect on these men. In a matter of seconds the quarrel between two men had become a general brawl and the hall was quickly becoming a battle field.

Edward rose to his feet and shouted: 'Order! In the name of the King . . .'

But his voice was lost. They did not hear it and even if they had he knew that they would have ignored him.

He felt frustrated and angry. A moment before he had seen himself as a triumphant king whose word was law. How different was the reality. He was only a young boy who shouted in vain and whose voice could not even be heard above the cries of battle.

It was Sir John and Mortimer who strode into the crowd. Edward would have followed them but his mother held him back.

'Release me, my lady,' he said authoritatively.

But she clung to him. 'They are in a dangerous mood, my son, I fear.'

He wrenched himself free and ran into the main part of the hall shouting: 'Desist. Desist I say. The King commands it.'

But it was Mortimer and Sir John who called order by shouting to their men to rally to them and stop their senseless fighting. It was some five minutes before there was quiet in the hall.

Then it was possible to see that in the sudden brief battle several men had been killed and many wounded.

Sir John cried out: 'Shame. You have come to fight the Scots not each other.'

His words were greeted with silence but the sullen looks of the Hainaulters and the truculent ones of the English as they surveyed each other showed that they were by no means penitent, nor were they ready to tolerate each other.

The King standing there felt young and inadequate. He had been unable to call a halt to the fighting and these men had dared to let it happen in his presence.

They would never have dared to do that before his grandfather.

And nor shall they before me again, he promised himself. How tragic it was to be a king and but fourteen.

The uneasy tension between the allies persisted.

Sir John talked a great deal to the young King and Edward listened. The affray had taught him that he had more to learn of warfare than he had realised. He was determined to be a great soldier; therefore he must learn all he could; he must forget he was a king and become a pupil; and he must never be too proud to listen. Sir John was a seasoned warrior. He had much to impart.

'The trouble with these men is that they have no heart for the fight,' he explained. 'They are not fighting in their own land. Men fighting in their land or for a cause in which they believe fight like lions. It is never the same fighting other people's battles. They fought in England because they were fighting for a beautiful lady whose husband had been cruel to her. So they fought well. Men want a motive if they are to fight.'

'The motive of many is to loot and ravage.'

''Tis true, lord King. But such a reason does not bring out heroic deeds. Those men seek an advantage and they will retreat if it is expedient for them to do so. No, my men must go home after this campaign. I have talked with them and I have promised that they shall do this. I said: "Make it a speedy campaign, my friends, and then it will be home."'

'And you think they will fight for that?'

'I do, my lord. This I am sure. Within a few weeks from now we shall have the Scots begging for mercy. Then will follow your fine treaty. Peace with the Scots for you and home for John of Hainault and his army.'

Yes, it was more pleasant talking with Sir John than with Roger de Mortimer. Sir John instructed in a most respectful way. There was something about Mortimer's manner which the King disliked and distrusted.

A few days after the fight in the hall messengers came from the North.

The Scots had crossed the Tyne and were advancing, ravaging the countryside as they passed through it.

'It is time I met Robert the Bruce,' said Edward.

And he with Sir John rode out from York with their armies, leaving behind the Queen and Mortimer with the royal children.

'You will soon be back ... victorious,' said the Queen as she bade her son farewell.

Edward noticed Mortimer standing by watching sardonically. Afterwards Edward thought it was almost as though he had foreknowledge of what was to come.

It was true that Robert the Bruce was a very sick man. The dreaded disease of leprosy was advancing rapidly and he knew that death could not be far off. It was for this reason that he was particularly anxious to make a lasting peace with England. His son David was little more than a baby and he dreaded what would happen to the child, heir to Scotland, when he was left, as he soon surely would be.

Bruce's illness was the result of never sparing himself during a life of hardship. He had lived in damp and draughty camps, and had suffered all the hazards of fighting.

By good fortune there were Scotsmen who were as eager to force the English out of the country as he was and with them he discussed the methods he wished to use against the enemy. The men he trusted most were Thomas Randolph, Earl of Moray, and Sir James Douglas.

Moray, being the son of his sister Isabel, was his nephew. He had played a prominent part at Bannockburn and had always been his uncle's faithful adherent. Douglas had been knighted on the field of Bannockburn and had also proved himself a strong supporter of the Bruce. He was a bold man and fierce fighter and a legend had grown up about him in the north of England. Mothers told naughty children that if they were not good the Black Douglas would get them. He was a flamboyant character, constantly calling attention to himself by some daring deed, and his dark eyes and skin had earned for him the name of Black Douglas which suited his reputation.

It distressed Robert greatly that he was unable to join his army. He was torn between the desire to make the effort and be there to conduct matters perhaps from a camp behind the army, and the fear that his emaciated appearance might undermine the spirit of his soldiers. It was due to his endeavours that the

Scots had driven the English out of Scotland with the magnificent climax at Bannockburn but Bruce was not the man to deceive himself and he knew that the victory had a good deal to do with the fact that Edward the First had died and his ineffectual son had taken his place.

Now he discussed with his two most trusted supporters the plan of action against the English.

'What I want to avoid if it is possible,' said Bruce, 'is direct confrontation.'

'We'd beat them then as we did at Bannockburn,' replied Douglas.

'Perhaps so, James, and perhaps not. It would mean that Scottish blood would be shed and I do not want that if it can be avoided. The advantage is with us. The English came laden with supplies and our men have learned to travel light.'

'Aye,' added Moray. 'A bag of oatmeal and an iron plate to bake it on. That and the cattle we can steal on the way keeps the men well fed.'

''Tis so,' said Bruce, 'and there I stress lies our advantage. My plan is that the English shall not come face to face with our army until we have lured them to that spot where a battle will take place if it cannot be avoided.'

'You mean retreat before them.'

'Not retreat,' answered Bruce. 'I like not that word. We shall leave England with them advancing towards us and as we pass through the English towns and villages we shall take their cattle and lay waste to the land. We shall be elusive. They will never catch up with us. And they will grow weary and exhausted trying to. Our plan should really be to bring about a peace treaty, which will free us from English domination for ever.'

Black Douglas was a little disappointed. He was hoping for another Bannockburn but like Moray he saw the wisdom of the King's remarks. If Scotland was to prosper it needed peace. War might be exciting to such men as Douglas but it was also destructive. Advantageous peace was what the country needed.

'The King of England has two sisters,' went on Bruce. 'They are about the age of my young David. You see what I am leading to. There is nothing like an alliance between countries to bring about a peace.'

Both Moray and Douglas acceded that this was true.

Plans were laid and thus when Edward with Sir John and their armies marched north in pursuit of the Scots they found evidence of them but they could not catch up with them.

They crossed the Tyne. Everywhere were ravaged villages but no Scots. The weather was bad; violent storms raged; the men grew restive and there was sickness in the camp.

'If we could catch up with the Scots and there was a real battle you would see a change in the men,' said Sir John to the King. 'This state of affairs has a debilitating effect on them.'

Edward said: 'It shows that the Scots are afraid of us.'

Sir John shook his head. 'I believe that Robert the Bruce plays a game with us.'

'He is a sick man. He is not with his army.'

'He directs operations, my lord. You can depend on that, and he is a man not easy to beat whether he be on horseback or a sick couch.'

Edward was discovering that war was not the glorious adventure he had envisaged. He had thought it rather like a tournament, a kind of *joust à l'outrance* when the opponents fought to the bitter end. He had visualised glittering armour, lances shimmering in the sun, great deeds of bravery. Instead of this he found sickness, torrential rain, flies, draughty camps and the frustrating habits of the Scots who mockingly were leading them along this exhausting path.

One day a man was brought to Edward's camp by Sir John of Hainault. The man had a story to tell. His name was Rokeby and he had been taken prisoner by the Scots and had consequently spent some time with them.

'As soon as I escaped I made my way straight to your camp, my lord,' said Rokeby. 'I can tell you exactly where you will find the Scots army.'

'Then,' cried Edward, 'we will find them. We will invite them to do battle. Then we shall have our revenge.'

He knighted Rokeby on the spot and as the man knelt to receive the accolade he laughed to himself. Edward was such a child really. He was easily deceived. He would tell Black Douglas that it hardly seemed fair, like cheating a baby.

Douglas would laugh. It had been his idea that Rokeby should bring the English army to the banks of the River Wear, for Douglas said he would have some sport with them.

In due course the army camp was set up on the banks of the River Wear in the county of Durham and true enough on the other side of the river the Scots were encamped.

'Now,' said Edward, 'we shall come to battle and I doubt not the day will be ours.'

'We should think of some way of surprising them,' replied Sir John.

'Nay,' cried Edward. 'I will fight with honour. They are on one side of the river, we on the other. I shall tell them that they must cross to meet us and I should consider it unchivalrous to attack them while they are crossing.'

'My lord king,' said Sir John with mild exasperation, 'this is war.'

'I intend to conduct war in an honourable way,' replied Edward. 'I will tell them that if they prefer us to cross the river we will do and the same terms will apply to us as I have offered them.'

Seasoned warrior John of Hainault shrugged his shoulders. He had come to the conclusion that the Scots were not eager to fight and when he considered the condition of his men, nor was he.

Edward waited for a reply from the messenger who had to ford the river to the Scottish camp. At last it came.

'We are in your kingdom,' it ran. 'We have laid waste to your land. If that displeases you, you must come and attack us. We shall remain where we are as long as it pleases us.'

What were they to do?

Edward said they must in honour now cross the river but Sir John shook his head wearily. 'The men are exhausted,' he explained. 'Supplies are running out. Our men do not travel with a bag of oatmeal and a griddle.'

'Then we must act quickly,' retorted Edward.

Edward had his way and they made plans to cross the river the following day. Through the night Edward lay sleepless. Across the water the light from the Scottish camp fires flickered in the darkness.

'In the morning we shall strike,' thought Edward, 'and victory will be ours. I shall return to my Court and people will no longer smile at my youth and inexperience. They will know that I am not merely a figurehead. I am a true king. I shall cease merely to reign and shall rule.'

But in the morning before he had risen Sir John burst into his tent.

'Come and look,' he said.

Edward followed him out. On the opposite side of the river the Scottish camp fires still smouldered but the army had gone.

❀ ❀ ❀

Again there were spies to tell them where. The Scots were still embanked on the same river but this time in a spot more advantageous to them. It was in a wood known as Stanhope Park, a hunting ground which belonged to the Bishop of Durham.

'The river,' said Sir John, 'is easier to ford here.'

'Then that is why they have moved,' cried Edward. 'Now we must prepare for battle in earnest.'

All through that day the preparations went on and by night time Edward was very tired. The end was nearly in sight he was sure, and as he lay in his tent he thought of returning to London. His first act would be to send for his ministers and tell them that he would not delay his marriage any longer. An agreement had been made with the Count of Hainault that he should marry one of his daughters. Well, he wanted that marriage to take place without delay. They would be pleased. They had always said that a king could not begin to get heirs too soon. It was a pleasant thought. He had discovered already that he was fond of the society of women and he had thought a great deal about Philippa who had clearly considered him to be wonderful. What a pretty girl she was, and she was charming and simple. In fact she was just the wife for him.

He drifted into pleasant sleep thinking of her.

He awakened with a start. There was uproar in the camp. He heard the horses whinnying, sudden shouts, running footsteps.

Then there was a cry of 'A Douglas! A Douglas!' and as Edward leaped to his feet he saw that his tent had started to collapse which meant that someone had cut the ropes. He ran out and as he did so he was aware of a dark-skinned man laughing at him.

One of his guards leaped forward.

'Run, my lord. Run, my lord,' he cried before he fell to the ground with a sword through his body.

Edward acted quickly. He knew what had happened. They had been outwitted by the Scots. Black Douglas had dared come to his tent perhaps to kill him or take him prisoner. The King of England a hostage! He had to run. It was ignoble. It did not fit in with his ideas of kingly actions; but he was unarmed and Black Douglas was waiting to catch him.

Sir John was shouting orders. The English had risen and the small party of Scots led by Black Douglas, which had invaded the English camp made its escape.

Consternation ensued. How had it happened? The watch had been careless. The King might have been killed or taken prisoner.

It seemed that the Scots got the better of them every time. 'This is the last though,' cried Edward. 'Tomorrow we attack.'

Sir John said they would need a day to reorganise. The raid had taken them by surprise and when they did attack the Scots they must be prepared in every way. There must be victory.

Smarting with humiliation, Edward was for immediate action.

He need not have worried. At daybreak it was clear that the Scots had decamped once more. There would be another journey to catch up with them. The Scots had fleet horses. They lacked the beauty of those of the English but they could move a great deal faster unencumbered as they were. Moreover wherever the English went there must go their supplies – saddle horses and wagons were very different from a griddle and a bag of oatmeal. It made progress slow.

News came that the Scots had crossed the Border. Edward knew he could never catch up with them. His men were exhausted, his supplies were running out and there were more quarrels between the English and the Hainaulters. It was a pointless depressing and humiliating experience.

Word came from Robert the Bruce. He would be ready to discuss terms for peace and he hinted at uniting the two countries through marriage. Edward had sisters; he had a son. Peace was often brought about more effectively through unions than battles.

Let there be meetings. Let these matters be discussed. And in the meantime let there be an end to hostilities.

Edward saw that they were right.

In the midst of this a messenger came to him with news from his mother.

His father had died peacefully in Berkeley Castle.

Well, perhaps it was God's will. Poor Edward the Second, his had been a life of failure. Perhaps he was at peace at last. It was a pity that he had not been with him at the end. He would have liked to hear him say again that he thought his son was right in taking the crown.

But he died at peace and it was for the best. Young Edward need no longer suffer the qualms of conscience. He was now truly the King.

But he must return to York where his mother would be waiting for him.

How different it would have been if he had come back a

triumphant hero, if he had won a battle which would have been like Bannockburn in reverse.

'Edward vindicates the English in Scotland,' he could hear them saying. 'It is his grandfather all over again.'

One day he would show them. But they would not always be comparing him with his grandfather. They should talk of Great Edward the Third as well as the First of that name.

In the meantime the Scots had outwitted him and he must return to his Court chastened but with a valuable lesson learned. War was not a tournament in which easy honours were won. It was a matter of life and death, of tricks and strategy, of discomforts and bloodshed.

He would remember that and it would stand him in good stead.

❁ ❁ ❁

As he travelled south to York Edward's mood lightened a little. At least he had not been defeated in battle as his father had. His mission had failed but that was because the Scots refused to fight. He tried to work out what he should have done and he could see that all that had been possible was to seek the enemy. True he was returning with nothing achieved; and when he thought of how it might have ended if the Black Douglas had succeeded in capturing him, he was filled with dismay.

But he was returning to York and the Scots had agreed to consider a treaty. True his army was not in the same form as it had been when it had set out, and the Hainaulters had force-fully intimated that there would be no more fighting for them. The next thing was to make an advantageous treaty and . . . what he wanted more than anything . . . to marry Philippa.

His family was waiting for him at York and with them like a shadow, Roger de Mortimer.

The King frowned. He knew very well that it was no use refusing to think of Mortimer and why his mother was so determined to keep the man at his side. Edward shut his ears to gossip and of course none would dare cast a slur on his mother in his hearing.

The Queen embraced him. She told him fervently that she was delighted to see him safely back.

Mortimer bowed and Edward was certain that he detected a gleam of satisfaction in his eyes.

'How well you look, my lord,' he said. 'Why, there is no sign of battle scars.'

'The dastardly Scots,' put in the Queen. 'Who would have believed they would refuse to fight!'

Edward said: 'The news of my father's death saddened me.'

'As it did us all,' replied the Queen.

'It was a peaceful passing,' put in Mortimer, 'and it has been said by those near him that the late King had longed for peace.'

The young King frowned. 'I would I had seen him at the end.'

His mother put her arm through his and lifted her face. 'My son,' she said, 'so do we all. But we must content ourselves with the knowledge that he is now at rest.'

Edward turned to his brother and sisters, who were regarding him with awe. He was not just their brother now. He was their King.

'Well, brother John, how fares it with you?'

John smiled and said it fared well with him as it did he hoped with his lord the King.

'Brother Edward to you, John.' Edward knelt down and took both little girls in his arms. How pretty they were with their wondering eyes and their smooth pink skins which reminded him of Philippa's.

Eleanor the elder of the two little girls said: 'They are making a banquet because you have come.'

'Is that so?' replied Edward. 'Then I must do justice to it, must I not?'

Six-year-old Joanna's eyes filled with tears suddenly. 'We have no father now,' she said.

The tears had started to spill from Joanna's eyes and both Eleanor and John were on the point of weeping. They remembered their father vaguely – a kindly man, who was gentle and quiet. They had not been afraid of him at all as they were of their mother.

'Now,' said the Queen, 'you must remember that your brother is now the King. You are not in the nursery you know.'

The sharpness of her voice sobered the children except Joanna who was unable to curb her tears.

'Take your sister away,' said the Queen. 'I am ashamed that you should so behave before the King.'

But Edward held them tightly to him. 'It is natural to mourn,' he said. 'I mourn with you. But, my little sisters, I am your guardian now. I am your King and your brother and I shall see that nothing harms you.'

Joanna threw her arms about his neck and again he was reminded of Philippa.

'Take your sisters away, John,' said the Queen authoritatively and when Edward released them they went.

'Poor fatherless children!' said Edward. 'They are aware of their loss.'

'My dear Edward, they saw so little of him. He had no time to spare for them.'

'He was kind to them when he did see them.'

'We know your father's failings. Let us not make a saint of him simply because he has departed.'

There was a sharpness to his mother's voice. It is her grief, I suppose, thought Edward. Perhaps she regrets their difference and herself wishes there had been time for reconciliation.

'You will wish to go to your apartments,' she said. 'You will be weary from the journey and I shall take you there now.' Edward nodded. 'Yes, my lady,' he said. 'Just you.' The words were addressed pointedly in the direction of Mortimer, who bowed and stood back.

When they were alone the King said: 'I wish to know how my father died.'

'It was as I told you. He died peacefully . . . in the night. He went to bed as usual and the next morning they went in and found him . . . dead.'

'My poor father, his was an unhappy life.'

'He knew himself to be a failure, Edward, as he was. It is no use pretending it was different now.'

'I know he was not like his father.'

The Queen's laugh had a note of hysteria in it. 'My dear, I understand your emotion. You feel sad about your father now that he is dead. Your grandfather was a great man. It was Edward's tragedy that he followed such a one. Had he come after . . . say John . . . his faults would not have been obvious. But he came after the Great Edward and he was a man of strange tastes. He is dead. Let him rest in peace.'

She put her hand on his arm and looked appealingly at him.

'Dear lady,' he said, 'you are right, of course.'

'You and I have worked together, Edward. I brought you to England. I made you a King.'

'Yes, my lady, but I was naturally one when my father died.'

'I made you one before your father died and because he was your father that made you uneasy. You must not be. Think of the wishes of the people. They did not want your father. They want you to rule them. Come, let us forget the past. Let us look forward to the future.'

'Let us do that. I am determined to marry without delay.' A dazzling smile crossed her face and he sensed her immense relief.

'It is natural that you should.'

'You made an agreement with the Count of Hainault.'

'It was necessary that I did. Without that agreement I could never have raised the army which brought us back to England.'

'I am glad you made it. I felt a great affection for Philippa.' The Queen laughed with excessive gaiety. 'It was a little noticeable,' she said. 'I shall never forget how the child burst into tears when she had to say good-bye.'

'She is charming,' cried Edward. 'So fresh, so natural.'

'Then why should not the marriage take place without delay?'

'That is what I think.'

She slipped her arm through his and walked to the window. 'The agreement,' she told him, 'was for one of the Count's daughters.'

'I shall have Philippa – no other.'

'Indeed you shall have Philippa but it has occurred to me that the Count may want his eldest daughter off his hands first. It is a custom. Margaret is the eldest.'

'I tell you I will have Philippa.'

'Pray do not grow so fierce. I will tell you what we shall do. We shall send our embassy to Hainault and we shall give instructions that the leader of it shall choose the most suitable of the four girls.'

'What if he does not choose Philippa?'

'He will because we shall tell him in advance that he must choose her.'

Edward laughed. 'That sounds a good project,' he said.

'Well then, we will set it in motion without delay. I'll send for Adam of Orlton. He is the man. He is with us now. He has always served us well. He is shrewd and clever. He will do exactly what is needed. I will send him to you. There is no reason why he should not set out at once.'

The King left his mother and immediately sent for Adam of Orlton.

Meanwhile the Queen had returned to Mortimer.

'Our lord the King has become somewhat imperious since his somewhat ignoble adventures in the North,' commented Mortimer. 'He clearly dismissed me.'

'You must not take that to heart, my love. He talked of his father. He broods on it, I believe. I had difficulty in getting him away from the subject.'

'He will hear no rumours.'

'None would dare. They know it would be most unwise. I have stressed that Edward is at peace now. I keep telling him that. He has no suspicions. He is in love with Philippa of Hainault and this occupies his mind, which is fortunate. He wants to marry without delay.'

'We must not stop him. Let his mind dwell on his marriage-couch rather than on the deathbed of his father.'

'So we will marry him without delay. Nothing should occupy him more exclusively than his little Philippa.'

'She will suit our young man very well,' said Mortimer.

'You thought her attractive?'

'Dazzled by the incomparable beauty of my Queen I scarcely saw her. She is a typical Fleming, I did vaguely observe. Plump already. She will incline to weightiness, you will see. But she is fresh enough and right I would say for the boy. She will be a good breeder, I doubt not.'

'I hope that he will not continue to talk of his father,' said the Queen with a shudder.

Mortimer put an arm about her. 'Ah, my love, you must stop brooding. Let us bring Philippa over. Let us have a royal wedding . . . babies. Can you believe it, sweetheart, you will be a grandmother.'

'I like not the sound of that.'

'The most beautiful and youthful grandmother the world has ever known.'

Adam of Orlton Bishop of Hereford stood before the King.

This was a man who had been the enemy of the late King and had served the Queen well. Shrewd, calculating and determined to go far in his profession, he had quickly realised that Edward the Second would in time become intolerable to the people of England and for that reason he had thrown in his lot with the Queen. He it was who had been largely responsible for Mortimer's escape from the Tower for, if the Queen had not been able to enlist his help and through him the two London merchants who supplied the boat and horses, the adventure would have failed.

As soon as the Queen had come to London with her army he had presented himself and had worked with her and Mortimer ever since.

Edward knew him as a faithful servant.

He now bowed before the King and Edward said: 'Pray be seated.' He felt a little awkward that such a venerable man should stand . . . while he sat. He would have to overcome such feelings. As usual he wished that he could grow up more quickly.

'My lord Bishop,' said the King, 'I wish you to leave at once for the Court of the Count of Hainault. As you know he has four young daughters and I have decided to marry one of these.'

'I will set off immediately, my lord,' the Bishop assured him.

'Pray present yourself to the Count and tell him of your mission. He will receive you with pleasure. He is eager for the marriage.'

'As he must be,' replied the Bishop. 'He has four daughters. Naturally your bride should be the eldest.'

'No, my lord. *No!* I have already met the future Queen of England and she is not Margaret the eldest but Philippa, the second daughter.'

'I see, my lord.'

'So when you are asked to choose the most suitable you will know which one to choose.'

'I shall choose Philippa, my lord.'

'And see that the rest of the embassy approves your choice.'

'I shall do that.'

'I knew I could rely on you, Adam.'

The Bishop smiled. 'I see it would bode ill for me if I returned with news of your betrothal to the wrong lady.'

'It could cost you your head, Bishop.'

The King spoke jocularly but the Bishop felt a shiver of uneasiness pass through him. One could never be sure with

31

these Plantagenets. The temper which had come through the line from Henry the Second was notorious.

'Rest assured, my lord. I shall keep it. It is too valuable an acquisition to be lightly cast aside. A matter has occurred to me, however, which no doubt you are aware of, my lord. There is a close relationship between you and the Lady Philippa.'

The King shrugged his shoulders impatiently. 'Kings have so many relations among noble houses,' he said.

'That is so, my lord, but this is close. You and the lady both have the same great grandfather in Philip the Third of France.'

'Well?' demanded Edward.

'I think it would be advisable for me to prepare for a mission to Avignon after I have settled matters in Hainault. I cannot believe the Pope will raise any objection to the dispensation.'

'I shall ignore him if he does.'

The Bishop bowed his head. 'That, my lord, I am sure will not be necessary. I shall set off at once for Hainault and my business completed there leave at once for Avignon.'

The King nodded, confident that soon Philippa would be with him.

Chapter III

THE KING'S BRIDE

Ever since Edward had spent a week at the Court of Hainault Philippa had never ceased to think of him. Before he had come she had been completely content with her life. Hers was a closely knit family and if it was a source of disappointment to the Count and Countess of Hainault that it consisted of only one son and four daughters they had showed no sign of it.

They had had one great tragedy in their life for there had been five girls. Their eldest, Sybella, had died when she was young; only the two elder ones remembered her, and they would never forget the deep sadness in the family at her premature departure.

The girls had always been aware that their mother came of a very noble family – the royal family of France, no less. Countess Jeanne was the daughter of Charles of Valois and her brother, Philip of Valois, was next in line of succession to the crown of France if the reigning King Charles died without a male heir. It seemed likely that he might for ill luck had been the lot of the Kings of France since Philip IV had persecuted the Knights Templars and their Grand Master, Jacques de

Molai, had cursed the Capet line while he was being burned at the stake. It did seem as though that branch of the family would die out; in which case the Valois would take over.

Countess Jeanne never tired of talking of her early life in France and the four sisters knew how much more elegantly life was conducted there than in Hainault and how the music and poetry composed there was the best in the world.

'Still,' she would add, 'I have known more happiness in Hainault than I ever had in France.'

That did not prevent her from introducing French customs and letting the girls know, if they ever acted in a manner of which their high-born mother disapproved, that they came from the royal house of France.

Philippa was sure that nowhere in the world was there such a handsome boy as Edward of England. Even France could not produce one so full of charm, vitality and kindliness, and since he had gone life had become excessively dull.

Every day was the same. It was made up mostly of lessons but there was also a good deal of exercise. The Count was a great believer in the benefits of outdoor life; they were all excellent horsewomen and their fresh complexions were an indication of their blooming good health.

It was a happy simple life they led and both the Count and his Countess had wished their girls to be first of all good women. They spoke their minds freely and saw no virtue in deception. They had been taught to be kind to those below them in rank and that, although they had been born without their own advantages, they were human beings and worthy of their consideration.

Countess Jeanne often smiled to think how differently she herself had been brought up; but she was wise enough to realise that the simple happiness of the Court of Hainault was infinitely more desirable than the sophistication of that of France.

The girls often discussed the visit of the Queen of England and her son who had since become the King. Philippa had a habit of bringing the conversation round to him and this usually happened at that hour of the day when they were at their needlework for they must set aside a certain time of the day to sew for the poor. They would all have preferred to work on some colourful tapestry but the Countess had told them that they must make themselves enjoy working on the rather coarse materials because they could think of the comfort it would bring to those less fortunate than themselves.

As she stitched Philippa thought of Edward and that made the hour pass quickly. She would sit smiling over the stuff and not see the strong thread but Edward leaping onto his horse, showing how far he could let an arrow fly, riding out with his falcon, and best of all arranging that he and she strayed behind a little or rode on ahead so that they could lose the party and be alone together.

Her sisters talked of him too. They had all found him attractive. And one day as they sat sewing their garments for the poor they heard sounds of arrival at the castle.

Young Isabella dropped her work and ran to the window. She looked out silently and Margaret said: 'Who is it?'

Isabella turned round, her habitually pink cheeks a shade more colourful. 'It is important, I think,' she said.

All the girls were at the window.

'Why,' said Margaret. 'Look at the pennant. They come from England.'

Philippa's heart was doing a wild dance; she could not trust herself to speak.

'I wonder what this means?' pondered Jeanne.

'Doubtless,' replied her eldest sister, 'we shall discover in due course.'

They stood at the window watching.

'Edward is not with them,' observed Isabella.

'As if he would be,' Philippa had found her voice. 'He is a king now. He has a country to rule.'

'Kings sometimes pay visits,' retorted Isabella. 'Do they not, Margaret?'

'Indeed they do. Edward must be one of the youngest kings that ever were.'

'Some people are kings when they're babies,' added Jeanne.

Philippa was not listening. Why had the messengers come from England? What could it mean?'

They were soon to discover. Later that day they were summoned to their parents' apartment and there they found the Count and Countess looking more sombre than they usually did.

'Come here, children,' said the Countess.

They came and stood before their parents, Margaret first, then Philippa, Jeanne and Isabella in order of age as was expected of them.

'You will have heard the arrivals,' the Countess went on.

'Yes, my lady,' Margaret answered for them all.

'They come from the King of England. You remember Edward who stayed here with his mother and whom your uncle John conducted to England?'

'Yes, my lady.'

'I believe you all grew fond of your cousin.'

'Oh yes, my lady.' It was Philippa that time, speaking a little ahead of the others.

'I am glad,' she said.

'I also,' said the Count. 'You girls will know that time must come when you must leave home to marry. Your mother and I know that you will not want to go. Alas, it is the fate of girls. The point is that the King of England is asking for the hand of one of you in marriage.'

'One of us!' cried Margaret.

'Which one?' Philippa's voice had sunk to a whisper.

'That is what has to be decided,' went on the Count. 'An embassy has come from the King and it is led by his Bishop of Hereford. Over the next day or so he will observe you and choose the one whom he considers most suitable to be the Queen of England.'

Philippa felt sick with fear. Oh, she thought, Margaret is prettier than I am; Jeanne is more graceful and Isabella has beautiful eyes; they are all cleverer than I. I shall die if they don't choose me . . . and how can they when my sisters are so much more attractive?

'I was not surprised,' went on the Count, 'when the embassy arrived for your mother and I had already agreed when the Queen and the King – Prince as he was then – were our guests, that we should put no obstacles in the way of a marriage between one of you and Edward. This is our bargain. We are very happy that the King, now he has his throne, has remembered it.'

'I am sure,' said the Countess, 'that whichever one of you is chosen, she will be happy. Edward is young – he is only a few months older than you, Philippa, and whichever one of you is chosen will quickly learn his ways and perhaps he some of yours.'

'When . . . when,' stammered Philippa, 'will the choice be made?'

'That is for the Bishop to say. He will watch you, I daresay and then he will come to us and tell us which one of you he thinks will suit his master best. There, now you may go. I think the Bishop will not want to delay long. So perhaps within a few days we shall know.'

For the first time in her life Philippa felt the need to hide her feelings.

She prayed that night. Oh God, let me be the chosen one.

Then she hated herself for being so selfish for it seemed to her that marriage with Edward must be the pinnacle of every girl's ambition and this would be denied to those who were not selected.

But I love him, she told herself. I was the one he rode with alone. *I* was the one he talked to. He said that he would come back for me. How could he send a Bishop to choose *one* of us!

Had he forgotten then? He must have. She meant no more to him than Margaret, Jeanne or Isabella.

One of the daughters of the Count of Hainault! Was that all that mattered?

It was a terrible time to live through. In her anxiety she looked less attractive than her sisters. She was clumsy at table. She saw the Bishop observing her gravely and she fancied he talked more to the others than to her.

He would not choose her, she was sure, and she would spend her life in misery. She would beg her parents to let her go into a convent. It was the only way. She could not marry anyone else.

They were once more summoned to their parents' apartment. Philippa was praying silently. 'Dear Lord, let me hide. Don't let them see my grief. I must not weep. I must kiss and congratulate Margaret . . . Jeanne or Isabella. But of course it will be Margaret. It is sure to be the eldest. The eldest always marries first. And *he* does not care. All he wants is a daughter of the Count of Hainault because he promised that he would marry one of us when he was crowned King of England. Which one was of no importance. Oh, why did I let myself care so much!'

Her father was speaking in a tender voice for he found the prospect of the marriage of one of his daughters deeply moving. Much as he wanted a grand marriage he did not want to lose any one of them.

They stood before him in order of age. They were all over-excited and the two younger ones were inclined to giggle. Margaret was serious for, like Philippa, she believed she might well be the chosen one. Philippa's emotions were too pent up to be described. She could only continue to pray that she, who had always been frank, did not betray them.

'My lord Bishop has come to tell us that he has chosen the future Queen of England,' said the Count. 'You will tell my daughter that she is the one you consider most suitable, I beg you my lord Bishop.'

The Bishop cleared his throat and frowned slightly. 'My lord and lady,' he said, 'your daughters are all charming. For me this has been the most difficult task. The lady Margaret . . .' He seemed to pause for a long time and Philippa thought: I cannot bear it. Oh how wicked I am. It is so wonderful for dear Margaret but I cannot bear it! 'The lady Margaret is gracious and charming. The lady Jeanne equally so as is her sister Isabella. I and my embassy have talked much of this and we have come to the conclusion that the lady Philippa being closer to the age of my lord the

King would be the most suitable to be his wife and Queen and it is for this reason, my lord Count, my lady Countess, that I beg, on behalf of my lord the King, for the hand of the lady Philippa.'

She was swooning. I am dreaming, she thought. It cannot be.

They were all looking at her. She had turned white and then red; she was trembling. Pray God the tears would not fall. So she was the chosen one. She . . . and because she was nearest to his age!

Her father had taken her hand and he was placing it in that of the Bishop.

'She is young yet, my lord,' he said.

'She will be an enchanting Queen of England,' said the Bishop.

❀ ❀ ❀

She was more important now, the betrothed of the King of England.

Her sisters talked all at once about the marriage. She was relieved that they did not mind too much. Isabella was a little regretful but then she was young and she had merely thought it would be fun to be a queen.

'Of course,' said Margaret, 'you are closest to him in age.'

'Of course,' she said demurely.

'I thought he would have asked for you,' said Jeanne. 'He seemed to like you best when he was here.'

'I daresay he forgot all about us as soon as he left,' put in Margaret. 'He had to get his crown didn't he, and there was something about his father. It seems strange not to be friendly with your own father.'

'Oh, there were reasons,' declared Philippa coming immediately to his defence.

'I thought *he* would have asked for you,' said Margaret, 'and not left it to his bishop to choose.'

No, nor had Philippa. It was a blow to her but never mind. She would not brood on it. She was to see him again. They would renew their friendship and it would be as though they had never parted.

She had to be happy, even though it was the Bishop who had chosen her and not Edward and it was because of her age.

There was another scare.

Her parents explained it to her.

'You know that your mother and Edward's mother are first cousins,' said the Count. 'Their fathers were both sons of the King Philip the Third of France. This means that there is a very close blood tie between you and Edward and because of this the Pope must give his permission for you to marry.'

'What if he does not?' she cried in dismay.

'There seems to be no reason why he will not,' replied her mother. 'We are sending an embassy at once to Avignon and we hope very soon to hear that the dispensation is granted.'

So there were further anxieties. How she wished that Edward himself had come for her. In her fantasies she imagined his coming and saying: 'Never mind about the Pope. Nothing is going to prevent our marrying.'

But all was well after all. The Pope readily gave the necessary dispensation and the King of England, now that his bride was settled on, wanted no delay. Philippa was to be married by proxy and immediately after that ceremony, to leave for England.

There was a great bustling preparation through the castle of Valenciennes for Edward was sending the Bishop of Lichfield to perform the proxy marriage.

Every morning when Philippa awoke she had to assure herself that it was really happening. She wondered how long it would be before she saw Edward. Over the intensity of her happiness there hung a faint shadow. It was there because Edward had not chosen her but had let his Bishop choose and the implication was surely that that idyllic week they had spent together had not meant the same to him as it had to her.

I will make him love me in time, she assured herself; but still the shadow persisted.

Her mother said: 'Your father is determined that you shall go richly equipped to England. Your husband-to-be is by no means rich, King though he may be. A great deal of his treasure has been spent in war and his father was not a provident man.'

'I do not care to be rich, dear lady.'

'My dearest child, I think you are very happy to be going to Edward.'

Philippa clasped her hands and said: 'I think I should have died if I had not been the chosen one.'

'Oh, my dear daughter, you must not speak so extravagantly. But I know your feelings for your husband and I am glad of them because whatever happens that love will remain constant I know and it will enrich both your lives.'

The Countess wondered whether to warn her daughter. She had betrayed her feelings too easily, and she wondered whether Edward would appreciate such blind devotion as Philippa seemed prepared to give. A little restraint should perhaps be practised. No, perhaps it was better that her daughter should behave in her natural way which had endeared Edward to her when he had come here as a prince.

'You are both very young,' went on the Countess. 'Fifteen years old. And you, Philippa to go to a new country!'

'But, my lady, it is not like going to a stranger.'

'No, dear child, and I rejoice that you are going to a husband whom you already love.'

It was better to leave it thus, the Countess decided. Philippa's frank nature, her inherent unselfishness and goodness would carry her through whatever lay in store for her. It was to be hoped that the boy King would recognise those qualities and appreciate them.

Her sisters revelled in the preparation; they were often present during the constant fitting sessions; they cried out with admiration at the richness of her garments.

'Just fancy our sister will be a Queen!'

'Oh Philippa, how does it feel to be a Queen?'

Philippa said that it was the most wonderful thing in the world. She was completely happy . . . well not quite completely because to go to Edward she had to leave them – and, she added to herself: he did not really choose me. It might have been any one of you.

As the days passed her happiness was more and more tinged with sadness at the thought of leaving her home. It would be so strange not to see her sisters and her parents every day.

'You must all visit me in England,' she said; and the thought struck her that in a short time all her sisters would be married and be gone from this lovely old castle in Valenciennes where they had been so happy. She saw the sadness in her parents' eyes; her sisters were too excited by all the fuss to think very much about the parting. How sad it was that there could not be complete happiness.

The days were passing quickly. Soon the time would come when she must really say good-bye.

'Your Uncle John will meet you when you arrive at Dover,' her mother told her, 'so it will not be like going to a land of strangers.'

She said it would be pleasant to see Uncle John again.

'He is greatly enamoured of England and the English,' replied her mother. 'He was a great friend to the Queen, Edward's mother.'

Philippa felt again a faint twinge of uneasiness. She remembered Edward's mother, the Queen – a strikingly beautiful woman, indeed one of the most beautiful she had ever seen. It was Isabella who had said of her: 'She is a witch, I believe, a beautiful witch. The sort Satan makes more beautiful than anyone else so that they can get the better of other people.'

Philippa also remembered a big man with flashing dark eyes and heavy brows who was always at the Queen's side and who also for some reason had aroused her misgivings.

But the excitement of those days swallowed up her uneasiness and she could think of little else but Edward.

At last the day came. The Count had said that it would be better for the family not to accompany her. They would say their farewells in the privacy of the castle and they would all go to the topmost turret and watch her ride away with the large company of knights, squires and ladies who would be her companions until the end of the journey.

Her parents embraced her with fervent affection, her sisters tearfully.

44

'How strange it will be without you,' said Isabella. 'There are only three of us now.'

And soon only two, thought their mother, for a marriage was being arranged for Margaret.

She looked sadly at her husband. She was reminding him of the inevitability of losing their daughters.

And so, riding at the head of the cavalcade, Philippa set out on her journey to England.

The crossing was comparatively smooth and in due course Philippa stood on deck and saw the starkly white cliffs coming nearer and nearer. And there looking out to sea was the fortress castle rising more than four hundred feet above the level of the water – formidable, warning off invaders and yet seeming to welcome her who came as a bride of the King.

As she came ashore there, as she had been told he would be, was her uncle Sir John of Hainault waiting to greet her. He embraced her warmly and said that this was one of the happiest days of his life. He had always wanted a link between England and Hainault and here was his dear little niece Philippa to forge it.

They would stay the night in Dover Castle and then they would travel on to London by way of Canterbury where of course they must pause to make an offering at the shrine of St Thomas à Becket, to thank him for their safe passage and to ask his blessing on the union.

Philippa slept little during her first night in her new country and she was ready at dawn to begin the journey to Canterbury.

Wrapped in furs to keep out the winter cold she rode with her uncle and from the villages they passed the people came out of their houses to stand in the roads and see her.

That they liked the fresh young face with the open smile was obvious, and on that journey Philippa first became aware that the people of England were ready to give her a warm welcome.

She was so young, so appealing, so ready with her smiles, and rumours about the late King's death and the Queen and her paramour Mortimer were beginning to circulate even in the remote country districts so that people wanted a change and they were more than ready to show great affection to the innocent young King and his bride.

By the time Philippa reached the outskirts of London it was Christmas Eve. There she was met by a procession largely made up of the clergy who had come to escort her into the city.

Eagerly she looked for Edward but he was not among them.

They are taking me to him, she thought.

Her uncle Sir John rode beside her and told her that he was very proud of her and happy because it was clear that she was making a good impression on the English. She said she was just being herself which made Sir John smile for he knew it was naturalness which the people were finding so appealing.

He delighted in pointing out the landmarks which he had come to know well. He showed her the Tower of London which she thought rather grim and hoped she did not have to spend too much time in the palace there. The river, though, sparkled in the frosty air and the gardens of great houses which ran down to the water's edge were beautiful indeed. There were so many trees – ornamental and fruit-bearing. Now their stark branches made a lacy pattern against the sky and their leaflessness made it possible to see the landscape more clearly.

Her uncle pointed out the abundance of green fields and he told her of the wells of London in which were waters proved to be beneficial to health. Holy Well, Clerken Well and St

Clement's Well. And there was Smithfield where every Friday – when it was not some great feast day or holiday – the finest horses in England changed hands. There was the Great Moor on the north side of the city which washed the edge of Moorfields and here a few weeks later in the depth of winter when the river was frozen, the young people would come out to skate.

All this he had seen; and he found the life of the capital city enjoyable indeed.

It was clear that Uncle John believed that the greatest good fortune which could have befallen his niece was her marrying into England.

In the heart of the City the Lord Mayor and his aldermen were waiting to greet her. It was a most impressive ceremony during which she was presented with a service of gold plate which Uncle John told her later was worth quite three hundred marks and was a sign of the people's joy in her arrival.

As the next day was Christmas Day she would spend that in London. She would be conducted to the Palace of Westminster and there she would remain for the next three days.

But why, she asked herself, was Edward not there to greet her?

In the palace she was taken to those apartments which had been restored with great artistry and expense under the direction of the King's great grandfather, Henry III. They were beautiful and had been especially prepared for her on the King's order.

But if only he had been here himself to greet her! Her uncle explained to her. 'We shall shortly be travelling to York where the King is with his mother the Queen.'

'I had thought to meet him ere this,' said Philippa, and her uncle noticed her despondency.

47

'Dear niece,' he answered, 'you must remember that you are married to a King. As eager as he is for your coming, he has State duties which demand his attention. He is involved at this time making a treaty with the Scots and it is for this reason that he cannot be with you. You have seen, have you not, how his people have welcomed you. Why do you think? It is because they have had orders from the King to do so.'

'So their welcome was not because they were glad to see me but because they were ordered to appear so,' said the logical Philippa.

'I tell you this to show the King's great regard for you. But one can always tell whether the people's welcome comes from the heart – as it never could if it were shown merely because it was commanded. Nay, my dear niece, you are the most fortunate of girls. Do not look askance at your luck.'

'I won't,' replied Philippa. 'I do understand that Edward has his State duties. And I am sure the people really like me. They could not be so warm and friendly if they did not.'

There were so many people who wished to meet her and so much feasting. The three days of Christmas had passed and, leaving the Londoners to continue celebrating their King's marriage to the pleasant little girl from Hainault, Philippa and her retinue began the journey north.

Edward's second cousin, John de Bohun, Earl of Hereford and Essex, had arrived to conduct her on her journey north and by New Year's Day they had reached Peterborough, where they rested awhile at the Abbey there.

The weather had taken a turn for the worse and their speed was considerably slackened on account of the icy roads; the winds were fierce and the quantity of baggage which travelled with them slowed them down even more, so it seemed a very long time to Philippa before she saw the towers of the Minster in the distance and knew that her journey was nearing its end.

Then she saw bearing down towards them an array of armour glistening in the pale wintry sun; pennants fluttered in the strong east wind for the cream of the nobility who were with the King in York had come out to greet her; and at their head rode the young King himself.

Philippa's heart leaped with joy as she saw him mounted on a fine white horse. Gloriously apparelled, taller than when she had last seen him, his flaxen hair adorned by a slender golden crown, he looked more like a god than a king and she was overwhelmed by adoration for him.

He broke away from the company in his eagerness to greet her. His horse was close to hers. His blue eyes were looking earnestly into hers as he took her hand and kissed it.

'Philippa . . . little Philippa,' he said, 'at last you have come to me. It has seemed a long time.'

'For me also,' she replied. 'I had thought to see you long ere this.'

'Oh, you are just the same. I feared you might have changed. How long it seems since we were together in the Hainault woods. I found the waiting irksome, but it is over now. We are to be married immediately. I'll have no delay.'

The glow of happiness which had settled on her made her beautiful but even in this moment she could not forget those days of anxiety when she had feared she might not be the chosen one.

'I was afraid . . .' she began.

'Afraid!' he cried. '*You* . . . of *me*!'

'Afraid that one of my sisters might have been chosen by the Bishop.'

49

Edward smiled at that. 'That could never have been.'

'Oh but it might have. Margaret is the eldest. I thought he was going to choose her.'

'He wouldn't have dared.'

'But I thought he was going to. He seemed to study her. I could have died with misery because you asked him to choose.'

Edward burst out laughing. 'Oh yes,' he said, 'the Bishop was sent to choose. It is the custom, you see. He must choose the most suitable. Kings have to follow customs, Philippa. But do you know what I said to him? "Bishop," I said, "if you value your head you will choose Philippa. Understand this now that I, the King, command you to choose Philippa." And of course he would dare choose no other.'

'Oh Edward, is it really so?'

'I swear it, my little love. I swear it on our marriage vows, on the tomb of St Thomas, on my father's bones. It is Philippa I loved in Valenciennes and I swore then and I swear now that I will take none other as my Queen.'

She was silent for a few moments. Then she said quietly: 'I had thought I should want to die if I had not been chosen. Now I feel I could die for very happiness.'

'No talk of dying please. You will live for me, sweet Philippa, and I for you and thus shall it be until the end of our days.'

It seemed to her that York was the most beautiful of all cities and she had never believed that there could be such happiness in the world.

The people cheered. They were so young – this King and Queen; they were so handsome and so much in love.

On the thirtieth of January, a month after Philippa had arrived in London they were married in York Minster. It was an impressive ceremony and it was attended not only by the leading members of the English nobility but by many of the great Scottish nobles also, for they had come to York to conclude the peace treaty which was being made between the two countries.

The young lovers were enchanted with each other. Edward would not be sixteen years old until the coming November and Philippa was even younger, but it was an age for early maturing and it had never occurred either to them or to anyone else that they were too young to consummate the marriage.

Although there were meetings with the Scots, and Parliament and the royal council were convened at York, still Edward was spending most of his time in the company of his bride. They rode out together and they were cheered wherever they went; they were in love with each other and the country was in love with them. Philippa made no secret of her adoration for her young husband and he of his love for her. They were ideally suited, it was generally said; and indeed the rich treasures which Philippa had brought with her into the country were very useful, for the English exchequer was very low at this time. Queen Isabella had necessarily spent much on maintaining her army and in keeping herself and Mortimer in the position they had taken up; the Scottish campaign had been costly; so in spite of the fact that the new Queen was the daughter of a mere Count she was, comparatively, a rich girl and welcomed because of it.

Philippa was delighted that her treasure should be so enthusiastically received. She wanted to give everything she had to her wonderful husband, and in her luggage were rich tapestries and cloth besides valuable jewels, for her father had not wished her to come as a pauper into her new country.

She was immensely popular with her young brother and sisters-in-law. Twelve-year-old John of Eltham who thought his brother the King the most wonderful being in the world immediately fell in love with Philippa; their shared opinion of the King made an immediate bond between them. The two little girls, ten-year-old Eleanor and seven-year-old Joanna, were ready to adore her.

'I like you,' Eleanor told her, 'because you are always smiling.'

'And I like you because your cheeks are so red,' added Joanna.

They were her dear little sisters, Philippa told them, and she was particularly happy to have them because when she came to England she had had to leave three sisters behind. And now she had two to replace them.

'There ought to have been three of us,' said Joanna looking apologetic.

'Never mind,' put in Eleanor. 'There is John. Will he do as well as a sister?'

Philippa said she thought he would do every bit as well.

When Edward was obliged to meet certain of his ministers and she could not be with him Philippa took the opportunity of going to the royal schoolroom. She was quick to sense that there was some uneasiness in her husband's family. It may have been due to the fact that she herself had come from such a happy home and that the honesty of purpose which prevailed there made her alert to something which was entirely alien to it.

That it emanated from her mother-in-law and the Earl of March she knew. She saw as little of them as possible for the truth was that they frightened her a little. She sensed a strangeness in the manner of Queen Isabella and she knew that the Dowager Queen and the Earl of March watched her intently. She fancied they were trying to find some fault in her. True, they were friendly towards her, in fact almost gushing in their attitude, and that was something she did not trust. The fact was that she did not understand them. The Queen made her very uneasy and it was not only her attitude which made her feel this. It even had something to do with Isabella's beauty. She moved with a grace and quietness which was almost feline, and would often appear suddenly in a room where Philippa had fancied herself to be alone. She endeavoured to make the young girl feel awkward, so that she was a little clumsy and somewhat hesitant in her speech. Philippa could not understand the effect the Queen had on her; yet she sensed in it something unhealthy, even evil.

As for the Earl of March, there was something in his cold features which told her that he was ruthless and brutal and she could not understand why he was treated with such respect by everyone – and most of all by the Queen. She believed that people were afraid of him and she was sure she ought to be wary of him.

One day, she promised herself she would speak to Edward about her feelings but she feared it would be rather churlish to say that about his mother which might be construed as criticism.

Moreover when she was with Edward they talked of themselves, how much they loved each other, and how wonderful life had been since they had married; they even talked of the children they would have, for they were certain they would soon have a child.

'It will be a boy,' declared Edward.

'And we shall call him Edward.'

Then they talked about this boy who, Philippa declared, must be exactly like his father or she would be most displeased.

Such nonsense they talked, Philippa said, but they laughed and kissed and made love and life was wonderful . . . far too wonderful to bring in sinister undertones which after all might only be thought up in her imagination.

But there was something unhappy even in the schoolroom. Philippa discovered this from the little girls.

They remembered so much that had happened. There was the time when they had been in the Tower and Lady le Despenser had been their guardian. Their father had set her over them and their mother was unhappy about it because she was the wife of Hugh.

Philippa knew enough about the recent history of her new country to understand that Hugh le Despenser had been a great favourite of the King and that Queen Isabella had been neglected for his sake. The people had hated him and he had been executed and later the King had given up his crown to Edward.

She did not talk to Edward about it because it was depressing and he was always sad when his father's name was mentioned.

'There was a lot of shouting in the streets,' Eleanor told her.

'And we were frightened,' added Joanna.

'And then the people came and took us to our mother.'

'We were still frightened.' Joanna's face puckered a little. Philippa realised that the little girl was greatly in awe of her mother.

'Once we saw a man swinging on a rope,' Joanna went on. 'He was dead.'

'He was Hugh's father,' went on Eleanor. 'They had done

terrible things to him. Then they hung him on the rope outside the castle . . . and he swung and he swung . . .'

Philippa said: 'It is all over now. I should not think of it any more.'

'I do sometimes in my bed,' said Eleanor. 'When it is dark.'

'I do too,' added Joanna.

'Then you mustn't any more. It's all over.'

'Have you ever seen a man hanging on a rope, dear sister?' asked Eleanor.

'No,' said Philippa firmly. 'Perhaps you didn't either. Perhaps it was a dream.'

The two little girls looked at her wonderingly.

'Yes,' said Philippa, 'that was it. A dream. Nobody worries much about dreams. They seem of no importance when the day breaks.'

The two girls seemed to like the idea of the hanging man being a dream. 'Yes, it was a dream,' they kept saying.

Joanna had something else on her mind. She wanted to know about marriage.

'What's marriage like?' asked Eleanor.

Philippa said that she thought it was the most wonderful thing that could happen to anyone.

'But you married Edward,' Joanna reminded her. 'I wish I could marry Edward.'

'You cannot marry your brother,' Philippa explained. 'Besides he is already married now.'

'When I was little,' went on Eleanor, 'they were going to marry me to Alfonso, the King of Castile. I never did though. Perhaps he didn't like me.'

'That could not be,' Philippa replied firmly. 'He never saw you.'

'Did you see Edward?' asked Joanna.

'Yes, I did.' She told them of his coming to Valenciennes and how they had ridden in the forest and fallen in love with each other and then Edward had sent for her to be his wife.

They listened avidly. She told it with such glowing enthusiasm that the little girls could not hear it often enough.

Joanna's face puckered with anxiety. 'They are going to make me marry the son of the King of the Scots.' Suddenly she turned to Philippa and buried her face in her lap. 'Don't let them, dear sister. I don't want to go to Scotland.'

Philippa stroked the little girl's hair. 'Oh you are too young yet. You will have to wait years and years.'

That comforted Joanna. 'I don't want to go to Scotland,' she said, 'even when I am old. It is a cold cold country and the Scots are our enemies.'

'That is why you will have to marry Robert the Bruce's son,' explained Eleanor. 'We always have to marry to stop people making wars.'

'He's only a little boy,' said Joanna scornfully. 'He's not as old as I am.'

'Oh, you are far too young,' Philippa assured her.

Then she told them more about Edward's visit to Valenciennes and although Joanna laughed and asked questions Philippa could see that she was not entirely convinced. She must have been listening to gossip. There was plenty of that and people were not always very careful of what they said in children's hearing.

When they were alone together Philippa talked to Edward about Joanna's fears.

'Poor little girl,' she said, 'she has had a very sad life. She and Eleanor seemed to be constantly expecting something unhappy to happen to them.'

Edward frowned. 'They were always well looked after in Pleshy Castle in Essex. Isabella de Valence was put in charge of them. She was connected with the family because she had married Ralph Monthermer after my aunt Joanna died. Johanette Jermyn was their gouvernante and she was a pleasant woman. They should have had a happy household.'

'I have no doubt their comforts were taken care of,' said Philippa. 'But I think they missed love. In my family our parents were always with us and we were all happy together.'

'Yours was an unusual family, sweetheart. That was why they produced you.'

She smiled lovingly at him but she pursued the subject. 'Is it really true that Joanna is to marry the son of Robert the Bruce?'

'It's part of the treaty. It's a good thing really. These wars with Scotland are costly in life and money. The country is too wild and mountainous for a complete conquest. Even my grandfather could not do it. I am all for a peaceful settlement between our two countries and this is what this treaty is all about.'

'The Scots agree?'

He nodded. 'Robert the Bruce is anxious for it. He is a very sick man. He has been slowly dying of leprosy for many years and the end cannot be far off. All that he leaves is a five-year-old boy, David, and David will be King of Scotland when Robert dies.'

'So the plan is to marry Joanna to him.'

'That is so.'

'As the boy is five and Joanna seven the marriage will not take place for years.'

'It will have to take place soon. Anything could happen in a few years. It has to be clear that there is union between England and Scotland and the only way of making this apparent is to celebrate the marriage.'

'Then Joanna will stay in her own country until she is older.'

Edward frowned. 'I'm afraid not. Joanna will have to go to Scotland.'

'Poor child! Then her fears are not groundless.'

'Oh come, Philippa, these things happen to princesses. They have to reconcile themselves to the fact that they are bargaining counters. It always has been so.'

'But such a child!'

'Princesses grow up quickly.'

He kissed her lips. 'I'll not have you worrying about these matters. Come, my love, I never have half the time with you that I want. Let us forget these tiresome Scots. They have been a thorn in our side for centuries. This matter may well settle the problem.'

She slipped into his embrace and forgot Joanna, but only temporarily. Later her anxieties concerning the child returned to her with those uneasy stirrings of apprehension which Isabella and the Earl of March aroused in her.

The treaty had been signed. Edward explained the terms to her. He was giving up his feudal claim to Scotland and the great stone of Scone which his grandfather had taken away from Scotland was to be restored to them with certain treasures which had been confiscated. The Scots were to pay twenty thousand pounds to the King of England over the next three years. But the most important clause was the marriage between David, son of Robert the Bruce, and Joanna, daughter of King Edward the Second, the marriage to take place four months after the signing of the treaty.

Philippa was horrified. So the poor child was to be sacrificed. She saw at once that there was nothing she could do about it. Isabella and the Earl of March were in favour of it. They had no desire for a lengthy war. They wanted to enjoy the spoils of their victory and that could not be done if treasure was to be wasted in fighting what could only be a prolonged war which might not bring success in the end. Edward the First, one of the mightiest warriors ever known, had been unable to subdue the Scots.

This was what Edward told her, but she did suspect that he was in some way under the spell of his mother. She could understand it in a way because Isabella was so beautiful and she made such a point of showing her affection for her son – though, thought Philippa sadly, she did not show the same to her other children. Poor little Joanna was in urgent need of comfort, for before the year was out, if this unhappy matter were carried out, the poor little girl would be in Scotland.

There was nothing Philippa could do. She was too young and inexperienced. She was glad that Edward was sympathetic towards his little sister, but as he said to Philippa, it had to be.

It was a mercy that there was a little time left to Joanna and with the resilience of childhood and for weeks at a time she forgot the ordeal ahead of her.

Easter had come and after the church service and celebrations the whole Court prepared to travel south.

As they came out of the city of York and into the village of Bishoppesthorpe, a strange incident occurred which seemed to indicate that already the people had begun to guess the nature of their new young Queen.

Philippa was riding beside Edward at the head of the cavalcade when a woman ran into the road before the oncoming horses and kneeling held up her hands.

The horses were brought to a sharp halt and the woman, ragged and unkempt, came straight to Philippa. She fell to her knees and Philippa leaning forward spoke to her gently and asked what she wanted of her.

'I have heard of your goodness, my lady,' said the woman, 'and it shines in your face. My daughter who is but eleven years is to be hanged by the neck. I beg of you, my lady, speak for her. Save her. She is my child . . .'

'What was her crime?' asked Philippa.

'She stole some trinket. It was but a childish impulse. Believe me, my lady, she is a good girl.'

Edward said: 'I fear my love, you will find many to beset you in this way.'

'I must help her,' replied Philippa firmly.

The Queen Mother said: 'Take the woman away. We wish to ride on.'

For a moment the two queens looked at each other. Isabella's gaze was impatient and then faintly disturbed. She had seen a hint of firmness in the wide candid eyes. Philippa had turned to Edward.

'You will want to please me, I know, my lord.'

'More than anything on earth,' answered Edward.

'Then,' said Philippa, 'we will call a halt here and I will look into this matter. I could not have our subjects believe that I

60

would not listen to a mother's plea. It is clear that this woman is deeply distressed.'

'Do as you will, my dearest,' answered Edward.

'How good you are to me,' she murmured.

So there was a stay at Bishoppesthorpe and Philippa herself saw the young girl who had stolen the trinket and she spoke to the stewards and marshal of the household in which the theft had taken place and the judge who had condemned the girl; and as a result the child was saved from the hangman's rope.

The mother fell to her knees and kissed the hem of Philippa's gown while Edward smiled on the scene benignly, and the people said: 'It was a happy day when our King brought good Queen Philippa to our shores.'

After that they continued their journey south and at last they came to the palace of Woodstock in Oxfordshire that most enchanting residence in sylvan surroundings so beloved of Edward's ancestor Henry the Second.

'We will rest here awhile,' said Edward, 'Philippa and I with a few attendants, for there has been so much state business and travelling since our marriage, and a little peace is due to us.'

So there they stayed at Woodstock and Philippa's attendants who had travelled with her from Hainault now returned to their native land. She retained only one. Walter de Manny who was her carver, because he had already shown himself to be a worthy knight and had sworn allegiance to the King.

'Now,' said Edward, 'you have left Hainault behind and are my English Queen. Are you sad, sweet Philippa, to see them go?'

'I have rewarded them well,' she said, 'and they are my friends. But I could not be sad while I am with you and you love me.'

The idyllic life continued at Woodstock.

❀ Chapter IV ❀

TREACHERY AT CORFE CASTLE

Isabella could not escape from the dark shadows which crowded in on her. Sometimes she thought she was going mad. She dreamed continually of her murdered husband, that he came to life and would not leave her, that he appeared not only in her bedroom at night when she lay beside her lover, but sometimes she thought she saw his face in a crowd, and once even at a conference table.

Mortimer laughed at her. Mortimer was strong and had little understanding of whimsical imaginings. Mortimer lived entirely for the present and if there were threats in the future he would not look at them.

Sometimes she thought of Gaveston and Hugh – both of whom had met violent deaths though neither could compare with what had happened to her husband – and how they had refused to see their fate approaching them. It had seemed clear enough to everyone else, but those two had continued to plunder the King and snap their fingers at the hatred of the people. If she were not besottedly infatuated by Mortimer, would she say he was the same?

He never wanted to talk about the possibilities of disaster.

He never wanted to take heed of warning shadows. He delighted in the pact with the Scots because Robert the Bruce was to pay Edward twenty thousand pounds. The first instalment arrived and Mortimer had taken charge of it, which meant that he would spend it. He was a great spender, Mortimer. He liked to live flamboyantly, and so did she. Well, they deserved it after all that they had suffered – he a prisoner in the Tower with an uncle who had died of starvation, as he might have done if he had not been so strong; and she, what humiliation she had endured for years, thrust into the background while all the favours were showered on her husband's men friends, bearing his children while she loathed him just because she had to give the country heirs.

Now, they were reaping their reward. Mortimer was the richest and most powerful man in the country and she and he ruled it together. Edward was such a boy and remained amenable.

She was uneasy though about Philippa.

She talked to Mortimer about it. 'Mortimer what do you think of Philippa?' she asked.

'I never think of her. What is she? A simple country girl, fresh and untutored. Why should we think of Philippa as anything but a nice playmate for our boy. He likes married life evidently. Well, let them enjoy it. It will keep them occupied.'

'That woman on the road . . . She insisted, you know, and Edward wants to please her.'

'She held us up yes. But it was of no great importance.'

'Only to show us that he will do a great deal to please her.'

'Of course he will . . . for a while. He is a boy; he experiences early love. It seems very important to him. Wait till she bears him children and he discovers that there are women in the world more attractive than his plump little Hainaulter.'

'At the moment she could guide him.'

'How could such an innocent guide anyone?'

'He is changing, wanting his own way. It could be less easy to control him.'

'Come, sweetheart, let us leave that problem until it arises.'

'This peace with Scotland . . .'

'I welcome it.'

Of course he did. It had brought money into his pocket.

'The people of London are rioting.'

'A plague on the people of London.'

'Do not say that. It could be disastrous to the country.'

'I mean I care not a groat for them.'

'They can be dangerous. They are saying the Scone stone shall not be given up and that it is a disgrace to send a baby to that barbarous land to marry the son of a leper.'

'She will be Queen of Scotland.'

'They do not like it. Mortimer, do you remember how they supported me? How they cheered me in the streets.'

'They always loved you. You only have to appear and they shout their loyalty.'

'Not any more.'

'It is a momentary matter. They don't like the wedding. They won't part with the stone of Scone. They have too high an opinion of their importance, these Londoners. It will blow over.'

'Yesterday someone shouted "Whore" as I rode by.'

'Did you see who? He could be hanged, drawn and quartered for that.'

'Yes, and still he did it. They are turning from me, Mortimer. They are turning from us.'

'Much should we care.'

'I wonder sometimes . . .'

He soothed her as he always did. He snapped his fingers at danger by refusing to see it.

He was the great Mortimer; she was the Queen of England. It was true there was another Queen – but she was of no importance, no more importance than her young husband. Edward and Philippa were the figureheads. The real rulers were Isabella and Mortimer – and so it should remain.

Every night Joanna cried herself to sleep. It was no use their telling her that she was going to be happy in Scotland. She knew she was not. She was going to have a hideous little bridegroom, two years younger than herself, David the Bruce, who was five years old.

She knew that many princesses were betrothed at her age and sometimes they had to go to the homes of their bride-grooms to be brought up in his way of life, but that did not help at all. Eleanor was older than she was and she did not have to go away. And now Philippa had come and she loved Philippa. Philippa was her new sister but what was the use of having a new sister if you were not going to be with her?

She heard the servants talking about how the new Queen had saved a girl from hanging, and how the King had indulged her although the Queen Mother and the Earl of March had not been very pleased and had wanted to continue their journey without delay.

Perhaps if she asked Philippa to save her from going to Scotland she could speak with Edward and as Edward could deny Philippa nothing – so the gossips said – then perhaps she would be saved.

It was her only hope. She would ask Philippa.

Philippa listened gravely. Yes, it was true Edward had allowed her to save the girl, but this was not a state matter. The marriage with Scotland was, and it might be that there could be no way of stopping it. But Philippa would speak to Edward.

She did. He was sorry but there was nothing he could do. It was a state matter and it was in the treaty.

'But when a child is so young surely she could be married by proxy and stay in her own home until she is of an age to leave?'

Edward could only say that it was in the treaty.

He himself was disturbed for he was fond of the little girl and her sister and his brother John. But he was so young himself and after his adventures in Scotland he felt loath to act on some matter of which he was not quite sure. He felt that he had looked rather foolish, marching north with an army and chasing the elusive Scots who had obviously been playing a game with him.

He had to be careful in future.

He hated to disappoint Philippa so he said he would go into the matter and see what could be done.

This meant talking to his mother.

Isabella was pleased that he should have consulted her instead of attempting to act on his own. She pretended to consider the matter but she was determined that Joanna must go to Scotland. It had been agreed upon and if the treaty broke down the Scots might demand the return of the money which Mortimer had already taken.

'We are dealing with barbaric people, my sweet son,' she said. 'You saw what they were like when you went up to chastise them. What a dance they led you.'

He flushed a little. He was very young. It was good to bring home to him in a subtle way how inexperienced he was.

'We could not say what would happen if we did not keep to the treaty. War might break out again.'

'The people are against this marriage, my lady.'

'The people sway with the wind. They know not what is best for them.'

'The Queen is worried about Joanna. She is but a baby . . . and to be sent away . . .'

Isabella stiffened imperceptibly. The Queen? My lady Philippa would have to learn that she had not come here to govern the land.

'Dear Philippa,' said Isabella, 'she is so soft-hearted. I saw lips curl with amusement when she allowed that woman to get the better of her.'

'You mean the woman with the daughter whom Philippa saved from the hangman's rope? I think the people loved her the more for that.'

'Criminals will, my son. They will say we can commit our crimes and be caught. Never mind. We'll make a plea to the Queen.'

'This was but a young girl . . .'

'Of course *she* is young, our dear Philippa. She will grow up. She will learn quickly I think. She is a charming girl. I am so happy for you Edward.'

Edward smiled. He loved to hear praise of Philippa.

'Dear Edward,' went on his mother, 'you know my thoughts are all for you. Everything I do is what I think is best for you. But you have always known that.'

Her beautiful eyes were moist with tears; he kissed her cheek.

She clung to him. 'It has not been easy for me, Edward,' she went on. 'Sometimes I look back over my life and wonder how I have come through it all. I was so petted in my young days at the Court of France and then when I came to England . . .' she shivered. 'And when I think of all I had to do . . . well, it was worth while because it brought me you. If I can see you secure on the throne, grown into the great King I know you will be . . . in time . . . I shall die happy.'

'Dear lady, you are not going to die yet . . . not for a long long time.'

'I pray it will be a long time . . . for I will refuse to die until you have become such a King as your grandfather was.'

She had successfully made him realise his youth, his dependence upon her. He accepted her word that the Scottish marriage must go through.

He told Philippa that he saw clearly that there was nothing he could do about it, and Philippa accepted his word.

Through the sultry July days the procession travelled north to Berwick. At its head rode Queen Isabella, beside the most wretched little girl in the kingdom.

Joanna often thought of running away and she might have attempted it if the Earl of March had not ridden beside her and she had not been so afraid of him. In fact she did not know whom she feared most – her mother or the Earl.

Her mother had spoken sharply to her. She must not be a baby. She must accept her fate. She was not the first Princess who had to leave her home. The Scots would make much of her. Didn't she understand that she would leave her home as a Princess and in Scotland become a Queen.

She would lie in her bed at the various castles in which they stayed during the journey and talk to her sister Eleanor. She was glad Eleanor had come. Eleanor tried to pretend that it was going to be wonderful in Scotland and marriage was exciting. Look how pleased Edward and Philippa were with theirs!

Sometimes Joanna was comforted by her sister; but there were occasions when Eleanor could think of nothing comforting to say and was only too aware that before long she herself might be in a similar plight.

It was sad that Edward and Philippa had not accompanied them. They had talked a great deal about the marriage and Edward longed to stop it. Once more he raged against his youth and inexperience. In his heart he felt the marriage was wrong, and yet he did not feel confident enough to stop it. If he had had a resounding success in Scotland he would have behaved differently.

It was not that he lacked strength of purpose; what he missed was experience; and if he could have convinced himself that there was a right thing to do, he would have done it.

Queen Isabella was hurt that he did not accompany them. She had tried to tempt him by arranging a mock battle and had had special spears made for him elaborately painted with his royal arms; she had others less glorious made for other combatants. It was the sort of entertainment Edward would have enjoyed taking part in and would have excelled at. But he was not tempted. In fact Isabella had misunderstood her son. The last thing he wanted was to be treated like a boy who is bribed with a special treat.

He did not like the idea of the marriage. He did not want to go to the North again where he considered he had recently been humiliated. He was uncertain and unhappy about Scottish matters. So he was going to stay in the soothing company of his beloved Queen.

Meanwhile the royal party arrived at Berwick and the ceremony of betrothal took place with a sad little bride weighed down with the magnificence of her jewelled garments and a little bridegroom who was even younger and seemed to be wondering what all the fuss was about.

It was a splendid ceremony but none was more magnificent than Roger de Mortimer who had brought one hundred and eighty knights to attend him and they in their turn were served by their squires; and all were elaborately and splendidly attired.

Days of feasting followed. There were pageants and tournaments and all these the little bride attended with wondering looks. She was less afraid now when she saw that her bridegroom was only a weak little boy who seemed very young to her because she had the advantage of being two years his senior.

In due course it was time for her to take her leave of the English party. Her mother embraced her and gave her some rich jewels which Joanna did not care very much about. Nor did she feel sad to say good-bye to her mother. She had always been afraid of her.

Isabella with Mortimer and the splendid cavalcade rode south while Joanna, who had been given into the hands of the Scottish nobles and their ladies, was taken to Edinburgh. There she was brought to the King of Scotland – an old old man who, though he was so feeble and could scarcely move, had brilliant eyes which smiled at her and a kindly look.

He was Robert the Bruce, her new father-in-law, and he gave orders that she was to be treated with the utmost care and it was to be remembered that she was very young and in a strange land.

There was something odd about him. He was dying, she

knew, of a terrible disease, but he did not inspire her with fear as her own mother and Roger de Mortimer did.

She was bitterly homesick. She wanted the nursery at Windsor. She wanted Johanette Jermyn and dear Isabella de Valance; she wanted her sister Eleanor and her brother John. And most of all she wanted Edward and Philippa.

She had to be brave though. She had to remember that this happened to most princesses. That was what they were born for. They had to make peace and stop wars.

She was not surprised when she heard herself referred to as Joanna Make-Peace.

Events in France had brought dazzling new prospects to the English crown. The history of France over the last few years had been overshadowed by the Curse of the Templars. Philip the Fair, father of Queen Isabella, had made the error of the century when, in order to take their wealth, he had destroyed the Knights Templars. The final act in that dismal tragedy was the burning to death of Jacques de Molai in the Ile de la Cité. As the flames licked his limbs de Molai had uttered the curse – no good should come to the King and his heirs and God would be revenged on them for this evil deed. This had been uttered in the presence of the thousands who had come to witness the end of the Grand Master. It was taken very seriously and, when within a year both the Pope (who had been deeply involved) and the King had died, it was accepted as certain that the curse would work. And so it seemed it had. Philip had three sons and one daughter Isabella, wife to Edward the Second. All three sons became Kings of France – Louis the Tenth le Hutin, the Quarrelsome, Philip the Fifth known as The Long because of his unusual height and Charles the Fourth, the Fair because of his good looks. They all reigned for short periods and none of them had left a male heir. This was generally believed to be due to the curse.

Charles the Fourth had just died and people were looking to Philip of Valois, son of Charles, younger brother of Philip the Fair, as the heir to the throne.

But, reasoned Edward's advisers, Philip had had a daughter – Isabella – and Isabella had a son Edward, King of England.

The Salic Law prevailed in France and that meant that a woman could not inherit the throne. Perhaps not, but what if that woman had a son? Why should he not have a right to the crown?

The matter was discussed in Parliament and the prospect of enriching the country and themselves was an agreeable one. Edward glowed with anticipation. He had failed to win Scotland but what a great prize France would be. And he could convince himself that he had a claim through his mother.

The French rather naturally had different ideas and elected Philip of Valois as their King.

There were hotheads in England who would have liked to raise an army and march into France. Edward himself longed to gain glory there. If he could win the crown of France he would have done something which even his illustrious grandfather had failed to do.

Isabella and Mortimer were against the enterprise.

'It is not as though victory – even if there should be victory – could be achieved in a few weeks,' said Mortimer. 'There would be a war. Do you think the French would accept Edward? They would put up a strong fight to keep an English King off the throne of France. It would go on for years. The country would be impoverished. *We* should be impoverished.'

Isabella agreed with him.

She talked gently to her son. 'The time is not yet ripe,' she said. 'You must grow up a little. You are not experienced in warfare as the Scottish exploit showed.'

'If the Scots had come out to fight . . .' began Edward hotly.

But his mother smiled lovingly at him. 'Those were the tactics of war, my dear son. They are something every commander has to be prepared for.'

She could bring Edward back to depend on her by reminding him of his youth and inexperience. 'The Scottish adventure has been a useful exercise,' she told Mortimer. 'A reference to it and he is prepared to take any advice.'

So the matter of the claim to the French crown was set aside. But only, Edward promised himself, temporarily. The time would come when he would make a bid for the crown of France.

Soon after his coronation Philip the Sixth called together his numerous vassals that, as a new King of France, he might accept their homage. Among these was Edward who must swear fealty for his French fiefs.

On receiving the command Edward called his Parliament together to decide what, in the somewhat delicate matter of his claim to the French crown, should be done.

After a great deal of discussion it was decided that he must go but that in doing his homage he should in no way renounce his claim to the throne. He must travel in great splendour so that the French might be aware of his riches, but the tricky moment would be when he came face to face with Philip in the ceremony.

Edward took a fond farewell of Philippa. It was the first time they had been separated since their marriage and he promised to be back as soon as he possibly could.

The King travelled through France to Amiens where he was greeted with great warmth to hide the suspicions the French must feel towards one who had declared he had a claim to the throne of France.

It was a hot June day when Edward came before the King of France to pay the necessary homage, most splendidly attired in a robe of crimson velvet embroidered in gold with leopards. His sword was at his side and on his head he wore a glittering golden crown and his spurs were golden to match it.

It was inevitable that the French King should be equally splendid. Seated on his throne, wearing *his* crown and clad in blue velvet decorated with golden fleurs-de-lis he looked askance at the King of England.

Philip murmured to his knight-at-arms that he did not expect his liegeman to do homage in a crown. All knew that Edward was King of England, but that fact was not a matter of concern on this occasion. He had come to pay homage for his lands in France and it should be done with a bare head and an ungirt sword.

'My lord,' said Edward, 'I can do homage only generally. I cannot set aside my English crown.'

There was much murmuring throughout the hall. Philip looked at this very young man – scarcely more than a boy and wondered what he had to fear from him. He decided to act with care.

'I will accept homage on your terms,' he said. 'But when you return to England I would have you search the records and if you find that full liege homage is due you will send letters patent to me of it.'

Edward said: 'This I agree to do.'

And the King of France answered: 'I accept your word on your honour.'

But before the homage proceeded, with Edward wearing the crown on his head and the sword at his side, he asked that those territories taken from his father should be returned to him.

'Why should this be?' asked Philip. 'These lands were taken from your father in war.'

There was a deep silence throughout the community. All realised how reluctantly Edward did homage to a King whose crown he thought he himself should be wearing. But his claim to the throne seemed so ridiculous to the French that they did not consider it seriously; and the fact that Edward was so young made it seem even more absurd.

But there among the nobles of France Edward came to a decision. At some time, when he was older and more experienced, he was coming over to claim what he was fast believing he had a right to.

The lesson of the Scottish enterprise had been well learned and he was going to tread warily. He agreed therefore to pay homage only for those lands which he held in France, so the ceremony proceeded and, according to the custom, Edward placed his hands between those of the King of France and Philip responded by kissing his mouth.

After the ceremony he was eager to return home to Philippa at Windsor and there was great joy in their reunion.

She told him how anxious she had been. She hated his going away from her and was terrified that something would happen to him. He laughed at her fears and expounded at great length on the glories of France.

75

'It is a wonderful country, Philippa, and as I rode through it I was saying to myself: "Mine . . . this should be mine."'

'They will never give it up,' said Philippa.

'No. I shall have to fight for it.'

She was uneasy.

'Do you not think I shall do it, Philippa?'

'I am sure you will do anything you wish to do, Edward. But I like not battles. For one thing they will take you away from me.'

Edward replied that he would forgo France for her.

He had only been in England four days when news came from the little castle of Cardross on the banks of the Clyde that Robert the Bruce was dead, worn out with continual struggles, and desperately ill with the fearful leprosy from which he had been suffering for several years.

Philippa stood by Edward when he received the news.

'The Bruce dead,' she murmured. 'This means that our little Joanna is Queen of Scotland.'

Isabella was growing more and more apprehensive. It was so different from when she had landed in England. It seemed to her that her friends were slipping away from her. Sir John of Hainault, that trusting adorer, who had been in love with her and had fought so well for her cause because of that, had returned to Hainault. She knew that those who had been with her in the beginning were turning away from her.

It was amazing how people blamed her for the marriage of Joanna. She knew they were saying it was cruel to have sent a child of seven into that northern land of harsh winters and barbaric people. To have married the little girl to a bridegroom of five whose father was dying of leprosy and who could very well have inherited the dreadful disease, was monstrous. But that, it could be argued, was a state matter; what could not be accepted was her flagrant behaviour with the adventurer Mortimer. Indeed a great deal of her unpopularity came from her association with Mortimer. Mortimer was a strong man, a fighter, a man who was without fear, but he could not be said to have a very subtle mind. He saw only the advantages of the moment and clearly there were many. He seized what he could get and no man – not even the favourites of the previous King – could have become so rich in so short a time. If there were lands and money to be had it could be depended on that Mortimer would find it and take it for himself.

And the reason why Isabella was being looked on with growing suspicion was due to her reliance on this man. It was as though he had bewitched her. She could see no fault in him. Their passionate sexual connection was as necessary to her as it had been in the beginning of their association.

If they had acted discreetly their relationship might have been accepted. The whole country knew how she must have suffered through the late King's deficiencies. But this affair with Mortimer was not discreet. It was blatant and becoming more so. One rarely appeared in public without the other and they behaved with such careless abandon that it was clear that they did not care who knew of their liaison.

Often she reminded herself of her achievements. Who would have believed it possible when she had gone to France, having lured her husband and Hugh le Despenser into agreeing to her departure, that she would have returned so triumphantly, have brought about Edward's removal, set her son on the throne and, with Mortimer, ruled the country through him? Everything they had planned had come to pass. Then why could she not enjoy it? Mortimer did. Oh, he was wiser than she was.

Of course there were her dreams and they were becoming more frequent. Sometimes they spilled over into the day. She wished she could stop thinking about her dead husband. She wished she didn't see him in her dreams. In that vague drifting between wakefulness and sleep she fancied she heard his screams when the red hot spit was entering his body.

'Oh God,' she cried, 'let me forget. Why do I have to be haunted? Why cannot I be wise like Mortimer?'

Mortimer was wise indeed. He cared for nobody – certainly not the dead.

'Let be,' was his motto. 'What's done is done.'

And he was right, of course.

What had happened to her? She, who was the daughter of one of the most ruthless men of the century, the despoiler and murderer of the Templars, should have inherited some of his ruthless strength. I am his daughter, she thought. Perhaps the curse has come upon me.

She was beginning to notice the change in people's attitudes towards her.

There was the Earl of Kent, for instance. As her husband's young half-brother, son of a French mother, he had been drawn to her from the day she had arrived in the country. He had clearly been impressed by her beauty as so many had and, when she had arrived in England with her army to stand against Edward the Second and put young Edward the Third on the throne, Edmund had been there to support her.

Yet only yesterday when she had been riding with him she had been aware of his coolness towards her.

He had talked about his brother. She remembered every word of the conversation because it had seemed significant.

'I believe he was not well treated at Berkeley,' he had said suddenly.

She had felt the tingling shrinking on her flesh which indicated fear and she was not sure whether it showed or not. A short while ago she would have given no sign but something was happening to her. She was becoming more and more tense and nervous and showing it.

'Oh . . . Thomas of Berkeley was very friendly with him.'

'He is a connection of the Earl of March, I believe.'

'Yes . . . through marriage . . .'

A silence had followed during which Edmund frowned deeply. She and Mortimer had always said that Edmund was a simple fellow. He had never been able to hide his feelings and he was very thoughtful now.

She had tried to change the subject but he had brought it back.

'Our cousin Lancaster and he were very amicable together when the King was at Kenilworth.'

She wanted to scream: 'Stop it. Stop. The dreams will come back tonight. They always do when I talk of him in the day.'

She desperately sought to change the subject. 'I have reason to believe that the Queen is with child.'

Edmund smiled. He was fond of the new Queen and of Edward. Isabella went on: 'It will be a blessing if it is so and I think the nation will go wild with joy if it is a son.'

Edmund agreed and to Isabella's relief they talked of the joys of parenthood. Edmund had four children of his own and he never tired of discussing them.

But just as Isabella was congratulating herself on having most happily changed the subject they came upon a group of people who stood back to let them pass.

There were no cheers for Queen Isabella as in the past.

But one voice was heard and what was said came very distinctly to their ears.

'Whore!'

Isabella had pretended not to hear but she saw the faint colour in the Earl's face. He looked disconcerted and she fancied she noticed a tightening of his lips.

She sought out Mortimer. In such circumstances she always turned to Mortimer. He would soothe her and know what to do.

'The people are turning against us,' she said.

'Why concern ourselves with them?'

'Dear Mortimer, they could rise against us.'

'They would never dare.'

Looking at him she could believe that. He looked so powerful, so important and so splendid. The glory of his apparel increased every day. He never went anywhere without an array of knights almost as splendidly clad as himself, proclaiming his wealth and importance.

She told him what the Earl of Kent had said. 'I could see speculation in his eyes. If the people turned against us, his royalty could make him a leader.'

'Kent! He would never lead anyone.'

'I believe he might,' said Isabella.

'The man's a fool.'

'That may be but he is Edward's half-brother.'

'The people have never liked him.'

'They have never disliked him.'

'No, he is neither this nor that.'

'But he would be a figurehead. Others would decide on policy. I fear him, Mortimer. He talked about the King. He has been making enquiries I believe.'

Mortimer narrowed his eyes. 'Maltravers, Gurney and Ogle are out of the country.'

'Yes, I know. What if he discovered where and they talked?'

Mortimer was silent for a while and then he said: 'We will make an example of one of them. We will let them see what happens to those who meddle.'

'An example of whom?' asked Isabella.

'My choice falls on Kent,' said Mortimer.

'Kent! The King's half-brother. Edward's uncle.'

'It is always best, my love, to strike at the top.'

Edmund Earl of Kent was twenty-nine years old. He had been six years old when his father, Edward the First, had died. He had seen very little of that great warrior who was always away from home on some military enterprise and he and his brother Thomas of Brotherton, Earl of Norfolk, who was just one year older than he was, had been brought up by their gentle French mother Marguerite.

It was only natural that when the new King, Edward the Second, married a French wife that he should be drawn to her. She was beautiful and gracious and everyone said what a good and docile wife she was to a husband who was far from admirable.

When Edward had become so unpopular through his association with the Despensers Edmund had become a member of Lancaster's party to stand against them, which meant being opposed to the King. He had been on an unsuccessful mission in France when Isabella had visited her brother's court and he had joined the malcontents who gathered round her. Thus when she came to England with her army he was with her; and he had been faithful to her cause until now.

Mortimer however was becoming intolerable. There was murmuring against him all through the country just as there had been with Gaveston and the Despensers in the previous reign. This Marcher Baron had set himself up as a king and even had he been a rightful king he would have caused discontent by his behaviour. Moreover he was Isabella's paramour and, although none would have raised any great objection if the liaison had been carried on with discretion, it was intolerable that Mortimer, freshly risen from Isabella's bed, should strut about as few kings had ever had the temerity to do.

It had to stop.

He had conferred with Henry of Lancaster, his cousin, and his brother, Thomas Earl of Norfolk, and they had agreed with him. At that same time they had reminded him that the King was very much under his mother's influence and that meant Mortimer's. The situation was full of dangers and they all agreed they must go warily.

It was at this time that a Friar called at the house of the Earl of Kent in Kensington and he asked for a private audience with the Earl for he had something to tell him which he was sure would be of the greatest interest.

As soon as they were alone together the Friar said: 'My lord, this seems incredible but I know it to be true. Edward the Second is not dead. He still lives.'

Kent was speechless and the Friar continued: 'I can tell you where he is, my lord. He is in Corfe Castle. The Governor of the castle is well known to me and I have his word for it that the King still lives. He is kept a prisoner there and he longs to be in touch with those whom he can trust. He looks to you, my lord, as his brother.'

Kent spluttered: 'I . . . I cannot believe this to be true. I must go to him at once.'

'My lord, forgive me, but you must act with the greatest care. The Governor goes in fear of his life. He regrets already having let me into the secret. If you did go to Corfe it would have to be with discretion.'

'Of course, of course,' cried Kent. 'What is their motive?'

'It is to tell the world that he is dead that they may rule through the young King as they wish.'

'But Edward gave up his throne to his son.'

'Yes, but young Edward was loth to take it and he could not happily wear the crown while his father lived. So . . . they devised this plan . . .'

'Isabella . . . and Mortimer . . .'

The Friar nodded.

'I will set out for Corfe without delay,' said the Earl.

'I will accompany you, my lord, but you will understand that our mission must be entirely secret.'

The Earl promised this should be so and did not even tell his wife where he was going.

During the journey the Friar told Kent that Edward was a prisoner and that Mortimer's idea was to get rid of him as soon as he could conveniently do so.

The Earl of Kent was a simple man. He had swayed from side to side during the troubles which had beset the country during the reigns of Gaveston and the Despensers. He had always been gullible and it might have been that was why Mortimer had selected him to be his example rather than his elder brother, Thomas of Norfolk. Norfolk had never been so embroiled in conflicts. Although he had supported Isabella on her return to England he had soon retired to his estates and had not taken a great part in the struggle. Kent was different: he was all enthusiasm one day and doubts the next.

Now he was ready to believe this story of Edward's captivity in Corfe, though when he arrived at the castle the reception he received would have warned any other man that there was something contrived about the whole matter.

At first the Governor did not wish to let him in and he reproached the Friar for having brought him, but at last after a great deal of talking the visitors were allowed inside.

'Is it true that you have my brother here?' demanded Kent.

The Governor floundered, stammered and looked down at the floor, up at the rafters and anywhere but at the Earl of Kent.

'I cannot believe it,' said Kent. 'There has been some mistake.'

'It is not so,' declared the Friar.

'It is all very strange,' said the Earl. 'Until I saw my brother here I would not believe it.'

'My lord,' cried the Governor, 'I dare not . . . I could not . . . I do not know whether . . .'

'You must tell me the truth,' cried the Earl.

The Governor at length said: 'If you would communicate with the King you must do so by letter.'

'So you admit that he is here.'

'I say that if you wrote a letter and it was delivered to the

84

one for whom it is intended then you would know for yourself whether the prisoner here is the King.'

'So you admit to having a prisoner.'

The Governor was silent.

A warning flashed into the Earl's mind. They were making such a mystery of this. Why? Of course they were making a mystery. The matter was mysterious. But he was not putting anything into writing until he was certain.

He said as much.

'My lord, I dare not take you to the King. He has refused to see anyone. He thinks all who come are his enemies, sent from the Earl of March.'

'I know,' said the Friar, 'that the King will see no one but would it be possible for my lord Earl to see the King . . . perhaps from some point where he himself would not be observed.'

'I will consider whether this could be possible,' said the Governor.

Edmund spent a restless night in the castle. It was all too involved and mysterious for comfort and he did not greatly care for the Governor.

At dusk the next day the Friar said that if he looked through a peep-hole above the room where the King was lodged he would see him for himself.

'Why should I not visit him?'

'My lord, the King has moments of desolation when he is not quite lucid. This matter of a rescue will have to be broken to him gently, by letter preferably. Come with us and assure yourself that it is your brother who is lodged in this castle.'

It was very strange, but the Earl told himself that if he could see Edward he would believe the story. He was conducted up a spiral staircase and taken to a room. Here a hole was revealed in the wall. It was small, just enough for an eye to peer through, and looking in the Earl saw a room with bed, table and a chair. On the chair sat a man. Although he was seated it was easy to see that he was exceptionally tall and his greying hair had been very fair. The resemblance was strong, but the light was feeble. However the Earl of Kent was very ready to be deceived.

He left Corfe Castle the next day to consider what he had seen, and thoughtfully returned to Kensington. He wondered whether he should tell his brother. Could he really have been the King, that man who was seated in the chair at the table in the room at Corfe Castle? But why should anyone want to deceive him?

For a few days he pondered and then he received another visit from the Friar.

'I have had a message from the Pope, my lord Earl,' he said. 'He has commanded me to tell you that he wishes the King to be rescued from Corfe Castle.'

'Then the Pope believes this story.'

'It is no story, my lord. Your brother lies in Corfe Castle, a prisoner of Mortimer. There are plans to remove him altogether. This is what the Pope fears will happen and he has commanded me to put this matter to you and to beg you not to delay.'

The Earl was thoughtful.

'First,' he said, 'I must write a letter to my brother.'

'That would be an excellent plan,' replied the Friar. 'If you will tell him that you are his friend as well as his brother and will rouse others to his aid. If you will tell him that you are determined to expose the wickedness of Roger de Mortimer you will put new hope into the King, my lord. Aye, and

Heaven will praise you, as the Pope implies, for what you have done.'

Edmund glowed with enthusiasm.

He would write immediately and the Friar should take the letter to Corfe. Could he be sure of getting it into the hands of the King? Indeed he could. The Governor would not be averse to passing on a letter.

Kent wrote at great length and indiscretion, explaining that he was at his brother's service and would raise an army to fight for him and against his enemies. He could, if he wished, be set back on the throne for it seemed as though he had given it up under duress.

The Friar took the letter and rode back to his lodging where he discarded his friar's habit. He would be well rewarded he knew. All had worked out according to their plans. He had the letter which was clear treason against the King if anything ever was. Who would have thought a man in the Earl of Kent's position would be so easily misled by a man who happened to bear a faint resemblance to the late King. The Friar set out for Winchester where a Parliament was sitting and Mortimer received him immediately.

He laughed as he read the letter.

'Well done, erstwhile Friar. Silly Kent has written enough to put a rope round his neck. He has been well deceived.'

'It was no hard matter, my lord, to deceive him. I never knew a man more eager to fall into a trap.'

'It will be the last time he shall fall,' said Mortimer fiercely. 'I have made up my mind to that. You have done well and shall not be forgotten.'

Now to it, he thought. I will summon the Earl of Kent to Winchester.

❀ ❀ ❀

The King and Queen were at Woodstock. They were as devoted as ever and they were especially happy at this time because the Queen was pregnant.

Edward was determined that the utmost care should be taken of her and he said he could trust her to no other than himself and in spite of pressing state matters he would not leave her.

Shortly before, she had been crowned. He had been so proud of her. He often thought how fortunate he had been. How many kings married women with whom they were already in love? How many secured such a woman as Philippa? She was loving, tender and good. His people appreciated her worth as he did. And when she gave him a son . . . She had admonished him a little, fearful of course that the child might not be a boy. But although he wanted a boy he would not care so very much if it proved to be a daughter. They were young in love and would have a host of children – many boys among them.

The coronation had not been as splendid as he would have liked. The exchequer was very low and he was beginning to feel very uneasy. His mother and Mortimer were taking too much of money and treasure which was needed for other things. He must examine these matters. He was concerned about his mother, though, and hated to upset her and she could be so easily upset nowadays. Any word of criticism however faint directed at Mortimer and she was ready to fly into one of those moods when she talked incessantly and sometimes not very coherently, and that worried him.

He was at Woodstock to forget such matters. He and Philippa could walk together and he could cosset her and they could talk of the baby which was due in June.

Messengers came from Winchester. There were alarming reports of treason, and his uncle the Earl of Kent was involved.

Oh not seriously, he thought. Uncle Edmund could never be really serious. He thought he was, of course, but he could be so enthusiastic about some plan and a few words could alter the course of his excitement completely. He did not take Uncle Edmund entirely seriously.

He would not go to Winchester. He was not going to leave Philippa. She was very young but then she was strong and so far she had had an easy pregnancy. He wanted to stay here and talk of the coming child for nothing could seem of any importance beside that.

The days were growing warm. Philippa was growing larger. Each day brought the arrival of that blessed infant nearer. Who could think about what was happening at Winchester?

The Earl of Kent was shown the letter he had written to the dead King. Was it in his handwriting? It was, he answered. There was no point in denying it. He had believed the dead King was alive and indeed had been shown a man in Corfe Castle who greatly resembled him.

'Did he tell you he was the dead King?' he was asked.

'I had no speech with him,' replied the Earl.

'Yet you believed he was the dead King and you wrote this letter to him. Do you know that this letter is treason. Do you know that your offers of service were to a man not our King whom you are proposing to set up against our true King . . . do you realise, my lord Earl, that this is treason?'

He knew enough to recognise that it was.

He also knew the penalty for treason.

Isabella and Mortimer talked of it when they were alone.

'You cannot sentence him to death, Mortimer,' said Isabella. 'He is the King's uncle.'

'I can and I will,' cried Mortimer. 'He has written this letter. He has condemned himself to death. He should not complain if the sentence is carried out.'

'You are forgetting he is royal.'

'Royal or not he goes to the scaffold. There is none who thinks himself so high that he cannot be brought low.'

'The King must be told.'

'My love, do you want to ruin our plan? You know what Edward would do. He would pardon his dear kinsman.'

'What then, Mortimer?'

'Execution,' replied Mortimer. 'Immediate execution.'

They had sentenced him to death and the sentence was to be carried out without delay. They had taken him into the courtroom presided over by the coroner of the royal household, Robert Howel, and he had been clad only in his shirt with a rope about his neck.

He pleaded for mercy. He wished to see the King, he said.

His accusers regarded him coldly. It was too late to think of repentance, they told him. He was a traitor to the King; he had committed treason; he had tried to arouse others to share his disloyalty; he had planned to raise an army against the King. What did it matter if he were closely related to the King? He was a traitor and deserved his punishment the more for being royal.

On Mortimer's orders he was taken through Winchester to a spot outside the walls. There the axe was awaiting him.

It was early morning for Mortimer had wished the deed to be done before the town was astir. He guessed that the execution of such a well-known man would attract crowds and there might be some to disagree with the verdict.

Half an hour passed and the headsman had not arrived. A messenger came from him. He had run away because he was afraid to do it, he had said, for the Earl of Kent was royal; he would not behead such a person. Who knew he might be blamed for it later.

Mortimer who was there in person to witness his enemy's end was furious.

'The knave!' he cried. 'Send for another. Anyone. But let there be no delay. The headsman had an assistant had he not?'

He had, was the answer, but hearing what his superior had done he himself had acted similarly. He also had decided that he would not take responsibility for beheading a member of the royal family.

Mortimer was fuming with rage. It was as though they were defying him, as though they said: 'Edward the King would not wish this deed to be done.' Of course he would not. That was why it had to be done with all speed.

'Find me a headsman,' cried Mortimer; and although one was sought none could be found. His knights and squires cast down their eyes lest he should command them to do the deed. He could not do that, for if he did it could be said that one of his men had murdered the Earl of Kent. It must be done by a man whose business was with prisons.

Noon had come and the Earl still lived. He was praying to God, telling himself that this was divine intervention. He was going to be saved because God would allow no one to behead him.

The afternoon wore on and still no one could be found to do the job. Then Mortimer had an idea. 'Go to the prison,' he said. 'Find a man who is condemned to die. Promise him freedom if he will act as headsman to the Earl of Kent.'

That was the end of the quest.

Life was a reward too great to be missed.

At five o'clock on that March day Edmund Earl of Kent laid his head on a block and that head was severed from his body.

The King was at Woodstock when he heard the news.

He could not believe it. His own uncle. To have been executed without a word to him!

A traitor they said. He was plotting to raise an army against his King.

It was the end of March and the child was due in June. Edward must leave Philippa and ride to Winchester to hear for himself what had really happened.

She did not want him to go, of course, nor did he wish to. She wanted to come with him, but he would not allow that.

True the winter was over but the roads were rough. How would she travel? Carried in a litter. That would not be good for the child.

'Must you go?' she asked.

'He was my uncle,' he answered.

'And a traitor to you.'

'Somehow I cannot believe that of my uncle.'

'You always thought he was not very clever.'

'Not very clever but he would not rise against *me*.'

'Something troubles you deeply,' she said.

'My love, my uncle has been beheaded, accused of treason against me. In truth I am troubled.'

'There is something more,' she said.

He stroked her hair back from her face. 'I am troubled that I must leave you,' he said. 'Never fear, I shall be back soon. I shall order that I am to be kept informed of your health every day.'

So he rode to Winchester, and there he found his mother and Mortimer.

'Fair son,' cried Isabella, 'how good it is to see you here.'

'I am not happy with my mission,' he answered grimly. 'I come to hear about my uncle Kent.'

Mortimer was there, smiling familiarly. One would have thought Mortimer the King and he, Edward, the subject.

'My lord, ever zealous in your service we could not allow one to live who was trying to raise an army against you.'

'I do not believe that to be true.'

'There was evidence. He admitted it. He had trumped up some story about a man at Corfe whom he believed to be your father.'

Edward was silent. He looked at this man and he thought: What happened to my father? How did he die?

His mother was watching him closely.

'Mortimer has been a good servant to you, Edward.'

'And to himself, my lady,' Edward replied; and his words sent shivers of alarm through Isabella's heart. She thought: He is growing up. He is growing up too fast.

'My dear son, your grandfather always dealt speedily with traitors so I heard. It is never good to let them live to ferment trouble.'

'My uncle was a fool but not a knave.'

'The actions of fools and knaves can sometimes run on

similar lines,' said Isabella. 'Oh, Edward, I know this is a shock to you, but it was necessary. Believe me. Believe me.'

She looked so wild that he had to soothe her. 'I know you have my good at heart,' he assured her.

'Have I not always loved you? Were you not everything to me? When you were a baby you made all that I had suffered worth while.'

'I know. I know. I do not complain of you.'

It was pointed but Mortimer shrugged it aside.

'Only a boy,' he said afterwards to Isabella. 'The Scottish campaign taught him that and it is something he will never forget.'

'What if he discovers that you set the trap for Kent? That you arranged for his downfall?'

'How could he? Has he discovered how his father died?'

'Not yet,' said Isabella.

'Oh, my love, what has come over you? You are so fearful these days.'

'I have a premonition of evil. Oh Mortimer, we should never have killed Edmund of Kent.'

'Nonsense. It has shown people that they should take care before they trifle with me.'

He drew himself to his full height. The complacent smile was always on his lips nowadays. What was wrong with the execution of Kent? Mortimer had taken charge of much of his possessions and grown the richer for it. All over the country people would be marvelling at the might of Mortimer.

'Take care,' they would say. 'Never offend the Earl of March.'

❦ Chapter V ❦

THE END OF MORTIMER

I
t was ten o'clock on the morning of June the fifteenth and
expectancy hung over Woodstock Palace.

Philippa was calm; her women about her declared that
that was extraordinary in one so young expecting her first
child. She was just seventeen years old.

'If the child is a boy,' she had told Lady Katherine
Haryngton, 'my happiness will be complete.'

'It is never wise to think too much about the sex of the child,
my lady,' was the reply.

'Oh do not think I should not love a girl. I should. And it is
not for myself that I want a boy, but for Edward. Imagine his
joy if I could bring forth a son. Everything has been perfect so
far, Katherine. I would just like it all to be crowned with a
boy . . . a perfect boy . . . a boy who looks exactly like Edward.'

'We will pray for that, my lady.'

'Dear Edward. He longs to be with me now and will be I
know ere long. In a way I am glad that he is not here. I may
suffer and that would make him unhappy. No, I want him to
arrive in time to see his boy . . . and not before.'

'My lady, you make great demands on fate.'

They were good friends, she and Katherine. Katherine was the wife of Sir John Haryngton of Farleton in Lancashire, herself a wife and mother and very well able to look after Philippa.

They discussed children and the best way to bring them up during those waiting days; and then came the fifteenth, that day which Philippa was to think of in later years as one of the happiest of her life for during the morning she gave birth to a child – a boy, who was perfect in every way and even at his birth showed himself to have the long limbs of the Plantagenets and that lusty air which Katherine Haryngton declared was obvious from the first moment she saw him.

Exhausted but triumphant Philippa held him in her arms – this wonder child, this fruit of her love for Edward.

'God has favoured me,' she said. 'Never was a woman more blessed. The news must be taken to Edward without delay.'

'I will send your valet, Thomas Priour, to him at once,' said Katherine.

'I would he were here. I would I could see his face.'

'He will be here. You will see his face.'

'I long to show him our boy.'

She did not have to wait. Edward came immediately. He had given the delighted Thomas Priour a reward of forty marks a year for bringing him the good news.

Now he strode into his wife's chamber, knelt by the bed and kissed her hand. There were tears on her cheeks.

'I never knew there could be such happiness,' said the Queen.

'Nor I,' replied the King, 'and only you could give this to me.'

They marvelled over the child. Edward had to assure

himself that the reports of him were true. Yes, there he lay in his state cradle decorated with paintings of four evangelists, big for his age, long-legged and with a down of flaxen hair. A true Plantagenet.

'An Edward,' said Philippa.

So that was the name he was given.

Edward was seventeen and seven months old when his son was born, and this event following so closely on the execution of his uncle which had been a great shock to him, jerked him out of his boyhood and into manhood.

There were certain facts he had refused to face before, and this was because of his mother's involvement. It was entirely due to her that he had not acted before. He had refused to look facts boldly in the face because he knew that if he did he would find something which would horrify him.

He was fast realising that he could no longer delay looking at the truth and in order to do so clearly he must forget that Isabella was his mother; he must escape from that spell she had cast on him from the days of his childhood. She had always been apart from other people; she was more beautiful than any he had ever seen; when she had ridden out with her as a boy and had heard the people's cheers she had seemed to him like a goddess. It was only now that he was forcing himself to see her as she really was.

The man he hated was Mortimer. For some time the Earl of March had shown that he considered himself the most important man in the kingdom. He had taken the money received from Scotland as though he were the King – only a King would not have used that money for his own personal needs — at least Edward would not. Edward had now heard the details of the Earl of Kent's execution. Mortimer had killed him because he had wanted him out of the way. There were rumours that Mortimer had set the scene for his death by trumping up a story about Edward the Second's still being alive.

Mortimer was a rogue and a villain and there would be no good rule in England while he lived.

But what concerned Edward was his mother.

Philippa was in a state of bliss, refusing to be separated from her baby, feeding the child herself, rushing to his cradle on awaking every morning to make sure that he had survived the night. If he whimpered she was overcome with anxieties; when he smiled her happiness was overwhelming. It was fortunate that the young Prince was a lusty child and gave little cause for anxiety.

Edward did not wish to disturb her at this time by imparting his fears to her. Yet he wished to confide in someone whom he could trust. There was one among his friends for whom he had a particular liking. This was William de Montacute who was in his late twenties — old enough to give helpful advice, but young enough to be almost of Edward's generation.

Montacute had been a good friend to Edward. He had accompanied him on the humiliating Scottish campaign and had travelled with him to France when he had gone to pay homage to the King there. Over the last two years the friendship had ripened and is was in Montacute that he decided to confide.

Montacute was quick to agree that Edward would never be the King in truth while Mortimer lived. He heard whispering which did not reach Edward's ears. The people were saying that Mortimer was the King and they did not like that. They wanted the country to be rid of Mortimer and their true King to govern them.

'I can speak frankly to you,' said Edward. 'There is my mother.'

'And do I have leave to speak frankly to you, my lord?'

'I see that we shall not advance very far without frankness.'

'Then, my lord, all the world knows that your mother is Mortimer's mistress. She is bewitched by him and this is why he has such power. She will deny him nothing and when he decided to murder your uncle of Kent, she agreed with him.'

'I know it,' said the King.

'Then my lord, imitate his tactics. Why should he not be arrested as he arrested Kent? Why should he not be submitted to a hasty trial and as hasty a death?'

'I would not want this country to be plunged into civil war.'

'Civil war, my lord! Do you think there are any men in this land who would fight for Mortimer? There is none so hated as he. Gaveston found none to stand by him. Nor did the Despensers. These favourites are hated by the people. Nay, my lord. It should be a simple matter. Arrest Mortimer. God knows there is enough against him. Lose no time. Seek the first opportunity. Bring him to trial. He will quickly be condemned and there be an end to him.'

'And my mother?'

Montacute was silent for a few moments, then he said: 'You will find out after Mortimer is gone, what is the best way to deal with her.'

'I am calling a Parliament at the end of the month. It shall be in Nottingham. Mortimer will be there. Meanwhile we will find out all we can of his evil deeds. It will not be difficult I am sure.'

'Then,' said Montacute, 'let us prepare for Nottingham at the end of October.'

❦ ❦ ❦

Isabella knew something was wrong. Edward was too young to hide it from her. He was aware of this and avoided her. She heard rumours of those who worked for her in secret that the King was planning something.

She warned Mortimer, but he was complacent as ever. 'Do you doubt my ability to deal with our boy?' he asked.

'Gentle Mortimer, I believe our boy has grown up considerably in these last few weeks.'

'My love, he is a father. I hear the new Prince is a lusty little fellow. It will be years before we need concern ourselves with him. But his birth has given our boy a feeling that he is at last a man. There's nothing more than that, my love.'

'He *is* a man, Mortimer,' said Isabella quietly.

When she was worried voices came to her in the night. Sometimes she would awaken and whisper: 'You are there, Edward, are you not? Mocking me in the shadows. Is it you who are sowing evil thoughts in Edward's mind? Do not harm Mortimer, Edward. He is my love, my life. I am bound to him as I never thought to be to any man. Do not harm Mortimer.'

She was always afraid she would awaken Mortimer. She dreaded his derisive laughter. He was always loving though – passionately loving. Sometimes she thought: Yes, I am a Queen. He needs me as I need him.

There was to be a Parliament at Nottingham. There was something special about this Parliament. Some of Mortimer's spies had discovered that the King was seeing a great deal of

William Montacute and one of their servants had overheard them, talking of taking Mortimer at Nottingham.

Mortimer laughed aloud when he heard. 'Let them try,' he said.

But Isabella was uneasy. 'We could refuse to go,' she said. 'You could feign illness.'

'Nay, my love. We'll go. We'll lodge in the castle there. It is the strongest fortress in the neighbourhood. We'll take possession of it and see what happens from there.'

Mortimer and Isabella rode to Nottingham surrounded by their retinue of knights, which grew more and more splendid every time they appeared, proclaiming as they did the wealth and might of Mortimer.

For all his bravado Mortimer was affected by Isabella's fears. He knew that a number of those who had supported him were now slipping away from him and it occurred to him that those who stayed with him did so because they were so involved in his schemes that they would be judged guilty even if they left.

It was too late now for them to leave. Too late. Those words had an ominous ring.

He had taken the precaution of reaching Nottingham before the King did and that enabled him to take possession of the castle there in the name of Queen Isabella.

It occurred to the Queen that the King might be given the keys of the castle so she set about having the outer locks changed. 'Every night,' she said, 'the keys shall be brought to me and I shall keep them under my pillow where I shall know that they are safe.'

The castle at Nottingham was indeed a fortress. It had been said that it was impregnable and could never be taken except by famine. It was built on the summit of a rock one hundred and thirty-three feet high and even before William the Conqueror had ordered the castle to be built there had been a tower there which had been used by the Danes against Ethelred.

Meanwhile Montacute had arrived in Nottingham, his plan being to seize Mortimer at the Parliament and then bring him to trial. By this time Mortimer was aware of what was about to happen and he knew what his fate would be if he were taken.

How wise he had been never to travel anywhere without his armed knights! There were one hundred and eighty of them – a little army, who would defend their master with their lives for what would they have if they lost him?

He would not emerge from the castle. He dared not. It was well fortified. It was well stocked. They could lay siege to it if they wished but they would not find it easy to take Mortimer.

The Queen was in despair. 'Who would have thought that it would have come to this?' she cried. 'I must speak to my son.'

'My dear,' replied Mortimer, 'it is too late to speak to him. He will never listen to us again. He is no longer our boy. He believes himself to be a man and a king.'

'Then woe betide us,' mourned the Queen. 'I hear that he is making enquiries about his father's death. Oh, I knew it would come.'

'Rest assured I shall find a way out of this. This is not the end of Mortimer. I have not come so far to go the way Kent went.'

'Oh Mortimer, Mortimer,' mourned Isabella, 'do not talk so.'

'Isabella!' admonished Mortimer. 'What has happened to you? Where is my brave Queen who was once ready to face the world?'

'It was before . . .' she murmured.

He did not ask her to go on. He knew. Before the murder of Edward. Before she had those dreams when he came to her in the dead of the night.

'Now,' he said briskly, 'we must think carefully. We cannot afford to make a mistake now.'

He sent for Sir William Eland, the governor of the castle.

'You understand,' he said, 'that we are now a fortress. Our enemies are in the town of Nottingham. A man in my position is certain to have enemies. I have reason to believe that Sir William Montacute is one of these. He may try to enter the castle, he is to be kept out at all cost.'

'Yes, my lord,' said Sir William Eland.

'I need hardly remind you,' went on Mortimer, 'that it would be dangerous to disobey my orders.'

'I understand, my lord.'

'Then all is well. We will remain in the castle. Let our enemies come. They cannot get in. The keys are to be delivered to Queen Isabella every night. Is that clear?'

'It is perfectly clear, my lord.'

Mortimer dismissed the governor and went to Isabella. 'We are perfectly safe here,' he said. 'All the passes of the castle are manned by my friends. They will never desert me because they have been my supporters for too long. Moreover they are certain that soon I shall outwit this little band who come to take me. Once you have talked to the King you will win him to our side. Have you not always done so?'

Isabella agreed that this was so, but she sensed change in the air. Her voices were coming to her very frequently now.

'We are safe while we are together,' said Mortimer. 'The King would never harm you.'

She was not sure. The King had changed. He was no longer the boy but the man.

🐯 🐯 🐯

The King had arrived in Nottingham. Montacute was already there and he acquainted Edward with what had happened. Mortimer, sensing what they were about, had taken possession of the castle and there was no way into him. He had skilfully arranged that all the gates were securely guarded by men whom he trusted, people whose fortunes would rise or fall with him. The keys had been changed and were in his mother's possession. Every night she slept with them under her pillows.

'What of the governor of the castle?'

'He feigns to be a friend of Mortimer, but we could sound him.'

'Who is he?'

'Sir William Eland.'

'He has always been a good and loyal knight.'

'He is doubtless afraid of Mortimer as so many have been. They know him as ruthless and brutal and for so long he has had his way. It is said that the only way to keep alive is to be on good terms with Mortimer. I shall find means of sounding him.'

That was not necessary. Sir William Eland came to them.

He was the King's man, he said. It was an unusual situation for the Queen Mother and her son were on separate sides whereas previously they had been together. He hated Mortimer. Who did not hate Mortimer? Who did not deplore his influence with the Queen Mother? And now that it seemed that there were two sides he would take that of his King to whom he had sworn allegiance.

'So, my lord,' he said, 'I come to tell you of a way into the castle which is known to very few people. There is a passage which is under the moat and comes up in the keep. It was made by a Saxon prince during the Danish invasions. You could enter through this hole and thus take possession of the castle.'

Montacute's spirits rose. He could see a satisfactory end of the enterprise in sight.

He planned with the King and Sir William to enter the castle that night.

In their bedchamber Isabella and Mortimer were preparing for bed. Isabella had placed the keys of the castle under her pillow and they were safe for the night, she believed.

We must be thankful for every night, she often said to herself. I have a terrible fear that some evil fate overhangs me.

It was for Mortimer she feared rather than herself. She could not believe that Edward would ever allow anyone to harm her.

Mortimer said he had thought of something he must say to the Bishop of Lincoln and his two trusted friends, Sir Oliver Ingham and Sir Simon Bereford, who were in the castle on this night. He would join Isabella later.

He never did.

As he talked with his friends, Montacute with an armed guard had come up through the secret passage and into the castle.

Mortimer heard the scuffle outside the door followed by shouts and groans. He opened the door and saw the armed men and several of his bodyguard lying dead on the floor.

'What means this?' he shouted.

He was immediately seized.

'It means, my lord,' said Montacute, 'that you are the King's prisoner.'

Isabella hearing the shouts came running out in her night clothes.

When she saw Mortimer held by the guards she gave a great cry of distress.

'Where is the King? The King is here. I know the King is here.'

No one answered her and she ran forward and would have thrown herself at Mortimer's feet, but two of the men gently restrained her.

'Where are you going? What are you doing? Release Mortimer.'

'My lady, the Earl of March is the King's prisoner.'

'Take me to the King. Take me to the King,' she sobbed. 'Oh sweet son, have pity on my gentle Mortimer.'

She slipped gently to the floor. She was moaning as they hustled Mortimer away.

❧ ❧ ❧

The King had issued a proclamation. He had taken the administration of the country into his own hands. He summoned a Parliament which should meet at Westminster on the twenty-sixth day of November and its first task would be to try the prisoner, Roger de Mortimer, Earl of March.

The whole country was talking of Mortimer. The people had long hated him. They had deplored his relationship with the Queen. There was scarcely a man in England who did not rejoice to see the end of Mortimer's rule. The King was now a man. He was his grandfather all over again. Thank God, they said, England at last has a King.

The story of Mortimer's capture was told and the secret passage into Nottingham Castle was named Mortimer's Hole and called so for ever after. This must be the end of Mortimer. He must go the way of other favourites who had taken so much of the wealth of the country and used it for their own benefit. England would have no more of him. England needed a strong King, a King who would restore law and order to the country so that it might trade and know justice and so grow rich.

There came the day when Mortimer faced the King and his peers.

The charges against him were that he had usurped royal power, that he had murdered King Edward the Second and Edmund Earl of Kent. He had taken possession of state revenues the latest of these being the payment from the Scots. For all these crimes he was judged to be a traitor and enemy of the King and the kingdom and was condemned to the traitor's death, hanged, drawn and quartered.

It was important, all agreed, that there should be no delay in carrying out the sentence. The Queen Mother had sent repeated appeals to her son but he would not see her until after the sentence was carried out.

Mortimer must die. The country demanded it.

So three days after his sentence Roger de Mortimer was taken to Tyburn and there, watched by thousands who had gathered to see the end of the most hated man in England, the terrible sentence was carried out.

Mortimer's reign of triumph was over.

Edward was distressed. He could not make up his mind what should be done about his mother. The old fascination she had always exerted over him was still there. She was guilty he believed of the murder of his father for she doubtless had connived with Mortimer to bring it about. He was hearing terrible rumours about the manner of that murder and surely any who could agree to such an act deserved the direst form of punishment.

Yet . . . she was his mother.

What could he do? He could not let her live in state. He could not allow her to be near Philippa and the boy. She must not believe that she could act in such a diabolical way and nothing be made of it. That would be unfair to his father.

He thought often of his father. He reproached himself for not being more watchful. He should have known when they put him away that some terrible fate was being planned for him. He could honestly plead his youth. A boy such as he had been had not dreamed such wickedness was possible.

He would not go to her just yet. He could not face her. She had murdered his father – she and Mortimer between them – and if rumour was true in the most horrible manner.

He could not condemn her to death as he had Mortimer. But he could not let her go free. He could not allow her to come to his Court. How could he? Every time he looked at her he would think of the terrible things she had allowed to be done to his father.

He talked the matter over with Montacute.

'My mother!' he murmured. 'My own mother!'

'It is a difficult situation in which you find yourself,' agreed Montacute. 'You will have to act promptly and wisely, my lord.'

'I know it. I shall strip her of all the wealth she has amassed – she and Mortimer together. Her ill-gotten gains must be restored to their rightful owners. But she is my mother, Montacute. I cannot forget that.'

'Nor should you. Let her have an adequate income of say three thousand pounds a year. That will keep her in the state worthy of a queen and yet without extravagance. Send her to one of your castles and let her stay there until you have decided what you should do in the best interests of all.'

'You have the answer, Montacute. I shall do that. And I think Castle Rising would provide the answer.'

'You mean that place in Norfolk not far from the town of Lynn?'

'That is the one. It is some distance from Westminster and from Windsor. It seems an ideal spot.'

'Yes, my lord, I think you have chosen wisely.'

Through the gloomy rooms of Castle Rising Isabella roamed as though she were seeking her lover. Sometimes she called to him.

'He is not dead,' she told her attendants. 'He cannot be dead. No one could kill Mortimer. Mortimer is invincible.'

They tried to soothe her. It was dreams which haunted her. Someone must sleep in her chamber and be there to soothe her when the nightmares came.

Once she fancied he was hanging on a rope at the foot of her bed. She had heard that long long ago King John had had his wife's lover mutilated and hung on her bed canopy so that when she awoke in the morning the first thing she should see was his obscenely assaulted body.

Then she would dream that they were doing to Mortimer what had been done to Edward.

At these times they said: 'The madness is upon her.'

It would pass and she would remember then where she was and why she was there. And how her son Edward the King had sent her there, making her his prisoner.

'He wants me out of the way,' she said. 'I have become an encumbrance to him . . . a reminder.'

Then she would be sunk in melancholy and she told them that her longing for Mortimer was more than she could endure.

She wept a great deal.

'It should have been so different,' she said. 'If I could but see my son . . .'

But Edward did not come near her. He was trying to find the murderers of his father. They had all escaped overseas but that did not mean they would not be found and brought back to justice. Then the questioning would start. She shuddered.

'Let be, let be,' she said. 'It is past and done with.'

That, she remembered, was what Mortimer had always said. And now he – the brave, the strong, the virile – the one being she had truly loved in the whole of her life – was past and done with.

The months went by. She did not see her son, nor his Queen and her child.

'One day,' she said, 'he will come. He will never desert his mother completely.'

There were days when she was well but her attendants never knew when the frenzy would come upon her or the madness return.

Sometimes they heard ghostly footsteps in the night.

'It is Queen Isabella wandering through the castle,' they said. 'Her madness is coming upon her again.'

Chapter VI

THE MARRIAGE OF ELEANOR

Edward was in a quandary. He had discovered the names of the men he suspected of murdering his father. William Ogle, he believed, had actually done the deed. When Edward considered that he felt sick with horror and his temper which he had inherited from his ancestors was ready to break out into fury, which it certainly would if he ever laid hands on Ogle. Nothing would be too bad for that man to suffer. 'And by God, he shall suffer,' vowed Edward.

There were others concerned. Sir John de Maltravers was one, Sir Thomas Gurney another. They had fled to the Continent the day after the murder, which was surely an admission of their guilt.

They shall be found, Edward promised himself, and when they are my father shall be avenged.

But these guilty men had disappeared. Mortimer had paid the price for his sins and Queen Isabella was living in Castle Rising from which she could not emerge without his consent. He had heard that her melancholy was so great that she was subject to fits of madness.

A just retribution, he thought. But she is my mother and it is not for me to add to her miseries. Her sins have created for her a hell on earth and it is for her to inhabit it.

Meanwhile there were domestic problems. He wanted his sister Eleanor to take up residence with Philippa.

Among all the evil things that had happened the brightness in his life came from his Queen and his child.

Little Edward was progressing well and proving himself to be the most beautiful and intelligent boy that ever lived. Philippa was a happy wife and mother and whenever the King felt in need of comfort he went to her. He found her delighting in a letter from the Court of Hainault. She had always been devoted to her family and there was a constant exchange of letters between the two Courts, so Philippa was kept informed of the family's health, excitement and sorrows.

'She writes so vividly,' said Philippa. 'When I read my mother's letters it is like being at home.'

This time she was more than usually excited. 'Such good news, Edward. My mother wants to visit us.'

'That will be wonderful for you.'

'Of course I tell her how happy I am, how wonderful you are to me and how ideally suited we are.'

'I'll warrant you also write of your son's perfections.'

'She will naturally want to hear of Edward.'

'What has the young rogue been doing of late?'

'Screaming now and then to attract my attention. Continuing to scream if the nurse picks him up because he wants his mother.'

'I don't blame him,' said Edward fondly.

'He knows exactly what is going on.'

'I am sure he knows all about the trouble with the Scots and the French and all our other affairs.'

Philippa noticed the sadness which crept into his voice, and she guessed he was thinking of his mother.

She said quickly: 'All declare there is something really wonderful about little Edward. He grows more like you every day.'

'Then it would appear that he is well on the way to becoming a paragon of all the virtues . . . in his mother's eyes at least. Now tell me more of these suggested visits.'

'She wants to see for herself.'

'Then we must make grand preparations for her.'

'Oh Edward, how good you are to me!'

He smiled a little grimly. The festivities would be paid for out of the money she had brought into the country. The exchequer was low. When was it not? They were an extravagant family, these Plantagenets. Some spent on themselves and their families like Henry the Third, some on their favourites like Edward. Some on wars like his grandfather. He himself was not averse to a certain extravagance in dress. In fact he liked it very much. A king, after all, must appear in royal splendour to please his subjects and to impress his enemies – otherwise people would begin to wonder whether he was indeed a king.

'We must make a really rich show for her. Your father will not travel with her, I suppose?'

'He could not leave Hainault. Isabella will stay with him. She is the only one of us who is unmarried.'

'I doubt she will remain so for long.'

'It must be lonely for her . . . with us all gone away. First me to you and then Margaret to Emperor Louis of Bavaria and then Jeanne to the Court of Juliers. It must be so different now.'

'Speaking of families reminds me. I want my sister Eleanor to come to you.'

'To come to me? To stay, you mean?'

'Yes, I want her to join your household. You see, Philippa, what has happened to our mother has been a shock to us all. I do not know how Eleanor feels, for I would not ask her. You are good and kind and sweet and I want you to take her under your care. I want you to comfort her.'

Philippa's eyes were gentle.

'My dear Edward, you can rely on me to do everything I can to make her happy.'

Edward regarded her with emotion.

Did ever a man have so perfect a wife?

It was a great comfort to the Princess Eleanor to join the household of her sister-in-law. Philippa welcomed her warmly and the friendly homely atmosphere which the Queen had brought to her Court was just what Eleanor needed at this time.

There had been so many shocks in her life. She had quickly learned that her parents were at war with each other. She had heard whispers which she did not understand about the Despensers. She remembered seeing a swinging body on a rope and she and Joanna had huddled together afraid to look out of their window and yet unable to stop themselves although they knew that their dreams would be haunted by that sight for a long time to come. Then her father had disappeared and her mother had come from France with the Earl of March; afterwards her father had died and then, most frightening of all, Joanna had been taken away from her and married to the Prince of Scotland. She had never really recovered from that shock for she and Joanna had always been together until then.

They had shared the same household. The Lady Isabella de Valence had been their guardian and Johanette Jermyn their governess, while John de Tresk had looked after their wardrobe. They had been a happy household and then gradually she had noticed an apprehension descend upon them. In those early days she had never thought of life without Joanna, and then suddenly her sister was whisked away. Poor sad little Joanna, who had been so frightened and clung to her at night and declared she would never never go. But the day had come and they had all travelled up to Scotland – except Edward. He would not come and people said it was because he did not like Joanna's being sent away.

And ever since Eleanor had realised that she might have been the one to be sent into that cold harsh country to live among strangers, away from her home, from Edward, Philippa, Lady de Valence and the rest. They might have allowed Johanette to go with her but after a while princesses' countrymen and women were always sent home. Philippa's had been but that was not important for Philippa had Edward and that was what she wanted; and now they had the dear little baby.

It was a joyful day for Eleanor when she heard that instead of being sent away to some foreign land she was to go into the Queen's household. This was balm; it would almost make up for the loss of Joanna; and it was Philippa's intention that it should.

There was the baby to be admired, for Philippa did not behave in the least as Eleanor's mother had. Eleanor had rarely seen Queen Isabella during her childhood and when she did there was so much to be remembered – curtseying in the correct manner, giving the right answers to the questions which were directed at her, and although few were she had always to be ready in case they might be. Philippa was quite different. She liked to sit with her baby in her lap with Eleanor on a stool while they talked of him and to him and marvelled at him.

Eleanor wished that Joanna could have been there so that she could have enjoyed this life before being taken away to Scotland.

Philippa did a great deal to soothe Eleanor's fears. She was sure, she said, that when Eleanor married it would be someone she loved as she, Philippa, loved Edward. Philippa never tired of telling of the romantic way in which Edward had come to her father's Court and how the four girls had liked him so much but that there was something special between her and Edward, and she told of how frightened she had been that she might not be the chosen one.

In time Eleanor's dreams ceased to be haunted by disaster. The days were pleasant. She saw more of Edward than she ever had before and she thought she was indeed lucky to have such a brother and a new sister who was good and kind and who helped her to understand what was expected of her.

The great excitement now was the coming of the Countess of Hainault. Philippa had not seen her mother since her marriage; her excitement was infectious and Eleanor was caught up in it.

Edward joined them and they excitedly discussed the arrangements for the entertainments they would give. Edward was determined that all due honour should be paid to the mother of his Queen. He loved to joust for he excelled at the sport. His long arms and legs gave him an advantage and since the death of Mortimer and retirement of his mother an aura of kingship had settled on him. Each day he grew more and more like his grandfather but he loved splendour far more than Edward the First ever had. Edward certainly liked to show off his handsome looks and figure with fine clothes and to appear before his people as a champion; but it was an understandable vanity and the people enjoyed it.

'There shall be tournaments in and around London,' he said. 'We will begin with Dartmouth and Stepney and the best of all shall be Cheapside. I will ride out through the streets with fifteen chosen knights and we will challenge any to come against us.'

'It will be magnificent,' cried the Queen.

'I shall have a gallery put up across the road and you ladies shall watch the joust from it.'

'My mother will be most grateful for your kindness in entertaining her so lavishly,' said Philippa, but she was thinking of the cost, for she had been amazed at the poverty of England – which was still feeling the effect of the extra-vagances, first of Gaveston, then the Despensers and after that Mortimer – when compared with the prosperity of Hainault which was so much smaller and of less importance in the world than England. She was sure that something should be done about it. But with the King glowing with anticipation at the pleasure in store this was not the time to talk about the country's poverty.

Philippa's happiness was complete when the Countess arrived. She and her daughter clung together for a while and the Countess was clearly longing to be alone with Philippa. When they were she said: 'Now I can look at you clearly. You look radiant, my dearest child. So it is all as wonderful as you told me in your letters?'

'I am perfectly happy,' Philippa assured her.

'I guessed you were. You could never deceive anyone, Philippa. It is not in your nature and I rejoice in that. Edward is a good husband to you, is he?'

'I could not have a better. I knew from the moment I saw him.'

'There are few who are as fortunate as you, dear child. Your father will be delighted when I return and tell him how things are here. There is some talk about Edward's intention to claim the crown of France.'

'He has a right through his mother,' answered Philippa.

The Countess shook her head. 'Philip would never give it up. It would be a long and bitter war.'

'I think Edward realises this. But he says there is a claim through his mother.'

'You know he would have the support of Hainault if you did go to war, but I hope it never comes to that. I fear little could be gained by it and it would mean long separations. It is never good for husband and wife to be apart from each other. Yet sometimes with kings it is necessary. And with wars . . .'

'Do not fear, dear mother,' said Philippa. 'Edward is wise. He is no longer guided by his mother and Mortimer. He has changed a great deal. You see, he was so young. He is not very old now.'

The Countess nodded. 'So many burdens on such young shoulders!'

'Edward is capable of carrying them. Of that I have no doubt.'

The Countess kissed her daughter. 'Now where is this wonder child?' she said.

Edward was produced and showed what both declared to be an extraordinarily intelligent interest in his grandmother.

118

They talked of the Court of Hainault and Philippa's sisters. The Countess was a little sad to lose her daughters. 'It is inevitable though and we still have Isabella. Though her turn will come I doubt not. Your father and I miss you all very much. But when I go home and tell him how happy you are it will be a great consolation to him.'

Days of feasting followed and the climax of the celebrations was to be the tournament in Cheapside between Wood Street and Queen Street. For days men had been at work preparing the site and a beautiful wooden gallery had been constructed on the King's orders. It stretched from one side of the road to the other and would place the ladies in the best possible position to witness the jousting.

Philippa was very anxious that Eleanor should enjoy the festivities and insisted on having the young girl beside her. It was thus that she found herself often in the company of Raynald, the Earl of Gueldres and Zutphen. The Earl, a handsome man of great charm, was clearly struck by the fresh innocence of the young girl. Philippa was delighted that he should notice her and Eleanor should appear to be so happy in his company.

'Alas, poor child,' she said to her mother, 'she has had such an unhappy childhood and as mine was so happy I feel I want to do everything I can for her.'

'You always had the sweetest nature in the family,' her mother told her fondly.

Philippa went on: 'She seems to enjoy Raynald's company. I think he admires her. It will be good for Eleanor to enjoy the society of such a man and she knows he is far too old to be considered as a possible husband. He has four daughters I believe . . . as you and my father did.'

'He has recently lost his wife,' the Countess added. 'So he may well be looking for a wife.'

'If Eleanor were older and he younger I would say they might fall in love.'

'You are so romantic,' said the Countess. 'You fell in love with Edward when you first saw him and I shall never forget how terrified you were that one of your sisters might be chosen to marry him.'

'My fears were groundless. There was never any question of one of them being chosen. Edward sent his Bishop to choose it is true but he told me afterwards that he warned the Bishop that if he valued his life he must choose me.'

'I thought it had happened that way,' said the Countess fondly. 'And you are indeed fortunate. I am so glad that you realise it and, my dear child, I shall pray that you continue with Edward as you are now.'

For three days the King with fifteen of his chosen knights rode through the streets of London challenging all comers to the Lists. Edward looked magnificent. He was nineteen years of age now and fully grown to his great height, almost as long-legged as his grandfather and with the same flaxen hair, bright blue eyes and fair complexion. He looked, as his people thought, just as a king should look. They were proud of him. He was like a god riding through their streets, his cloak of green embroidered with golden arrows and lined with red silk. His squires rode behind him in white kirtles with green sleeves. It was, said the people, a goodly sight. The bright September sun shone benignly on the scene and at the windows of every house people watched the riders flash by. They cheered the King; they delighted in him. At last he had come to power and manhood. He had destroyed the ruthless brutal grasping

Mortimer whom they had all hated. He had acted with discretion towards his mother; he had never forgotten that she was his mother and, although he had realised that she was guilty of great crimes, he had set her up in some small state in Castle Rising where she would remain for a while until time showed him what to do. It was said that none dared criticise her in his hearing, which showed a good loyalty; and on the other hand he had not seen her since the death of her paramour; she had remained in Castle Rising.

And there was the Queen – rosy-cheeked, a little buxom, kindly and splendidly gowned, her crown on her head, her silk gown embroidered with pearls and gold, her cloak of velvet trimmed with ermine. She might have lacked the outstanding beauty of the last Queen, but no one wanted to be reminded of her; and if there was something a little homely about Philippa's countenance it shone with the softness of a good and kindly nature. She had made their King happy; she had given them their Prince; and already people were remembering little acts of kindness and the girl whom she had saved from execution.

The people of London were content with their King and Queen and little Prince. So they flocked to the Lists and they wanted to see their King triumphant.

It was like the days of great Edward all over again.

Philippa with her mother, Eleanor and a few of the noblest ladies mounted the tower, seated themselves and prepared to watch the pageantry.

The trumpets were sounding; the crowd were cheering; the royal procession to the Lists had begun.

The musicians walked before the horsemen, playing as they came. These were followed by the squires of the King's household in their shining livery. Then the King himself.

Edward's love of dress was clearly shown, as for each day of the tournaments he had chosen different costumes. He had decided that on this day he and his knights should be disguised as Tartars, and ferocious they looked in long fur cloaks and high hats.

As he rode in the Lists Edward's first glance was for the Queen in the gallery, seated there with her mother, his sister and the ladies of the Court. The King bowed low and the Queen immediately rose to return his greeting; as she did so everyone in the gallery rose too; and as they sat down there was a creaking sound, followed by a scream from one of the ladies, for the gallery seemed to reel and cave in and suddenly it had collapsed in a cloud of dust.

There was a moment of silence before pandemonium broke out. The King had dashed to the falling structure. Philippa, her gown covered in dust, her bright cheeks smudged with it, stood up. She was unharmed. The gallery had been made of light wood; it was too flimsy for the weight of the ladies and it had never been tested to see if it would take the weight of so many people.

'Philippa,' cried the King, 'are you hurt?'

She laughed at him. 'No, my lord. A little shaken. It was so sudden. I was not expecting it.'

It was a relief to discover that no one was hurt. People were crowding in on the scene and Edward shouted to them to stand back. He was clearly shaken and concerned for the ladies and in particular his wife.

'How could such a thing happen?' he demanded.

'Well, we are safe,' Philippa reassured him. 'Only a little shaken and our gowns dirty. Oh, Edward, I hope it has not spoilt the day for you. You must not let it.'

She had seen a frown gathering on Edward's brow and she knew what that meant. He was angry. She dreaded his anger. She had seen very little of it and it had never once been directed against her, but she had heard of the Plantagenet temper. It seemed most of them had it, and in some it was more violent than in others. Henry the Third and King John used to lie on the floor and bite the rushes in their accesses of rage; Henry the Third had only mildly possessed it and Edward the First had had it under control, as this Edward would; but there were occasions when it would break out and this was one of them.

'I want the men who built this gallery found and brought here to me,' he said. There was a brief pause. 'Find them,' he shouted, 'and bring them to me without delay.'

Philippa said gently: 'It is all over. We are not harmed. Such accidents can happen.'

'Such accidents can happen only once in my kingdom,' he retorted. He looked at her pleasant face smudged with dirt and her torn gown. His Philippa, who might so easily have been killed. The thought of what could have happened to Philippa enraged him still further.

'Why is there this delay?' he shouted. 'Find those men. Bring them here. By God, they will wish they had never been born.'

Philippa laid her hand on his arm but he shrugged it aside. He was intent only on giving vent to his anger.

The men had been found. They came fearfully and the expression on their faces when they saw the fallen gallery and dishevelled ladies set them trembling. The King, looking ferocious in his Tartar's robes, demanded to know why this had happened.

The men could only stare blankly.

'Why was it not tested to see if it would stand the weight?'

'My lord . . . there was not time,' said their spokesman. 'It was only finished an hour or so before the joust was to begin.'

'You fools, you knaves . . . do you know this could have cost the Queen her life?'

Philippa said quickly: 'My lord, it was light and flimsy. We could have had a fall at the worst. See, I am not harmed at all.'

But the King would not listen. He was whipping himself to fury, exaggerating the damage, intent on inflicting the utmost punishment on these careless men whose shoddy work had spoilt the day and could have caused harm to the Queen.

'Take them away from here,' he shouted. 'Put a rope around their necks and let them be hanged until they be dead.'

There was a hushed silence in the crowd. One of the workmen, only a boy, fell to his knees and began to whimper.

The King turned his face away and shouted: 'Take them away. Let it be done.'

Philippa was horrified. She thought of the families of those men, robbed of the breadwinners; she thought of the loves of wives for their husbands and mothers for their sons and she would not let it happen.

She knelt suddenly before the King. She took his hand and said: 'My lord, you have said that you love and honour me. You have showered many gifts on me. There is nothing I want more than the lives of these men. If they die by the rope I shall remember them all my life. I have suffered no harm. Nor have these ladies. The gallery was erected in a hurry. Please, my lord, I beg of you, as you love me, spare these men.'

The King looked at her, with her hair loose about her shoulders and her dear kind eyes full of tears; the grief apparent on the face which he was accustomed to see merry and content.

He hesitated and she waited, watching him.

Then she said: 'My lord, if you will not grant this request, I shall never be completely happy again. I shall always remember what was done to these men who wished me no ill and are your loyal subjects.'

The King said: 'Let the men go free. My Queen pleads for them with such passion that I cannot resist her.'

The Queen covered her face for the tears of joy were streaming down her cheeks. There were sudden deafening cheers. They filled the streets; the people were surging forward.

'God bless the Queen!' they cried. 'God bless good Queen Philippa.'

The Countess returned to Hainault happy with her visit to England. There could be no doubt of Philippa's happiness and she certainly seemed the most fortunate of princesses to have enjoyed a happy childhood and to slip so easily into a happy marriage.

There was one matter of concern to Philippa. She knew that the celebrations given in honour of her mother had been very costly, and her frugal outlook on life would not let her accept this. She compared her own country with England; a small country but with a rich economy; she decided it was because the people of Hainault worked harder than the English.

She talked to Edward about this and he was at first amused by her but after a while he saw that she was talking sense. It was true that the economy of the country was not flourishing. There was a great deal of poverty in certain areas. Through the reign of his father and of Mortimer there had been no thought of making the best of the country's resources; wealth was appropriated and absorbed by favourites who used it not for the good of the country but for their own pleasure.

She had seen at once that the wool produced in England, which was reckoned to be the best in the world, would be more profitable to the country if it were made into cloth instead of the wool's being exported to the Low Countries, there to be made into cloth and brought back to England.

Edward considered this and could see the logic in it.

'Our people are not weavers,' he said. 'They do not care to work as hard as the people of Flanders. They like to keep their sheep, watch over them, and wait for the shearing time.'

'They would be more prosperous if they worked harder. A country needs prosperity, Edward. It is happier because of it.'

He conceded this. 'Tell me what you have in mind,' he said.

'I want to send for some cloth weavers to come to England and set up a colony of weavers here. Then we can make our own cloth . . . a little at first, and then increase it. I would like to see English cloth – not only wool – the best in the world.'

'Well, my wise Queen, let us proceed with this.'

'So I have your permission to write to one I know who excels in the craft?'

'My dearest wife and Queen, you have indeed.'

Philippa immediately wrote to a certain John Kempe of Flanders. If he would come to England with his servants, apprentices and everything he needed to carry on his business he would have the protection of the King; and it was his wish that they should build up a flourishing cloth-weaving industry in England.

Philippa was delighted because she fully believed that hard work was the way to prosperity.

There was a great deal that John Kempe wanted clarified before he could take this great step. But the project had started and although it took a year or so to be put into action, Philippa's wisdom was in due course responsible for the setting up in Norfolk of a cloth-making industry which was to bring prosperity not only to Norfolk but to the whole of England.

The Princess Eleanor was to be married. Oddly enough the prospect excited her. There was something about the Earl of Gueldres which fascinated her. It might have been that she heard so much from Philippa of the romantic meeting between her and Edward, how they had loved at first sight and the evidence of her own eyes told her how happy that had turned out to be.

Eleanor was only thirteen years old but many girls were married at that age; Philippa herself had not been much older and it seemed that the King was satisfied with the Earl of Gueldres as a husband for his sister.

Philippa wondered whether Edward still thought about taking the French crown. If he did he would need friends on the Continent. Her own marriage had really come about because of an alliance between two countries. If Queen Isabella and Mortimer had not needed an army they would never have consented to a match between Hainault and England. Philippa shuddered at the thought of how much her happiness had depended on chance.

Eleanor discussed Raynald with Philippa and Philippa encouraged her for she knew from Edward that he had decided on the match; therefore if Eleanor could fall in love with her future husband Philippa would be delighted.

'There is something rather exciting about him,' said Eleanor with a smile.

Philippa agreed that there was indeed.

'Of course he is rather old . . .'

Eleanor waited for Philippa to defend age which she did promptly. 'There is a great deal to be said for experience,' she commented.

'Would you have loved Edward if he had been married before?'

'I should have loved Edward whatever had happened to him,' said Philippa vehemently.

'Suppose he had had four daughters?'

'I should have loved them as I did his sisters.'

'I suppose daughters are different from sisters.'

'It would have made no difference,' declared Philippa. 'If one loves nothing can make any difference.'

'Do you think he is handsome?'

'Very!' said Philippa.

'They call him Raynald de Swerte in his own country. Do you think he is swarthy? He is very dark of complexion is he not?'

'It is most attractive. It makes him seem strong, a little fierce . . . as a man should be.'

'You must prefer fair men. Edward is so fair.'

'I do not love him for the colour of his hair.'

'No, one does not. In truth I think a little swarthiness is rather attractive.'

'And so do I,' said Philippa. 'But don't tell Edward.'

Eleanor laughed. How comforting they were, these conversations.

Philippa encouraged them and each day she was preparing Eleanor for her coming marriage. In private she was often a little uneasy and she discussed Raynald with Edward and asked him if he really thought the match was a good one.

'I must find a husband for Eleanor,' he said. 'You know I have tried for Alfonso of Castile and for the son and heir of the King of France. I have tried too for the son of the King of Aragon. All these have been considered and have come to nothing. Eleanor has been rejected three times. I begin to think this might tell against her. I should like to see her married soon before it is believed that there is some spell working against her. I would not want her to remain unmarried.'

'It seems wrong that she should marry this man because other offers came to nothing. Is it not true that this so happens in royal circles?'

'Indeed it does, but I want Eleanor married and I can do with Raynald's help. It is an astonishing thing but these small provinces seem to have more than I have myself of the things I need ... money ... arms ... men ... all that is necessary to succeed in conquest. And it may well be that if I do not have to contest the crown of France I may have to go to Scotland again some day. I shall need help, Philippa, and I am more likely to get it within my own family than anywhere else.'

'Raynald is a somewhat ambitious man.'

'All rulers worth their salt are ambitious.'

'I did not like what he did to his father.'

'My dear gentle Philippa, you are too good for this world. Have I not always said that Raynald's father was a weak man. Had he continued to reign there would have been nothing worth-while for Raynald to inherit. So he forestalled destiny that was all.'

'By imprisoning his own father! I have heard that he kept him in prison for six years and he was an old man.'

'We must admire Raynald. He took over a tottering province . . . Had he not done so there would have been nothing for him to take over.'

'He kept his father in prison until he died.'

'Yes, yes, but what did he do? He ruled well, with immense skill and vigour. And the result. Now Gueldres, though small, is one of the most important of the minor European countries. What he has done is admirable, Philippa, even though it meant supplanting his own father. In fact all he did was take six years earlier that which would have in time been his and he took it before it could be rendered useless. He has shown himself a good soldier and wise ruler. He is highly respected in Europe and I tell you this: even the King of France would think twice before entering into a disagreement with him. I shall welcome him as my brother-in-law.'

'I think Eleanor is quite happy.'

'I doubt not that you have helped her to recognise her good fortune.'

'I have. But I do hope he will be kind to her.'

'Of a certainty he will be kind to my sister.'

'He is an ambitious man and she is not yet fifteen. He chose his first wife for her wealth I believe, for I heard that that exceeded her rank, and that the marriage took place when the bride's parents promised to pay all his debts.'

'Of one thing we can be sure. Eleanor's brother will not be able to oblige him in the same manner.'

'This time he marries a Princess of England.'

'Ah, my Philippa, you are too gentle and loving for this world of ambition. Not that I would have you otherwise. Eleanor like her sister must marry where she can best help her country. I am delighted that she is not displeased with our swarthy hero. But had she been, there would have been no help for it. To Gueldres she must go as poor little Joanna went to Scotland. The fate of Princesses, my love.'

'I know it well and I thank God that I was able to follow my heart. I shall never cease to thank Fate or God, or whoever ordained it, for the day when you came riding through the forest of Hainault; and I only had to look at you to love you.'

'As I did you. As soon as I saw you I said: "There is my Queen," and I made up my mind in that first moment.'

'I shall pray that Eleanor knows as much happiness as we do.'

'But you know, my love, that is impossible for no one could.'

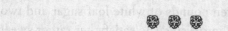

Edward was determined that his sister should go to her new country well equipped and there was great excitement in her apartments where her wardrobe was being made ready with Philippa presiding over it. She made Eleanor try on her clothes and laughingly pointed out that she herself could not have done so. She was far too plump and very different from the willowy Eleanor. How beautiful was the cloak of blue Brussels cloth edged with ermine, the robe of Spanish cloth of gold which the young girl would wear on her wedding day; there were pelisses worked with gold thread and sparkling with silver beads and surtunics of velvet and cloth of silver. The King had presented her costly jewelled ornaments; there were coronals set with pearls and diamonds and several zones artistically wrought in rubies and emeralds.

Not only would she take with her clothes and jewels but also many items of furniture, chief of which was the bridal bed, a magnificent object with Tripoli silk curtains most exquisitely embroidered and decorated in gold with the entwined arms of England and Gueldres. There was a chariot, another gift from her brother, decorated with her coat of arms, and lined with purple velvet spattered with golden stars; and there were chairs, tables, carpets, curtains and gold and silver plate; even tankards, table knives, dishes and spoons were to be taken with her.

Edward was determined that she should go into her new country equipped as a royal princess.

Nor was it only clothes and furniture which Eleanor took with her. Three tons of provisions were prepared for her including cinnamon, saffron, ginger, rice, dates, one hundred and twenty-seven pounds of white loaf sugar and two hundred pounds of Cyprus sugar to satisfy her rather sweet tooth.

Eleanor made sure too that she had a good supply of sandalwood, which finely powdered was a fleshy shade of red, for she was very pale of complexion and, admiring the natural rosy cheeks of her sister-in-law, liked to touch her own up with sandalwood to give her a healthy glow.

Several vessels were needed to convey everything across the sea and these were already being loaded in Sandwich.

The day arrived for her to set out. She took a fond and rather tearful farewell of her brother and Philippa. As a last-minute present the latter gave her a magnificently furred robe and Edward presented her with six altar cloths which she might give to the churches she passed on her journey to her new country.

It was a splendid cavalcade which travelled down to the coast. Eleanor rode at its head and among the company were one hundred and thirty-six men servants – pages, salterers, poulterers, sumpterers, chamber women, washermen, stewards, knights and esquires.

All along the route people came out to see the procession pass. This was very different from the marriage of Eleanor's sister, Joanna. That marriage had not pleased the people at all. But Eleanor was clearly not unhappy.

The people were pleased with their new King so it was cheers for his sister and the match with Gueldres.

Philippa missed her young sister-in-law, but she was deeply absorbed in her own life because to her joy she had become pregnant again.

She had gone once more to Woodstock where her precious first-born Edward had made his appearance.

'I have a fancy,' she said, 'that Woodstock is lucky for me.'

And Edward was, of course, only too happy to indulge her wishes.

Preparations were made for the birth of the child and the two cradles were ready awaiting their occupant. One, the state cradle was very grand and of course would be used only for state occasions when the nobility would wish to inspect the child. This cradle which bore the arms of England and Hainault was beautifully lined with gilded taffeta and had a fur coverlet made from six hundred and seventy skins which could hardly be used until the baby was a few months older and winter had set in.

And on the sixteenth day of June of that year 1332 Philippa gave birth to her second child. This time it was a daughter, as beautiful and physically perfect as her brother had been.

The King was delighted and if he would have preferred another boy he did not show this. He loved the little girl as much as he loved her brother and no child could have come into the world with a greater welcome.

The King had been thinking a great deal about his mother. He had in fact on one occasion visited her at Castle Rising where he heard from her attendants that she suffered from bouts of madness and how her grief was so great at such times that they feared she might do herself an injury. He spoke to her gently, for he could not forget all she had once meant to him, and he gave orders that never must she be treated with less respect than was due to her rank and none must forget that she was his mother.

It was necessary, of course, to keep her at Castle Rising and he did not wish to see her too often for, although his conscience troubled him concerning the fact that she was virtually a prisoner, whenever he saw her horrible thoughts came into his mind about the death of his father. All efforts to find the murderers had so far come to nothing, but he believed that in due course they would be delivered to him; and when they were and he had avenged his father perhaps he would feel easier in his mind.

His mixed feelings of sorrow and uncertainty about his mother led him to suggest that his daughter be named after her. He suggested it tentatively to Philippa who immediately understood his feelings.

'It is a beautiful name,' she said. 'Yes, I should like our first daughter to be named Isabella.'

Young Isabella flourished. She was placed under the care of Sir William and Lady Omer, while a young girl named Joanna Gaunbun was put in attendance, her duties being that of a rocker and her pallet bed was placed beside the cradle so that at any hour of the night she could attend to the baby if need be.

Philippa nursed the child herself. She could not bear to pass it over to any other; and, unlike her predecessor, she spent many happy hours in the nursery.

Chapter VII

THE EXILES OF CHÂTEAU GAILLARD

Nearly four years had passed since the Princess Joanna had come to Scotland as the bride of David the Bruce. They had been uneasy years for Joanna. She did not greatly care for her bridegroom who had seemed such a child to her, being two years younger; only five years old when she had arrived.

The country was cold and bleak, the winds harsh, the people dour, and she bitterly missed her brother, her sister Eleanor, and her new sister-in-law Philippa.

The old King had been kind to her, but he was suffering from a terrible disease which had distorted his appearance in a dreadful way and he frightened her in spite of his kindness. She longed for her home and she used to tell her little husband about it and how much she wanted to go back there.

Robert the Bruce died and then David was King and she was Queen which made them very important.

Soon after the death of Robert they had been solemnly anointed and crowned and then they knew they were really King and Queen. David had been anxious as to what he would have to do, but he was told that he need not worry. All he had to do was what he was told and there were plenty to tell him that.

The two chief men whom they must obey were the Regents. One of these was Lord James Douglas and the other the Earl of Moray. Robert the Bruce had expressed a wish that his heart should be carried to the Holy Land because during his lifetime he had made a vow to go and fight the Infidel. With all his responsibilities it had never been possible for him to carry out his vow but he believed that if his heart was taken there, he would be absolved from his broken vow. He trusted Lord James Douglas as he trusted few men and when Douglas agreed to undertake the mission he knew he would do his best to carry it out.

Lord James Douglas had been an impressive figure in Joanna's eyes right from the first. He was a very big man, tall, broad-shouldered with masses of very black hair which had earned him the name of Black Douglas. However when he spoke – and oddly enough with a slight lisp – he betrayed a rather quiet courteous nature and although none could be fiercer in battle in his personal relationships he was a gentle man.

Joanna had begun to love him for he showed her clearly that he was going to look after her. He understood just how she felt in leaving her family and he wanted her to know that while he was near her she would have nothing to fear from anyone.

So it was a great relief to know that he had been appointed one of the Regents of Scotland and he would be in close contact with her and the young King.

But alas there was this vow he had made and he must set out with the heart of Robert the Bruce in order to keep his promise.

When he came to say good-bye to them he showed them the casket of gold in which the heart of Robert the Bruce was carried. The children held it and marvelled at it and Black Douglas told them what a brave heart it had been.

'The Scots will never forget what they owe to Robert the Bruce,' he told them.

Joanna was fearful though when he left. A loneliness came over her which was almost like a premonition of evil.

'The Earl of Moray will watch over you,' he had comforted her. 'All you have to do is what he tells you. And soon I shall be back.'

Thomas Randolph, Earl of Moray was the cousin of Robert the Bruce. He had served with his uncle and had been closer to him than any man and he had made him Regent with Douglas to help him, on his death bed. Moray was an honourable man; there was no one Robert the Bruce could have placed greater trust in. There was a dignity about Moray and a determination to do what his uncle would expect of him, and Joanna felt as safe with Moray as she had with Douglas.

So when Douglas set out on his mission she felt that while one of those who were so important to her and David had gone, the other remained and as Douglas said he would come back soon.

Alas, there was sad news of Douglas.

Moray came to the children that he himself might tell them what had happened.

He sat down and drew them to him and as they stood beside him he placed an arm about each of them.

'There is sad news of Black Douglas,' he said quietly.

He felt Joanna start and went on gently: 'I know you loved him. He looked fierce sometimes, didn't he?'

Joanna nodded. She had heard the story of how he had almost captured her brother. She had thought him a fearful man until she met him and he himself had told her the story. 'It was war,' he had said. 'War is a terrible thing, my Queen. We want to avoid it all we can.'

'He was not really fierce,' said Joanna. 'When will he come home?'

Moray shook his head. 'You are a King and a Queen,' he reminded them, 'and when there is bad news it is better for you to know it at once. Douglas will never come back. He is dead.'

'Dead,' cried David shrilly. 'He cannot be dead!'

'Alas, my little lord, he is. He took the heart of your father from this land as you know. He went to Alfonso the King of Castile and Leon because he knew that he was fighting a war against the Saracen King of Granada.'

'I thought he was to go to the Holy Land,' said Joanna.

'It matters not, my lady, whether a knight goes to Jerusalem or Spain as long as he fights for Christ against the Infidel. So there will be just as much merit in God's eyes to fight in Spain as in Jerusalem. So to Spain went Black Douglas. He fought bravely on the plains of Andalusia but when the battle was won he pursued the fleeing Moors. He went too far and suddenly he was cut off from his friends. He carried the Bruce's heart and knowing of course that he could not come out of this affray alive he flung the heart from him into the midst of his enemy and followed it as he had followed Robert the Bruce during his lifetime.'

'They . . . killed him,' whispered Joanna.

Moray nodded. 'But the Moors respected a brave man. They will send his body home to Scotland and we shall bury it here.'

Both children were crying. They would never see Black Douglas again; but Joanna who was the elder thought: He will not be there to protect us any more.

But they had the dear Earl of Moray. They were safe while they had him.

❁ ❁ ❁

That there was some trouble afoot Joanna was aware. No one told her of course but she could sense a certain tension in the castle. She listened to the conversation of attendants and servants, for she felt it was important to know what was going on now that Black Douglas was dead and the Earl of Moray had to be away so much.

There was one name she kept hearing mentioned and that was Baliol.

'Who is Baliol?' she asked one of her women who was the sort who liked to gossip and who, Joanna had discovered, was more likely to impart information than some of them.

'Baliol, my lady. You will be meaning Edward Baliol. He is the son of John Baliol, who was at one time King of Scotland. I dareswear Master Edward thinks he has a right to the crown. That would not surprise me.'

'But David is King. He was crowned and so was I.'

'That's true enough, my lady, but when people think they have a claim to something they try to get it.'

'Do you mean this Baliol will try to take the crown away from David?'

'That would never be allowed.'

'The Earl of Moray will stop it and so would Black Douglas have done . . . if he had been here. Never mind, the Earl of Moray will never let it happen. Tell me more of this Baliol.'

But the woman had realised that she had already said too much. The Lady Joanna was too knowing. At one moment she seemed nothing but a child but the next she was asking questions to which perhaps it was better not to give her the answers.

'I know nothing,' said the woman pursing her lips. The old sign, thought Joanna in exasperation. They all came to that when something was becoming interesting.

Later she heard more from another source of gossip.

Baliol was stirring up trouble in England and the English King was not so hostile to him as might have been expected considering his sister was the Queen of Scotland.

It seemed there were some barons who had lost their possessions through supporting the English against the Scots and being very dissatisfied were joining up with Baliol.

It all sounded very disturbing and Joanna talked about it with David who, being two years younger than she was, listened intently and when she said she thought they might be trying to take their crowns away from them, he shook his head. They couldn't do that because his father had been Robert the Bruce and whatever Robert the Bruce had said must be done, was done.

'But he is dead,' said Joanna. 'He is dead like Black Douglas.'

The thought that she would never see that fierce dark face again made her feel ready to burst into tears. She was fearful too until she remembered the Earl of Moray.

'It is all right,' she said. 'We still have the Earl of Moray. He would never allow anyone to take our crowns away from us.'

Moray came to see them soon after that and she asked him questions.

When she mentioned Baliol's name he wanted to know who had told her this. She answered that she listened and heard people talking.

'Well,' said Moray, 'there is often trouble in countries. It very often happens that when there is a crown some people want to take it from those to whom it belongs and keep it for themselves.'

'*We* have it though,' said David.

'Yes, my King, you have it, and on your head it shall remain while I have an arm to fight to keep it there.'

'Then it will always remain there,' declared Joanna.

'Thank you, my lady.'

'We have lost Black Douglas but we still have you,' said Joanna. 'I would never be afraid while we had you.'

The Earl was touched. He kissed her hand and said he would serve his little Queen with his life.

'Will this man Baliol come here to fight?' asked Joanna.

'He might well do that.'

'He will never win,' said David, 'will he?'

'We shall not let him,' answered Moray.

'My brother would not let him either,' put in Joanna.

The Earl of Moray was silent; but Joanna did not notice. She was too absorbed in the memory which the mention of her brother's name had brought back.

Very soon after that Moray took his leave of them.

'I shall see you soon,' he said. 'Whatever you hear do not be afraid. All you have to do is what I tell you. And if I say you are to go to such and such a place you know it will be for your safety and you will do it, won't you?'

'Yes,' said Joanna speaking for David as she so often did.

'All will be well.'

'Yes,' said Joanna confidently, 'while we have you to look after us.'

Moray rode away to Musselburgh and a few weeks later a

messenger arrived at Edinburgh Castle. He wished to see the King and the Queen.

They knew him for one of the Earl's squires and the gravity of his face struck terror into Joanna's heart.

'You come from my lord?' said David.

'My lord, I have sorry news. We had come from Musselburgh to Wemyss when he was taken ill suddenly. He died that very night.'

The children were amazed. First Black Douglas and now the Earl of Moray. Their two protectors taken from them one after the other.

They were too stunned to cry. That would come later. All they could think of now was that they had lost dear Moray.

Nothing could seem the same again. There was a great deal of whispering. Joanna listened and in her bed at night she lay trembling because she feared something dreadful was going to happen.

She must learn all she could. She felt so young, so ineffectual, and David was even more so.

She was not surprised when she heard the lowered voices, when she caught the word: 'Poison!'

'No doubt he was poisoned,' they said. 'Edward Baliol would have men everywhere. So easy . . . a little something in his food. Something in his wine. Nothing will be the same now that Moray is dead.'

Edward was well aware that there was going to be trouble in Scotland. He still smarted with humiliation when he remembered that campaign of his. He had been so young, so inexperienced. It would be different now, he promised himself, if the opportunity should arise.

He often thought that he would like to carry on with his grandfather's work. He would like to be the one to subdue Scotland; instead of which, during his father's weak reign, Robert the Bruce had been able to consolidate his successes. But Robert the Bruce was dead and a little boy was on the throne. True he had had two strong men to stand beside him – Moray and Black Douglas – but now they were both dead.

He was musing on affairs in Scotland when Henry de Beaumont asked leave to see him. Edward was alert. Beaumont was one of those barons whom the Scots had robbed of his possessions because he had sided with the English.

He received him without delay.

'My lord,' he said, 'Edward de Baliol is without. I have come to ask you if you will see him.'

'Edward de Baliol!' cried the King in surprise. 'For what purpose?'

'That is something he would wish to tell you himself.'

'Then I will see him.'

Baliol! A weak son of a weak father, thought Edward. What did he want? Edward could give a quick answer to that: The crown of Scotland.

Edward waited to hear his request.

'My lord,' said Baliol, 'the Regents of Scotland have both died recently.'

'They say Moray died of poison. Is it so?'

'That, my lord, I could not say.'

Will not, you mean, thought Edward. I'll swear it was one of your agents who administered the fatal dose.

'And Douglas, in that foolhardy action! I should have thought he would have realised that his duty lay in his own country.'

144

'My lord, he died as he thought fit. What I have come to say to you is that Scotland is in turmoil. These two men who were governing – ably some say – are no more. You will know that the King and the Queen are but children.'

'I should since one of them is my own sister.'

Baliol flinched a little. Was it folly to ask the King of England to act against his own sister?

'They have selected the Earl of Mar to take the place of Moray. He is a weakling. The state of the country is too weak for him to handle.'

'And what would you have me do about it?' asked Edward.

'I would ask your help, my lord. My father was the King of Scotland. I am his heir. If you will help me to regain what is mine I will pay homage to you as my overlord.'

Edward was silent. That would be a step in the right direction. It would take him back to the position in which his grandfather had stood. It would mean deposing his sister; it would mean dishonouring the treaty he had made; moreover he was bound to pay the Pope twenty thousand pounds if he broke the treaty.

'My lord,' said Baliol, 'the marriage of your sister and David Bruce has never been consummated. If I were King of Scotland there could be a dispensation. I would marry your sister. I would give you Berwick.'

'Enough,' said Edward. 'I cannot help you. Nor can I allow you to march through England.'

'Is that your final word?'

Edward hesitated just a second or so too long and Baliol's hopes soared.

Edward said: 'I shall have to put the matter before my Parliament.'

Edward was watchful. Meanwhile Baliol had collected together a fleet in England, and Edward had made no objections. In due course he sailed to Fife, landed at a place called Dupplin Moor and rather unexpectedly beat the assembled Scottish forces. During the battle the new Regent Earl of Mar was killed and there was nothing to stop Baliol marching on to Scone where he was crowned King of Scotland.

David and Joanna heard of what was happening and wondered what would become of them. Joanna was of the opinion that her brother would save them.

'He will come marching into Scotland,' she said, 'and Baliol will run for his life, you will see.'

What did happen was that Baliol sent a messenger to them. 'My lord,' said the messenger, 'the King of Scotland offers you a proposition.'

'How can that be?' asked David haughtily. 'I am the King of Scotland.'

'It would seem no longer so, my lord,' was the answer. 'King Edward de Baliol sends his greetings to you and wishes you to know that if you will renounce your right to the crown he will offer you a safe conduct out of Scotland or allow you to remain in any part you wish.'

'This is generous of him,' said David with sarcasm. 'Tell Edward de Baliol that we deplore his insolence and the Queen and I will remain where we wish in our own dominion.'

The messenger departed and Joanna urged her young husband to write without delay to her brother. She was certain that he would come marching up to Scotland to help them.

Baliol's letter to the King of England arrived first. He

reminded him that he was willing to marry Joanna, to increase her dower and if she declined to marry him he would pay her ten thousand pounds for her portion should she marry elsewhere. All he asked was that she resign her right to the throne of Scotland which came through David the Bruce.

Edward was wavering. In the meantime he had received the urgent call for help from his young brother-in-law.

He would not help him. His excuse was that some of his nobles had been deprived of their inheritance by the Scottish Kings and he could not therefore take sides against them.

Baliol's triumph was short lived. Many Scots loyal to the young King rose against him and attacked him with such fervour and success that the erstwhile King was obliged to abandon his recent conquest and fly to England.

Edward allowed him to do this and even received him with certain friendliness at his Court. When the news of this reached Scotland the anger of the Scots was intense, and to show their indignation many of them resumed old tactics and crossed the Border with the object of harassing the English, burning down villages and making off with the cattle.

Edward was not altogether displeased. This gave him the opportunity he really wanted, for the thought of setting Baliol on the Scottish throne as his puppet appealed to him. He would not fail as his father had done. There would be no Bannockburn for him. All the same there was the treaty; there was the Pope to think of; and there was the fact that his own sister was married to David the Bruce.

But this was the opportunity to win back what had been his grandfather's and to carry on with those plans to subdue Scotland for ever which had been the main object of Edward the First's life.

He had to go carefully though. He was in a delicate position. First he demanded the return of Berwick and that Scotland should render feudal homage to him.

Young David was bewildered; so was Joanna. She had believed that as soon as he heard she was in distress Edward would come to her. He had been so fond of her. He had kissed her so tenderly on parting and had told her that she must always remember that she was his sister and they were friends for ever. Did he mean that she must help him if he needed her but if she needed him that was another matter?

David, primed by his ministers, was given a speech to learn. Joanna listened to him as he practised it. It was depressing that her brother Edward was seen in the light of an enemy.

'Neither my father nor any of his ancestors acknowledged submission to England, nor will I consent to it . . .' David's voice droned on. 'If any other prince should do us wrong, you should defend us, from the love you bear your sister and our Queen.'

Joanna could not bear to listen. Edward! she thought. Oh Edward, how can you do this to us! She wished that she could go to him, see him, explain to him. If only she could talk to Philippa.

The Scots had broken their treaty, declared Edward. They had raided Border towns and they had refused to give up Berwick which Baliol had promised him. If he did not act they would soon be marching further south into England. He was justified in what he was about to do.

He wanted to vindicate himself. He wanted to wipe out for ever the depressing memory of his first campaign against the Scots.

While he was preparing his armies for the march north Philippa declared that she could not let him go alone. Edward was delighted. His grandmother had accompanied his grandfather on his campaigns and he was growing more and more eager to be like him.

'There are the children,' said Philippa uneasily.

'Ah,' replied Edward. 'You will have to choose between us.'

It was the saddest choice Philippa had had to make during her married life. There was one characteristic she had observed about Edward. He was a faithful husband, she was sure, but she had seen his eyes follow attractive women and she had noticed that he liked to lead them in the dance, to linger at their sides. There were great temptations of that nature in the life of a King.

Edward loved her deeply. He gave evidence of that. But at the same time she would be a very foolish wife indeed if she allowed temptation to come his way while she herself was far away from him.

Edward was so vital, so virile. He was so handsome. All women must admire him; and in addition to his extreme masculinity and his outstanding good looks he had about him that aura of royalty which so many women found irresistible.

Philippa came to the conclusion that she would place her children in good care and follow her husband into battle.

She chose guardians whom she thought could be trusted and sent the children to the palace of Clarendon; and she set out for Scotland with Edward.

❀ ❀ ❀

When they arrived in Knaresborough there occurred another of those incidents in which Philippa was able to show her kindly nature, and once more she saved someone from the gallows. This was a woman known as Agnes who had stolen a surcoat and three shillings. When she was being taken to the gallows the Queen was riding nearby with the King and the woman's young daughter threw herself at the Queen's horse and might have been run down if Philippa had not pulled up sharply.

The sight of a child in distress could always move the Queen deeply, and when she heard that the condemned woman was pregnant Philippa implored the King to give her a reprieve at least until her child was born.

Edward gallantly acceded to her request and there were cheers for the Queen. But that night as they lay in Knaresborough Philippa was deeply concerned as to what would become of the motherless child when after it was born the hangman claimed his victim.

'She must live to care for her child, Edward. And it seemed to me a terrible thing that a surcoat and three shillings should be considered worth a life.'

'This does seem so,' said Edward thoughtfully. 'But we cannot allow thieves to flourish. In the days of my great ancestor, William the Conqueror, no traveller need fear taking to the roads. The penalty for stealing was not death but the loss of ears, hands, feet, eyes . . . Which ever was judged applicable. Under the weak reign of Stephen when this penalty was abolished the roads swarmed with thieves – and worse. Travellers were kidnapped and taken to the castles of robber barons to be robbed and tortured and to make cruel sport for the guests of these wicked men. It is easy to say the price of a surcoat is death but it is not merely one surcoat we are considering.'

Philippa was silent. 'I know this well,' she replied at length. 'But I shall grieve for that child. I believe that the woman stole to feed her living child. Edward, you often wish to give me some jewel to show how you love me. I would rather have this woman's life than any jewel.'

So Edward said the woman should be pardoned; and the people crowded round the Queen when she rode out and blessed her with tears in their eyes and she was called Good Queen Philippa.

❈ ❈ ❈

The King of England was on the march. Robert the Bruce was dead and King Edward looked and acted like his grandfather. There was no Scottish army worthy of the name. It had never been easy to discipline Scotsmen. They needed a William Wallace or a Robert the Bruce, and they had neither. Moray was dead. So was Black Douglas. They were without those leaders who could have led them to victory.

Sir Malcolm Fleming came to Edinburgh. He knew what Edward planned. He would set up Baliol as a puppet King and take David and Joanna back to England. There they would live comfortably – but as prisoners. It must not be. David must remain King of Scotland and if he ever fell into Edward's hands who could say what the English King would inveigle him into promising.

Sir Malcolm's plan was that he should convey the young King and Queen to Dumbarton, which was reckoned to be the strongest castle in the country, and he was its governor. There he would keep the royal pair; and if it were necessary for them to leave the country he could have a ship waiting for them and they could leave for France, when danger came too near.

This seemed a good plan and the children set out with Sir Malcolm.

So to Dumbarton, that grim fortress set on a point of land formed by the Clyde and the Leven from where it would be possible to take ship easily if the need arose.

It was an adventure riding through the night with the kindly Sir Malcolm, though David hated to leave his castle and – even more – the possibility of leaving Scotland itself. He was the King and they were trying to make him not a King. It was all the fault of Joanna's brother. He was sullen and would not speak to her. She did not care for that but she was deeply hurt that Edward should have marched against Scotland while she was its Queen.

'There need not have been a marriage,' said David. 'It was supposed to be to make Edward our friend.'

'He *is* really our friend,' Joanna tried to explain. But alas she could find no argument to back up that statement.

They settled in at Dumbarton and David forgot his animosity towards her because it was all rather exciting. Messengers were constantly arriving at the castle and they used to sit at the window and watch the ships dancing on the water. There were always men to load them with goods so that, said David, we could step into them and be gone in an hour.

'We should have to wait for the tide,' retorted Joanna.

'Of course we should wait for the tide.'

'Then it might be more than an hour.'

'Don't be silly. I'd like to go on that ship.'

Joanna considered. Yes, she thought she might like it too.

And then one day they did so. Sir Malcolm came to them and said: 'Make ready. We are sailing with the tide.'

'Where are we going?' cried David.

'To France, my King.'

Hastily they prepared. They were glad they had been told

weeks ago to make ready. They would be less likely to forget something important.

Soon they were going on board. And then . . . away to France.

❁ ❁ ❁

It was a difficult crossing but the young people were too excited by the prospect before them to notice the rigours of the sea. David felt it was wrong to be excited for he was leaving his kingdom; he would be a king in exile and his knowledge of history told him that that was not a very good thing to be. Joanna was depressed by the thought that she was running away from the approaching armies of her own brother.

Still, the tedium of life in Edinburgh was no more and it was becoming very adventurous.

When they arrived at Boulogne a messenger was sent to the King of France to tell him of their arrival and in a very short time he sent a company of Knights to bid them welcome and to bring them to the Court of France.

The friendly concern of the King of France was a great comfort to the Scots and they lost no time in accepting his hospitality.

Philip the Sixth had already proved himself to be a mighty monarch and the contrast between him and his three predecessors, the sons of Philip the Fourth, was marked and the change had put fresh hope into the hearts of his subjects, particularly now that they believed that the Templar's curse was worked out. It had been directed at the Capet line; and with the death of Charles the Fourth the Valois had taken their place as the ruling house.

True the King's father had been the brother of Philip the

Fourth but this was a new branch on the royal tree and the curse was finished.

It had been clear from the first that Philip was a strong man. He immediately set about pulling France out of the morass into which three weak kings had led her. Already he had subdued the Flemings and had commanded the young King of England to do homage to him. It was true he felt a certain uneasiness because of young Edward's claim to the throne of France, ridiculous though it might be, but all the same Philip believed they must be prepared for trouble. Through Edward's marriage with Philippa of Hainault he had made sure of the friendship of the Low Countries. Philip had heard that the English Queen had notions of improving the trade of England.

'What is she?' Philip said. 'A tradesman's daughter!'

'The Lowlanders are traders by profession,' was the mocking answer.

Still Edward must be watched. He was popular in his own country and since he had rid himself of Mortimer and taken the reins into his own hands, there had been improvements. He had heard that Philippa was importing weavers to England and that they were becoming prosperous in this little community.

Yes, Edward must be watched.

It was good that he should be kept occupied in Scotland, for while he was using his energies there he could not turn to France. The last thing Philip wanted was to have war, the object of which would be to prove whether he or Edward had a right to the throne of France. Preposterous as the suggestion was it would mean a long and disastrous war and, if Edward really were growing more and more like his grandfather, he could be a formidable enemy.

He would therefore make much of this little Scottish King.

Puppet he might be, but he could be tutored and who knew some good might come of it.

Philip himself rode out to meet the cavalcade as it made its way into Paris.

He embraced Joanna and complimented her on her beauty. He treated David as though he were a great King. So both the children were enchanted by the King of France.

There was to be a feast in their honour, he told them and one should sit on either side of him. There was food such as they had never tasted before, music and elegant dancing. The French Court, it seemed to both of them, was a sort of heaven, and the King the most charming man in the world.

Their apartments were luxurious – very different from those sparsely furnished rooms in Scotland, and even grander than many in England.

There was nothing, it seemed, that the King of France would not do for their comfort.

'You poor children,' he said embracing them, 'how glad I am that you came to me for comfort.'

'Will you help me to regain my kingdom?' asked David who every now and then remembered he was a king.

'With all my heart,' replied Philip. 'Of course I know that you are a proud king. You will accept my help and my advice but you will want to do something for me in exchange. I can see you were about to say this.'

'It is true,' said David.

'Then just promise me this. You will never make peace with England without first obtaining my consent for you to do so. There. That is not much to ask is it? And I make the request because I can see your pride demands that you give something in return.'

'I willingly agree,' said David eagerly.

'Now I shall give you an income while you are with me so that you can live in the state which is due to you.'

'My lord, your kindness overwhelms me,' cried David.

'Nay. You are young and brave and I like not to see my friends exploited on account of their youth. This beautiful lady . . .' he turned to Joanna . . . 'should be happy and gay and that is what I intend she shall be during her stay in France.'

It was impossible not to be grateful for so much so graciously given.

The King suggested that they should have a private establishment during their stay in France, and he offered them Château Gaillard, that fortress built on a high rock, which was symbolic to both England and France. It had been built by Richard Coeur de Lion and it had been the pride of his heart. King John, in his folly had lost it to the French; and since then it had had a sad history and become more a prison than a royal castle.

They would bring gaiety into Château Gaillard, said Philip; and it amused him that he should offer that castle which had been built by an English King to these two young exiles from Scotland.

Philip himself conducted them to their residence and there he said he would allow them to entertain him and his knights in their home.

This delighted David in particular. It was not that the King of France did not enchant Joanna. The trouble was that all the time she kept thinking that he was an enemy of Edward. But Edward had deserted her. Her own brother had made war on her country. It was foolish, as David said, to think of him any more with affection.

The benign King of France was never anything but kind to them. They gave a lavish banquet for him all provided for by him and prepared by his servants; but he kept calling it the hospitality of the King and Queen of Scotland.

He told them about French wines and made them try them.

'Who knows,' he said, 'one day we might raise an army in France and win back Scotland for you. What would you do if we did? I know. You would want to pay feudal homage to France for your kingdom, would you not?'

'I should be so grateful,' said David, guilelessly.

'Then you will do it. Is that a promise?'

'It is a promise.'

'Then I am going to say that you hold Scotland as fief of France. That means you are under my protection. I think that is a very happy state of affairs, do you not agree?'

David feeling very happy and sleepy nodded.

The King raised his goblet. 'My friends,' he said addressing the whole community. 'My friend the King of Scotland has made me very happy this night. He has just declared that Scotland is a fief of France. Let us drink to this, my friends.'

There was much drinking and chatter.

The King of France kissed first David and then Joanna.

'There,' he said, 'we have sealed our pact in this goodly company.'

Somewhat reluctantly Philippa agreed to stay at Bamborough Castle while Edward went on to Berwick.

It would be necessary to lay siege to the castle for naturally it would not be easily given up. There could be heavy fighting and the Queen might be in danger.

'If you are there that is where I would wish to be,' she told him.

'I know, my love, but I should be thinking of your safety and not the battle.'

When it was put to her like that she could not refuse, so she settled in at Bamborough to await his return.

The ancient fortress had been erected long before the coming of the Conqueror and its position on a rock which was almost perpendicular and looking straight out to sea made it an invaluable stronghold.

Here Philippa must settle down to await the King's return. He sent her messages frequently so that she might know how the campaign was progressing. He was after all only about twenty miles away. He did not anticipate that the siege would be a long one, and he had had unexpected good fortune which he hastened to impart to the Queen. Some of his men had found two young boys riding in the forest and had brought them to him. On questioning them he had discovered that they were the sons of the Governor of Berwick Castle.

'You see, my dear, what a good weapon Fate has placed in my hands. I hold these two boys hostage. I do not think the Governor will want to hold out too long when he hears that I have his sons.'

While she recognised the lucky fate which had given Edward this advantage, Philippa could not help thinking of the poor parents of those boys and what they must be suffering at this time. She was sure that they would never allow any harm to come to them, and if it shortened the siege she supposed it was all to the good and would bring Edward back to her all the more quickly.

It was soon after that, looking from the turret window on the land side, she saw a band of men approaching. As she watched she saw more and more. Then she recognised the

Scottish pennants and knew that the enemy was marching on Bamborough Castle.

She hurriedly summoned the guard. Everything must be securely locked. The guards must take their places for the defence. The enemy were about to lay siege to Bamborough.

'We must get a message through to the King somehow,' she said.

There were several volunteers, and she decided that more than one should go in case there should be difficulty in getting to the army outside Berwick.

When Edward heard that Philippa was being besieged in Bamborough his first impulse was to fly to her aid, but even before he could make preparations for departure he realised that this was exactly what the Scots wished. They wanted to draw him off Berwick, to let in reinforcements, to make the taking of the town impossible. The object of this campaign had been to take Berwick and if he failed to achieve it another failure would be marked up to him.

He was in a quandary. He was very anxious for Philippa's safety; and at the same time he knew that it would be folly to leave Berwick. Philippa was wise; she was well protected. The siege of Berwick would soon be at an end. It was Scottish strategy to draw him away just when he was on the brink of victory.

Uncontrolled rage seized him. Philippa in danger and he unable to go to her! A curse on the Scots. That ungovernable Plantagenet temper had never been so strong in him. He had to wreak revenge on someone.

The Governor of Berwick! By God, he had his two boys. The hostages!

He summoned his guard.

'Slay those boys,' he said.

The guard stared at him in dismay. He could not believe he had heard correctly for the two hostages had been treated rather as pets in the camp. They had played games with the soldiers and the King had spoken kindly to them often. They were all fond of them. They were two innocent boys.

'Go, you fool,' shouted Edward. 'You heard me. Do you dare refuse to carry out my order?'

'My lord . . . I cannot believe I heard right.'

'You heard me say, "Slay the boys." Kill the hostages. I have had a trick played on me and no one plays tricks on Edward of England. Cut off their heads and bring them to me so that I can see that the deed is done. Go. Or do you want the same sentence meted out to you?'

The guard went.

In less than ten minutes he returned with the two young heads and as Edward stared at them his anger passed and terrible remorse came to him. He wondered if he would ever forget that blood-stained innocence.

It had to be, he told himself. It had to be. There is no room for softness.

Now, to Berwick. He would storm the place. There should be no more waiting.

He was a soldier. He knew that now. He would vie with his grandfather for battle honours. There was nothing soft about him. He was going to win.

Berwick fell into his hands with astonishing ease. And as soon as he had set his garrison in it he turned to Bamborough, the vehement fighting mood still on him.

He slew the Earl of Douglas who had led the troops to Bamborough, and routed his troops with ease; then he went into the castle.

Philippa was waiting for him, calm, certain that he would come to rescue her.

They embraced with fervour.

'I knew there was nothing to fear,' she said. 'I knew you would come.'

'Berwick is mine,' he said. 'I have won what I came out to win. I will take you in to Berwick tomorrow and you will ride through the streets in triumph with me.'

'Oh Edward. I am proud of you.'

He had to tell her himself about the boys for he did not want her to hear of it from anyone else. He tried to explain to her, to excuse himself. 'It was a trick to draw me from Berwick and by God, Philippa, I almost fell into it. I almost did what they wanted me to. Then I saw that I must stay at Berwick.'

'Of course you had to stay at Berwick. Of course you did right.'

'A madness came over me. To think I must stay while you were in danger.'

'The castle is a great stronghold. I was in no danger. I could have hung out for weeks.'

'Yes, I know. But in my fury I ordered the hostages to be slain.'

'The hostages . . . The . . .' He saw the shudder run through her. 'The little boys . . .' she went on.

'It was because you were in danger. A great fury seized me. It was like a frenzy . . .'

She tried to hide the horror in her eyes. She thought of the boys' mother. Poor poor bereaved woman to lose both her sons.

'Philippa, it was because of you . . . *you* . . . in danger.'

She understood. Philippa would always understand.

She said quickly: 'It was an ill fortune of war.'

'Yes,' he agreed, 'an ill fortune of war.'

He was going to forget it. It was necessary. No one was going to think he could be trifled with.

He had won Berwick. His feet were now set on a certain path. He was emerging gradually as the man he would be and in these last weeks he had taken a step forward.

Men were going to tremble at the mention of his name as they had at that of his grandfather.

There would be two Great Edwards for men to marvel at.

The object achieved there was no longer any need to be parted from their children. Berwick was in English hands where Baliol had promised it should be. That was enough for the time. It would show the Scots that when the King of England had a purpose he achieved it. Another Edward had arisen to hammer them into submission.

Philippa was delighted to be returning to her babies. She had not mentioned the death of the hostages again and Edward had convinced himself that a soldier must harden himself to brutality when it was necessary and when men died by the hundred and thousand in battle life was not so very precious.

When they arrived at the castle of Clarendon they were amazed to find that the place seemed almost empty. They surprised one or two serving men lolling about and Philippa immediately noticed that there was something unkempt about the place. A terrible fear seized her; she feared for the safety of her children.

Edward thundered: 'Where are the guards? Where are the attendants?'

But Philippa was already running to the nursery.

Three-year-old Edward was seated on the floor, rolling pewter platters around and chuckling with glee as he caught them. One-year-old Isabella was crawling after him. Both the children were unwashed, their garments stained and torn.

The Queen ran to them and picked up Isabella who screamed in protest but Edward recognising his mother ran to her and clutched at her skirts, smiling his delight.

She knelt down and put her arms about them, assuring herself that in spite of their neglected condition they were well.

They had been fed. There was evidence of that on their clothing but how could they be in such a condition? Where were the governesses, the attendants?

In a short time Edward had summoned to the hall all the attendants and servants who were in the castle and in a stern voice demanded to know what this meant.

There was a deep silence; all were afraid to speak until Edward thundered that it would be well for them to give him some explanation of their conduct before his temper was such that all would pay with their heads for what they had done.

It was one of the minor servants who spoke, feeling himself no doubt without blame as his only duty was to obey those who were set over him.

'We were told, my lord, that we could not have what we needed because there was not enough money to pay for it.'

'It was true,' said another. 'We could not provide what food was necessary for the household. So it was taken from the neighbourhood and the people got very angry.'

'You mean you stole from the villages round here to feed yourself . . . and my children!'

'Well, my lord, there was not enough money to pay for what was wanted.'

'This is a sorry state of affairs. And does that account for the neglected state I find my children in?'

There was silence.

'By God,' cried Edward, 'some of you will be sorry you flouted my wishes.'

Philippa said: 'The children are well. It seems they have been fed. They have been left to themselves and have not been washed and tended – that is all. My lord, all I wish is to be with them, to look after them. If you dismiss these people it is punishment enough that they will have nowhere to go and no employment. We can bring others in to take their place.'

Edward, who had felt that rising anger beginning to stir in him, was haunted suddenly by the sight of two headless children. He must govern this temper or his life would be strewn with regrets for violent actions taken impulsively.

Philippa was right. No harm had been done to the children. They had not been starved or ill-treated. They were happy enough.

He turned to Philippa.

'I will leave you to deal with the household,' he said. 'I will summon those villagers and hear their version of this sorry tale. They must be reimbursed for what they have lost. And let me warn you all that if it is brought to my ears that you have behaved in this disgraceful way again, you will know no mercy from me and what you have done at this time shall be considered against you.'

Edward learned from the neighbourhood that five hundred pounds was owing. This he ordered should be paid at once.

Philippa had been deeply shocked by the sight of the children but in a short time she herself had washed them and put them into fresh garments. Edward chattered away to her and she was relieved that he had no idea that he had been so neglected.

Philippa was thoughtful. She had made up her mind that she would have to be very careful about leaving them again. She would never have a moment's peace if she did. Yet on the other hand she did not want to leave Edward.

She prayed for peace that would allow Edward to remain at Court with her; but she knew that the time would come when the difficult choice would have to be made.

To her great joy she discovered that she was once again pregnant. The King was delighted. Their two children brought him great joy and she noticed that although Edward was his pride, it was Isabella on whom he doted.

Isabella was a very pretty child, wilful and more demanding than Edward but that seemed to amuse the King. He liked her to sit on his knee and talk to him in her baby way; she clearly enjoyed being made much of and always ran to her father as soon as he appeared.

Philippa rejoiced to see Edward with the children so it was a great happiness to know that there would soon be another.

With Berwick in English hands, there could be a respite from the Scottish wars and Christmas was a jolly occasion and they spent it at Wallingford. Philippa at this time was heavily pregnant, the baby being due in February.

The Court was in London at the time of the birth and the baby was born in the palace of the Tower. Perhaps it was for this reason that Philippa decided to call her Joanna in memory of that other Joanna her aunt, who had been born in the Tower and was now living in France with her husband, David the Bruce, under the protection of Philip the Sixth.

However Joanna was a welcome addition to the family and Edward was more than ever delighted with a loving and fruitful wife.

He was however beset with problems. Trade had suffered considerably from the Scottish war. Foreign ships avoided coming to England for fear of being taken and robbed of their cargoes. Edward had quickly seen that if he was going to have a contented country it must be a peaceful one. Trade was what the country needed. He issued letters of safe conduct to all merchants and gradually the ships were coming back into English ports. The weavers who had come to England on Philippa's suggestion were settling in Norfolk, although they faced some hostility from the local people who found them too hard-working for their liking. But they were a quiet people and so industrious that in spite of certain opposition they flourished. Moreover they had the blessing of the King and Queen and the natives were afraid to be too openly hostile.

Baliol was now back on the throne of Scotland with Edward's support. He had agreed that Edward should have the whole of the South of Scotland below the Forth and by accepting him as his liege lord for the North he was allowed to reign over that part. It was not to be expected that Scotsmen would consider this a very happy state of affairs. Baliol was weak and needed continually bolstering up which meant that for Edward during the months that followed there must be continual journeys back and forth to the North. After her experiences at Clarendon Philippa would not leave her children, so she and the children, even baby Joanna, were constantly on the move. There was one occasion however when she could not have them with her and after much soul-searching she decided that she would leave them at Peterborough Abbey where she knew they would be safe.

The Abbot, Adam de Botheby, was taken aback. The Abbey was no place for young children, he pointed out. Yet the Queen pleaded with him. She told him of her experiences at Clarendon and she also mentioned Edward's need of her. So eloquently did she plead that, after consulting his monks the Abbot agreed to take the children.

They could not expect great comfort, he said. They would be disciplined and expected to follow the rules of the Abbey.

At least Philippa knew they would be cared for by these good men. She was amazed however when she returned to find that they had completely changed the life of the Abbey. She found young Edward seated on the shoulders of the Reverend Abbot and Isabella had one of the monks on all fours while she rode him as a horse. Joanna was rocked to sleep by one of the cellarers and would have none other to do this task, expressing loud disapproval if any other tried.

The children were reluctant to leave Peterborough and the Queen discovered that if they had been neglected at Clarendon, they had been utterly spoiled by the monks.

'I must keep them with me,' she told Edward. 'I must.' It was not long before another child was born. It was a boy this time whom the Queen wanted to name William, to which the King immediately agreed. His was a sad little life. He lacked the vigorous health of his brother and sisters and after a few months he died.

The Queen's grief was great and long after the little boy was buried in York Minster she continued to mourn him.

Edward consoled her. They had three healthy ones. They must be thankful for them – and there would be more.

There was sad news from Scotland where Edward's brother the Earl of Cornwall, known as John of Eltham after the place of his birth, had gone to help subdue the Scots who had risen against the Baliol-Edward régime. There was nothing unusual in this, because trouble was continually breaking out and it was to deal with this in his brother's name that John had marched to Perth. He had been there some months when fighting had broken out and during it he had been killed.

Edward was overcome by grief. John had always been a good brother to him. He was only twenty years old and had never married, although alliances for him had been proposed. It was terrible to think, said Edward, that he had died without really living. It was different for children like William who never knew what life was; but John had lived for twenty years and then suddenly death had taken him.

The loss of his brother set Edward thinking about his childhood when they had been in the nursery together. They had not often seen their parents then and when they had Isabella had seemed to them like a goddess. They had never seen anyone as beautiful. It was true she had ignored John but she had always made much of Edward and looking back Edward realised that he had always taken her attention as his right. Poor John. He hoped he had not minded too much; but their sisters had shared that neglect too. Poor Eleanor and poorer Joanna. He wondered how Eleanor was faring with her elderly husband. How splendidly equipped with material goods she had been when she had gone off, but that would not make for happiness. She had a little son now, Raynald after his father; he guessed that Eleanor would make a good mother. But poor young Joanna, what was life like for her in the Château Gaillard with her young husband who was not very prepossessing or charming.

How lucky he was with his Philippa.

Being depressed by trouble in the family, he had thought a great deal lately about his mother, and decided he would go to Castle Rising and see her.

There was no doubt of her pleasure when he arrived.

She embraced him and wept a little and he noticed with relief that she was more serene than he had seen her ever before.

'Ah,' she said, 'you are indeed a King now.'

'I have grown older – and perhaps more quickly than most.'

'It was necessary. You were such a boy when the crown was placed on your head.'

'Tell me, my lady, are you content here at Castle Rising?'

She was silent for a while and he wished he had not asked that question for it had set her looking back into the past.

'There is peace here,' she said.

'Peace . . . ah peace! Is that not what we all long for?'

'I never wanted it when I was young. It is only when you are old and wise that you realise its virtues. You, my dear son, would not like to be shut away here in Castle Rising. I see very few people but I have good servants. I ride a little. I go out with my falcon now and then. I hunt the deer. I read a great deal and I pray, Edward. I pray for the remission of my sins.'

'You are . . . better than you were?'

'You mean do I still have my fits of madness? Now and then, Edward, now and then, but I fancy they are less frequent nowadays and of shorter duration. I see visions in my dreams but not in my waking moments. Sometimes I lie remembering all the evil deeds of my life.'

'An unhealthy occupation which would do none of us much good, I fear.'

'Some of mine will need a great deal of prayer for forgiveness. And now your brother is dead. I think about him, Edward. I was never a good mother to him.'

'He thought of you as a goddess. He said not long ago that he had never seen a woman whose beauty compared with yours.'

She shook her head. 'I scarcely looked at him. I wanted children for the power they would give me. Oh, I am a wicked woman, Edward. John's death has brought that home to me.'

'You must not brood on it, my lady.'

'At least it has brought you to see me.'

'I should have come before.'

'You have been lenient with me, though you killed Mortimer . . .' Her voice broke at the mention of that name. 'I must not think of him,' she said quietly, 'or I shall have bad dreams. Edward, I want to come to see you sometime. You . . . and the children and your good Philippa.'

He went to her and kissed her brow.

'You shall come to us, Mother. Philippa would wish it. You should see young Edward.'

'He is like you when you were his age. I am glad you called him Edward.'

Questions came into her mind. She wanted to ask him if his father's murderers had ever been discovered. But she dared not. She did not want him remembering what part she had played in the most horrible murder in history.

She knew that the long exile could be over if she wished. She could go to Court. People would forget.

They talked of John for a while and it was clear that she mourned this son though she had never loved him in life. His death had brought home to her another of her failings. She had been a bad mother to her children . . . all except Edward and she had led him to depose his father.

Edward took an affectionate farewell of her.

Life could change now if she wished. He had come to see her; he was telling her that whatever she had done she was his mother and he had loved and admired her until he discovered her true nature.

He could forgive her.

Her spirits were lifted. But she would have one of her attendants sleep in her room this night. She was afraid that the ghosts would come.

Edward had revived memories.

❀ Chapter VIII ❀

THE KING AND THE HERON

Count Robert of Artois, Queen Isabella's cousin, had arrived in England. He had quarrelled with the King Philip and came as a fugitive, having escaped from France disguised as a merchant.

Robert of Artois was a man born to make trouble. It had been his lot in life never to achieve what he thought was his by right; he suffered from a permanent envy and a desire to bring misfortune to those who possessed that which he would like to have.

His great animosity was directed against the King of France. He was a great grandson of Robert the first Count of Artois, who had been a younger brother of St Louis, and it was frustrating for a man of Robert's temperament to be descended from the royal tree and yet not of the main line. He constantly reminded himself of how different everything would have been if instead of being a younger brother his great grandsire had been the elder.

Moreover Philip, the present King, was not of the direct line. Yet there he sat on the throne, elected by common consent as the nearest to Philip the Fair since his father was brother to that

King. Philip's three sons, Louis, Philip and Charles had reigned ignobly under the shadow of the Templar's curse and now Philip son of Charles de Valois had become the King of France.

For some years Robert had had to sue for what was his by right – that was the countship of Artois which had belonged to his great grandfather.

Philip the Fair had refused to grant him these lands and had tried to fob him off with others and during the reigns of Philip's three sons he had tried again; he had even married Philip's sister; but it was no use. Philip had shown clearly that he was not interested in his kinsman's claims.

When Queen Isabella had been in France he had been struck by her beauty and had become one of her ardent partisans. At the time when her brother was finding her presence at his court embarrassing, it was Robert of Artois who had hastened to warn her to get away and had helped her to reach Hainault.

The fact was that Robert could never resist being involved in any intrigue. He liked to be at the heart of it and if he could not enjoy the estates which he believed were his due, he could at least enjoy trouble.

If there was anything likely to bring that about he would seize the opportunity to be in the thick of it. He could only soothe his envy for the King of France by making the position more difficult for him to hold.

Again and again sources of disaffection would be traced to him; and there came a time when the King decided he would have no more of it.

There would never be peace in a realm while Artois was there to make trouble so the King called together a court of peers to examine the case against Robert of Artois with the result that he was banished and his property confiscated.

Robert was not the kind of man to go meekly. He lingered. He sought further means of making trouble until the King was so exasperated that he sent guards to arrest him. If Robert would not live peaceably in freedom, he would have to be put somewhere where he could do nothing to disrupt the country.

It was then that Robert, having warning of his intended arrest, disguised himself as a merchant and took flight.

Where should he go? Where but to England. But for him Edward might never have had his throne, so he believed.

He presented himself at Court in most dramatic fashion. Edward was dining at the time in the great hall of Westminster with a large company of people. The Queen was seated beside him and as was the custom the people were allowed to walk in and watch the King at his meal.

There was a sudden commotion among the crowd and a merchant stepped forward. As he had come very close to the table the guards moved in to restrain him.

Edward, his knife in his hand, had been in the act of conveying a tasty morsel of lamprey to his mouth.

'What means this?' he demanded.

The merchant came forward. 'Allow me a word with the King,' he said.

The guards stood hesitantly awaiting the King's orders. All eyes were on the merchant.

'My dear dear cousin,' he said. 'I have come from afar to seek hospitality at your Court. I know you will not deny it.'

Edward stared in astonishment. 'It is. It can't be. But yes . . . Robert . . . Robert of Artois!'

'Your own cousin . . . your loyal friend. It warms my heart to see you in the midst of your devoted subjects.'

Edward rose, embraced Robert and made him sit beside him

and eat of the food, which Robert did with great heartiness while he talked a great deal about the wickedness of the King of France.

He was so different from Robert's dear cousin of England. The just requests which he, Robert, had made had been denied him. He never wanted to return to France while Philip of Valois sat on the throne. He would go back though when that unworthy monarch was ousted from that position.

This was a reckless manner in which to talk in public but Robert had been born reckless.

'This Foundling!' went on Robert. 'That is what they call him in France. He had no idea that he would ever come to the throne . . . nor would he but for a course of mishaps. First the father and then the sons . . . one by one. It was clear was it not that they were a cursed line? And who is Valois? The son of a King's brother. Methinks there are others who come before him.'

There were sly looks at Edward who was flushed a little – either with this suggestion or with the excitement of the reunion.

Philippa studied this flamboyant man who looked as though he had seen a great deal of the world and was dissatisfied with it.

She did not greatly like him. Something told her that where he was trouble would follow.

She was right. Robert immediately became a member of that intimate circle about the King. He was after all royal. He hunted with the royal party and declared his intention of helping in the war against Scotland. He had a certain charm and was experienced, being a good many years older than Edward. He had many fascinating anecdotes to tell of his adventures and he became a favourite particularly with the women. He travelled with the royal cavalcade up to Scotland, but war was not his idea of enjoyment. Certainly not the war with Scotland.

He talked a great deal to Edward about Scotland. 'Why concern yourself with this poor little country? This Baliol – why bolster him up? He is doomed to be a failure, that man. He will never hold the country together. Philip has not been a very good friend to you, has he? He has shown clearly his preference for your enemies. Look how he keeps the young King and Queen of Scotland at Château Gaillard.'

'He has certainly been no friend to me, that is clear enough,' admitted Edward.

'My dear friend and lord, it is a sad state of affairs when your own sister is the guest of the King of France, and in flight from you.'

'I have offered them a refuge here. I have promised that on the death of Baliol their throne shall be restored to them.'

'Ah, but they do not take advantage of your goodness, my lord. Why? Because the King of France tells them not to. Do you realise that this wily enemy of yours has taken those two children under his wing for the sole purpose of making trouble for you in Scotland?'

'I know that, Robert.'

'Scotland!' Robert snapped his fingers. 'What is Scotland? This is a poor little country . . . and yet so much blood has been shed to get possession of it. I marvel at you, Edward. You waste your energies on Scotland when there is a far greater crown waiting for you. It is not as though you had no right to it.'

'The crown of France!' said Edward. 'There are many who would say I have no right.'

'The Valois would! Naturally. He wants it for himself. The Foundling King!'

'He was chosen by the people to reign. I hear he is a good King.'

'Any king would be called good who came after the last three. Mercy be that their reigns did not last long. Your beautiful mother was the daughter of Philip the Fair. Her three brothers ruled – if you can call it rule – and she is the next in line and through her, her son.'

'You know full well the Salic Law prevails in France.'

Robert snapped his fingers. 'I do not ask that Isabella should rule. No. But she has now a son, a son who now carries the crown of England. Why should he not, instead of wasting his skill, his men and his arms on petty little Scotland, seek a worthier crown?'

'Ah, Robert, you almost convince me. But think of the bloodshed there would be. It would not be something which could be settled in a month or a year. I could see it going on and on . . .'

'Nothing that is worth while comes easily.'

'It is good of you to concern yourself with my welfare.'

'Oh, this is but justice.'

They were in the forest and when someone came to speak to the King, Robert rode on. He had said enough for the time being. His words would have their effect and it would be a deeper one if the poison was administered in small doses. It must be allowed to seep into the mind gradually so that it was allowed to take a firm hold before the subject realised it.

It would be amusing to start a war. Philip feared it. He wanted to make his country rich, to get it sound again after the

177

last disastrous reigns. What would he say if he had to start a war to hold on to his crown?

Robert was at his favourite trick – mischievously moulding events to his pleasure.

A war! he thought. A war between England and France. Philip was wily; Edward was young; but Edward would prove to be the better general.

He was pleased with himself. He had never done anything as big as this before.

Edward had realised from the first that his chances of turning Philip from his throne and taking it himself were not great. To carry war into a foreign country was always an undertaking and even defending French provinces had drained the energies of English kings since the Conqueror. The Scottish conflict had impoverished his grandfather and some said worn him out; and although he himself had left Baliol with a defending force in Scotland he did not expect the peace to last there. It was a pleasant idea to consider himself as rightful King of France but whether he should make an attempt to win that crown needed a great deal of examination. Robert d'Artois was constantly at his elbow pointing out the simplicity of the task; but Edward was experienced enough to know that war was only simple in the mind.

There was a great deal at home to demand his attention. Since the death of Mortimer he had made several attempts to bring his father's murderers to justice. Berkeley had been arrested as the deed had been carried out in his castle; but he had successfully proved that he had been nowhere near the castle when it had been committed. He was in disgrace but no punishment had been inflicted on him. His crime had been to turn away from what was happening in Berkeley Castle, when he should have called attention to the way in which the King was being treated. He could scarcely be executed for that.

Sir John Maltravers had disappeared into Flanders and it seemed was doing all he could to promote trade there for England. Therefore it was best that he should not be disturbed. Sir William Ogle however had been arrested in Naples.

Edward dreaded his arrival in England when the whole terrible story would be brought to light, for Ogle, with the connivance of others and having been ordered to behave as he had by Mortimer and the Queen, was the actual one who had carried out the grisly sentence.

Ogle could not be allowed to live.

Edward's commissioners knew his wishes, and that because there was Queen Isabella to be considered, the King did not want his mother's misdeeds to be brought out into the open.

It was arranged that Ogle should die on the journey from Naples to England. Thus he would expiate his sins with the least inconvenience; and there would be no revival of the old story in which Queen Isabella stood in such an evil light.

She was living quietly now at Castle Rising and seemed to have lost all that fiery ambition and pride which had made her the woman she had been.

Let these matters be laid to rest, thought Edward. It would be better so for the peace of the realm.

Meanwhile Robert d'Artois was constantly at his elbow. Robert was lively, amusing and knew exactly how to charm Edward. He had settled at Court and often said he would go back to France once the rightful king was ruling there.

'We are two of a kind, Edward,' he said. 'We both have to

179

regain our inheritance. I know this: When you are King of France, the Artois estates will be back where they belong.'

'You may rest assured, Robert, that they will be.'

Robert talked a great deal about his wrongs but he always did so in a light and amusing way.

'The battle of Courtrai should never have taken place,' he said. 'If it had not my grandfather would not have been killed and my estates would never have been taken from me. Imagine, Edward, this poor little orphan – myself – too young to defend himself. My father died soon after I was born. Oh, it was a devious business. Surely a father's possessions should pass to his son and then from son to son throughout the generations. So should it have been with Artois. But because I was but a fatherless child and the King was married to my aunt Mahaut's daughter, they were given to Mahaut.'

'That was most unfair,' cried Edward.

'Unfair! Of course it was unfair. It was said that Mahaut showed documents written by my grandfather in which he had said that she should succeed, not I.'

'Were they forgeries?'

'I am sure they were, but when Mahaut died the estates went to her daughter, the wife of the King. So you see what it was all about. Oh, I have been most shamefully treated, my lord. But I am not the man to stand aside and allow people to browbeat me.'

'Indeed you are not.'

'Nor would you be, my brave king. You are fortunate. You came into your inheritance . . . or part of it. England is yours but you will have to fight for France. And you will win it I know. Once you bestir yourself to get it.'

'What made your grandfather leave his estates to your aunt?'

'He did not. The documents were forgeries. There was a woman in his household who had always been a good friend to me. Her name was La Division.' Robert smiled reminiscently. 'Oh yes, she had always been a good friend to me. When I put it to her that the documents had been tampered with and my aunt's name substituted for mine she swore this was true and she produced new documents in which I was named sole heir.'

'And what did you do about it?'

'You can guess I would not let the matter rest. The present King had by this time ascended the throne. He was different from his predecessors. They were content to let matters drift. Not Philip. I put the case to him and his answer was to arrest La Division. Poor woman she was ready to stick to the truth but the torture broke her in time. She told them under pressure that she had been lying and the documents in which I was preferred were forgeries. It was what they wanted her to say, you see; and the poor woman, out of her mind with pain, agreed with anything just to make them stop the torture. She was burned at the stake. But that was not enough for Philip. I was still there. I knew too much, so he wanted to be rid of me too. It was proclaimed that during the questioning of La Division they had uncovered evidence that she — on my command — had poisoned Mahaut. I saw what was coming. That was when I disguised myself as a merchant and came to you. Oh, he is a wicked one, this King of France. He then set it about that a wax doll resembling him had been found in my castle and that in this doll red hot pins had been stuck. He said I was dabbling in witchcraft.'

'It seems he is determined to persecute you.'

'Not content with having taken my estates he has now made it impossible for me to live in France. It is a fact, you know,

Edward, that some people hate those they have wronged. Philip of Valois is one of them. Never mind, his day will come. Wait until the armies of Edward of England are astride France. That is the day I am longing to see.'

'Ah,' replied Edward, 'that could not be achieved in a day.'

'Perhaps in a month . . .'

'My grandfather who is reckoned to be one of the greatest warriors of all time could not subdue Scotland. My ancester Richard Coeur de Lion never reached Jerusalem, even the great Conqueror did not succeed in bringing Wales under his control. When one talks of conquest one forgets the long marches through rain and mud, snow, slush and blistering heat. One forgets the rigours of camp life. Before a campaign is undertaken it is necessary to decide what will be gained by victory and what lost by defeat.'

'Is this the way a great commander talks? I did not think the thought of defeat ever entered his mind.'

'He is no great commander if it does not. A leader of an army must consider everything that could befall his men and himself. He must be prepared. True he goes into battle with high hopes; at the moment of fighting he will believe he must be victorious. But in his meditations before the battle he must not be bemused by over confidence.'

'You surprise me, Edward. I have thought of you as one of the greatest generals the world has ever known.'

'Why should you since I have not yet proved myself to be so?'

'You have about you an aura of greatness.'

'Come, Robert, I am old enough now not to take flattery to heart. I have yet to prove what I am to myself and the world.'

'Shall I tell you something? The King of Naples told me that he has consulted the stars and he has discovered that the King of France can be defeated in battle . . . and by one man, the King of England.'

'Is this so?'

'My dear Edward, I swear it. It is written in the stars that if you – and you alone – led your troops against the King of France you could not fail to be victorious. Philip has heard this. He trembles, Edward. He trembles lest you march against him. I promise you this: if you went into battle this time next year the crown of France would be yours.'

Edward listened intently and Artois believed he was making some impression.

Edward was thoughtful. It was very pleasant to hear Artois tell him that he was a warrior destined for greatness.

He talked the matter over with Philippa. She was uneasy. Now that the Flemish weavers were settling in, Norfolk trade was increasing. There was nothing like a war to impoverish a country. Philippa believed in peace. Moreover she wanted to keep her family with her. She would never forget her horror on returning to her children and finding that they had been neglected. She would like the family to remain together. She hated leaving the children and on the other hand it was not always possible to take them with her on her travels. Then would come the terrible decision. Should she go with Edward or remain with the children?

'Philip is not like the sons of Philip the Fair,' she pointed out. 'The reports of him are that he is wily and shrewd. He will not lightly surrender his kingdom.'

'There will be a war, there is no doubt of that.'

'There have been so many wars between England and France.'

'Which is one reason why there should be a final one to settle the matter. If I had the crown of France then England and France would be as one country and the wars would cease.'

'But there would be a long war before you were victorious, Edward.'

'Artois thinks I should achieve victory in a few months.'

'Artois is obsessed by his hatred of the King of France. There might be others who do not dismiss him so easily.'

''Tis true. And Philip I am sure would be a fierce adversary. But there has been a prophecy, Artois tells me. The King of Naples has consulted the stars and they tell him that if I go against the King of France in person the crown of France will be mine.'

'Countries have to be won even if prophecies are to be fulfilled, Edward. I beg of you give great thought to this matter.'

'My dear Philippa, you may rest assured that I will do that.'

She seemed a little more satisfied; and the more Edward thought of the project the more he wanted to shelve the matter. If he decided to act against France he would have to be sure of his allies. He reckoned he could count on his father-in-law, William of Hainault, and Philippa's uncle John had always been a good friend.

Young Joanna, though scarcely more than a baby, was promised to the son of the Duke of Austria. That might ensure Austria's help.

Edward went on turning over these matters in his mind and nothing definite was arranged. Artois was becoming desperately impatient.

Am I going to stay here in exile all my life? Artois asked himself. Will Edward never make a move to gain the crown of France?

How he longed to see Philip brought low. He hated Philip as he had never hated anyone in his life and he was a man of violent passions. Philip of Valois to be King of France! The Foundling King who was on the throne because of a series of accidents! It was unfair. It should be stopped. And to think that Philip had upheld those who had robbed him of his estates and had made it clear that while he was on the throne they should never be restored to him.

Throughout Artois' life he had always had some project which he pursued with passionate intensity. He would never allow himself calm reflection. He enjoyed working himself up into a passion of hatred or love. He had to indulge these violent emotions; he had to live adventurously.

Out of his hatred of Philip of France had grown the idea of toppling him from his throne; and here was a ready-made solution. Through his mother Edward might by some be said to have a claim to the French crown. Others might say it was a flimsy one since it came through his mother, and the Salic Law prevented women coming to the throne. Edward was her son, a man . . . but still his inheritance came through a woman. The claim would not be regarded very seriously in France. But of course those who passionately wanted it to be so, could convince themselves that it was a good one.

Yet Edward would not move. Edward was cautious. Edward himself perhaps did not believe in his claim. It might be that he was considering what an undertaking it would be to go to France and fight the French, the object being to displace Philip from the throne.

Edward had had an uneasy beginning as a warrior in Scotland. He was not going to act rashly again. He could have been said to have set aside that first humiliation by later success but there was nothing spectacular in his military exploits so far.

Again and again Robert had pointed out the differences in France and Scotland. The Scots were a wild people; they had their mountains to help them. It was difficult to keep the Border fortified. How different it would be in France. He imagined the crown being set on his head, the French people acclaiming him.

Would they? wondered Edward. Why should they?

Because they hated Philip, the oppressor, the usurper, the Foundling King.

But they had put him on the throne and by all accounts France had been more stable under his rule.

How exasperating Edward was! Artois was getting very impatient and when he was impatient he was reckless.

He rode out alone in a fever of impatience and as he came through the forest he saw a stream and wading in the water looking for food was a slate grey bird with a thin black crest which curled down the long neck. Its pointed yellow beak was like a dagger poised ready to spear some unsuspecting creature. A heron!

Robert watched it quietly for some time. He must be still he knew for it was one of the most timorous of birds. A coward bird he had heard it called. Then an idea came to him.

He freed his hawk and very soon he held the heron in his hands.

Laughing to himself he returned to the castle.

The King and Queen were in the dining-hall. Artois was late. The King was on the point of asking for him when Robert entered. Behind him walked two women carrying a dish and in this dish was the heron which he had ordered to be roasted.

'What means this?' asked Edward preparing to be amused for Artois was notorious for the tricks he liked to play.

Artois went up to the King and bowed low. 'While hawking in your forest, my lord, I found this bird. I thought it would please you, my lord. It must be a favourite bird of yours.'

'A heron. Why so?' asked Edward.

'My lord,' said Artois speaking so loudly that everyone in the hall could hear and all were eagerly listening now to what the Count had to say. 'My lord, the heron is the most timid of birds. Everyone knows this. And you are a King who is not ready to fight for what is his. A timid bird . . . a timid King. There must be a certain partiality. So I have brought this bird to you for though he is but a bird and you a king you are alike in one respect.'

Edward rose, his face scarlet. Philippa trembled for the first signs of the Plantagenet temper were beginning to show themselves.

Artois folded his arms and studied the King mockingly, and to everyone's surprise Edward burst into laughter.

'You are a rogue, Artois,' he said.

'Yes, my lord,' replied Artois meekly.

'You have compared me with the heron. You call me a coward.'

Artois said nothing and all marvelled at his temerity. Whatever else he was he was a brave man.

Edward cried: 'It is true that I have a claim to France and I swear on this heron that I will take an army there and I shall give battle with the King of France be his forces twice the number of mine. Come, my friends, we will all take a vow on this heron. We will all swear together. We shall go to France. We shall take the crown from the head of the imposter Philip and we shall not rest until it is placed where it belongs. Never shall the Count of Artois compare me with a heron again. Come, those who love me, those who would serve me, take the vow of the heron.'

And one by one all the great nobles present advanced to the table and they vowed themselves to the French adventure.

Artois stood by smiling benignly. At last he had succeeded.

Chapter IX

JOANNA'S BETROTHAL

Now that he had decided on war with France, Edward knew that he was to make sure of his allies. The most important of these was Philippa's father, William of Hainault, for Edward believed there was one on whom he could rely.

Philippa was worried about the health of her father for the letters which came regularly from her mother were disturbing. Count William was, she wrote, mightily sick of the gout and he could not leave his bed.

But his support for Edward's claim was strong. This was a good sign for although some might say that naturally he would be on the side of his son-in-law, his wife, Philippa's mother, was the sister of the King of France so his ties with both countries were very strong. However, he came down on the side of Edward and as, though only a small country, by reason of its hard-working people and their concentration on trading it was one of the most prosperous in Europe, it was therefore a very worthwhile ally.

Austria was important and for this reason young Joanna who had been promised to the son of the Duke of Austria could no longer delay leaving England for her new home.

When her governess, kind Lady Pembroke, had told her she was going to leave England with her parents, Joanna had been delighted for she had not then known the significance of this journey.

It was her sister Isabella who told her. Isabella was very pretty and had always been spoilt by her father. She could not understand why she should be left behind. She knew that her mother hated leaving any of them and would not do so unless it was for some special reason, but she and Edward were to stay in the palace of the Tower with Lady St Omer and Joanna was to go with her parents. What could it mean? Isabella was only six years old – just over a year older than Joanna but she was very much the big knowledgeable sister.

'You are going to your husband,' she said. 'That is why you are going.'

'I am not,' replied Joanna. 'I am not old enough to be married.'

'Girls go to their husbands and grow up with them, do they not Edward?'

Edward said they did, and Joanna was plunged into misgivings.

Then her hopes were raised. Her mother would never let her go, she was sure. Yet it was strange that she was to travel with her parents and Isabella and Edward were not to go with them.

When she next saw her mother she clung to her hand and Philippa immediately guessed what was wrong. The child had been listening to gossip. She had wondered whether it would be wise to tell her what lay in store and prepare her or to wait until later. Now she had no alternative.

'Yes, my dear child,' she said, 'you are going to Austria. You see you are going to have a husband and he is the son of the

Duke of Austria. As your husband is Austrian it seems best that you should be brought up in their Court so that he would not be a stranger to you when you marry. I was brought up in Hainault and then I came to England and I had to learn how to be English. You will learn right at the beginning to be Austrian.'

'I want to stay English,' said Joanna.

'My love, you will laugh at that in time. You will want to be just what your husband is. I wanted to be English when I married your father.'

Joanna listened but she was afraid.

'Your new family wanted you to go over a long time ago but your father would not allow it,' Philippa went on. He said "No, she is too young and I must keep my Joanna here with me."'

'Perhaps he will still say it,' suggested Joanna eagerly. 'He is going to Europe himself and so am I and you will be with us. Your father would not let you go without him. He loves you so much.'

'Then perhaps he will keep me.'

Poor child. The hope in her eyes moved Philippa to pity. Why did this have to happen to young children? They were torn from their homes for political reasons. How could she explain to this little girl that she was going now because her father needed the help of the Duke of Austria and dared not offend him by keeping Joanna with her family any longer. How fervently she wished that there had never been this claim to the French throne! How she wished that Robert of Artois had never come to England, had never caught his symbolic heron!

But it had happened and she was forced to leave her two elder children behind and travel with Edward to Europe, taking this pathetic child who was going to be removed from her family and given to strangers.

Philippa tried to interest her in the clothes she was taking and the pallet bed which she would sleep on when she was on the ship. Joanna studied them with only mild interest. She could not stop thinking of leaving Isabella and Edward and wondering what her husband would be like.

But there was the journey first and during that she would be with her parents and that was what she liked better than anything. Isabella had pouted and cried when they left and demanded to know why she should be left behind. Then their father had kissed her and said next time he would take her with him and she had to be content with that.

When they set sail and it was all so new and exciting Joanna forgot where they were going; she loved the sea and her pallet bed and in spite of her apprehension it was all very interesting.

It was a hot July day when the party landed in Antwerp. There was no royal residence where they could lodge and a Flemish merchant of the name of Sirkyn Fordul offered them shelter. He was very honoured, he said, to have them in his house and he and his wife set about entertaining them in as royal a fashion as they could.

It was an exciting adventure for the little Joanna especially when in the night she was awakened by her mother who snatched her up in her arms and ran with her out of the house. Joanna clung to her mother in terror; the smoke choked her and she could scarcely breathe until she was out in the cold night air in her mother's arms, and her father was beside them. The house in which they were spending the night was a mass of burning timber.

Then Joanna saw hooded figures coming towards them. It was an abbot with his monks who suggested that the royal party should go with them to their convent of St Michael where they could shelter for the rest of the night.

To Joanna it seemed like a strange dream – all part of the adventure of going to a husband. Philippa was most distressed because of the disaster their coming had caused Sirkyn Fordul and his wife, for the conflagration had been started because of all the fires they had had to make to deal with cooking for so large a number. Edward comforted her and assured her that he would repay them for all the damage and then the worthy couple would have enough money to build a new house.

It was an unfortunate beginning to the adventure and Edward was worried about Philippa who had become pregnant again. Had it not been that she had insisted on accompanying Joanna to her new country he would have persuaded her to stay in England.

The next few days were spent in Antwerp where they were able to take trips along the river Scheldt and to visit the town and its many churches.

Edward was greatly concerned because he knew that he needed allies on whom he could rely and he had heard that Louis of Bavaria was wavering and might well decide to become the ally of the King of France.

'I must see him and talk to him,' he told Philippa. 'I can at the same time take Joanna into Austria.'

'I will go with you,' said Philippa.

'My dearest, remember your condition. I trembled for you during the fire. That sort of thing is not good for the child.'

Philippa had to agree with this.

'You may trust me,' he said, 'to look after our daughter. I think it is better for her to part from one of us now and the other later. It will break the shock of losing us both together.'

Philippa agreed that this might be so; and indeed she was

feeling the usual discomforts of pregnancy which were not helped by the hardships travel necessarily imposed.

An idea had occurred to her. 'I will write to Margaret,' she said, 'and ask her to keep an eye on Joanna.'

It seemed an excellent idea for Philippa's elder sister Margaret was now the wife of Louis of Bavaria.

This soothed Philippa's maternal heart considerably. And they set out for Herenthals where they would rest a night before the parting when Edward and Joanna would go on to Bavaria and Philippa would return to Antwerp to await the birth of her child.

There was no place at Herenthals worthy of their rank and they were lodged at the house of one of the peasants. Overcome by the honour done to them Podenot de Lippe and his wife Catherine, realising that their house would not hold so many people, decided that the only thing they could do was to serve supper in the garden.

This appeared to be an excellent idea until it was seen that the grass and the plants were ruined by the press of people for not only were there the attendants in the royal party but crowds who came in to pay their respects to them.

The crestfallen faces of Podenot and Catherine de Lippe were so reproachful that Edward immediately offered to compensate them for the damage done, so it turned out to be a very expensive supper party.

However there were other matters of greater concern to them for it was time now for Philippa to take leave of her daughter. The child clung to her mother and Philippa found it difficult to restrain her tears.

'Your father is still with you, my love,' she said. 'There is a long time for you two to be together. I shall think of you every day. I shall pray for you and I know that you will be happy in your new country. Your aunt Margaret will be there. She will look after you. You remember my telling you of my sister Margaret and all the fun we used to have together when we were children in Hainault.'

Joanna nodded mournfully and Edward lifted her in his arms and kissed her.

'You will be safe with me, daughter,' he told her tenderly.

Philippa watched until the cavalcade was out of sight; then sorrowfully she returned to Antwerp.

Joanna was young enough to enjoy the journey and forget what was waiting for her at the end of it. She adored her father. He was always kind to her; he loved all his children dearly but had always been more inclined to favour his daughters and since he knew that the parting with her mother had so upset Joanna he made every effort to compensate her for the loss. So at times Joanna was quite happy. It was exciting to ride on her little horse beside this magnificent man who was her father and to see how everyone paid great respect to him — and to her, simply because she was his daughter. They rode with sixty-six archers who made an impressive show and then there were their personal servants so they were a large company.

The scenery was beautiful. Joanna loved sailing up the Rhine while her father pointed out the castles on the banks and the rock on which the Lorelei had lured sailors to their destruction. She did not fear them because her father was by her side and she was sure he would get the better of anyone — even Lorelei.

At Bonn they landed and there were the guests of the

Archbishop of Cologne who had his residence there. They had a peaceful night there and then went on staying at various places where they were entertained and fêted until they came to Coblenz where the Emperor Louis himself was waiting for them. With him were the various princes of the Empire, among them the Duke of Austria, the father of the boy who was to marry Joanna.

With Louis was his wife who immediately took Joanna by the hand and said that she was going to look after her.

This was Joanna's Aunt Margaret.

'Your mother has written to me and asked me to take especial care of you,' she told Joanna.

Joanna's spirits were a little uplifted for during the past few days she had not been able to forget that soon she must say good-bye to her father. She clutched at this new hope. Her aunt was here and she was her mother's sister – and, yes, she did look a little like Philippa. She had the same bright complexion, the same plump face; but she was not quite Philippa. Joanna was quick to detect the difference. She lacked that clear candid gaze which was so comforting. She was kind and she smiled, but Joanna felt instinctively that she was not really like her mother.

However, there was so much to see. The Emperor had ordered that two thrones be set up in the market-place and here he and Edward sat during some very long ceremonies.

Aunt Margaret was beside Joanna during these and asked a few questions about her sister. She would write and tell her, she said, that she loved her little daughter on sight and was going to look after her until she was old enough to go to the Court of her future husband's father. Duke Otho was kind too, though Frederic, the future bridegroom, was very young and he regarded Joanna with the same suspicion as that which she bestowed on him.

'You will get to know each other and love each other,' said Aunt Margaret. 'But in the meantime you shall stay with me.'

Edward could see little of his daughter during the few days before their parting. His main purpose in coming so far had been to meet the Emperor and Duke Otho, and persuade them to support him in his claim to the French throne against Philip.

They were both cordial but inclined to be evasive, Edward thought, though he believed the marriage alliance would make sure of their friendship. He soon realised that however long he stayed he could do no more, so he prepared to leave. Before he did so he bestowed costly gifts on the Emperor and his wife and the Duke of Austria. These were intended as two-way bribes. In exchange he wanted their co-operation against France and for his daughter to be treated with the utmost kindness.

The gifts were readily accepted and assurances of friendship were exchanged so that Edward could leave feeling that the pact between them was secure and his daughter would be in good hands.

Duke Otho wanted to take the child with him to his Court but Margaret intervened. 'She is too young as yet,' she declared, 'and my sister has asked me to keep her with me for a while.'

Duke Otho would have liked to protest. After all Joanna was going to marry his son; but he dared not offend the Emperor who would naturally be influenced by his wife. Moreover Edward was delighted with the arrangements. 'It will be better for the child to be with her aunt,' he said. 'She is very young and loves her already.'

So it was arranged that Joanna should stay in Bavaria with

her Aunt Margaret until such time as she could join her young husband-to-be.

It was an emotional farewell. Joanna wept and Edward had difficulty in restraining his emotions. 'All will be well, dearest child,' he said. 'I and your mother will be thinking of you. No harm will come to you. Lord John de Montgomery will look after you. He will make sure that everything is well. There, my little one, you will be with your aunt and I know you already begin to love her. I shall tell your mother you are going to be happy here – otherwise *she* will be sad. You would not want that, I know.'

Joanna clung to him and he found it difficult to withdraw from her embraces. He almost felt inclined to take her back with him. That of course would be the end of friendly relations between him and the Emperor and the Duke. And he needed them.

For a few moments he wondered why he had embarked on this venture. He wished he had never made friends with Robert of Artois and allowed him such freedom that he could goad him with his heron.

That was nonsense. A King's life must not be dedicated to his family however much he loved them. He had a crown to win and he was going to do everything in his power to get it.

So at last he left Joanna and started on the journey back to Antwerp and Philippa.

In due course Edward arrived in Antwerp where Philippa was eagerly awaiting him. She wanted to hear about his parting with Joanna and was delighted that Margaret had taken her under her wing and yet she had certain misgivings. Few could know Margaret as well as she did and she could not help being aware that during their childhood Margaret had always contrived to get the larger share of any good things which came their way and to shrug off on the others anything that did not appeal to her.

But then she had been but a child – the eldest of the girls and somewhat conscious of her superior position. She would have mellowed and settled down and she would love Joanna for her sister's sake. Moreover Philippa had made sure that some costly gifts went Margaret's way for she knew how Margaret loved jewels.

All would be well.

Edward was a little depressed by the journey. He was not at all sure of Louis of Bavaria. There had been something rather shifty about him and though while in his presence Edward had believed in his friendship, he was not so sure of it when he was away.

If he could count on Louis he would have the support of the German princes for naturally they would follow the Emperor. The Count of Gueldres had married his sister Eleanor so there was a close tie there and he thought he could rely on him.

But the King of France had some strong allies. Navarre, Sicily and Luxembourg were with him. The Pope however wrote to Edward chiding him for making an alliance with Emperor Louis who had been excommunicated. Edward could hardly expect support from the Pope who, installed in Avignon, was a creature of the King of France. Still, if those he believed he had acquired remained faithful to him he was well placed to make his attack on France.

He conferred a great deal with Philippa. What he needed was money and he had already pawned a great many of the jewels Philippa had brought with her from Hainault.

'I am afraid,' he told her, 'we shall have to raise what we can on your best crown.'

Philippa shrugged her shoulders. If it must be, it must be and the contentment of her husband and family meant more to her than any jewels. But she deplored the prospect of war and yearned to be at home with her family. She thought constantly of Edward and Isabella and she wondered if they were being well cared for. There would always be this anxiety when she was separated from her children, and, but for the war, little Joanna need not have gone just yet.

In November her child was born. It was a great delight to her for it was a son. She decided he should be called Lionel after the lion in the arms of Brabant. It would be a compliment to the people who had been so hospitable to them.

Although he was long-limbed and beautiful and typically Plantagenet, the baby suffered from some very slight chest trouble and Philippa insisted that the doctor who had attended her and her family in Hainault should be sent for to look after the child. Philippa had great faith in him.

Her father had died and it had been a great blow to her but she had known it was inevitable; and her mother, who was alone now, for all the girls were married, had decided to retire to a convent. Therefore Philippa had no conscience about bringing the doctor to look after little Lionel.

He came and to Philippa's joy in a very short time Lionel was a lively healthy baby – the biggest of all her babies including Edward who had been a very healthy child.

Edward had a very good friend in Jacob van Arteveldt, a most extraordinary man who because of his outstanding character and undoubted integrity had became the Governor of Flanders. He was a man of some fifty years and in his younger days had lived in fairly affluent obscurity. His father Jan had been a cloth worker who had been Sheriff of Ghent. Jacob was widely travelled, having been in the service of Charles of Valois, the brother of Philip the Handsome, and had, with him, journeyed into Italy, Greece and Sicily. Returning to Ghent he had immersed himself in family life, his weaving business and that which his wife had brought to him – a factory in which sweet beer was brewed. He himself was by no means poor; his family had been hard workers and had accumulated wealth and he lived in a fine house in the Calanderberg over which he could display his family escutcheon. He was, in fact, a man of substance.

He was a big man in both senses of the word, a reformer by nature and a fervent patriot. He saw a great deal of what was wrong in his country and he believed it stemmed from incompetent rule. Count Louis of Flanders was the tool of the French King and the French were eager that the weavers should be dependent on their wool and Jacob believed that because of French interference the weaving trade was not as flourishing as it might have been.

The alliance which had come about with England when Queen Philippa had arranged that Flemish weavers should go to England had seemed to Jacob a promise of better things; and if the Flemings could throw off the French yoke which Count Louis of Flanders had put on them through his friendship with France, he was sure there would be better times ahead.

In the streets of Ghent weavers who had no work gathered to talk together. Their families had not enough to eat; their houses were small and cramped and overcrowded. They were a hard-working people and it seemed bad luck that they who were so ready to earn a living should be unable to keep themselves and their families.

Then they began to hear of a man named Jacob van Arteveldt who believed he could find a solution to their difficulties. The whole of the town was talking of him; everywhere his name was mentioned. He was well known in the town; a man who had always treated his workers well; a patriot who loved his country.

'Let us hear what he says,' cried the people.

The outcome was that Jacob agreed to speak to them and if they would assemble in the grounds of the monastery of Biloke he would be there to address them.

The grounds of the monastery were crowded with eager citizens, and there Jacob spoke to them with great eloquence and what seemed to them sound good sense.

He begged them not to forget the might and glory of Flanders. Who should dictate to them? They knew full well that the King of France was trying to prevent their trading with England. What had they to fear from France? All the communes of Brabant would stand beside them, as would those of Hainault, Holland and Zealand. So it was folly to be intimidated by the French.

'What I want to see and what I know will make our trade flourish is freedom to pursue fair commercial intercourse between Flanders and England, and at the same time assure neutrality if this threatened war between England and France should break out.'

The people cheered him. There was something solid about this man with a great girth and eloquent words. He was known as an honest trader. He was a good citizen. He was the sort of man they wanted to manage their affairs.

It was not long before all the representatives of the various communes had joined with Jacob van Arteveldt in Ghent and together they visited Louis the Count of Flanders, who seeing their determination, immediately agreed to support them, and a treaty was signed at Anvers to which Jacob had invited the English ambassadors. They agreed on three main articles. First that they should be able to buy wools and any other merchandise from England. Secondly traders from Flanders visiting England should be free in their persons and their goods and thirdly they should not meddle in any way by assistance in men and arms in the wars between Edward of England and Philip of Valois.

Philip was of course very disturbed by all this and he sent a message to the Count of Flanders to tell him that this dangerous man von Arteveldt must be removed, or, he added ominously, it would be the end of the Count of Flanders. However the Count's attempts to get Jacob assassinated came to nothing. The people were determined that their saviour should live and when the Count summoned Jacob to his hotel he was accompanied by so many of the citizens that Count Louis saw he could not easily dispose of him. All he could do was try to explain to Jacob that if he would persuade the people to love the King of France much good would come to him, whereas if he failed to do this he might be in a precarious position.

Jacob was not the man to be impressed by bribes or threats. He replied that he wished to do what was best for the people of Flanders and for no one else. It was they who had elected him for this task and he intended to carry it out.

It was impossible for Count Louis to harm Jacob for the people were with him to a man.

They must arm themselves against attack, Jacob told them. There should be trained bands throughout the towns. They were not arming for war but to preserve their rights. This was armed neutrality.

This hostility between France and Flanders was naturally to Edward's advantage and he realised that he must do all in his power to increase trade between the two countries. That was what they wanted and what was good for them both.

Philippa had understood this so clearly when she had brought the weavers to England; then there had been established between the two countries a great friendship which was now standing him in good stead.

'Ah,' said Philippa, 'if it were not for the state of war, how prosperous all our countries would be.'

She was sad as she reflected on Edward's absorption in this battle for a crown.

She had always thought how much better it would be to have a prosperous England than an England at war; and even if there was success for Edward and he won the crown of France he would only gain a country devastated by war.

But what could a woman do? Nobody would listen to her and they would dismiss her beliefs as woman's thinking. Yet if they had stopped to think they would have to admit she was wiser than they were.

When Prince Edward and his sister Isabella had been left in England they had both been disappointed. It was unfair, Isabella said, that Joanna should go with them. 'She is younger than I,' grumbled Isabella. 'Why should she go and I remain behind?'

Edward pointed out that Joanna had gone for a reason. She was to be left at her future husband's court. Poor Joanna had not been very happy about that.

Isabella certainly had no wish to leave her parents. Her father made too much fuss of her and secretly she delighted in the fact that she was his favourite.

Edward looked at her with tolerance. He himself was growing very tall and handsome. He was only ten years old but his attendants said that he looked all of sixteen and they had seen many women glance his way with approving and hopeful looks in their eyes.

Edward was unaware of them. He was interested in horses and he was very skilful in sword play. It was said that he would be a commander like his father and great grandfather and the King and the country should be very proud to have such a promising heir to the throne.

The Prince already was aware of his responsibilities. He was now Earl of Chester and Duke of Cornwall and since his father had left for France he had been appointed Guardian of the Kingdom. He was naturally too young for this to be anything but a title but it did mean that he was forced to attend meetings and although all he had to do was sit and listen, people turned to him with great respect and he must appear to give his consent to certain measures which really meant doing what he was told.

It was however good preparation for what would one day come to him. Nor were his studies neglected. Dr Walter Burley of Merton College, Oxford was his tutor and no easy taskmaster. A prince had great responsibilities, he was told, and he must not shirk them.

Not that he had ever shirked his duty. He had a great desire to excel. He had heard whispers of his grandfather's infamous life and unfortunate end and it was his duty to make sure that he did not inherit the weakness that had appeared in that sad King.

There seemed little likelihood of that.

He was in the palace of the Tower when Dr Burley sent for him to give him some news.

'My lord,' said the Doctor, 'I have had instructions from the King regarding you, and you must now prepare yourself for a journey.'

'I am going to join my father?' asked the Prince eagerly.

The Doctor nodded.

'When?'

'As soon as your journey can be arranged.'

'That means at once. For rest assured I shall not delay.'

'You should know that the King is anxious to celebrate your betrothal.'

'I am to have a wife?'

'The marriage is necessary to the King's plans. He is eager to strengthen his alliances on the Continent and is arranging a marriage between you and Margaret, the daughter of the Duke of Brabant.'

Edward was taken aback. He had wanted to go into battle, not matrimony.

'Am I to be married at once?'

'No, no. But the King needs these alliances.'

The Prince was thoughtful. Well, it was what happened to members of royal families. Their spouses were chosen for them and they must needs accept them. He wondered what this Margaret was like. At least when he married he would not have to leave his home and family as poor little Joanna had.

'The marriage would not be consummated immediately,' said the doctor.

The Prince understood. There would be some ceremony

206

and he would go on just as before. He could shrug the thought of marriage aside.

'I hope,' he said, 'that my father does not finish the war before I arrive.'

'I doubt you will be allowed to join in battles, my lord.'

'Do you think the war will be over before I am old enough to join in?'

The Doctor did not answer. He believed that this war would go on and on for many years. The King of France against the King of England and the battle fought on French soil! It was slow in starting, so perhaps both sides were realising what a difficult task faced them. Philip's was the easier. He was defending his homeland.

The Doctor in his sagacity thought that it was a pity Edward had ever embarked on such an undertaking. He lacked the means; he was in constant need of money; moreover there would certainly be trouble on the Scottish border if ever he became too involved on the Continent.

But the Doctor's talents lay not in war; it was his mission to educate the young heir to the throne. And he was not displeased with his job. Edward was showing signs of becoming a credit to him.

Edward left him and immediately began his preparations.

Isabella had heard the news and she came into his apartments. It was typical of Isabella that she came unannounced, always presuming that everyone would be delighted to see her.

Now her eyes were blazing, her cheeks scarlet.

'They say you are going to France,' she cried.

'It's true,' said Edward. 'I shall leave perhaps tomorrow.'

'And I am to stay here.'

'That is what I have heard.'

She stamped her foot. 'It's not fair. Why should I be left behind? Edward, take me with you.'

She flung herself at him and clung to him, but he coolly set her aside. 'How can I take you? There were no orders that you should come.'

'Our father promised . . . he *promised*. He said when he left that he would take me one day.'

'That day has not yet come.'

'Oh, it is cruel. I hate it here.'

'You know very well you do not hate it. Lady St Omer is very kind to you and takes good care of you.'

'I want to go to France,' sobbed Isabella.

The Prince turned away impatiently. He had no time to dally with his spoilt sister.

He left the next day watched by a sullen-eyed Isabella, but he was too excited at the prospect to think much about her. The crossing was good and it was a thrilling moment when he stepped ashore. He deplored his youth; he longed to be old enough to prove himself as a soldier. But it was a good sign that his father had sent for him.

He was as delighted to see his mother again as she was to see him. She embraced him and was almost overcome by her emotion. Philippa rarely gave way to her feelings but on this occasion at the sight of this handsome first-born she was so deeply moved.

How he had grown! He was quite a man. He was so like his father with his light-coloured hair, his high cheek bones, his aquiline nose which was just a little blunted at the tip – so like his father's – and those all-seeing blue eyes. He was a son any mother could be proud of. He was all that a future King should be.

208

She was glad she had called him Edward.

'You grow more and more like your father,' she told him.

The King was delighted too. Such a son was enough to warm any father's heart. Little Lionel too was becoming stronger every day and growing fast. His nurses said that they had never seen a baby grow as Lionel did . . . even Edward had not been so big.

If only he could have been as happy with the progress of the war as he was with his family, Edward would have been a very contented man.

Young Edward was very anxious to hear about the progress of the war and his father saw that he was wondering why it had not yet been won and the King of England was not also the King of France.

'My dear son,' he said, 'you have much to learn. Wars are not easily won. When I was your age I thought the same. I became King too young and I went to Scotland where I learned a bitter lesson. Wars swallow up money. Soldiers have to be paid, arms have to be found, friendship has to be bought.'

'I did not think friendship would be true friendship if it depended on gifts,' said the Prince.

'I see the good Doctor teaches you wisdom. I have to buy allies, Edward. I call them friends but as you so rightly point out they are not truly my friends and they could be my enemies if someone came along with a better proposition. Now, Edward, you are here in Brabant to be seen by the Duke. He will decide then whether you are a fitting bridegroom for his daughter.'

'Is the Duke one of these friends who have to be bought?'

'I need his help, Edward. This is a mighty task.'

'Do you need the French crown so badly, Father?'

'I need not to be deprived of my rights.'

The Prince saw the point of that.

'We will take it. I long to fight beside you.'

'One day, my son. One day.'

The Prince was not very sure that he liked being inspected as a future bridegroom. He did not see Margaret. That would come later. So much depended on the war. If Edward had had a few successes every prince in the neighbourhood would be eager to be his friend. What he needed was success. But first of all he must have money.

Money, money, money! It was the crying need. So much to be spent, so many bribes to be given, so much lavish entertaining.

The Prince wondered if this was the way to win a war.

He found himself riding side by side with a very handsome man some ten years his senior. There was something honest about him and the Prince at this time, brooding on what his father had said about bribing for friendship, was deeply concerned with honesty.

The young man asked him how he liked being out of England and Edward replied that it was good to be where important events were going to happen.

They chatted awhile of trivial matters and then Edward asked the young man what he thought about the delay in fighting. Did it seem to him that there was a certain reluctance on both sides?

The young man was thoughtful. It did seem so. There had been so much talk of war that it was certainly strange that no battle should have taken place. He thought that it was due to lack of money. He had been present he said at the banquet when Robert of Artois had produced the roasted heron. Perhaps the King had made his vow before he was ready to fight.

Then they talked about the claims of the King through his mother and how Philip was not really in the direct line.

Edward found it most interesting and very much enjoyed the company of the young man.

He asked his name.

'It is John Chandos,' he was told.

'Well, John Chandos,' he said, 'I hope we shall ride together again.'

John Chandos said he was at the Prince's disposal and as the days passed the Prince saw more of John Chandos, and when he deplored the fact that he was so young and therefore would not be allowed to join in the battle, John pointed out that there were always compensations in every situation. 'Just imagine,' he said, 'if you were four or five years older they would be marrying you to Margaret of Brabant.'

'And I am not at all sure that I want to marry her, John.'

'That is what I mean. So be thankful that you cannot just yet.'

The Prince laughed. And his friendship with John Chandos grew.

Philippa noticed it and was pleased. It was good for Edward to make friends and although Sir John Chandos was not of the most noble birth, he was of good family and an honourable man who had given the King good service. One of his sisters, Elizabeth, had been maid of honour to Philippa at one time. She had liked the woman, just as she liked her brother.

John Chandos could teach Edward a good deal.

Philippa was deeply concerned with other matters. Edward had said that he thought he would have to go to England to raise some money.

She sighed. Money could be spent in so many better ways

than in war. She was very sorry that Edward had ever thought of laying claim to the throne of France. If he had not they might all be together in England.

She thought constantly of her family. She worried about Joanna and Isabella. If only they could return to England where they belonged and settle down to live in peace.

She had a fancy that she might be pregnant again.

Joanna was desperately unhappy. Because her aunt Margaret looked a little like her mother she had expected her to act like her. When her father had ridden away the little girl had burst into tears and continued to sob bitterly.

Her aunt looked at her with some distaste and said rather sharply: 'Now, child, you are not a baby you know. What are you making that noise for?'

Joanna stopped crying to look at the Empress in astonishment.

'I want my father,' she said, 'and my mother.'

The Empress turned away impatiently. 'Pray make the child wash her face,' she said. 'The sight is offensive.'

Joanna was astounded. She had thought her aunt would understand. She had been so kind when her father was there and she had told him how generous he was to have given her such lovely jewels.

'You can trust me to look after your daughter,' she had said.

And now she could not understand how miserable Joanna was. Surely she knew that there was never a father in the world like hers, nor a mother like her sister Philippa? And was it not reasonable to suppose that any daughter who had lost them would be miserable?

It was a sad realization that all might not be as she thought.

When she next saw her aunt she was composed and it was a ceremonial occasion. The Emperor and the Empress were together before a banquet and Joanna was taken to her because the Empress had wished it. She was all smiles and friendliness. 'My dear child,' she said, 'ah, you look well now. It was a sad parting was it not?' Then to someone at her elbow. 'The daughter of my sister the Queen of England, is a little sad just now, being parted from her parents, but she will be happy and well with me. Will you not, Joanna?'

Poor Joanna was bewildered. She wondered if she had heard correctly on that other occasion.

Sometimes she rode beside the Empress on her little pony and people smiled at her and seemed as though they were pleased to see her.

Duke Otho was kind and she was presented to Frederic who was to be her husband. She did not greatly care for him.

'Oh,' said the Empress being kind now, 'it will be a long long time before you are old enough to marry.'

'I hope I never do,' said Joanna.

'That,' replied the Empress coldly, 'is a very stupid statement.'

She was looking at Joanna with cold dislike again and Joanna felt a great impulse to cry like a baby for her mother.

It was a little bewildering when one was not very old to leave one's family and go away to strangers, even though it had always been stressed that princesses had to grow up more quickly than other people.

She was thankful to Lord John de Montgomery although she could not confide in him, but he did give her the feeling that she was being looked after.

She had a few attendants and it was comforting to talk to them but she saw that as the weeks passed they were becoming rather uneasy. There was often very little to eat — in fact not enough for the household and she heard the attendants talking together and saying that if Queen Philippa knew how her sister was treating the little Princess she would never forgive her.

After her first show of friendship the Empress rarely came near her niece. In fact she seemed to have forgotten her existence. Joanna was deeply hurt; she had expected very different treatment from her mother's sister.

Lord John came to see her and he told her that it was no use pretending that she was being treated properly at the Imperial Court and he proposed writing to the King and telling him what was happening to his daughter.

'I suggest, my lady Princess,' he said, 'that you write to your mother.'

Joanna's eyes were round with terror. 'What if the letters fell into *their* hands?'

She imagined terrible things happening to her, things of which she heard whispers in corners. How traitors were cast into dungeons to live with the rats, how they died . . .

Lord John realised then how deeply the child had suffered and a great anger arose in him against the selfish Empress and he thought how different she was from her sister.

He said: 'Never fear, they shall not fall into their hands, and if they did, no harm could befall the daughter of King Edward of England.'

'They can give her very little to eat and be unkind to her,' retorted Joanna with logic.

That was true. Lord John agreed, but if she would write of

what had happened to her he would see that the letters fell into no other hands but those of her mother.

To write letters in secret gave a new excitement to life – and hope too. If her mother knew she would never let her stay in this horrible place.

In due course the letters had the desired effect.

The King of England now wished his daughter to be put into the care of her future father-in-law, Duke Otho of Austria.

The Empress shrugged her shoulders. She had forgotten about the child in any case. The costly gifts which the King had bestowed on her were also forgotten.

'Let the child go,' she said.

Life was a little more comfortable for Joanna after that although she was very homesick and longed to be with her mother. Bickering with Isabella now seemed like perfect bliss and she did long to see her brother Edward. She wanted to be lifted up in her father's arms and put her cheek against his; she wanted to run into her mother's arms and be held tightly.

Would she never see them again? Lucky Isabella, who although older was still at home!

Duke Otho was a kindly man. He thought his new little daughter charming. He seemed very old to Joanna but perhaps that was because he was ill.

Here of course she saw Frederic almost every day. He was not nearly as handsome as her brother Edward but that would be asking too much. He was an arrogant little boy and he told her that husbands were always the masters and their wives had to obey them.

'Nobody obeys such *little* boys,' replied Joanna, which made Frederic angry.

He was growing up fast. His servants said so. He was going to be seven foot tall and then he would show her.

Joanna's consolation was that it would be a long time before he was old enough to marry. In the meantime she had to share lessons with him and speak all the time in their hateful tongue.

Frederic's Uncle Albrecht was frequently at the ducal court. Joanna did not like him at all. He lacked Duke Otho's kindliness and she fancied he looked at her with a certain amused dislike which was very unpleasant. Everyone was very deferential to him, and he used to come to the schoolroom and sit there listening with that supercilious smile on his lips whenever Joanna spoke.

At first she had been relieved to be rid of her Aunt Margaret, now Uncle Albrecht and Frederic made her wonder whether the change had been such a great improvement.

Albrecht had a loud booming voice and an air of being always right. Once Joanna heard him say to his brother: 'This could be a mistake.' And she instinctively knew that he was referring to her betrothal to Frederic. 'The English won't have a chance against the French,' he went on.

Duke Otho murmured something inaudibly but Joanna guessed that he was defending the proposed marriage and his alliance with her father.

A few days later Duke Otho was very ill. There was a hushed atmosphere throughout the palace.

'They say the Duke is dying,' said one of her attendants.

'Then,' said another, 'Frederic will be the Duke.'

'Yes, but we know who will be the real ruler. Duke Albrecht.'

'There will be some changes.'

'I have heard it said that he is hand in glove with the King of France.'

The King of France! thought Joanna. Her father's enemy! But it was because her father wanted Austria to be his friend that she was to marry Frederic.

It was a sad day when Duke Otho died. Joanna had been fond of him and it was yet another tragedy to lose him; and as the days passed she realised that more and more the attitude towards her was changing.

Frederic told her that her father had no right to the throne of France. He must have heard that somewhere for he would never have thought of it himself.

'It is my father's,' cried Joanna, equally ignorant of the facts, but sure that her father was right. She would defend him even if it were dangerous to do so.

'Your father will be driven out of France,' cried Frederic.

'Who says so?'

'My Uncle Albrecht.'

She knew it of course. Duke Albrecht had always disliked her. Now his dislike was more than ever apparent.

Lord John came to her and when she heard what he had to tell her she was almost delirious with joy.

'I have written to your father,' he said, 'to tell him of the death of Duke Otho and that the sympathies of Duke Albrecht, the Regent, are with the French. I have now heard from him that we are to leave at once and join the Queen in Flanders.'

Joanna was speechless with joy.

It was over then, this nightmare. She was going home. She wanted to run through the palace telling everyone.

She would start preparations immediately but Lord John warned that she must wait a little until Duke Albrecht himself spoke to her of her departure.

She saw him that very day. He was with Frederic as he often was. It was said he was teaching Frederic how to govern.

'Why, here is our little bride,' he said. 'She looks radiant today, does she not, Frederic?'

Frederic said nothing. Oaf, thought Joanna. How happy I shall be when I do not have to see *him* again.

'Tell us why you are so happy, little lady.'

'You will know that my father has sent for me,' she replied.

'And the prospect of leaving us makes you happy?'

No need to placate them now. No need for anything but the truth. 'Yes,' she said. 'It does.'

'Is that not a little ungracious?'

'It is the truth,' she answered.

'Shall I tell you another truth, my Princess? You are here with us and here you will stay until we say you may go. Let us appeal to the Duke. Is that not so, Frederic?'

Frederic smiled his silly smile.

'Yes,' he said. 'She cannot go until we say so.'

Cold terror seized Joanna. All the brightness had drained from her face. She turned and ran from the room.

🐾 🐾 🐾

'Duke Albrecht will never dare to flout your father,' said her attendants, but she could see that Lord John was not so sure.

There was no attempt now to hide the fact that Austria was going to be on the side of the French in the coming struggle and all the rich gifts and the proposed marriage might never have been given and arranged.

Frederic, who was very much under the influence of his uncle, told her that the French King was the greatest in the world and he would soon make the English King wish he had never thought of trying to take what did not belong to him.

Joanna refused to argue with him. She was sick at heart wondering what would happen to her now.

Looking into her sad little face Lord John tried to comfort her.

'You know your father is a man who always gets what he wants.'

She did know that.

'Well now he wants you to leave Austria and go to your mother. He has asked for your return and since you have not left he has sent another letter which I have taken to the Duke. In this he *demands* your return.'

She had great faith in her father. But still Duke Albrecht would not let her go.

'Is he going to make me marry Frederic then?' she wanted to know.

She talked of it with her attendants.

They were silent and she knew that meant they believed he might.

'Why? Why when they hate me?'

She had to grow up. She had to learn that sometimes princesses were married to princes whom they hated and who hated them because of some political reason.

She heard someone whisper 'as a sort of hostage, do you mean?' and the answer, 'Well, yes, it could amount to that.' And she knew they were talking about her.

The weeks passed, tension was rising. Every day there was some mention of the coming conflict between her father and the King of France and she knew that she was among her country's enemies.

Her father would come to rescue her, she promised herself, and she used to lie in her bed thinking of that wonderful day when she would see her parents again.

And one day, Lord John came to her in some excitement.

'I have just taken a letter to Duke Albrecht from the King your father. I do not think the Duke will dare refuse to let you go when he receives it.'

'He does not care for my father. He thinks the King of France will defeat him.'

'He is afraid of your father as all his enemies must be. I do not think he will dare hold any longer.'

Lord John was right.

Duke Albrecht did not come to her nor did he send for her.

One of his equerries came and told her to make ready. She was to leave Austria within the next few days to make the long journey up the Danube to Munich, through Coblen to the Castle of Ghent where she would join her mother.

On a glorious April day she rode forth. Never was there anyone in the world, she was sure, as happy as the Princess Joanna on that bright April day.

This was an anxious time for Philippa. She was heavily pregnant and in a strange country. She was very worried about Joanna. Being well aware that her sister was not the most unselfish of women, she had thought at first that her affection for her sister and her compassion for a very young girl far from home would have induced her finer feelings. She had been presented with costly gifts in the hope that these would remind her that she owed her sister something, but Margaret had hardened she was sure now and the selfish little traits of her childhood had magnified. Philippa had been horrified by Lord John's account of the neglect poor Joanna had had to suffer and she had long wanted to prevent the marriage and bring Joanna back.

'It is so unnatural,' she had complained to Edward, 'to send a child so young away from her home.'

Edward agreed but it was necessary to find allies if he were to win the crown of France.

The crown of France! thought Philippa. That bauble! What was that compared with the heartbreak of a little girl and her mother. And even if he won it – which could she was certain only be after years of struggle, suffering, privation and endurance – what then?

How she longed to leave the Low Countries. She thought longingly of Windsor – the forests, the river and the castle which she had grown to love. Now her child would be born in a foreign land.

Edward was worried too. The campaign was so costly and nothing at all had been achieved so far. It was disconcerting that those whom he had taken such pains to please and at great expense were now turning towards France as the more likely side to be the victor.

This infuriated him. Moreover he must raise more money and how could he do this in Flanders?

He came to the conclusion that he would have to return to England. He must persuade Parliament that he needed money for his armies. He had to pay his soldiers; he had to keep them supplied with arms.

He told Philippa this and it added to her anxieties. True, he had sent to Austria demanding the return of Joanna and she was hourly expecting news that her little daughter was on her way to her. What a happy day that would be when she could hold the child in her arms.

The time came when Edward could delay no longer. He must have money and would have to pay a brief visit to England in order to get it. He was uneasy about leaving Philippa behind but she assured him that she would be capable of looking after herself. Moreover she had good friends in Ghent, the chief of these being Jacob von Arteveldt for whom the King had such regard.

'How I wish I could come with you,' said Philippa sadly.

The King shared her regret but reminded her that just as his duty lay in finding money for arms and men, hers was in giving England heirs and so far she had made an excellent job of that.

'For your greater safety,' said the King, 'I am going to send you to the Abbey of St Bavon. You will be safe there and when I see you again our child will be born.'

So Philippa retired to the Abbey of St Bavon in the town of Ghent and Edward left for England.

Within a month of his going Philippa gave birth to a boy. He was a fine healthy child and she decided his name should be John. He quickly showed himself to be a lusty Plantagenet and he became known as John of Ghent which the English, using the Anglicised form of the name, called Gaunt.

As each day passed Joanna's happiness increased. It seemed strange to her to be making the same journey as she had made before in the company of her father. Then her heart had been heavy with foreboding. Now she was light-hearted, full of joyful anticipation.

Everything seemed so much more beautiful – the silver

Rhine, the grey stone castles, the towns and villages through which she passed and where the people ran out of their homes to stare at her.

She smiled at them, gaily, happily. Joanna loved the whole world during that journey to Ghent.

It was eighteen months since she had seen her mother and it seemed a lifetime to the little girl.

At length she came to the city of Ghent and Lord John was told that the King was in England and at first her heart sank; but when she heard that her mother was at St Bavon's Abbey, her spirits revived.

And there it was, the old grey stone Abbey and as they rode towards it she saw her mother and she thought her heart would burst with happiness.

She leaped from her horse. There could be no ceremony. She could not endure that.

She ran to her mother and threw herself into her arms.

Philippa was holding her tightly, murmuring words of endearment. 'My little one . . . It has seemed so long . . . I thought you would never come back to me.'

'Dearest dearest lady mother . . . I am here . . . at last. It is like a dream.'

Philippa stroked her daughter's hair. She had changed. She had had so many experiences since she had left home . . . and not happy ones.

'My love,' crooned Philippa, 'there is so much to tell you, so much to show you. You have a little brother.'

Joanna was laughing with sheer happiness.

'Another brother !'

'Little John. He was born here in Ghent. They call him John of Gaunt . . . He can already give a good account of himself.'

'And my father?'

'Alas, he has had to return to England.'

'Then I shall not see him.'

'He will be back soon.'

'Perhaps,' said Joanna, 'to have seen him too would have been too much happiness all at once.'

'You have that joy to come, my dearest child.'

So they were together; and Joanna could only think of the happy present.

And the Queen rejoiced that she had her daughter back.

❀ Chapter X ❀

TROUBLE AT THE TOWER

As soon as Edward had conferred with his Parliament and persuaded its members to grant him more funds for carrying on the fight for the crown of France he went to see his daughter Isabella in the palace of the Tower.

It was a tearful Isabella whom he found there. She threw herself into his arms and clung to him.

He was deeply touched. Dearly as he loved all his children, Isabella was the favourite. Edward very much enjoyed feminine society. He had been a faithful husband but that did not mean he was unaware of beautiful women and there had been times when had he been less determined he might have strayed. One of his greatest pleasures was jousting, with himself the champion of course and riding triumphantly round the field being aware of the applause and admiration of the ladies. He enjoyed wearing splendid garments to show off his outstanding good looks. This side to his character was in direct contrast to the great warrior and dedicated king, but it was nevertheless there and he was liked for this weakness which emphasised his strength in other directions.

Proud and delighted as he was to have begotten healthy sons, it was his daughters whom, in his heart, he secretly loved best.

Isabella was well aware of this and because she was self-willed, imperious and liked to have her own way she made good use of it.

When she had shown him how delighted she was to see him she asked why it was that she alone of the family was unable to be with her mother in Flanders.

'Dearest child,' said Edward, 'we are at war you know. You are safer here in London.'

'I don't want to be safe,' she retorted. 'I want to be with you all.'

'So you shall be . . . in due course.'

'But I don't want to wait for due course.'

'I'll tell you something, Isabella. Your sister Joanna is coming back from Austria. Our plans there did not work out as we expected. Soon she will be coming to join you here with Lady St Omer.'

Isabella frowned. She did not want Joanna. She wanted to share in the adventures. Life was so dull here, she pointed out. Besides, it was so long since she had seen her mother and if she were in Flanders she would see her father often would she not?

'Oh dear dear father, I have missed you so.'

'My love,' replied Edward, 'do you not think I have missed you?'

'But exciting things happen to you. Here it is lessons and sitting over needlework. I am not like Joanna who always wants to be stitching and making embroidery.'

'Poor little Joanna, she has had a sad time I am afraid.'

'At least it has not been dull for her. She has travelled and almost married.'

'But she has been very unhappy. Soon, I trust, she will be with your mother.'

'While I stay here . . .'

Edward took Isabella's face in his hands and kissed her. 'It is not safe for you to travel, little daughter.'

She stamped her foot. 'I don't want to be safe. Besides, you promised . . . You said next time you came you would take me with you. You promised. You *promised*.'

'Listen,' he said, 'as soon as this war is over, I will take you with me to France.'

'It can be years and years . . .'

A feeling of depression came to Edward then. Years and years! He had always known that taking the French crown was not going to be an easy matter, but there were times when it seemed an insuperable task.

'And you promised . . . you promised. You said people should never break promises. You couldn't do that, could you? You couldn't break your promises to your own daughter . . .'

'I am thinking only of your safety.'

'Oh, my dear lord, I am so miserable . . . Please . . . *please* . . . take me with you.'

He hesitated and she was quick to see that. She twined her arms about his neck. 'I cannot *bear* not to see you. I want to see them all – my mother, my brothers, and Joanna . . . but most of all *you*, dear father. And you *promised* me . . .'

Edward made a sudden decision.

'Very well,' he said. 'I shall take you back with me.'

He was deeply moved to see the transfiguration. She was radiant.

He held her tightly in his arms and added: 'Because I could not bear to be without you.'

Philippa uneasily waited in Ghent for the return of Edward; and when he did return she knew that confrontation with the French would be close at hand. Often she thought with regret of Robert of Artois and his heron. She could see that it was largely due to that man's hatred of the King of France that he had almost forced Edward into action. Edward should have stood out against the temptor. Let him call him coward. There was not a man in England who did not know that that was the last thing Edward was. He was brave to recklessness; he would fight at the head of his armies. But secretly Philippa wished it was for a more worthy cause. She had been despised by some for her mildness; people did not realise that the very mildness had grown from her knowledge of what was best in life. Harmony was more to be desired than discord, peace than war; love could triumph over hatred at any time and how much happier were those who could take advantage of this.

If only she and Edward could return to England and waive this claim to the throne of France how much happier they would all be.

Sometimes Edward seemed to her like one of her children. She smiled at his vanities, his love of fine clothes and admiration; his delight in a tournament when he showed himself possessed of greater skill than others. Yes, like a child. Yet on the other side was the strong man, the great king, the wily general, the wise ruler.

She did not know for which she loved him more – his strength or his weakness.

And her role in life was to smooth the way for him, to care for him, to be at hand whenever he needed her most, to stand beside him, to hide from him her sometimes greater wisdom; to be always at his side when he needed her.

So now she was in Ghent, in some danger, for the knowledge that Edward had gone to England had reached the French who naturally thought this might be a good time to harry his Queen.

She was unafraid but Jacob von Arteveldt was anxious. He feared that the French might capture her and hold her captive. What a prize she would be with her young ones!

Jacob strengthened the defences about the Abbey of St Bavon and prayed for the speedy return of the King. He was particularly interested in little John whose godfather he was. The friendship between the Arteveldts and the Queen had become very firm. Philippa liked Jacob's wife, Catherine, and in turn became godmother to her son who was christened Philip which was as near to Philippa as could be, considering the sex of the child.

There were skirmishes in the neighbourhood between the French and the English and Philippa was greatly distressed one day to learn that William de Montacute, who three years before had become Earl of Salisbury and was one of Edward's greatest friends, had been captured and taken to Paris.

Jacob was very grave when he told Philippa the news.

'I fear for the Earl of Salisbury,' he said. 'He is known to be very close to the King.'

Philippa was deeply distressed. 'They have been friends for so long,' she said. 'In fact I think that William could be said to be his greatest friend. I hope that no harm comes to him.'

'The mood of the King of France is not very benign towards the English at this time.'

'How I wish Edward were here. He might be able to do something.'

Jacob shook his head. 'There is little to be done, I fear. We can only hope for the best.'

There was even greater cause for concern. The French fleet was assembling to intercept Edward on his return to the Continent, and its strength would greatly exceed anything that Edward could muster.

Rumours of the assembling of the French fleet reached Edward and he was dismayed – not for himself, for he welcomed the opportunity of meeting the enemy – but on account of his daughter.

He should never have been so weak as to promise to take her with him. When he was away from her he realised that he spoilt Isabella. Philippa was aware of it and tried to curb his generosity towards their eldest daughter, but he had never been able to withstand her wiles. He smiled, thinking of her soft delicate skin, her pretty hair, those clear eyes that could cloud so quickly with passion when she was in a rage. Naughty Isabella! But he would not have her other than she was.

And now what? He could not break his promise to her. That was out of the question. Why, he thought indulgently, she would never forgive me!

He gave orders that three hundred of the bravest men at arms and five hundred archers should be assigned to protect the little Princess and a train of countesses, ladies, knights' wives and other demoiselles were chosen to travel with her that she should do so in the utmost comfort.

So they set sail and as they came near to the Helvoetsluys the King, from the deck of his ship, had his first glimpse of the great fleet of French ships which were assembled to intercept him.

His own fleet was small but it was either a matter of going on or turning back which was unthinkable.

'I have long wished to meet them,' he cried, 'and now by the help of God and St George, I will fight them. They have done me so much mischief that I will be revenged on them.'

It was true that he welcomed the conflict; his only fear was for his daughter. He sent word to those who guarded her to do so with their lives, for if aught happened to her they would have to answer to him.

There was exultation among the French when they saw the English because of their greater numbers and they believed it would be an easy task to overcome those paltry two hundred English ships.

Edward was never better than when at a disadvantage and he had learned a great deal since the days of his first campaign in Scotland. He was now showing those signs of generalship which had distinguished his grandfather; and he never ceased to think of him when he went into battle. He had read of his campaigns; he had inherited his spirit and though the old King had been dead before he had been born he felt that he knew him well.

The fight had begun. Isabella, in her cabin surrounded by her ladies, listened to the tumult and wondered whether she would ever see her family again. She did think fleetingly that she should not have coerced her father into taking her for she knew that while he should be thinking only of the enemy he would be concerned for her.

'But,' she said confidently, 'he will win. My father will always win. He will fight even harder because I am here. So it is a good thing after all.'

Isabella had learned that it was pleasant to believe that what she did was for the best. She was not one to suffer great remorse.

All through the long hot day the battle raged. The noise was deafening; the ship rocked and there were times when it seemed as though it would sink. But as the day wore on the heat grew less intense and so did the battle.

Isabella was not surprised when she was told that the English had sunk countless French vessels, that the rest were in flight, and the result was victory for her father.

Such triumphs gave especial gratification to the winning side because they had successfully come through when it had seemed almost impossible that they could.

Edward ordered special thanksgiving services on each ship and he said they must cruise along the coast for a while to make sure that the French fleet did not have an opportunity to rally and fight again. Battles had been lost more than once when the victorious had retired from the scene of conflict too soon.

He came to Isabella and asked her how she had fared.

'Such a lot of noise,' she said, 'and the ship rocked back and forth.'

'So you thought you were going to sink, did you?'

'I knew you wouldn't let that happen.'

Now Philippa would have pointed out to the child that only God was omnipotent and what had been achieved had been done with His help. Edward was different; he could not help basking in his daughter's admiration and he did not want God to have a share in it.

'I'll warrant you wished you were back in the Tower.'

'How could I when you are here! I want to be in all the battles you win, dear father.'

'I could not risk that,' he told her.

232

And she smiled contentedly, knowing how precious she was to him and that, even if he refused her something in the first place, she would always get it in the end.

After a pilgrimage to Ardenberg to give thanks to the Virgin there for this great victory, Edward and his train set out for Ghent.

With what joy was Philippa reunited with her husband and her eldest daughter. Isabella was beside herself with delight.

She looked with mild interest on the new brother John; even two-year-old Lionel was a stranger to her. Her brother Edward seemed a great deal older than when he had left England and Joanna had undoubtedly changed. She was quiet and there was a certain sadness about her which was doubtless due to the unpleasant time she had had in Austria.

When Philippa was alone with her husband she broke the news of William Montacute's capture. Edward was deeply distressed.

'William was always a good friend to me,' he said. 'In fact I know of none other outside my family whom I love so well. I trust he will not be treated badly. I must do what I can to get him released.'

'It will not be an easy matter,' the Queen pointed out, 'for all know him to be one of your most faithful friends.'

Edward wanted to know how he had been taken and was even more distressed to know that it had been in a mere skirmish near the town of Lille.

'I must set about getting him released without delay,' he declared.

'It will not be easy. Philip will not readily let him go.'

'But I must do my best. I shall send a message to Philip immediately.'

Philippa was certain that after suffering a disastrous defeat during which his fleet had been routed Philip was very unlikely to parley for the return of one of Edward's friends.

After a few days she broached the subject of the family with Edward.

'They are all here in Ghent,' she said. 'Is that wise?'

'I was thinking how delightful it is for us all to be together though it is only for a short time.'

'So it is,' said Philippa, 'but the people will not like it if the entire family is out of England. They will be restive. You know how it is. They might turn against us.'

Edward pondered this and in his heart he knew it was true. He had been very foolish to have allowed Isabella to accompany him. She should have stayed in the palace of the Tower and Joanna should have been sent to join her.

'Isabella pleaded so earnestly . . .' he began.

'I know,' replied Philippa indulgently, 'and she can do as she wills with you.'

'Our daughter is such an enchanting child.'

'Still,' said Philippa, 'I think that she and Joanna should return to England. The little boys must stay with me, of course, and Edward must be with you here. But the girls should go back. It is no place for them here and they will be an extra anxiety for you.'

'They will hate to go. Joanna has only just come back to us.'

'I know, I know. But, my dear lord, they must go. Isabella will forget her disappointment in comforting Joanna.'

Edward knew that she was right.

Shortly after – although Isabella protested – the two

Princesses set sail for England. To please Isabella Edward made sure that she travelled in great style. She had three ladies-in-waiting while Joanna as the younger had but two; they had new gowns and cloaks bordered with fur and fashioned in the German style which was new to them. Isabella was a little placated and as her younger sister was put into her care and she could feel her importance she accepted her fate.

'Ere long,' the King promised her, 'we shall all be together.'

Although Edward had routed the French and destroyed the naval power of France it was beginning to be borne home to him that to win this war was a near impossible feat. If it had not been necessary to fight on foreign soil transport problems would not have arisen. Constantly victory was either snatched from him or he was unable to consolidate his gains because he must pause to wait for supplies. This was the case at Tourney which he had besieged and violently attacked but which he had to abandon because of lack of supplies for his army.

Suddenly it seemed to him that there was one way only to settle this dispute and that was to challenge Philip to single combat.

Edward delighted in this because he had been a champion of the joust all his life and nothing could have pleased him more than to parade before a glittering assembly with his opponent, the King of France.

Philip however had no such ambitions and declined to meet Edward, his reason being that Edward had addressed him as the Duke of Valois when his title was the King of France. It was an excuse of course, said Edward. And it was true that all knew of the prowess on the field of the King of England.

Even had Philip been inclined to accept the challenge he would have had to heed the many warnings which came his way. Not that he would have accepted it in any case. He was far too wily. Settled by single combat! A crown! He had never heard such folly.

His sister Jeanne, Countess of Hainault, who was Edward's mother-in-law, warned her brother not to take part in any such combat for she had seen Edward in action and she knew that Philip would be killed.

She had heard from Philippa and knew how her daughter deplored this war which she believed could bring nothing but misery and death to both sides. Countess Jeanne was at this time in a convent, her husband being dead and her daughters settled in marriage, and she made up her mind that she was going to do all she could to stop this senseless conflict between the members of her family.

When Edward heard what was afoot, he was dubious. He had had his great sea victory and had succeeded in crippling the French navy, and would have liked to have gone on from there.

But Philippa pointed out to him that the cost of providing the means to go to war was so great that she doubted the people would endure more taxation.

Edward at last agreed to consider the proposals the Countess had put forth and to the relief of Philippa and many others a truce was agreed upon. He left Robert of Artois in command of his army and prepared to return to England.

'This will give us a little respite,' said Philippa. 'Oh how I long to be in England with the children!'

To her great delight they made preparations to leave Flanders.

❀ ❀ ❀

It was November before they left – not the best time to cross the Channel and they had scarcely lost sight of the French coastline when a terrible storm arose. The ships were tossed and buffeted and all thought their last hour had come.

Some fell on their knees and prayed to God for His help. Many were certain that French witches had stirred up the elements and produced this fearful tempest so that the King might perish or even if he lived, be so terrified that he would never cross the sea again.

Edward was not likely to be so deterred when there was a crown to be won. They should know that he had only agreed to the truce because he needed the respite. Scotland was beginning to give him many uneasy qualms, and he knew instinctively that he had been away from England too long.

He was depressed. He would have liked to come home with the fruits of a decisive victory. Important though the naval battle had been it was far from that. The French might have lost sea power but they seemed to be unbeatable on land.

Philippa noticed how angry he looked as they rode to the Tower. She was always deeply conscious of his moods and when the black temper started to rise she was the only one who could soothe him and stop its breaking out into that full fury which could bring trouble to anyone with whom he came into contact.

As they approached the Tower they were surprised to find that the place seemed deserted. Edward's brow darkened still further.

'What can have happened?' he muttered and there was great anxiety in his tone, for his thoughts immediately went to his daughters who should be guarded in the fortress.

He had given special instructions to the Constable of the Tower, Nicholas de la Bèche, that there should always be a guard round the Tower; he had assigned twenty men at arms and fifty archers to him for this purpose. Where were they now?

The King rode into the Tower. Had he been a stranger he could have done so unchallenged.

'Where are the Princesses?' he roared, but there was no one to answer him.

In a fury he dismounted; one of his attendants took the reins and, with Philippa beside him, he strode into the Tower.

There was no sign of anyone. The fortress was completely unguarded.

Isabella appeared suddenly and with her Joanna.

Seeing their father and mother the girls ran to them and Isabella threw herself into her father's arms, Joanna into her mother's.

For a few seconds Edward's expression softened and then as he thought of the danger these precious children might have been in, unattended as they were he shouted: 'Where are the guards? Where is the Constable?'

'We like to be here by ourselves,' said Isabella.

'By yourselves ! Do you tell me that you are here alone?'

'We have three of the ladies with us and some servants and the others will all be back soon. They have only gone into the town to see their friends.'

Edward cried: 'By God, someone shall pay for this.'

The palace was now full of noise and bustle as the King's attendants settled in. Edward himself grimly awaited the return of Nicholas de la Bèche.

When the Constable returned he was white with horror. He guessed that this would be the end of his career, perhaps his life. He had deserted his post; he had left the King's daughters unprotected; it was an act which must certainly arouse the Plantagenet temper to its wildest heights.

'So,' cried Edward, 'you have seen fit to return to your duty.'

'My lord,' stammered de la Bèche, 'I have been close all the time . . . I kept the Tower in sight . . .'

'You were not close enough to witness our arrival or you would have come scuttling back long ere this, I doubt not. And your guards, man, where were they? Carousing in taverns I doubt not! Oh, you will be sorry for this day, I promise you.'

Nicholas de la Bèche was trembling so much that he could not speak.

'Take this man away,' roared the King. 'I will decide what shall be done with him. And his guards too who deserted their posts but he is the prime culprit. By God's teeth, Constable of the Tower no more, you will regret this day's work.'

Edward paced up and down trying to devise a punishment horrible enough to fit the crime.

Philippa came to him. 'Dear lord,' she said, 'this matter is spoiling your delight in your family. It has made you forget that we are all here together and in England, and it has been so long ere this has happened.'

'All the more reason why he should suffer.'

'I have discovered that he visited his mistress.'

'Villain.'

'I doubt she thinks so,' said the Queen. 'Edward put aside your anger. It grieves us all. The Constable is beside himself with grief and remorse.'

'And terror I doubt not, as I would have him. He contemplates what awaits him and I promise you it shall not be pleasant.'

'My lord, promise me something else.'

'What is this?'

'That you will forget your anger and look at this matter calmly.'

'Calmly! When my daughters were in peril.'

'They were not. The people of London love them. So do the attendants. They left their posts briefly and if there had been trouble would have been back to guard the children with their lives. I believe that the Constable and his guards have suffered enough.'

'I intend to make an example of them. His head shall be on the bridge that all may see it. I'll have him flayed alive . . .'

'Oh, my lord, such a bitter punishment . . . !'

'Well, perhaps it'll be the traitor's death. He has assuredly been a traitor to me.'

Philippa shivered. 'My lord, I beg of you, please me in this.'

'Do I not always do my best to please you?'

'You do and that is why I know you will do so now.'

'Philippa, you are constantly pleading for wrongdoers.'

'I want the people to call you their merciful king. There is nothing so appealing as a man with power who shows mercy. That is a sign of greatness.'

Edward was silent and at that moment the door opened and Isabella came in.

'Oh it is wonderful. You are home. Both of you. We are all so happy,' she cried.

The King's mood softened at the sight of his daughter. He said: 'And think you that I am not happy to be with my family?'

'You have done nothing but glower ever since you came,' scolded Isabella. 'Oh, dearest father, do not harm the Constable. He is such an amusing fellow.'

'He does not amuse me.'

'He has told us of his mistress. She is very beautiful . . . and ardent, and a little light so that if he does not visit her she might find another lover. And he asked my permission to visit her and I gave it . . . so you see, dearest Father, you cannot blame *him*.'

'*You* gave it.'

'I was the mistress of the Tower was I not, in your absence? I said to him: "Go to this ardent mistress of yours, Constable," and of course when he had gone I told the guards they could go too. That was all it was, Father. And they are saying that you are going to do terrible things to him. Oh please let him go free. You see if you do not *I* shall be unhappy and it is all my fault and I shall never smile again.'

'You are a foolish girl,' said the King.

Isabella put her arms about his neck. 'But you love me just the same. In spite of my folly. Oh, you do, don't you, because if you don't I shall . . . *die*.'

'What shall we do with this daughter of ours?' asked the King.

'I think on this occasion you will give her what she asks,' replied the Queen.

'Well,' said the King, 'if I say that the Constable shall go free will that please you?'

Isabella kissed him fervently. 'You are the best father in the world and I love you dearly.'

'But,' said the King, 'not today. He shall fret and sweat in his terror all through the night.'

'But in the morning he shall be free,' cried Isabella. 'Oh, you dear good King. And we shall all be together for Christmas shall we not? I have planned such games.'

Philippa noticed that the King's ill humour had completely disappeared.

'Let us join Edward and Joanna,' she said, 'and hear all about these plans.'

Thus the Constable of the Tower resumed his duties and marvelled at the leniency of the King while he vowed that never would he be so foolish again and would serve Edward and his family with his life if need be.

🌹 Chapter XI 🌹

THE KING FALLS IN LOVE

hat there was change in the air was apparent throughout
Château Gaillard where the King and Queen of
Scotland lived as guests of the King of France.

The most unhappy person in that castle of Normandy was
the Queen – Joanna, sister of Edward King of England. She
had always been disturbed by the conflict between her husband
and her brother and now that Edward was engaged in a
struggle with the King of France it grieved her that David
should side with her brother's enemy and had even gone into
battle with the French against the English.

She had heard the sad story of her namesake's adventures in
Austria. Poor child, she could understand and sympathise with
her for being taken from her country at a tender age. Had it not
happened to her? Perhaps people with the name Joanna were
unfortunate. She could almost make herself believe that the
name itself brought bad luck.

She certainly had had very little good luck.

She hoped her sister Eleanor was happier with the Earl of
Gueldres than she was as the guest of the King of France.

She was almost nineteen years old now and David was

sixteen, not too young to have had love affairs with some of the women in the castle. They had never really liked each other although she had tried to make a show of affection for him. He was a petulant boy and arrogant. He was constantly reminding people that he was a king, as though, because he was an exile from his country, they might forget it.

Being the son of the greatest King Scotland had ever known was a handicap. People constantly compared him with his father and naturally he must suffer in comparison. David was aware of it and it bothered him; he liked to taunt Joanna with remarks about her own father who was as different from Robert the Bruce as a man could be. Poor Father, who had died mysteriously and she feared ignobly in Berkeley Castle.

But that King's son and her brother now reigned and he was a source of great irritation to David. Sometimes she fancied he flaunted his infidelity more before her because she was the sister of Edward of England.

It was as though he said I shall do as I please. What care I for your noble brother about whom men are now beginning to talk as they did about your grandfather.

David enjoyed the life at Château Gaillard. There was dancing and jesting, plays and feasting. The King of France had said: 'You must look upon me as your friend and France as your home.'

And David had done so; not so Joanna. She could never forget that their host was the enemy of her brother and she was ashamed of accepting his hospitality.

Visitors from afar had come to the castle. The news they brought was exciting. The Scots had naturally taken advantage of Edward's absence in France. They had risen and there had been none to stop them, certainly not the token force Edward had left with them. They had ousted Baliol who was no more than Edward's tool. He had quickly left Scotland and had sought a refuge in England.

An embassy arrived at the Château Gaillard, led by Simon Fraser who had been David's tutor and in whom he had had great confidence.

That was an exciting day at the château for Simon laid before the exiled King plans for his return to Scotland. For the last year or so the Scots had been scoring victory after victory over the English. The absence of Edward in France had been a boon to them, and he had to admit that they had enjoyed a great deal of help from the King of France who was pleased that the English should be harried on the Scottish Border so diverting them from their activities in France. Now the Bruce party had succeeded in ridding themselves of Edward's puppet Baliol and therefore it was time David returned to take up his rightful place in the kingdom.

David was excited at the prospect. Life at Château Gaillard had been pleasant enough, but he was a king and wanted to rule his country. He could not forget that, even though the King of France had treated him as a visiting King, he was still dependent on his bounty.

'When can I leave for Scotland?' he asked Simon Fraser. Simon replied that he thought it would be advisable to visit the Court of France, make the King aware of his subjects' request for him to return and ask his help in doing so.

It would be readily given, they were both sure.

And so it proved to be.

Smarting from the defeat at Helvoetsluys, Philip was only too pleased to add to Edward's troubles; and he knew that the

245

greatest of these would be a war in Scotland which must necessarily keep him out of France.

'It is good news that they have driven out that traitor Baliol and Scotland is no longer England's vassal,' cried Philip. 'You must keep it so, my lord. David the Bruce is the King of Scotland and not Edward Plantagenet.'

'I want to go back and regain my kingdom. Then I will protect it from the English.'

'That is as it should be,' said the King of France. 'Now, as you know, I lost many of my ships in conflict with Edward. He will know that you are proposing to leave for Scotland and what your arrival there will mean to him. He will use all his power and cunning to capture you before you arrive. We must be careful or you and your Queen will find you have left happy Gaillard for a less pleasant castle in England. You have been my honoured guests. You would be Edward's prisoners. Leave this to me.'

David returned to Gaillard and the King of France gave orders that strong ships should be built to escort him back to Scotland. The shipwrights of Harfleur were working day and night; in fact all over France men were working on the ships and all the accoutrements necessary to convey a monarch home.

It was very flattering but David was to learn that the wily Philip was not expending all this time and money on him. The ships were in fact replacements for those lost in the battle of Helvoetsluys. Philip sent a secret message to Gaillard to the effect that David and the Queen were to make for the coast ostensibly to inspect the ships which were being made. They should pretend to begin to journey back to Gaillard and instead make for a quiet spot on the coast. Here they would find two humble vessels waiting for them. They should embark on these and sail for Scotland.

The English would be quite unaware that they had left France until they were safe in Scotland.

David was a little annoyed to realise that all the grand preparations were not for him. He would have liked to sail home surrounded by the might of the French navy. The English would then have determined to intercept. He was vain and arrogant but he was not a coward and he would have looked forward to such an encounter.

Joanna saw the wisdom of what the French King had arranged, and on the first day of June they set sail.

Their journey was uneventful and they arrived on the second day of June at Inverbervie, a small harbour in Kincardineshire.

Although their landing was scarcely noticed, when the Scots heard that David the Bruce, their rightful King, had come back to Scotland, they went wild with joy.

Now they would turn the English out of their country for ever.

🌼 🌼 🌼

David and his Queen were brought in triumph to Edinburgh. He found that the weakness of Baliol and his subservience to England had aroused the spirit of those men who longed to see a return of the strong rule of Robert the Bruce. There was a handful of men who were great fighters and had to a large extent the quality of leadership; these were rallying round the young King. There was Sir William Douglas, the Knight of Liddesdale, Robert the Steward, Murray of Bothwell and Randolph; and the determination of all these men was to rid

Scotland of English domination. The fact that Edward had determined to make a bid for the crown of France had inspired them with greater hope than they had known since the death of Robert the Bruce.

The help they had received from France had been an inspiration. They were grateful to Philip for the hospitality he had shown to their king although they were of course aware of the reason for this.

They were stirring days in Scotland which followed the return of the King.

It might have been that they were a little disturbed to note his Frenchified manners. He loved fine clothes – such as were never seen in Scotland. His manners were French; he had developed a love of luxury and young as he was indulged with a freedom and abandon in his light affairs which was, they believed, a reflection of French customs. They were sorry for the young Queen, but she was after all English and the sister of King Edward, and no doubt she had other matters with which to concern herself than her husband's infidelities.

Success followed success, castle after castle was recaptured in the name of the King and David was complacent, and as he had not yet been called upon to take part in any really serious battles his lack of judgement was not obvious.

He was surrounded by strong men and there seemed little doubt that victory was in the air.

It was hardly likely that Edward would allow matters to go on in this way.

Edward and Philippa determined that that Christmas should be a memorable one.

'We have promised it to the children,' said Edward. 'Isabella was insistent that we all spend it together.'

'And,' added Philippa, 'last Christmas poor little Joanna was in Austria.'

'Well, there shall certainly be revelry this Christmas, otherwise I shall be in trouble with our daughter.'

'Not too much indulgence, Edward, I beg of you.'

'Oh, they are young yet. Let them be happy while they can. It will be necessary to arrange marriages for them soon. That is something I cannot relish.'

The plans began to be carried out and there was a great deal of excitement in the Princesses' apartments. Joanna was embroidering gifts for her family – a pastime in which she delighted and she knew that her parents appreciated what she did. There were purses for them both decorated with dragons and birds, worked with exquisitely coloured silks. Isabella was not inclined to do such work; she sent her treasurer to buy gifts for her parents. They revelled in their new gowns – scarlet and purple scattered with pearls. They would wear their hair hanging down their backs because that was how their father liked it. They had surcoats of fine cloth of gold with patterns of birds and beasts on them; and beneath these they would wear a close-fitting gown of very fine material. Isabella loved to try on her gowns and indeed she had a great admiration for herself. As for Joanna she was so happy to be home that she was ready to laugh at everything – even Isabella's vanity and her determination to have the best whenever there should happen to be a choice.

Never mind. This was Christmas in the palace of the Tower and a rare occasion because for once the entire family were all altogether.

Philippa was contented to be with her children and she was expecting another in June. She had a fine family and she was proud of it. One of the joys of her life had been her ability to give Edward these children whom he so dearly loved.

Perhaps some women would have been jealous of his devotion to them. Not Philippa. She rejoiced in it.

So it was indeed a happy Christmas. Edward had summoned the most talented of his minstrels, a man named Godenal who was famous throughout the Court for his music, his singing, his mimicry and his ability to amuse.

The pleasure of the children was a joy to behold, even young Edward joined in and they remarked afterwards that he was growing up fast and none would believe that he was only eleven years old.

I could die tomorrow, thought the King, and I should have a worthy successor.

But he had no intention of dying. There was so much he must do. More children to have. He was a man who could not have too many children. The more he had the more dear they would become to him. He hoped this one was a little girl. They had Edward, Lionel and John; and little girls were so enchanting.

Isabella was now nestling up to him and he drew Joanna close lest she should think he favoured her sister more than he did her, which perhaps he did, but he loved them both dearly.

Godenal's performance was greeted with great joy by the children and the King whispered to them that they should reward the minstrel with a present.

'Six shillings and eightpence from each of you I believe would be adequate,' he said.

He smiled benignly as the children gravely paid the minstrel for his services.

That was a happy Christmas, but soon after came news from Scotland which was disturbing.

Edward realised that there was no help for it. It was no use leaving others to deal with the Scots. He must go and do so himself.

He reflected sadly that the last time he had gone his chief companion had been William Montacute Earl of Salisbury. Poor William, still languishing in a French prison! He had made several attempts to bring about his release, but Philip must know how great his friendship was for the Earl and he was determined to demand a great deal for his release.

Whatever it was, it must be paid.

But Philip was dilatory. After all, why should he put himself out to please the King of England?

After Christmas it was necessary to say good-bye to the children. They would remain in the palace of the Tower until the Queen left for Langley where she had decided she would go for her next confinement.

Edward in the meantime must busy himself with getting an army together to march on Scotland.

In June at Langley, Philippa's child was born. Another boy – healthy and with as good a pair of lungs as any of his brothers possessed. He was named Edmund.

Edward marched north and was encamped at Berwick. The months passed with neither side making much progress. Edward was prepared to make a big onslaught after Christmas and in the great fortress of Berwick his thoughts went back to the happy Christmas he had spent with his family the previous year. How different in Berwick! He was determined to settle the Scots; but then of course he had the French matter to deal with.

Philippa would like him to stay in England, to govern that country well and forget Scotland and France. But Philippa was a woman, devoted to her home. He thought of her as she had been when he had first met her in her father's castle of Hainault and what a happy domesticated atmosphere there had been there.

The old Count had not been ambitious – neither had his wife albeit she was a daughter of a King of France. Dear Philippa – rosy-cheeked, strong, plump, born to be a wife and mother.

And, by God, he thought, where could I have found another such as she has been to me? I have been singularly blessed in my marriage.

Often he thought of his mother who was now living in some luxury at Castle Rising but he rarely visited her. He found that too depressing, but when he did so, he gathered that her lapses into mental confusion were less frequent and that although she was not at Court she lived royally. When he had been with her he had been surprised at the plenteous and expensive foods on her table. Swans, turbot, lampreys and other delicacies abounded. She said that the people of the neighbourhood delighted in giving her presents. They were so pleased to have a Queen in their midst.

He wondered if she ever thought of Mortimer, that lover to whom she had been so passionately devoted, or of his father and did he still come to haunt her dreams?

He would go to see her when he left the North. She was after all his mother.

One of the guards came to tell him that a young man had ridden to the camp and was begging to be allowed to see him.

'What young man is this?' demanded the King.

'Scarcely more than a boy, my lord. He said he comes from the Castle of Wark which is under heavy siege by the Scots. He has come to beg your help.'

'Wark. Why that is Salisbury's place. Bring him to me without delay.'

The boy was brought. He had a look of his father. Edward was concerned to see him so distressed.

'My lord,' stammered the boy, 'we need your help. My mother and I have tried to hold the castle and have done so. We cannot hold out much longer. I fear they may take my mother as a hostage.'

'You may be sure,' said Edward, 'that I shall drive the Scots away and save your mother from falling into their hands. There is no time to lose.'

Catharine Montacute, Countess of Salisbury, deeply mourned the absence of her husband. Theirs had been an unusually happy marriage but like all wives she had had to accept the fact that there would be times when they were separated. William had long been in the service of the King and although she herself had never met Edward she felt she knew him well from William's talk of him.

There was a bond between Edward and William. They were both happily married – rare in their circle where marriages were often made in the cradle which was likely to result in certain resentments as young people grew up and found they had no choice in whom they should marry.

How fortunate she had been.

As Catharine Grandison, daughter of the first Baron

Grandison, she had been considered a suitable wife for the eldest son of the second Baron Montacute. William was a man of great charm and Catharine would have been guilty of false modesty if she had not admitted to being a beauty. In fact wherever she went her exceptional good looks aroused attention. She was not only a beautiful woman, she was wise, possessed dignity, courage and a lack of vanity which in one so gifted was particularly admirable.

Their union had been blessed with several children, two of whom were sons, William and John. William the eldest at this time was almost fourteen years old.

Her husband had gone far in the King's service for Edward had taken a fancy to him from the first and when he was little more than a boy it was William whom he had taken into his confidence when he had realised he must rid the country of Mortimer.

It was William who had found a way into Nottingham Castle and had been present at the arrest of Mortimer. The boy King had looked to the older man for friendship and advice for William was almost eleven years older than he was. It had been a lasting friendship and a few years before Edward had shown his appreciation by creating him Earl of Salisbury. He had chosen William to go to France to state his claim to the French crown; and Catharine knew that Edward had been most distressed to hear of his capture.

Nothing had gone right since that day. The possibility of what might be happening to him in some dark French prison haunted her dreams; every morning when she awoke her first thoughts were for him. She could only find consolation in taking charge of his castles and his affairs so that they should not suffer from his absence.

Wark Castle was on the south bank of the Tweed and being immediately on the border between England and Scotland could scarcely be in a more vulnerable position. So far it had been too formidable a fortress to have come under attack; and it probably never would have if Catharine's brother-in-law, Edward Montacute, had not disconcerted the Scots by getting the better of them after one of their raids on English territory.

Since the return of David the Bruce these forays were becoming more frequent. The Scots were particularly suited to this kind of warfare, travelling as they did on small sure-footed horses very different from the magnificent creatures which the English rode into battle; but they were very well suited to the rough country. Each man carried a small griddle and a bag of oatmeal so that he could feed himself for long periods at a stretch even if he could not augment this with the spoils snatched from the villages which they ransacked. It gave them a great advantage. They could lie low for days unhindered by the need to look for food. And there was no doubt that these raids were having a great effect on the English inhabitants. They never knew when they would occur; Catharine realised that in the past many of them had made pacts with the Scots simply because they could not bear to go on living in uncertainty.

When recently there had been a big Scottish raid on Durham and Edward Montacute had had warning of this, he had taken a band of men from Wark Castle and lain in wait for the enemy. The Scots came to rest in a wood; they were weary with travelling; and they had brought with them the valuable articles which they had stolen from the town.

While they were sleeping, Edward Montacute and his men suddenly appeared among them, taking them completely off their guard. It had been a successful raid. Two hundred Scots were killed for the loss of one or two English and Montacute rode back to Wark with twelve horses laden with Durham spoils.

It was hardly to be supposed that the Scots would forgive such an attack.

A few days passed. Nothing happened and Edward Montacute was called away on the King's business. Two days after he had gone the Scottish army arrived at Wark and were at this time camped in the surrounding fields.

The siege had begun.

Catharine was determined to hold the castle for her husband, but although after the raid she had made certain preparations, she soon began to see that she was in a vulnerable position.

She needed help. The King was in the neighbourhood. When she had last heard he had been in Berwick; and in fact that was the town which he had always made his headquarters. If she could get a message to him she was sure he would send help.

Her eldest son was eager to see if he could break out of the castle but she was reluctant to allow him to try. Young William however had strong determination and she rather feared that if she forbade him to go he would all the same. He had his father's spirit and was determined to break out and get help. He had heard that there were jokes being circulated in the Scottish camp about his mother. It was being said that she – so far-famed for her beauty – would be more of a prize than the castle. Their King David, who had an eye for women, would appreciate her; and the fact that her reputation for virtue was as great as that for beauty would make the matter doubly amusing.

Young William had made up his mind and at night under cover of darkness, knowing the secret doors and passage ways of the castle, he managed to escape unseen. It was not difficult to acquire a horse, for those in the neighbourhood had benefited often from the goodness of the countess and were ready to help. Very soon he was on his way to Berwick.

Riding at the head of his army Edward saw the grim towers of Wark in the distance. He thought it would be a simple matter to rout the Scots. And when he returned to Westminster he would renew his attempts to get William Montacute released.

In the meantime there was the Countess to think of. Edward knew how William loved his wife. They had compared their wives so often. Two virtuous women, two women who loved them. He would rescue Catharine Montacute for William. Edward laughed aloud when the Scottish camps came into sight. Enough to frighten a lady alone in a castle perhaps. He would make short work of them. One of his men suggested that they rest before the attack but Edward would hear nothing of that.

'There is a lady waiting eagerly to be released,' he said. 'It would be churlish to let her remain so one second longer than is necessary.'

So the attack began and as Edward had anticipated it did not last long. The English were vastly superior in arms and numbers, and in a short time the Scots had been routed and were flying in disorder.

Seeing the approach of the English, Catharine's first impulse was to give thanks to God. So her son had made his way to the King for there fluttering in the breeze was the royal standard so she knew who her deliverer was.

The relief was intense. The Scots would have no chance against him. Briefly she let herself think of what might have happened to her. The humiliation of being taken prisoner by the uncouth Scots. She had heard rumours of the King's profligate ways; she knew that there had been obscene talk about her in the Scottish ranks and in her heart that was what she had feared more than anything, although until now when release seemed certain she had not allowed herself to think about it.

The King would be victorious. So certain was she of this that she went to the kitchens and told them to prepare what food was left and do their very best for she believed that before the end of the day the King would be eating at their table.

They must wear their best livery. They must make a brave show. They were no longer the besieged. There must be adequate celebration of victory.

She went to her bedchamber and commanded her women to bring out her finest garments. Her hair was combed and displayed in all its rippling golden glory, her close-fitting jacket of golden-coloured velvet revealed her small elegant waist and over it she wore her spangled surcoat with its fashionable long hanging sleeves.

Then she went to a turret window to watch.

It was as she had known it would be as soon as she had seen the royal standard approaching.

The Scots were fleeing in disorder and the King was ready to enter the castle.

She gave orders that the drawbridge should be lowered; and as he rode across it she was waiting to greet him.

He dismounted and came towards her.

She made a deep curtsey and lifted her grateful eyes to his.

'My lord,' she said, 'welcome. My heart is too full to give you thanks just now.'

The King did not speak. He continued to look at her. His eyes were intensely blue she noticed; he was more handsome than hearsay had made him.

She stood up and their eyes met. Still he did not speak.

He seemed bemused. She repeated her thanks.

Then he said slowly: 'Lady, I am at your service . . . now . . . and always. Never in my life did I see a lady as beautiful as you.'

'My lord is gracious,' she answered. 'May I conduct you into the castle which your timely rescue has saved for my husband.'

He did not seem to hear her and she walked beside him into the castle.

Edward, bemused, dazzled, told himself that having seen this perfect woman nothing could ever be the same for him again.

Wark was not the finest of the country's castles. It was indeed primitive compared with the grandeur of those to which Edward was accustomed. But he was not aware of it. He could only think of the beautiful Countess. Her fine abundant hair, the contours of her face, the small waist, the dignity of her walk, her elegance.

The Countess was uneasy. She had been afraid of capture and what would happen to her at the hands of the rough Scots, but now a new fear had come to her. She realised what had happened more quickly than Edward did, for she had aroused similar emotions many times before. When William was with her, he could protect her, but William was now a prisoner in Europe and this was the King.

'My lord,' she said, 'I fear we cannot entertain you here at Wark in the manner to which you are accustomed.'

'There is nowhere I would rather be at this time than in Wark,' he answered.

He did not notice that the place was little more than a fortress. He knew these buildings, hardly worthy of the name of castle. They had been built by the Normans nearly three hundred years ago and never been improved on since. There was the hall with its high vaulted roof and the rooms were small cell-like places set along the outer walls.

'I will conduct you to the room I have hastily had prepared for you. It is small, I fear, but the best in the house. You will not find it unbearably cold I trust . . .'

'I know,' he said, 'that I shall find it to my liking.'

'My husband will want to thank you for what you have done for us this day.'

He did not answer. She saw the slight frown on his brow which increased her dismay.

'My lord, if you will give me permission to leave you I will go to the kitchens to make sure that the best we can offer is laid before you.'

His eyes had never left her. She thought: I must get away. She curtseyed again and this time he took her hand and kissed it.

His lips were hot and fierce on her skin.

God help me, she prayed.

She withdrew her hand and to her amazement he had released it. Then without looking back she turned and ran from the room.

She went to a room on the other side of the castle. There she stood for a while leaning against the door.

I must be wrong, she told herself. It could not be. William had always talked about his devotion to Philippa. If only William were here!

It was early evening. There was the rest of the day to live through and then he would retire to the room she had prepared . . . her room . . . the only one fit to offer to the King.

She would sleep as far from him as possible.

There was no bolt to this door. She would choose another room.

Absurd precaution. It was not so. It could not be so.

'The King is devoted to the Queen,' William had said that again and again.

'And he never looks at other women?' she had asked.

'He looks. He has a certain fancy for them. He told me once that except when he must discuss going into battle or state matters he preferred the company of women. He says they are wiser in many ways and he likes so much to look at them. Yet he is the most faithful husband in the country. He loved Philippa the moment he saw her and she follows him into battle so that she is never far away.'

Oh Philippa, thought the Countess, where are you now?

But it is a mistake, she assured herself. I imagine this. He has just driven off the enemy. He is overjoyed to have routed the Scots. He is pleased with me because I have given him an opportunity of doing this and being chivalrous it pleases him to help a lady in distress.

There. That was the explanation.

It must be the explanation.

❀ ❀ ❀

Alone Edward sat on the bed. Her bed. He knew she had given him her room. The previous night she would have slept here.

He had never seen anyone like her. Naturally he had not. There *was* no one like her.

What perfections! He noticed many women, beautiful women, women with whom he would have liked to make love. Oddly enough, in spite of his position which would have meant even easier conquests than his outstanding good looks would have brought him, he had abstained from indulgence. Often using great restraint.

Always he thought of Philippa. There was something about Philippa which had made him loath to betray her trust in him. A sweet simplicity which had attracted him from the first. A gentleness, a kindness, a homeliness. No one could have been a better wife to him.

But never before this day had he been confronted by a goddess. For that was what Catharine Montacute seemed to him. Her beauty was blinding. Why had William not told him? Obviously because he wanted to keep her to himself. Why had William not brought her to Court? Ah, that was clear enough. He would have been the same if he had been in William's place.

For the first time he was glad that William was a prisoner.

He was amazed at himself. He could not stop it. A raging desire had taken possession of him. He had been a good husband; he had never strayed from his marriage bed. But then he had never met Catharine Montacute before today.

She had changed everything. All his good resolutions had fled. This urgent need of her was fighting his conscience, subduing it, destroying it.

He had no conscience. He had only his desire for this woman.

Someone was at the door. He did not see them.

They had come to help him dress for soon he would go down to the great hall where they were doing their best to set forth a feast worthy of a king.

The table was ready; the knights were entering the hall. The King was not among them. His squire said that he had left Edward deep in thought and he had not even answered when he had reminded him that it was time to descend to the hall.

'I think, my lady,' said the squire, 'that he awaits your coming that you may escort him to your table.'

It was indeed an old custom and with misgivings Catharine went to that bedchamber which had recently been hers.

She knocked on the door and the King himself opened it. When he saw her a smile of great delight spread over his face. He took her hand and drew her into the room shutting the door after them.

She saw that he was as he had been when he arrived and had not removed all of his armour.

She said: 'My lord, I must leave you to take off your armour that you may come down unencumbered to our simple meal.'

'I have thought a great deal since you left me,' he said. 'I have thought of nothing but you . . . and of myself . . . and of what this meeting means to me.'

'My lord, it has meant my rescue and I am sure my lord of Salisbury will bless you for ever for what you have done for his lady this day.'

'I was not thinking of him,' said the King. 'He has been your

263

husband. That is reward enough for any man. Nay, I would think of you and me. For this day that has happened to me which has never happened before. I have met the most gracious and most beautiful lady in the world and to tell the truth I find I love her with all my heart.'

She smiled, pretending to treat the matter lightly. 'My lord shows his gallantry in speech as well as in actions. You speak kindly of me and now I would show you what we have prepared for you to eat for I am sure you must be suffering from hunger.'

'I hunger for one thing only, lady. For you.'

'There are hungry men below, my lord, and they cannot start without your presence.'

'Let them wait. I can wait no longer to tell you that your beautiful face, your perfections, your manners have so affected me that I cannot know another moment's peace until you tell me that you do not look unkindly on me.'

'How could a faithful subject look unkindly upon her King.'

'I do not wish this subject to look upon her King but on her lover.'

'My lord, you amuse yourself thus, but I pray you, consider this. Your presence in this room and mine with you will give rise to gossip. It may be that your good Queen will hear of it and be much distressed.'

The mention of Philippa affected him a little, she saw; but he would not be diverted from his purpose.

'I beg of you,' she said, 'come to our table.'

'We will talk more of this later,' he said.

'Yes, yes,' she answered, for she knew that she must get away from this small room, away from those ardent eyes, the eager straying hands.

'My lord,' she said, 'I will return to my guests and tell them that you will join us in a few moments.'

With that she escaped.

🌹 🌹 🌹

He was silent during the meal but everyone noticed that he could not take his eyes from the lady of the castle.

He must be entertained of course in accordance with the custom and it was Catharine who must sing and play the lute for him.

He watched her all the time, his eyes bright, his feelings for her obvious for all to see.

He expressed a desire for dancing and she must lead the dance with him beside her.

He held her hand firmly.

He whispered to her: 'We must be together this night, for I cannot live another hour without you.'

'I beg of you, my lord,' she said. 'Consider what you say.'

'Of what moment is it . . . but to us two.'

'There are others to consider,' she answered. 'My husband, a prisoner in your service, your wife the Queen. My honour and duty to my husband, yours to your country and your family. All your subjects who look to you to set an example. I beg of you, my lord, go from here. Forget me.'

'You ask the impossible. Do you think I will ever forget you? Do not be cruel to me, lady. I have never wanted anything in my life as I want you. The crown of England, the crown of France, I would give them all up for one night with you.'

She laughed as lightly as she could. 'And the next go to war to win them back. My lord, I know you well. My husband talked much to me of you. He loves you dearly. Would you betray him when he has become a prisoner in your service?'

'I would not think of him. I would forbid you to do so.'

'Not even a king can guide a subject's thoughts, my lord. I should think of my husband as long as I live.'

'I shall not rest until you tell me that you love me as I love you. And when a man feels as I do – even if he be the noblest in the land – he will not rest until he has obtained the object of his desire.'

'And when a woman is determined to maintain her honour until her death she will do so, my lord.'

'You fill me with despair.'

'Alas, my lord, I must.'

The dance over, the King expressed his desire to retire and he looked to the lady of the castle to conduct him to his bedchamber.

Catharine took his hand. Now she was afraid for she had seen the resolution in the King's eyes. Others had noticed it too.

But the determination in Catharine's eyes was equally strong.

He drew her into the bedchamber and turning to her put his arms about her.

'Come, my love,' he said. 'Hold off no more.'

She was rigid in his arms and he released her.

'So you continue to resist?' he said.

'My lord, I must, for the sake of mine honour and yours.'

'Honour beside . . . '

She answered for him, 'Lust.'

'I call it love,' he answered.

'It is not love that comes in a few moments,' she answered.

266

'Not that true love such as I have for my husband and you have for your wife.'

'I tell you this. There was never one who affected me as deeply as you do.'

'Nay, my lord. I am a woman like others. You like my face and form. That is all. Of me, the true woman, you know little.'

'I know that you are as brave as a lion and as stubborn as a mule.'

'Then, my lord, I beg of you, turn your thoughts from me.'

'I could take you if I wished. You might protest never so much and none would heed you if it were the King's pleasure that they did not.'

'That is true,' she said, 'but I know that you never would.'

'It seems you know as little of me as you say I know of you.'

'I see in your eyes, my lord, that though you would break your marriage vows and ask me to do the same, you would not violate a woman. You would respect her will for you know full well that gratification you seek would never be yours if you did so and all you would know would be shame.'

'You are bold, Countess,' he said.

'As you are, my lord.'

He took her hand and pressed his lips to it. 'Methinks I love you more with every passing minute,' he said.

'My lord, I will wish you good night. It is better so. You will agree with me. I shall pray to God to preserve you and drive from your noble heart those villainous thoughts which have temporarily possessed it. I am ever ready to serve you as your faithful subject, but only in that which is consistent with your honour and mine.'

She withdrew her hands and opening the door went out.

She went to the room which she had selected. She drew the

bolt and lay down on the bed. She was exhausted but no longer so fearful.

He would never take her by force so she had nothing to fear.

For she would never break her marriage vows.

Edward left for Berwick next morning.

He was silent and it was clear that his thoughts were far away from the war with Scotland.

He would never be contented again, he told himself. How could he be when Catharine was the wife of another man and he was married to Philippa?

His disloyalty struck him forcibly. He wished that he could stop thinking of Philippa. He could not. She was so much a part of his life, the mother of his beloved children. Yet he would have dismissed her, their children and their life together for Catharine Montacute.

It would not have been like that. He and Catharine could have been lovers and Philippa need never have known anything about it.

The thought made him smile wryly. How many people in Wark last night had slyly noted his obsession? They would be talking of it, whispering of it, nodding their heads over it. They had always marvelled at his fidelity to Philippa.

How noble Catharine had been! She was the sort of woman who would die for her beliefs and she believed it wrong that he and she should break their marriage vows.

She was not only beautiful, she was peerless. The arch of her eyebrows, the pure line of her profile, the way she held her head . . . all this he could see quite clearly and would remember for ever.

If she were his Queen he would be the happiest man on earth.

Philippa seemed to stand before him – her calm eyes sorrowful. She would understand of course. Philippa had always understood. Poor Philippa, she had never really been a beauty. He realised that more than ever when he compared her with the incomparable Catherine – plump Philippa, with her shining rosy cheeks and the goodness which was apparent in her very expression! He had always thought he had the best wife in the world . . . but now he had seen Catherine.

And so it went on.

He was wretched. He had no heart for the fight. He was tired of the Scottish war. He wanted to go south, to put as much distance between himself and temptation as possible. He would go to France. Fight for his crown there. Sometimes he felt the Scots would never be subdued. They could always retire to their stronghold in the mountains and the strife could go on indefinitely.

There was news from Philippa. She was pregnant again. He should rejoice for he loved his children and could not have too many of them. But the thought of Philippa so disturbed his conscience that he felt more uneasy than ever.

Philippa reminded him that she had heard nothing for some time from their dear sister Eleanor, the wife of the Duke of Gueldres, and as Eleanor had corresponded frequently with her she hoped that was not a bad sign.

It was a relief to let his thoughts stray momentarily from his own affairs. Raynald of Gueldres, his sister's husband, had been his firm ally in France. It was eight years since Eleanor had married him and she now had two healthy sons and had always appeared to be happy. Of course his sisters had had a very different childhood from that of his children. Perhaps memories of his early days had made him especially tender with his own children. How different his parents had been from himself and Philippa! His father had not been unkind but never interested in them and his mother had cared nothing at all for the girls and only for himself and his brother because of the importance they could be to her. So when Eleanor had gone to Gueldres she had been prepared to adjust herself. She had never been indulged as his own daughters had – particularly Isabella.

There must be some simple reason why she had not written. He was sure all was well in Gueldres.

Philippa's news had steadied him a little, reminded him of the felicity of his family life so far. Catharine was right. It would have been wrong to disrupt it. Many of his ancestors had had mistresses and it had been considered quite a natural state of affairs. There had even once been a breath of scandal about the Conqueror. His grandfather had been a faithful husband and so had his great grandfather. They had set an example to the family. His own father had disgraced it, but even he had been faithful to his lovers.

As the days passed he began to see that Catharine had been right. Neither he nor she were the kind to indulge in a light love affair. Theirs would have been too deep a passion for that. And Philippa, how she would have grieved!

He made a decision. The first thing he would do would be to bring Catharine's husband back to her. That would show her the nature of his devotion.

He had made several attempts to bring his friend out of captivity but the price demanded by Philip had been too high.

He immediately sent messengers to France to ask Philip

which prisoner he would like in exchange for the Earl of Salisbury.

Philip asked for the Earl of Moray, whom Edward had captured a short while before with great elation for Moray was reckoned to be one of the finest Scottish leaders, a man who would be a great asset to young David the Bruce.

Philip would naturally ask a great price.

Edward agreed to it.

'The Earl of Salisbury is one of my greatest friends,' he said.

And when he thought of how he had attempted to seduce his wife he was ashamed. But his desire for the beautiful Countess burned as strongly as ever.

The Earl returned to England and Edward made a truce with the Scots and marched south.

✿ Chapter XII ✿

THE JOUST AT WINDSOR

There was a sadness in the palace of the Tower of London. Philippa had given birth to a little girl. They had christened her Blanche but it was said of her that she had hardly time to open her eyes before she was dead.

A great depression had seized Philippa. She had several beautiful children but she could never bear to lose one. And this was a little girl. Edward loved girls.

There had been uneasy rumours which had disturbed her. No one had told her of course, but she had caught whispered words; she had seen furtive looks; and she could not help knowing that Edward had conceived a passion for the Countess of Salisbury and that the Countess was a virtuous woman who had repulsed his advances, and only because of this the affair had come to nothing. But it had changed everything. Often she had marvelled at his devotion to her. She had always realised that she was not a beautiful woman, and child-bearing had not improved her figure. In the last years she had grown over plump and she had always had a tendency to put on flesh. It was a characteristic of her race. Edward himself was very handsome. Not as tall as his grandfather,

Edward Longshanks, had been but well over medium height; blue-eyed, fair-haired, and with his love of finery he always presented a magnificent figure to the world. Moreover there was that aura of royalty about him which many women would find irresistible. The Countess of Salisbury apparently had not.

Edward, great king that he was, often seemed to her a child. His enthusiasms, his impulsiveness – the manner in which Robert of Artois had goaded him into the struggle for the French crown was an example of this – his love of pageantry, his delight in the joust when he wanted everyone to see him as the champion . . . all that seemed to her the actions of a lovable child. And this desire of Catharine Montacute was part of the pattern. She was one of the most beautiful women in England, Philippa had heard. Well, Edward's Queen was certainly not that.

Poor Edward, he had been disappointed of his prize!

To her he was like one of her children, and her nature was such that she looked for the fault in herself rather than in him.

She had failed him. Failed him by not being beautiful like Catharine de Montacute.

She forgave him, but it was the first time he had strayed – or tried to stray – and it seemed to her like the end of a certain pattern in their relationship.

And now she had lost her baby.

Edward had arrived at the palace.

It was the first time she had seen him since the relief of Wark Castle.

He came and knelt by her bed and kissed her hands fervently.

'You must not fret, my love,' he said. And she wondered whether he was referring to the loss of the baby or his unrequited love.

'A little girl,' he said. 'Dear Philippa, I have been so anxious for you.'

That was real concern in his eyes. Remorse, of course. She wanted to comfort him. To tell him to forget what had happened. They had been too happy one with the other, and together too long for anything to spoil what had gone before.

He talked of the child they had lost. 'We'll have more, Philippa. And how blessed we are in those we have already.'

They talked awhile of the children and she knew that he was telling her that he would always love her. Even though he had seen the most beautiful woman in England and would never forget her, it could make no difference to his love for Philippa.

Baby Blanche was buried in the chapel of St Peter in Westminster Abbey. All the family were present at the ceremony – Edward Prince of Wales, Isabella, Joanna, Lionel, John and Edmund.

Cloth of gold tissue was laid on her tomb and prayers were offered up for the reception of her soul in heaven.

Edward remained with his family for a while. He was anxious for Philippa to know how he esteemed her.

❀ ❀ ❀

Philippa had been right when she had guessed that there was some reason why her sister-in-law had not written from Gueldres.

Eleanor had, at first, been very happy in Gueldres. There had been some doubts about her marriage because her husband had been a widower at that time and much older than herself; but Eleanor had found him a kind and considerate husband, and when her sons were born she had been completely content.

After her somewhat desolate childhood when there had been whispers and innuendoes in the nursery she had not been very happy and then her sister Joanna at a very early age had been sent away to Scotland to marry David the Bruce. Life had scarcely been very happy for them. So that when she came to Gueldres she had enjoyed a contentment which she had not known before.

And when the elder of her sons, little Raynald, had been born there had been great satisfaction for the Duke's children by his first marriage had all been girls. She had been only sixteen at that time, for it was eight years ago; and since then she had given birth to another boy.

All was well until suddenly she developed a strange skin complaint which turned her very pale skin into an extremely highly coloured one. She could not understand what had happened and none of the ointments or unguents she used had any effect.

Then she noticed a coolness in her husband's attitude towards her. She rarely saw him and when she did it was only briefly in the day time.

One day she was out riding when her attendants asked her to look at a house some distance from the ducal palace.

'For what purpose?' she asked, and she could tell by the unhappy looks of her attendants that she had asked an embarrassing question.

The Duke's chamberlain, who had joined the party, explained to her: 'It is the wish of the Duke that you take up residence here, my lady.'

'Take up residence here! My place is in the palace.'

'That is the Duke's wish . . . the Duke's *order,* my lady.'

She was nonplussed and overcome with fear.

'And my children?' she asked.

'They are to join you here.'

She could not understand what this meant, nor was she allowed to see her husband to ask him what his intentions were. She did not write to Philippa and Edward as she had been wont to do. She would not know what to tell them, for she had no idea what crime she was supposed to have committed.

She had never taken lovers so there could be no question of infidelity. She had always been a loving wife. It was incomprehensible.

The slight skin infection which had changed her colouring had now disappeared and her skin was as white and perfect as it had ever been. She had grown thin with anxiety, and her only comfort was in her children.

Her faithful attendants could not make up their minds whether it would be wise to tell her of the rumours about her relationship with the Duke or to let her remain in ignorance. But one of them, considering what was involved decided to tell her.

'My lady, you must not let this happen.'

She wanted to know what.

'They say that the Duke plans to divorce you and disinherit your sons. He will take a new wife and hope to get sons by her.'

'This cannot be true. Why does he not tell me himself that he has ceased to love me?'

'It does not seem that he has. It is said that what he must do he does sadly.'

'Perhaps I should write to my brother. I do not understand. The Duke and I have never quarrelled. He seemed contented with our union. And my boys. You say they are to be disinherited?'

'There have been a lot of rumours, my lady. You know how leprosy is dreaded.'

'Leprosy!'

'Yes, my lady. They were convinced that you were suffering from this disease. It began with change in the colour of the skin. The Duke wished to be separated from you before it had too big a hold and became contagious. They say too that a mother passes it on to her sons and for that reason the Duke wants a divorce and sons from a mother who can give him healthy ones to carry on the line.'

'So that is what it is all about. Why wasn't I told? Leprosy! Do I look leprous?'

'Not now, my lady. Your skin is as fair and clear as it ever was.'

'What I had was a mild disorder. I finally cleared it up with herbs and lotions. It has completely gone. I must ask the Duke to come and see me.'

The woman looked dubious but Eleanor was undeterred.

She sent a message to the Duke but he would not receive it, so great was his fear of infection.

'So,' cried Eleanor, 'I am to be discarded without a chance to show the truth.'

It seemed this was so.

She had no friends in Gueldres, only her attendants but at least through them she understood what was at the root of her troubles.

The Duke, her husband, had been a keen supporter of Edward's claim to the throne of France but there were many nobles in Gueldres who inclined to the French. If they could rid the Duke of his English wife who was actually a sister of Edward, they could arrange a marriage with a bride put

277

forward by the King of France and thus bring about what so many of them sought: to break the link with England and forge a new one with France.

It was imperative that she must stop this. How dared they insist that she suffered from leprosy! They had alarmed the Duke to such an extent that he had refused to see her. That did point to the fact that his love for her was not very strong. But she believed she could revive that if only she could see him.

She realised that if she appealed to Edward it could have the reverse effect of what she wanted. Now she alone must do what had to be done for the sake of her children, herself, and her brother.

She had heard that there was to be a meeting of the nobles in the palace the following week and accordingly she laid her plans.

On the day when the meeting was to take place she put on a light tunic which exposed most of her body; over this she wrapped a cloak and taking her two sons with her set out for the palace.

No one attempted to stop her so taken by surprise were they to see their Duchess and she went through to the council hall where the nobles were assembled. The Duke was seated on his throne-like chair and holding a child by each hand she went to him and throwing off her cloak and exposing much of her fair, delicate and perfect skin, she cried: 'Oh, my lord, I have come to you to show you that the stories of my leprous condition are entirely false. If I were in that condition would it not be clear for all to see? Look at me, my lord. Look at me, you nobles, some of whom have spread these tales about me. I am whole and in good health. I insist that your doctors examine me. Here are your children, my lord. You cannot doubt that they are yours. They look like you. If you allow these calumnies to obscure the truth then, my lord, I will tell you this: you will regret our divorce and you will see the failure of your line.'

There was silence in the hall. All eyes were on the Duchess, who wearing nothing but her tunic, displayed an utter denial of the rumours of leprosy.

The Duke rose and going to her placed his hands on her shoulders. Then he picked up her cloak and wrapped it round her.

'My lady,' he said, 'you are right that I have been listening to calumnies. I feared leprosy and what effect it would have on you and your sons. I dared not risk infection. But they were lies . . . I do not wish for divorce. I thought it was my duty, for I must provide heirs.'

'You have your heirs,' she cried. 'And here they are.'

'It's true. This meeting is over,' he said addressing the company. 'I will take my wife to our apartment.'

He then led her and her children out of the hall and as they mounted the stairs he told her how pleased he was that she was back, how he had deplored the need to divorce her which so many of his nobles had forced him to consider.

There were many questions that she might have asked but she did not wish to. It was good enough that the nightmare was over. She was back in the palace and the Duke could not do enough to show her how delighted he was that the trouble was over.

Now Eleanor could sit down and write to Philippa and tell her of the strange episode which had now ended happily.

Poor Eleanor, thought Philippa. And she chided herself for feeling that inner resentment because Edward had briefly preferred another woman.

Edward showed clearly that he did not wish to be separated from Philippa. He took great pains to display his devotion to her which she found very touching. She had never mentioned to him that she knew of his feelings for the Countess of Salisbury and he never spoke of that lady to her. Everywhere he went he wanted her beside him; and he always insisted that she was as magnificently attired as he was – and since he took very great delight in fine clothes they made a splendid pair indeed.

He decided that he would hold a great tournament at Windsor and to this would be invited all the champions of Europe. He hoped that among these would be included the French knights; and it amused him to contemplate King Philip's chagrin in knowing that his greatest nobles were competing on an English field.

Edward, like his grandfather, had always felt a great interest in the legends of King Arthur and his knights, and he decided that for this occasion there should be a round table and that there the fairest ladies of the land, led by the Queen, should be seated with their knights whose object should be the exercise of chivalry.

Safe conducts were given for all knights no matter whence they came and this applied in particular to the French. They began to arrive from all over Europe.

This was going to be the most magnificent joust of all times. The Princesses Isabella and Joanna were to be present and there was great excitement in their apartments as they were fitted for the glittering garments they would wear. They were to be seated with the Queen in the ladies' gallery and from there they would select the knights they most admired and perhaps one of them would wear a favour from one of them which would proclaim the lady whom he honoured.

Their father's cousin Joan was with them. The fact that she was twelve years old – four years Isabella's senior – gave her a certain authority and she seemed very knowledgeable to the two Princesses. There was an aura of romance about Joan. In the first place she was outstandingly pretty. Isabella had noticed with dismay that whenever Joan was present people looked at her, smiled at her, were ready to indulge her. That irritated Isabella for even her father had a fondness for the girl because she was so pretty.

In fact she was called the Fair Maid of Kent. Another reason why she seemed so romantic was because of her father, the Duke of Kent, who was royal by birth being the son of Edward the First, had been executed before he was thirty years old at the order of the old Queen and Mortimer. Joan herself did not remember him for she was only two years old at the time – but this fact and her beauty made her an outstanding personality.

Joan was very much aware of her charms and already she had admirers. One was William de Montacute, eldest son of the Earl of Salisbury, but when in his household she had made the acquaintance of Sir Thomas Holland, his father's steward, and she was not sure which one she preferred.

'My sister Joanna has been betrothed and almost married,' Isabella reminded Joan, 'and there have been arrangements for me.'

Joan tossed back her beautiful fair hair and smiled tolerantly at them. 'Poor little Princesses,' she said, *you* will have to marry Princes who are chosen for you. You will have to go away to their countries and be very docile. I shall never be that, I assure you.'

She had no need to assure them. It was clear that Joan would have her own way.

She then told them about William de Montacute whose father was a prisoner of the French and whose mother was said to be one of the handsomest women in the country. 'Of course she is old,' added Joan complacently.

She was not sure whom she would marry, she told the Princesses. If she married William de Montacute she would be Countess of Salisbury when his father died and life in a French prison was not the sort of condition to prolong life was it? On the other hand she had Sir Thomas Holland, and he could be very rich. So the Princess would see it was a hard choice for her. On the whole she thought she preferred Thomas and being as royal as they were the title of Countess meant little to her.

Isabella was a little disconcerted that Joan's affair should be the main topic of conversation. It was annoying that when Joan tried on her glittering garments she looked so much more attractive than they did. Joan was well aware of this and could not resist calling attention to her own charms.

Isabella whispered to her sisters that she did not believe these stories about Joan and her lovers. She would have to marry where she was told – as they would – and there would be no choice for her in the matter.

But when their brother came to their apartments he was immediately attracted to Joan and sat on a window seat with her talking and laughing where she behaved as though she greatly honoured him for allowing him to speak with her.

'What airs she gives herself,' said Isabella. 'One would think she were a king's daughter.'

Young Edward, however, seemed to find her very atractive and when they rode out it was true that she had three attendants – the Prince himself, William de Montacute and Thomas Holland.

There could be no doubt that Joan, the Fair Maid of Kent, was a very fascinating creature.

There was a new arrival at the joust. He came straight to the King and when Edward saw him he was overcome with emotion.

'William!' he cried and embraced his friend.

The Earl of Salisbury said that he thought he should lose no time in presenting himself to his sovereign lord who, he knew, had made such efforts on his behalf.

'I waited only to see my family and hearing that my son had already left for the joust I knew that you, my lord, would wish me to join you.'

'You are welcome, William. It does me good to see you.' The King hesitated. 'Tell me, is the Countess with you?'

'My lord, she begs your indulgence. An indisposition.'

'Nothing serious?'

'Nay, my lord. She assures me of that. But she felt unfit to make the journey.'

The King did not know whether he was bitterly disappointed or relieved. She had done the right thing he was sure – as her tact and discretion would always insist. He longed to see her and yet had she come it would have been embarrassing with her husband just returned from captivity and the gossip which he guessed existed although none would dare let it reach his ears.

'Come,' he said, 'you must show yourself to the Queen. She has been greatly concerned about your imprisonment. Then you must let us know how you were treated. Not too ill, I would guess, by your looks.'

'No. Philip gave instructions that I was to be well treated. But you know I have had to swear not to take up arms against him again.'

'I know. It was part of the terms. We will talk of it later. Now let us go to the Queen.'

There had never been such a joust as this one.

It was January and there was a sharp frost in the air. The Queen with her daughters and her ladies seated in the gallery was a sparkling figure, her gown decorated with pearls and jewels, her velvet cloak edged with finest fur. The King beside her was in red velvet and the entire company glittered.

It was Edward himself who must be the brightest star. He must be the champion of the joust. None should surpass him; nor would it be easy to for he had made himself a master of the field.

The emphasis on this occasion was chivalry. As his grandfather had, he wanted to return to those days when knighthood meant chivalry. And nowhere was this more stressed than in the legendary tales of King Arthur and his Round Table. True knights he proclaimed must respect pity and defend all weaker than themselves and that meant a glorification of that sex which was said to be the weaker. Each knight liked to carry a lady's favour into the fight. A true knight must believe in and defend the Church. He must show strict obedience to his overlord except where this could conflict against his duty to God. He must always fight the forces of evil.

Edward would wear the Queen's favour and wear it ostentatiously so that all the whispers about him might be suppressed and he could convey to the company that it ill pleased him that there should be calumnies concerning his relationship with the Countess of Salisbury.

How the people cheered his victory! How he enjoyed riding round the field and coming to rest at the royal balcony and there making his bow to the Queen. Philippa, smiling tenderly, knew what this meant. Contrition. He might stray in his thoughts but she was his Queen, the mother of his children and he loved her dearly.

He kept the Earl of Salisbury by his side and it was clear that he considered him to be his very dear friend. This did not surprise William de Montacute because he had always considered himself to be very close to the King; they had shared so many adventures together, and it seemed natural that having so recently returned from captivity in the King's service Edward should show his appreciation.

In due course William made his appearance in the lists. It may have been that he was weakened from his imprisonment but to the King's dismay he was felled by his opponent.

A deep silence was on the assembly and many hurried forward to offer succour to the fallen Earl.

The King ordered that he should be carried into the castle and his own royal doctors should attend him. There was a strange tension in the air. It was not unusual for such accidents to happen on such occasions – and they could result in death – but that at this time the victim should be the Earl of Salisbury seemed somehow like an act of fate.

The Earl was not dead, but badly bruised and certain bones were broken. The doctors said that if he rested there was a faint hope that he might recover.

The King said: 'He is not old' – he was in fact forty-three years of age – 'certainly he will recover.'

It had been the most magnificent joust he remembered and his pleasure in it was increased because Philip of France was furious because many of his knights had attended it. Philip had endeavoured to have a similar entertainment at his Court at the same time – which had turned out to be a failure. This was inevitable because many of the French champions having been given safe conduct to Windsor had been present there.

'But for Salisbury's accident,' he said to Philippa, 'it would have been perfect.'

'Poor man,' replied the Queen. 'Perhaps we should send for his wife.'

Edward did not meet her eye. 'Oh that will not be necessary,' he said quickly, 'he will be about in a week or so . . . none the worse for this. It was nothing but a fall.'

He really was contrite, thought Philippa. And he did not think Catharine should be here to tempt him. He was very young and guileless and she loved him dearly. She longed to comfort him, to ease his conscience and to tell him that she knew she lacked the fascination of women like Catharine of Salisbury and she understood his admiration and desire for them. He must not fret. She would love him the more because he had resisted temptation for her sake. Or was that true? Was it the high morals of the Countess which had saved him from infidelity or his own stern conscience? She did not know. Nor did she want to.

'I am going to make this an annual occasion,' said the King. 'I shall send for carpenters and builders and I will build a round table at which two hundred may sit and it shall be here at Windsor in commemoration of this occasion.'

The Queen thought it would be an excellent idea. Chivalry should be encouraged. It was good to remind the people of those glorious legendary days of King Arthur when the task of the strong was to defend the weak.

'Nothing but good can come of it,' she declared.

The work was immediately set in progress and a great Round Tower was begun at Windsor.

The King threw himself into the project with enthusiasm. It was a joy to be able to plan something other than war. The Queen agreed with him. A truce with France, a truce with Scotland. It was a satisfactory state of affairs. There should be a Round Table once a year, declared the King; and he would command all knights to attend. No one else should set up a tournament while the Round Table was in progress, so that none could have an excuse for not attending.

The whole court was excited about the project. Then it was realised that the Earl of Salisbury's injuries were more serious than had been realised.

He became very ill and in a few days died, as the doctors said, 'from his bruises.'

So the beautiful Catharine was now a widow. Edward thought of her often and let himself imagine that now she was free she would not be breaking her marriage vows. But he knew in his heart that such was her moral code she would never be a partner in adultery.

Philippa had become pregnant again and he spent a great deal of time with her. He could not remember a period in their lives when he had been able to be so frequently with his family.

He was so eager that Philippa should be well cared for and that she should not believe for one instant that his deepest concern was not for her.

It had occurred to him that if she died he might, now that Salisbury was dead, marry Catharine and he let himself wonder what the country's reaction would be if he did. But to think of life without Philippa was intolerable. No, not for anything, would he want her not to be beside him. He did not forget for one moment what he owed to her and if some thought her simple then it must be the simplicity of wisdom for he had never known anyone so capable of being happy and making others happy as his Queen; and surely happiness was at the heart of success.

Perhaps that was no way for a king to think. But it was the truth.

Robert of Artois had been severely wounded in France and had been brought home to England to die. He was buried with much ceremony in St Paul's and the King was deeply grieved. Robert had been dissatisfied from birth; he had always believed that fate was against him; he had been a stirrer up of trouble yet he had had great charm and the King had enjoyed his company. Edward often thought that but for Robert he would never have embarked on this immense task of taking the crown of France. Sometimes when he thought of it he could see warfare stretching on through the century bringing no definite conclusion. Many lives would be lost in the struggle and what would be the end? Success for England would mean a changing of crowns. Success for France retaining it.

This year he had remained in England. He had had his family around him and it had been one of the happiest and most prosperous years he had ever known.

October came. The Queen had retired to Waltham near Winchester there to await the birth of her child.

In due course the child arrived. There was great rejoicing

for it was a healthy child and after the brief appearance and exit of little Blanche there had been certain apprehensions.

The King was delighted to have a daughter and the Queen rejoiced with him.

They christened her Mary.

It was a wonderful day when the rest of the children came to their mother's bedchamber to inspect their new sister. Even two-year-old Edmund was there to gaze in wonder at the new baby. They now had seven healthy children and had lost only two – little William and Blanche.

It was a goodly tally, said Edward.

He was well content with his family and union with the Countess of Salisbury was just an impossible dream.

🌸 Chapter XIII 🌸

CRÉCY

Prince Edward was now almost a man. At fifteen he was tall, mature for his age, and was eager to show his father that he was a man.

Edward delighted in him. Dearly as he loved his daughters he must admit that everyone looked to his sons and at the head of them was Edward. He could be proud of them all: Lionel a big sturdy fellow; John – who was always called John of Gaunt even in England and was always ready to attract attention and give a good account of himself; and Edmund who was a baby yet, but growing up like the others. Yes, he was a lucky man to have such sons.

Events of course did not stand still. Edward believed that the best place to start the attack on France must come from the North. The nearer he was to England, the easier was it to get the necessary supplies. He had no intention of falling into that trap which had proved to be the disaster of many a commander. Victory in the hands and nothing to hold it, success quickly turning to wretched failure. No, Edward wanted an open way to transport behind him. Therefore it would be the North and he looked to the Flemings for help.

There was uneasy news from Jacob van Arteveldt.

The Flemings were restive. Prosperity was waning and they were now grumbling among themselves and accusing Jacob of not keeping his promises.

An idea had occurred to Edward. Why should not Flanders be made a Duchy and Prince Edward become its Duke? The more he thought of it, the more the idea appealed to him. With Flanders in his hands through his son as its Duke, he would be in a good position to attack France. He could imagine Philip's rage and chagrin when he heard of such a *fait accompli*.

But first it had to be brought about. Jacob van Arteveldt was in agreement with Edward when the matter was broached with him and he assured Edward that he could win the support of the main towns whose consent would be necessary. He had brought the people of Flanders to his side with his eloquence and honesty and he could do so again for he sincerely believed that union with England was the best hope for Flanders.

Delighted Edward summoned his son and explained to him what he hoped for. Young Edward, eager to fight beside his father, was excited at the prospect. Indeed he was chafing against the delay in getting to France and wresting the crown from Philip and placing it where he believed it belonged, on his father's head, and he knew that in time that should mean on his, too.

'We must prepare to leave at once for Flanders,' said the King, 'but without too much noise. It should not be known what is in our minds until the Flemings send to us to welcome us into Flanders. We want no trouble from our enemies. I trust van Arteveldt with all my heart and he will let us know as soon as his countrymen are ready to receive us. My plan is to take very few men with us. We will ride quietly to Sandwich and there take ship. The *Swallow* will be waiting for us. But remember, my son, quiet is the word. I have told your mother and a few others, no more. Now prepare.'

Philippa had listened to the project with a certain apprehension. It meant that the peaceful months were at an end. Heartily as she wished that Edward would abandon his project for the conquest of France she said nothing; but a little sadly said good-bye to her husband and son, and on the last day of June the two Edwards set out on the journey for Sandwich.

The following day they embarked on the *Swallow*.

Jacob van Arteveldt, however, was finding it was not as easy as he had thought. When he had first arisen the citizens of the main Flanders towns – Bruges, Ghent and Ypres – had welcomed him as their saviour. He was one of them; he was a good honest workman, a man of ideals and the courage to present them; an honest man; a leader of stature. Perhaps he had been a little too hopeful. Perhaps he had set his dreams of prosperity too high. The fact remains that a great deal of what he had promised had not come to pass.

He talked to the people in market squares. They were dissatisfied with their Count who worked against them with the French but, they wanted to know, why should they exchange him for a foreigner, an English boy of whom they knew nothing? No, they would keep what they had. Who could say which might be the lesser of two evils?

Meanwhile Edward and his son remained on board the *Swallow* in Sluys awaiting the call from van Arteveldt. It was long in coming but Edward was certain of Jacob's influence with the people and he believed it would come in time. He had forgotten that it was a long time since he had been in Flanders and reputations such as that of Jacob van Arteveldt, acquired so hastily can evaporate with equal speed.

Jacob's success in Ghent had aroused a great deal of envy among his fellow citizens. Who is this man who sets himself up to be our leader? they were asking. He is only one of us. What has he that we haven't?

He was an excellent business man. He had acquired a small fortune. But who was he to dictate what Flanders should do?

Then the whispers came. He was working with the English. He wanted to depose the Count and set up the son of the King of England in his place. *He* wanted to choose their rulers. He was a traitor, wasn't he?

When Jacob returned to Ghent they were waiting for him. He sensed their hostility immediately. He saw murderous looks directed in his direction so he made haste to his house and once there barricaded himself in.

It seemed that no sooner had he done this than the mob was at his door. He heard them shouting for him to come out and he knew that if they were determined they would, in time, break down his doors. It was an ugly mob.

It was his eloquence which had won them in the first place so he would try it again. He went to the topmost window of his house and looked down on the crowd.

Some of them carried clubs and others had picked up whatever article they could find to act as a weapon. He realised that they hated him now as fiercely as they had once loved him. Such was the emotion of the mob.

He opened a window and called to them to let him speak.

'My friends and countrymen,' he cried, 'will you listen to me . . .'

But they could not hear him so great was the noise they made.

'Come down and face us, Jacob,' they chanted. 'We will show you what we will do with you.'

'Have you not prospered of late?' he shouted. 'Have I not made it easier for you to sell your goods? Did I not arrange . . .'

But he could see it was useless. They had not come to listen. They had come to destroy him.

Several of them were climbing up the side of the house.

'I can bring you prosperity,' he cried.

But they could not hear. They did not want prosperity at this moment. They only wanted to satisfy their lust for revenge on one of their own kind who had risen far above them, who had set out to be a leader and who made contracts with kings.

A hand reached out and grabbed his arm. He was half way out of the window. Other hands seized him and pulled him down to the ground.

They were trampling on him; they were kicking him. They were raining blows on him.

It has all been in vain, he thought.

And so he died.

Eagerly awaiting a message from Jacob van Arteveldt, making his preparations for his and his son's entry into Ghent, Edward received the messenger.

He could not believe what he heard.

Van Arteveldt dead! Murdered by the people of Ghent. But he was a man who had done so much for Flanders. Murdered. It was impossible.

"'Tis so, my lord,' replied the messenger and told the King how the people of Ghent had turned against Jacob because he wanted to set a foreign Prince over them and how they had clubbed him to death.

Edward was subdued.

'He was a good man,' he said. 'He was a man who served his country well and would have gone on doing so. An honest man, rare in these days.'

He saw it was the end of a dream.

He rewarded the messenger and dismissing him, summoned his son.

'You see, Edward, how in this life that which we thought to be within our grasp will often elude us. We should never count on anything until we hold it in our hands.'

'Should we not go and avenge the death of this good friend, Father?' asked the Prince.

The King shook his head.

'Jacob is dead. Nothing can bring him back. We are engaged on a war to win the crown of France. We cannot involve ourselves in minor wars which would divert us from our purpose. I had hoped to attack with the Flemings beside me. Now we will forget that and start from another point.'

'What shall we do now?'

'My son, we shall return to England. There we shall prepare ourselves for a mighty campaign against the French.'

There should be no more delay.

He would depend on none but himself. The next months should be spent in preparation and this time next year he would be in France with the finest army he could muster.

295

Thank God for the truce! Preparation time. It should be well spent.

Philippa was delighted to see them back. She mourned the death of Jacob van Arteveldt, a man whom she had greatly admired; she wondered about his son Philip who had been her godson. 'Poor fatherless boy,' she said. 'And Jacob was such a good man. Why cannot people understand that such as he did not seek honours for themselves but only the good of their country?'

She was glad though that she had her husband and son back if it was to be only a short respite. She had not wanted young Edward to take the title of Duke in Flanders. Men like her husband could never see how dearly such honours were bought and that the world would be happier without them.

Now throughout England workshops were busy. Bows and arrows were being made in their thousands. The blacksmiths shops throughout the country rang with activity; they were making horse-trappings for the horses which would go to war. Carpenters and tentmakers were working full speed, and this brought prosperity to the country.

Every man knew what they were working for. It was for the excursion into France. It was to set the crown of France on the head of Edward Plantagenet for, every Englishman believed, that was where it rightly belonged. Was not their King's mother a daughter of a King of France and had not her brothers died . . . every one of them? The French said that no woman could inherit the crown of France. That was their Salic law. Well why shouldn't a woman's son inherit? In any case this was what they wanted to believe and they were going to believe it.

Their Edward was the true King of France not Philip of Valois. And they were going to fight to give him what was his by right.

By the following summer there was an army of twenty thousand men ready to follow the King to France. And each day they practised with their bows. They were determined to be the finest archers England had ever known. Lance, sword and battle-axe. They would know how to use them against the French when the great day came.

Philippa hid her grief at parting. She was once more pregnant or she would have gone with the King to France.

She smiled tenderly on her husband who was now so eager to be gone. He was certain of victory; it was characteristic of him that he should be. Again it seemed to her that he had never really grown up, a trait which often served him well. His unfailing optimism had carried him through many a difficult situation. Edward always believed in victory and he had the gift of making others believe in it too; and when his dreams failed to come true he never brooded on their failure; he began the next campaign. Thus cheated of the dukedom of Flanders he turned his efforts to the crown of France.

Fondly he embraced Philippa. 'I leave you, my love,' he said, 'regent of this realm. The Earl of Kent will stand beside you. And Lionel shall be Guardian of the Realm.'

Lionel who was summoned to the King's presence listened gravely to his father's injunctions. It sounded wonderful to be Guardian of the Realm. He did not quite understand what it meant but it was something to boast of to his brothers and sisters and it gave him a chance to score over Isabella who always thought she was the most important person in the family because she was their father's favourite.

When he asked his mother what he would have to do she

reassured him by telling him only what she told him to. He might have to sit at meetings and when he did so remember that he must keep quiet and try to listen, or seem as if he were listening.

That did not seem insuperable and was a great comfort to the eight-year-old boy.

So they said good-bye to the King and Prince Edward, and the Regency had begun.

Shortly afterwards the Queen went to Windsor for her lying in and very soon gave birth to her daughter Margaret.

Prince Edward stood on deck with his friends William de Montacute, who had become the Earl of Salisbury on the death of his father, and Sir John Chandos. He admired John Chandos more than anyone he knew and he was proud of his friendship with him. John being older than he was had taught him a great deal and he seemed to the Prince the perfect knight. He was brave yet gentle; he hated oppressing the weak and showed no fear of the strong. Edward delighted in his company. He felt differently towards William de Montacute who was two years older than he was and inclined to stress the superior wisdom of seniority. Moreover there had been a certain rivalry between them over the fascinating Joan of Kent who, at the joust of the Round Table, had played one against the others, with Thomas Holland in spite of his being of lesser rank seeming to be the favoured one. But perhaps that was just Joan's perversity.

Both William de Montacute and Edward had yet to attain knighthood and this was their immediate ambition. The Prince was envious of William for he was to command the landing of the first batch of the invaders – a task which Edward had thought his father might have given to him.

William was preening himself, determined to make a success of it and listening to the advice given by John Chandos.

Edward shrugged his shoulders. Well, if he were going to be the perfect knight like John, he must not show envy but wish all success to William which, somewhat grudgingly under the eye of John, he did.

And then to land and the beginning of operations.

There was some opposition by the natives but they were unarmed and William, a noble sight charging among them brandishing his sword, had little difficulty in putting them to flight and the operation assigned to him was carried through smoothly.

Edward was to land with his father and stood beside him awaiting the moment.

The King was carried shoulder high to the shore and as he sprang to his feet he miscalculated in some way and fell sprawling.

There was a shocked silence. Men about to go into battle were always looking for omens and for the King to fall as he set foot on land seemed like a deadly one.

Edward burst into loud laughter.

He stood up and held out his earth-stained hands.

'Behold, my friends,' he cried. 'The very land of France cannot wait to embrace me as its rightful master.' He looked at those solemn faces and he went on: 'When my great ancestor came from Normandy to England, he fell on landing just as I have done. He told his men what I have just told you, and lo and behold did it not come to pass that he conquered that land? Now it is changed. I come to conquer France as he once came to conquer England.'

Yes, they remembered the story of the Conqueror. It had been passed down through the ages.

It was a sign from Heaven. Edward was going to conquer France.

It was important, Edward believed, to imbue his son with that aura which men such as himself and his grandfather possessed. It was a pity Edward was not a few years older. Sixteen was so young. He was not even a knight yet. That could be remedied and it would be a good dramatic gesture to knight him here and now in the first hour on French soil. Then these men would know that if their King fell in battle there was another whom they could follow, ready to step into his shoes.

He summoned the Prince to him and there on a knoll made him bend his knee. He touched his shoulder with his unsheathed sword, fastened the belt about his hips and the golden spurs at his heels. Your Prince, he was telling the watchers, is no longer a boy.

He knighted one or two others on that spot and among them was William de Montacute, the young Earl of Salisbury. Edward felt a rush of emotion as he applied the naked sword to the shoulder.

He wished that the boy's mother could see this ceremony. She would know then that he thought of her often and that he was determined to honour and do all he could to advance her family.

The march across the north of France had begun and there was little opposition in the first weeks. Barfleur, Valonges, Carentan and St Lo quickly fell to Edward. At the last place a thousand tuns of wine were discovered and these so refreshed the English army that they were unable to move for some time.

'But,' Edward explained to his son, 'one must consider the needs of the men. This night they will be thanking God that they came to France and pitying those who stayed behind. Let it be so, they will not always harbour such sentiments, for war, my son, is not all seeking a woman in the village and getting tipsy on discovered wine.'

After St Lo they came to Caen which he took with ease and from Caen he marched to Lisieux.

By this time Philip, realising what had happened, was gathering together a large force; he intended to put one double that of the English into the field if he could and in one mighty battle smash the fighting power of England. He would show Edward that it was one matter to take a defenceless town and another to score a victory over a well trained army.

Edward meanwhile marched on, encountering here and there French resistance but nothing serious. He knew what was happening and very shortly he would have to stand and fight the great army which Philip was bringing to meet him.

Edward chose his spot with great foresight. He set his men to occupy the right bank of the river Maye. To his right was the river and the village of Crécy; he had ordered that wagons be piled up on the left flank where the army might be vulnerable and these provided a measure of protection. From the front he commanded the Vallée-aux-Clercs.

Thus he had built himself in to a very desirable position.

Edward knew that he needed it. He was going to face an army vastly superior to his own in numbers. He had landed with twenty thousand but during the march to Crécy with its attendant skirmishes several men had lost their lives; others had been incapacitated by sickness. He had taken several towns but it was inevitable that some men should lose their lives during these operations. He had had to send some home because their attacks of dysentery had made them a burden to the army.

So he lacked the fine army he had set out with, but in his optimism he assured himself that he was left with the best. The survivors of the rigours of the last weeks must be the strong and the brave.

Philip however came with his army in full force. It was estimated that he had some fifty thousand men which was thirty thousand more than Edward had set out with for naturally he had had to leave men at home for the defence of England whereas Philip could draw from the whole of his domain.

It would be a hard battle but Edward was not the man to be oppressed by the thought of numbers.

'Our men have had the experience of warfare in the last weeks,' he told the Prince. 'They will be prepared for battle. And know this: one Englishman is worth three Frenchmen so that will make us roughly equal in numbers.'

The Prince was longing to go into battle, to prove himself, to show his father that although he was but sixteen he could fight as well as any man.

The morning of Saturday the twenty-sixth of August dawned and there was still no sign of the French army, though scouts had brought the news that Philip and his men were in the vicinity.

The King and the Prince heard mass as did most of the army; and they set themselves to wait. The Prince wore black armour which distinguished him from all others. The King was a little uneasy for it would soon be discovered who he was and he feared for him, inexperienced of battle as he was.

'I wish to be recognised,' said the Prince. 'I care not who comes to me, I will give a good account of myself. I should despise myself if I feared to be known.'

The King was torn between his fears for his son and in his pleasure in his bravery. He would not have wished for a coward. Better a dead son than an unworthy one.

It was Robert the Bruce who had gone into battle with a golden circlet on his head that all might know he was the king. Edward Longshanks had been recognised by his unusual height and had never sought to disguise it. And so the Prince would follow these examples and show himself as the Black Prince of Wales.

It was midday when the French discovered they were almost face to face with the English.

The hour of battle was close.

Some of the French thought it should be postponed for a day as their men had ridden hard all the morning and would be weary but this suggestion was thrust aside by the King's brother and the battle began.

Through the afternoon the conflict raged, swaying this way and that and, if it had not been for the skill of the English archers, there would have been victory for the French. The sun was hot but suddenly the sky was overcast and a terrible storm broke. The sky was then black; forked lightning shot across the sky and the rain teemed down. The position of the English which Edward had so carefully planned was a help to them. It was different with the French. They took the brunt of the storm and, when suddenly a number of crows rose up and cawing loudly circled over the French army, there was alarm in their ranks.

Everyone was amazed at the sight – the sudden darkness, the downpour, the lightning, the deafening thunder and then the crows.

Edward cried: 'This prophesies disaster for our enemies. Victory will be ours. Heaven is telling us this.'

Quite suddenly the storm was over and the blazing sun was seen again. It shone in the face of the French and was behind the English which was an added advantage.

Young Edward, conspicuous in his black armour was in the thick of the fight. He was surrounded by the enemy and there was not a man among them who was not longing for the honour of taking the son of the King of England dead or alive.

Sir John Chandos had questioned the wisdom of wearing such a distinguishing armour, but for once the Prince would not listen to his friend. Salisbury had won honour by landing the first batch of men; he was going to win greater honour in the battle of Crécy.

Suddenly he was down. His horse lay wounded, he almost beneath it.

'It's the Black Prince!' he heard the shout, and he knew his enemies were all about him. He would fight to the end. He would never let them take him alive. It seemed now that all his dreams of glory were to end on the field of Crécy.

Someone was standing over him straddled over his fallen body wielding an axe. He was shouting, 'Edward and St George. Edward *Fils du Roi*.'

Before he had fallen, but seeing him surrounded, Sir John Beauchamp had galloped to the King.

'My lord, my lord,' he cried, 'the Prince is sorely pressed.'

'Is he dead?' asked Edward quietly.

'Nay, nay. But he needs help . . . without delay he needs help.'

'Is he badly wounded then that he needs help?'

'He is not wounded, my lord. But knowing he is the Prince they are pressing him hard.'

'Sir Thomas,' replied the King, 'as long as my son lives he will fight. I say this to you: Let the boy win his spurs. I would have the honour of this day be his.'

Sir Thomas rode off. One did not question the King's orders, but as Edward watched his departing figure a terrible fear touched him.

What if he could have saved the boy? What if Edward were killed or taken prisoner? How could he face Philippa? She would say: Our boy was in danger and you did not send help to him.

I wanted him to prove himself. I wanted him not to be ashamed after this day, not to have to say I should have failed if my father had not sent to help me.

'Oh God of battles,' he prayed, 'let the boy earn his spurs this day.'

❧ ❧ ❧

It was John Chandos who led the charge. He galloped forward scattering those who would have taken the Prince.

'John . . .' cried Edward.

'Up on this horse, my lord,' said John. 'We must pursue the enemy.'

How good it was to be mounted again. To have come close to death and to have felt no fear.

He rode beside John. The warmth of the sun enveloped him; the grass wet and glistening after the recent rain smelt fresh.

'I'll never forget this day, John,' he said.

'I doubt any of us will ever forget the field of Crécy, my lord,' was the answer.

The French were defeated but would not concede victory. Again and again they threw themselves into the fight. Even the King of France was wounded and it was only the urgent pleading of his faithful friends which decided him finally to depart. He had lost a battle, they said, but a battle was not a war. He must retire, give the English this victory and live to fight again.

Sound advice which Philip followed.

And so, against overwhelming odds, the victory was Edward's.

He was exultant. 'As long as men shall live,' he declared, 'they will speak of Crécy.'

Then he turned to Edward standing beside him in his black armour and he embraced him. 'You are truly my son,' he said in a ringing voice. 'This day you have borne yourself right royally. You are worthy to be a King and a King of England.'

The Prince murmured that he owed his life to many and all men here today had contributed to the victory of Crécy.

And they cheered him for his bravery and his modesty and they said that when people talked of Crécy they would link with that great victory the name of the Black Prince.

❀ Chapter XIV ❀

NEVILLE'S CROSS

Philippa had heard the news of the victory at Crécy when Edward had written glowingly of the bravery of their son and how proud he was of him and how, young as he was, men were already looking to him as their leader. When she heard of how near the Prince had come to death she shivered with apprehension.

'Oh God,' she prayed, 'let there be an end to this warfare. Bring them home safely to me.'

They had been victorious at Crécy, but what next. How many more battles would there be in which her family would fly defiantly in the face of death? How often could they hope for God always to be merciful and answer a frightened mother's prayers?

She had little time for brooding on what was happening in France for events in England began to claim her attention.

It began when the young Earl of Kent came to her in great haste. He was her co-regent, and with little Lionel as the figurehead, she and he were governing the realm.

His news was alarming.

'The Scots are attacking and David has marched over the Border.'

'This means war,' said Philippa.

'It does, my lady, and there is little time to lose. Philip, having been routed at Crécy is determined to attack us through Scotland and, as his ally, David dances to his tune. We must send what men we can muster to the North immediately. I will get the army on the march and keep you informed.'

'There will be no need to keep me informed,' said Philippa, 'for I shall be there.'

The Earl looked amazed but she went on, 'When the King went into battle I was never far behind. I know what it means, my lord, to go to war. The King is alas not here. I must take his place. I cannot hope to inspire the men as he would but I fancy they will be pleased to see me with them.'

When David heard that the Queen was marching north at the head of an army he laughed aloud.

'This will be amusing,' he said. 'I shall be interested to meet the lady.' His eyes shone as he relished an easy victory. 'Nothing shall stop me,' he cried, 'nothing . . . until I reach the gates of Westminster!'

He was lost in a dream. At last here was his revenge. He would face the facts and admit that he stood little chance against Edward at whose name Scotsmen shivered; they feared him as they had his grandfather. But Edward was away and in place of the mighty warrior was a weak woman.

Victory would certainly be his. How amusing to take London! What news to send to France where Edward was fighting for the crown of France! What a pleasure it would be to inform him that not only had he not gained the crown of France but he had lost that of England.

He spent the night with his mistress who would travel with the army.

His wife Joanna was apprehensive. Naturally she would be. He always suspected her of divided loyalties. The King of England was after all her brother and like most people she seemed to think he was some sort of god. This would show them and her. What would the god do when he realised he had lost his kingdom?

He couldn't resist taunting her. Sometimes he hated her. She was so calm; she never uttered a reproach though sometimes it was there in her manner. He had made no secret of the fact that he preferred his mistresses to her. It soothed him to do so largely because she was the sister of the King of England.

'Perhaps,' he said, 'I'll take you to London with me. It will be like returning home to you, will it not?'

'You have many battles to win first,' she answered, 'and I think you may not find the conquest easy.'

'Of course you think that. Your noble brother would stop me, you think. Well let me tell you this. He is fighting a war which he will never win. The King of France is my friend. He was always my friend. Have you forgotten how he put Gaillard at our disposal? And what a good life it was there!'

She was silent and turned away. He shouted after all: 'This is the end of Edward's kingdom. This is the defeat of the English for ever. Even my father could not do what I shall do now. This is the hour.'

'Do not be too sure, David,' she said quietly and left him.

'A curse on the English!' muttered David.

He had gathered together three thousand cavalry and about thirty thousand other troops, many of them untrained and mounted only on ponies but they were sure-footed beasts.

William Douglas warned him that there must be no delay as

the summer was over and if the campaign were long it would extend into winter.

'I promise you, Douglas, that there will be no long campaign. Before the winter comes I shall be in London.'

William Douglas replied that they must expect some opposition.

'Opposition! The King's army is in France fighting a hopeless war.'

'You have heard of Crécy, my lord.'

'I have said I will have the head of the next man who talks to me of Crécy, William Douglas.'

Douglas bowed and asked leave to retire as there was much to be done.

He went out thinking how different was the son from the father. He could hardly believe great Robert the Bruce had sired this braggart.

But David was the King and must be obeyed.

Within a week the Scottish army was marching south ravaging the country as it went. The savage Highlanders had no respect for the churches and abbeys which lay in their paths and the monks mourned among the ruins and cursed the invaders and called on the saints to avenge the innocent who had suffered at their hands.

Some of the Scots were afraid but David laughed at the prophecies of evil.

It was armies, he said, not saints who decided battles.

The news of what was happening reached Philippa. She had been gathering together an army which she was preparing to send to France where Edward was planning to lay siege to Calais. Discussing this with the Earl of Kent she decided to divert that army and send it north for the need to defeat the

Scots she realised was greater than that to besiege a French town.

Soon a considerable army was marching north.

Moreover it was not to be expected, that the people of the North would stand by and allow the Scots to use them as they fancied, and the lords of the North, Neville and Percy, were mustering men to meet the Scots and, when Philippa came with her army from the South, together they made a considerable force.

The Scots were less disciplined than the English; they were brave in the extreme but only under the control of a skilled commander such as Robert the Bruce could they work as a team. David fell short of that. They would not take orders, and consequently they were not the well trained army that the English could put in the field – even though it was a secondary one.

The English had reached Durham, and there Philippa addressed the men.

'The King will be proud of the manner in which you rallied to his banner. I would he were here this day to see you, loyal to a man, eager each one of you to serve your King and your country. These Scots have ravaged our land, they have burned and looted and taken our women. We will not allow this to continue. I know the King will want to thank you all for what you have done this day. I am only a woman, but your Queen, and I stand for the King in his absence. My friends, I know you will do him honour this day.'

The men cheered her. A noble lady, who had brought nothing but good to the country. The weavers of Norfolk had prospered through her; she had brought trade to England; she had been a true and faithful wife to the King and had given them their Black Prince and other bonny children.

Long live the Queen!

They respected her for coming north but they would not, she knew, wish her to join them on the battlefield, where the care of her would hinder more important work.

They were not far from the town of Neville's Cross where it seemed likely they would meet the Scots, and Philippa would remain in Durham where she said she would pray for success.

William Douglas, in search of food and straying from the main Scottish army with a small band of followers, rode to the top of a hill and to his amazement he saw an army camped below.

He recognised the English pennants and was filled with dismay.

So near and what an army! Not merely a handful here – a considerable force.

He lost no time in going back to the Scottish camp and seeking out the King.

David listened sardonically. 'It is nonsense,' he cried. 'The English are in France. There are no men left in England but monks, swineherds, tailors and tanners. Do you think my soldiers will be halted by such?'

'I tell you, my lord,' insisted Douglas, 'that I have seen an army encamped not two miles from here.'

'You were dreaming, Douglas. Are you a coward man? Do you fear to match the English?'

To hint that a Douglas was a coward was an insult not to be taken lightly.

He bowed and retired without asking permission.

'I never liked Douglas,' commented David. 'He fancies himself more royal than I am.'

One of Douglas's companions came to him to repeat the story.

'Swineherds tending their animals!' cried the King. 'We'll have some succulent pork tomorrow.'

'My lord,' said the man, 'these were no swineherds. They were strong men and looked as though they were ready for the fight.'

'You know what is wrong with you, man,' said David angrily, 'you have been asleep and dreamed. Get you gone. I want none of your foolish imaginings. If you and Douglas are afraid, you may go back to Scotland. There, I give you leave. I want no cowards in my army.'

The man went back to Douglas. 'He will not listen,' he said. 'What will become of us?'

'We shall fight as good Scotsmen and who knows we may defeat the English. It cannot be the pick of the English we face for they are in France. But what are we fighting for? That is what Scotsmen ask themselves. For David the Bruce? Who would have thought he could be his father's son?'

It was dawn next day when the English attacked and David, taken unawares, was rudely shown how foolish he had been not to listen to Sir William Douglas.

Seized with fury, determined to show the English and his own men that he was invincible, he shouted for his armour and his horse and brandishing his sword called to his men to follow him.

There was no question of his bravery, but he was foolhardy in his recklessness. His officers sought to restrain him. He had no plan of action. All he wanted was to kill the enemy and win glory for himself. He would lead his army, exposing it and himself to a hundred dangers in doing so.

In vain was he warned of the skill of the English archers to whose deadly aim the victory at Crécy was due. The bowmen of England were notorious. It was said they whittled magic into their bows and arrows. He would not listen. He was the King. He was tired of hearing of the fame of Robert the Bruce. Now men should begin to speak of David.

But it was not to be. Defeat closed in on the Scots, for lack of training and their King's erratic leadership was their undoing. David was wounded twice by English arrows. He did not care. He grew more and more reckless now that he realised defeat was close at hand and Douglas had been right; he preferred to die rather than give in.

An Englishman was bearing down on him, intent on winning the glory of capturing the King. David's horse fell and he was down.

This was the end. This was disgrace. All his enemies would be gleeful and not only the English. His own people would whisper together: 'I told you so. He was never the man his father was.'

The man bending over him was grinning at him. David was almost helpless but in a rush of fury he shot his gauntleted hand into the grinning face. There was a crunch and a groan and he saw blood on the man's mouth.

William Douglas had come to his rescue. Oh the degradation of that. Douglas fought valiantly but men had seized him.

Douglas was a prisoner of the English.

And so was David to be. Death! he thought. Death is preferable.

But the man with the bleeding mouth had his sword.

'You are my prisoner,' he said.

And so on the field of Neville's Cross the captivity of David of Scotland had begun.

314

There could be nothing more humiliating. David was overcome with wretchedness. Sir Malcolm Fleming and the earls of Fife and Monteith with William Douglas were all in the hands of the English.

And he himself had been captured by a mere squire. John Copeland was his name and the man was beside himself with glee. He would let no one come near the King of the Scots. David was his booty and he was going to cling to him.

So he was Edward's prisoner. Even when he was away from home the King of England was invincible.

And now what? he asked himself.

Was God never going to smile on him? For years he had been in exile in France; then he had come home and after a few years he was the prisoner of the English.

Of one thing he was certain: they would not lightly let him go.

Philippa was overjoyed at the result of the battle of Neville's Cross. She had been afraid that without Edward the troops would falter. Not so. They had gone into battle determined to fight and there had been a resounding victory.

She heard that the man who had captured David was a certain John Copeland a Northumbrian Squire and she sent for him to come to her and bring his prisoner with him. She had been amused to hear that Copeland had taken David to his house and had him well guarded there, so fearful was he that he might escape, although that was hardly likely considering how badly wounded David was. Moreover Copeland would let no one go near him but himself.

'He is a good jailer,' said Philippa with a smile.

She was told that they had wanted to bring David to her but Copeland would not let him go.

She nodded and sent for John Copeland.

He came – a plain simple man, she realised, unversed in court manners.

'I congratulate you on your capture,' she said. 'The King will, I am sure, wish to reward you. I will take the King of Scots to London and would have you bring him to me here.'

John Copeland shook his head.

'Oh no, my lady,' he said. 'Oh no.'

Philippa was amazed. 'What mean you?' she asked.

'I took the King of Scots captive for my master, the King of England.'

'I know that – and nobly done it was. Bring him to me and I will write immediately to the King and tell him that I have David of Scotland in my hands.'

'No, my lady, when I say I deliver him to none but the King, that is what I mean. The King is my master. To him I swear fief for my lands. To none other. And not to Duke, Earl or woman will I deliver my prisoner.'

Philippa did not lose her temper though she thought the man a fool.

'You must know that I am acting as Regent in the name of the King.'

'I know naught of such matters, my lady. All I know is that I owe allegiance to my King and none other and only to him will I deliver up my prisoner.'

'The King will be displeased that you flout me,' Philippa warned him.

'That must be as it will. I shall give up my prisoner to him and him alone.'

Philippa dismissed him.

The Earl of Kent came to her. He was angry. 'But my lady, he insults you. Shall we arrest him? The man is a traitor. He refuses to obey you. The King will have him hanged. We shall arrest him and then bring the prisoner to you.'

The Queen shook her head.

'There was something in him I admired. He is a true servant of the King. There is no doubt about that. Let it be. I will write to the King and tell him of this strange attitude of his. I have already written to tell him of the victory of Neville's Cross, and he will know that David is in our hands.'

'I know the King's nature,' was the answer. 'He will be furious with one who has insulted you.'

'Perhaps not when I explain to him how this man spoke of his loyalty to the King. I think he will understand as I do. I shall try to put it clearly.'

The Earl was astonished. He wondered how many women would have taken Copeland's insults so mildly.

Edward's answer was prompt.

David was to remain well guarded in Copeland's house and Copeland himself was to leave England immediately and present himself to him.

When Copeland received these orders his wife was thrown into a panic.

'You fool, John,' she cried. 'See what you have done. You should have given up the King of Scots. It was the Queen who asked, wasn't it? Oh my dear lord, I shall never see you more.'

Copeland was uneasy. He had heard of the temper of the King and his devotion to his wife. He liked people to do homage to her. The more he thought of it the more he realised how deeply he had insulted the Queen.

Edward was at this time outside Calais. He planned to take the town and knowing it would be a long task he had hastily erected dwellings to house himself and his army.

As soon as Copeland arrived he was taken before the King. Edward, always vain about his appearance, looked magnificent at all times and the squire was overcome by awe and trepidation.

'Welcome, my squire,' said Edward. 'I hear of your valour in capturing my enemy, the King of Scots.'

'My lord, it was honour to serve you in this as I would at all times.' The squire remained on his knees raising his wondering eyes to the King. 'God has been good to me, a humble squire,' he went on, 'in allowing me to make such a capture. I felt, this being a king of our enemies, I should hand him to no one but yourself. I meant no discourtesy to the Queen but the Queen is not the King, my lord, and it is to the King that I have given my oath.'

Edward laughed. The simplicity of his own nature gave him an immediate knowledge of the way in which the minds of his humbler subjects worked. This man was a loyal servant. He had need of such. Everything he had done had been in his opinion in the service of his King. Poor Philippa, she had been humiliated, but she understood as well as he did.

'Get to your feet, John Copeland. Perhaps we shall from henceforth call you Sir John Copeland. You will return to England where you shall have lands to the value of five hundred pounds.'

'My lord . . .'

The King held up his hand. 'But we must placate the Queen. I doubt not that she was surprised when you would not give up the King of Scots to her. Take him to her. Give him into her hands and make your excuses as best you may. I believe she will accept them.'

'My gracious lord, I would I had the chance to die for you.'

'Ah,' said the King, 'who knows, some day I might even ask that. Now begone. I like well those who serve me with their hearts and if maybe there are times when they are mistaken in their acts then that is a small matter compared with good and honest loyalty.'

It was a very happy Sir John Copeland who returned to England and immediately delivered David of Scotland into the Queen's hands with muttered excuses which she kindly deigned to accept.

Smarting with humiliation David lay in the small chamber in the Copeland house. From one aspect it was fortunate for him that he was so badly wounded, for it prevented his brooding too bitterly on his position. Copeland's wife tended his wounds herself and he was too exhausted to protest.

Gradually they began to heal and by the time John Copeland arrived home flushed with the triumph of knighthood and new lands, it was decided that he should be taken to London. John Copeland himself made sure that the King of Scotland was securely guarded for, as he said to his wife, now that he was getting better who should say what tricks he would be up to.

The humiliation for David was bitter. Seated on a black horse, the son of Robert the Bruce was led through the city of London at the head of a procession of twenty thousand composed of the city companies in their state liveries and the people of London and those of the surrounding districts who rode with him.

He was the symbol of defeat. Now perhaps there would be peace on the Border, no more ravaging of English towns; no more threats from the unruly Scots. This was a day of rejoicing.

It was a pity the King was not there to see it. Nor was the Queen.

Edward had summoned her to join him in France and she had already gone.

Humiliation of humiliations he was taken before the council and there seated on the throne of state was the eight-year-old Prince Lionel, Duke of Clarence, to condemn him to his prison in the Tower.

His dream of riding triumphantly into London had been bitterly reversed.

Chapter XV

JILTED

Edward's reputation had been greatly enhanced after the Battle of Crécy and the Flemings having murdered Edward's friend Jacob van Arteveldt greatly feared his wrath and when he sent ambassadors into Ghent to discover the means and cause of the murder of Arteveldt their apprehension grew and they sought about for a means of placating him. Yes, they admitted, the murder had been committed and the reason was that the people had objected to van Arteveldt's seeking to depose the Earl of Flanders who was after all their true ruler. They knew that Edward had wished his son to become the Duke of Flanders but to attempt to enforce this was certain to mean bloodshed. Why should not the matter be amicably settled by the marriage of the new Earl of Flanders who had just succeeded to the title? They did not stress the fact that his father had been killed by the English at the Battle of Crécy. The new Earl was young, unmarried and would be an ideal bridegroom for the eldest daughter of the King of England.

This seemed to Edward an excellent idea. Much as he hated the thought of Isabella's marrying, he must not, he knew, shelve the matter altogether. If she married into Flanders they could meet often. He was constantly in Ghent and it would not be difficult for her to come to England.

Moreover the King of France was eager that Louis of Flanders should marry Margaret of Brabant which would mean an alliance favourable to France. Oh yes, Edward could see the advantages of this marriage. He wrote at once to Philippa. He was outside Calais where he would remain until that town had fallen into his hands. He told her that he was arranging a marriage for Isabella with the young Earl of Flanders. The burghers of Flanders were agreeable to the match for their prosperity depended upon England's supplying them with wool from which they wove their goods and without this concession their trade would suffer. Always eager to stimulate business the Flemings saw the point of this. They needed English wool; therefore young Louis should marry Isabella.

'Leave England without delay,' wrote the King. 'The Scots can give us no more trouble. We have their King thanks to you and the army at Neville's Cross. I am anxious that this marriage shall be made as quickly as possible before Philip is able to bind Louis to him through Margaret of Brabant.'

When she received the letter Philippa went at once to her daughter in the palace of the Tower and there told her that she must make ready for a journey.

The Princess Joanna, who was with her sister, listened apprehensively. Poor Joanna, she dreaded being sent to a bridegroom. She would never forget her unhappy experiences in Austria and feared that one day they would be repeated. She knew that negotiations were in progress to marry her to the son of the King of Castile and she lived in terror of hearing that she must prepare to leave for Spain.

Isabella felt quite different. She was so sure of herself, so certain that she was the most fascinating creature in the world that she had no doubt of her ability to charm anyone.

'Your father wants us to leave at once,' the Queen said. 'No, not you, Joanna. You will remain here with the others. Isabella is to be married to the Earl of Flanders.'

'Only an Earl!' cried Isabella, dismayed.

'My dear child, this is a most important marriage. Your father is most anxious for it. The Flemings have a great influence, particularly now when your father has to win his French crown. He is particularly anxious for this marriage because it means you will be within easy reach of him. There. That is what he said.'

Isabella was placated. 'I knew he would not want *me* to be too far away.'

'So now we shall make sure that you are properly provided for. I must see the seamstresses without delay.' Isabella was elated.

She was fourteen, old enough for marriage, and had supposed that a bridegroom would soon be found for her. She had expected a grander one it was true but it would be pleasant to be not too far from her father and she was sure that this Earl of Flanders must be overcome with delight at the prospect of marriage with the eldest daughter of the King of England.

So, in a state of great excitement she made her preparation. Inordinately vain of her appearance she revelled in the beautiful garments which were made for her, for she had inherited her father's love of finery, and she could scarcely wait for the journey to begin. With her she was taking a company of ladies of the Court, many of whom had husbands or sons serving in the King's army, so it was a time of happy reunion for them.

Edward welcomed them ashore and when he saw his daughter he was overcome with pride and emotion.

There would be great rejoicing in the camps throughout the temporary town Edward had built outside the walls of Calais, and if it seemed strange to rejoice and celebrate a betrothal at that spot when so near, within the walls of the city, the people were starving and were waiting anxiously for rescue, Isabella did not think of it.

She was the beloved daughter of the great King of England and her bridegroom elect would fall in love with her as soon as he set eyes on her. She was absolutely sure of that.

She might have been disturbed if she could have known the circumstances in which that bridegroom now found himself.

Having been brought up at the French Court, young Louis was in outlook a Frenchman, and Philip realising his importance as a pawn in the marriage market had always shown friendship towards him. Louis had enjoyed the elegance of the French Court which seemed to him so much more attractive than that of Flanders, and he thought like a Frenchman, dressed like a Frenchman and acted like one. The French King had sung the praises of Margaret of Brabant. Louis had met her and prompted by the wily Philip had found her a girl to his liking.

He would marry her, he promised himself; and indeed he had thought he would.

Then had come the battle of Crécy. Louis would never forget that day for he had ridden out with the French army beside his father, at whose side he had been when the English arrow had pierced the Earl's heart and it was in his son's arms that Louis the elder had died. He would never forget the agony on that once proud face; he would continue to hear the groans from those distorted lips; he tried not to think of the blood . . . his father's blood.

'Oh God,' he had cried, 'how I hate the English.'

He would always remember that it was an English archer who had robbed him of his father.

He was astounded when the representatives from the main towns of Flanders visited him and told him that they were in favour of a marriage with Isabella, daughter of the King of England.

'Marry the daughter of my father's murderer!' he cried aghast. 'You must be mad to suggest it. I never will.'

'My lord,' explained the burghers, 'a union with England will be good for Flanders. We need English wool if we are to keep our weavers working. The marriage is necessary to the prosperity of the country.'

'I have already agreed to marry Margaret of Brabant.'

'That is what the French want, but my lord, the English are more necessary to our country than are the French. This marriage with Isabella is important. She is a lively girl of considerable beauty. You will not be disappointed.'

Louis's eyes blazed with anger. 'I will not be forced into a marriage which is distasteful to me,' he said.

'My lord, my lord,' they cried, 'how can it be distasteful when you have not set eyes on the girl? She has a charm and beauty unsurpassable, so we have heard.'

'From her father doubtless. That murderer who comes here and tries to snatch the crown of France from its rightful owner!'

The burghers were dismayed. They feared trouble ahead. Louis must see reason.

'My lord,' said the leading burgher sternly, 'you should watch your words. If you arouse Edward's wrath this could be disaster for Flanders. You have become too much the Frenchman and it would be well for you to remember that that is not the country to which you owe allegiance.'

'I will hear no more of this,' said the young Earl haughtily. But the burghers had surrounded him almost menacingly.

'What means this?' cried Louis.

'It means, my lord, that you are not free to leave this castle.'

'What! You would make a prisoner of me!'

'Not a prisoner, my lord. You will be free to hunt and hawk. But there will be guards with you as we do not want you flying back to your friend, the King of France – who is no friend to your country. We Flemings must look to the English. We shall keep you here with us until you see reason and agree to a betrothal with Isabella of England.'

The Earl was furious with rage but he could see that he was in the hands of his subjects and he must bide his time. He must listen to their wearying diatribes. In the meantime he could enjoy his favourite sports.

But marry the daughter of his father's murderer, never!

Resentfully he submitted to the kind of luxurious captivity he was offered. But though he might enjoy the comforts to which he had been accustomed he was constantly aware of the irksome presence of guards. He realised that these had been selected with the greatest care. There was not one among them who could be seduced into plotting against those who held him. Every one of the men set to watch over him believed fervently in the need for alliance with England.

A few months passed in this way and then Louis capitulated.

He sent for the chief members of the Council and told them

that he had changed his mind. He would agree to a marriage with Isabella.

He was congratulated on his sound good sense. He would find the Princess a delightful creature. Everyone sang her praises. She was the most beautiful Princess in the world. He would never regret having shown such good sense.

Messengers were sent to Edward and it was at this stage that he told Philippa to bring his daughter to Calais.

It was a rather bleak March day when Isabella and Louis were brought face to face. The encounter took place at the monastery of Bergues and it was to be a very ceremonious occasion.

The highest ranking Flemings were in Louis's entourage and Edward could be relied upon to see that his daughter was surrounded by even greater pomp and glitter.

Edward said that before the meeting of the young people he would like to speak with Earl Louis alone and he received him in one of the apartments of the monastery.

An impressive figure at all times, Edward on this occasion was even more magnificent than usual. He wore his robes of state and he looked a mighty king, as he endeavoured to, for it was important to overawe Louis.

Louis however was not so easily overawed. He was a young man of some spirit and he was filled with a smouldering resentment against those who had forced him into this situation. Edward knew very well what great efforts had had to be made to get Louis to agree to the marriage and he applauded the boy's sentiments. His father had died in his arms on Crécy field and being a family man capable of sentiment, Edward understood Louis's feelings.

He came straight to the point. 'My lord Earl,' he said, 'I

wanted to speak to you first before the ceremonies because I wished to tell you with my own lips that I am guiltless of your father's death.'

'It was at Crécy,' murmured Louis with a hint of defiance.

'I know it. And that was a resounding victory for my armies. And there your father died. I did not know that he was with the French army. It was only when the battle was over that I learned of his death. I understand your feelings. I have children whom I love dearly and I know that had I died on the field of Crécy they would feel against the King of France as you do against me. I am guiltless of the death of your father. You must see this. Had I known that he was there, had I come across him in need of help, although he was on the side of my enemy, I would have spared his life. You must understand this, and bear me no grudge.'

But even as Louis looked at this man of commanding appearance he could think only of his father lying back in agony. He could only see the horrible blood . . . his father's blood.

Edward laid a hand on his shoulder. 'Let us forget, my dear lord, that your father and I were on opposing sides. Come, let me be the father you have lost. I swear to you that you will never regret it.'

Louis's eyes were glazed with emotion and the King moving towards him embraced him.

'All is well between us, my son,' said Edward. 'Now, let us talk of this wedding we are going to have.'

The Flemish nobles marvelled at the power and charm the King of England displayed in winning over their stubborn lord, for they had known that although he had given in to their wishes he had done so most reluctantly.

Isabella and her prospective bridegroom stood face to face. She was magnificently attired, a glittering Princess. She smiled at him, inviting his admiration.

The daughter of my father's murderer! he thought. How vain she is! Pretty enough, but why should I allow them to choose my bride for me?

Isabella thought: He is handsome. I like him. He must be thinking how beautiful I am and what a lucky man he is to have an alliance with England and . . . me.

They talked a little. He told her of Flanders. She did not listen very intently. She was eager to tell him about England and how she and her sister travelled about on occasions, and that she had three ladies-in-waiting while her sister had only two, that she was the eldest and her father was inclined to spoil her.

Indeed, thought Louis, that at least is obvious. The King and the Flemings looked on benignly. 'Methinks our happy pair are pleased with each other,' said Edward.

They were betrothed with great ceremony. The wedding itself must be a very grand affair. It would take place in two weeks time which, said the King, would give everyone time to prepare. He wanted it to be an occasion which all would remember.

Isabella left Bergues with her parents, and Louis returned to his captivity because, said some of the wily Flemish nobles, they knew their Prince to be of a stubborn nature and they being cautious men were determined that care should be maintained until that day when Isabella was truly Louis's wife.

Louis, seeing the day of his wedding coming nearer and nearer, decided to take a chance. He had become very friendly with two of his guards and he confided to them his misgivings about his future. He believed the Flemings were wrong, he hinted, in seeking this firm alliance with England. Did Edward think he was going to seize the crown of France? True there was Crécy but how much nearer to the crown had that brought him?

Louis reckoned that ere long they would see that the King of France would drive Edward out of his country and then what would happen to those who had supported Edward?

The guards liked to argue, and so forceful was Louis that he began to bring them round to his way of thinking. There came a day when they were ready to risk anything to please him and he began to plan.

It must of course be carried out with the utmost speed for there was only a week before the wedding was to take place. He was allowed to go hawking with his guards and it might be that they had grown a little lax now that there had been a formal betrothal to Isabella.

It was a simple plan. He would ride out with his guards and his falconer should release a heron. The two hawks would be sent after them. He would gallop off in the normal way but instead of following the way of the hawk he would go to a spot where the two guards had horses ready. He would change to the fleeter steed and they would ride with all speed to the Flemish frontiers.

It should not be impossible. In fact it seemed infallible.

Out he came with his guards and falconers. The heron was released as planned; he freed his horse and shouting to them he rode on . . . and on and on . . .

It was even simpler than he had thought. He had completely foiled them. They had believed he was sincere when he had promised to marry Isabella. What a surprise they would get!

Across the border he rode into the province of Artois and then on to Paris.

The King of France was highly amused at the exploit. He said he longed to hear what the effect would be on Edward when he heard of the absconding bridegroom.

Isabella could not believe it.

Jilted. She, Isabella, the most desirable of brides, the beautiful Princess, her father's darling!

The Queen had come to her to tell her the news.

'There will be no wedding,' she said.

Isabella listened incredulously. 'So he . . . ran away. He ran away from *me* . . .'

'It was not from you, my dear child,' said Philippa. 'It was from the marriage with England.'

'The . . . traitor,' cried Isabella. 'I hope he makes a disastrous marriage with his Margaret of Brabant.'

'It is as well you did not marry him,' replied her mother. 'I can only rejoice that he showed himself in his true colours *before* the wedding.'

The King came in. He took his daughter into his arms and held her tightly against him.

'My dearest child. This rogue . . . this *criminal* . . .' He could not speak coherently, so great was his rage. He cared more about the insult to his daughter than the loss of an alliance which would have been useful to him.

'He ran away from me!' said Isabella blankly.

'Not from you,' replied Edward. 'You must not think that.'

'I have explained to her,' replied Philippa. 'It is not Isabella he does not want. It is the alliance.'

'My dear child,' said Edward, 'we shall have entertainment outside Calais. We shall show everyone that we snap our fingers at this oaf.'

'Yes, Father,' said Isabella meekly.

She had already assured herself that he was not running away from her; she would dance gaily; she would show everyone she did not care that she had been jilted.

❀ Chapter XVI ❀

THE BURGHERS OF CALAIS

I t had been a fearful winter for the inhabitants of Calais. During all the bitterly cold months they had been attacked from without; arrows had rained into the town; the walls were constantly in need of repair lest there should be a breach which would let in the enemy. The greatest hardship was cold and hunger. Many of the inhabitants were dying of starvation, but they were determined to hold out. 'Succour will come,' said the people of Calais. 'Our King will not forget us.'

The siege of Calais was proving to be the most difficult operation of the war. The place was so well fortified. Its importance to the other side was evident. Edward believed that if he could take it it would not be long before his ambition was realised; Philip knew that to lose it would be a greater blow than the defeats at Helvoetsluys and Crécy.

Edward had sent word to England that he must have more supplies. He needed more ships to blockade the harbour for great hopes had arisen in the town when Philip had managed to get supplies in to the people.

That must never happen again, declared Edward and ordered the Earl of Warwick to keep command of the Channel.

For this purpose he had eighty ships under his command. Philip however must endeavour to reach his starving subjects and made an attempt to land forty-four ships most of them victuallers. But they were spotted by Warwick, and the Earls of Northampton and Pembroke were informed. Between them they succeeded in capturing some of the ships and sinking the others, so there was no relief for the starving citizens of Calais, and the town continued in extreme suffering. All the corn, meat and wine had long disappeared; they were living on cats, dogs and horses and even the supply of these was running out.

Philip must come to their aid.

He made preparations for the attack. He was growing very unpopular because he had taxed the people of France so heavily to pay for the war; and when he ordered a muster of troops many of the nobles showed a great reluctance to come forward.

Edward, meanwhile, had the support of his people. They were beginning to regard him as a king to be proud of. His magnificent appearance, his displays of grandeur, that special Plantagenet charm which had been his grandfather's and was perhaps even more apparent in him, the courage of his son and heir the Black Prince, the victor of Crécy – for Edward had had it proclaimed that that success was largely due to the skill and generalship of his beloved son – all this had made the English rally to their King and they were prepared to pay for a share in the glory he brought to England. They talked of Helvoetsluys and Crécy and they wanted to boast of Calais.

Therefore they were ready to pay for their King's war.

They despised the French. It was generally believed that the men were like women, that they spent a lot of time combing their hair, that their skins were pale unlike the healthy ruddy

Englishman's; they minced and simpered and their manner of speaking was more attuned to a lady's boudoir than to a battlefield. They were highly immoral and each man, however humble, had a dozen mistresses. They would soon be vanquished by the superior strength and virility of the English.

The French naturally despised the English. 'They are the dregs of men, the shame of the world and the least of all things,' they declared. They were barbarians; they ate great quantities of food and did not greatly care how it was cooked or served; they swilled ale instead of fine wines. What had cultivated Frenchmen to fear from such as these?

All through the winter and spring the wretched inhabitants waited for relief. The summer had come and the heat seemed worse than the cold.

They knew they could not hold out much longer when the cheering news came that Philip was on the march. He was bringing an army of two hundred thousand men to relieve them.

Edward awaited their arrival. Which way? he wondered. There were three routes Philip might take: By way of the dunes, by Gravelines or across the marches by way of the Bridge of Nieulay.

Edward made sure that whichever way Philip tried to take he should find it almost impassable.

They came by way of the sandhills and saw at once that it was impossible to get nearer than within a mile of the enemy. Edward had arranged his defences so skilfully that the only way for the French to approach the English was over the narrow Bridge of Nieulay which would mean they would fight against tremendous odds.

Philip had one recourse. He must ask Edward to come out into the open country and fight.

When Edward received this message he laughed aloud.

He told the messenger to go back to his master, Philip of Valois, who wrongfully kept him from his inheritance and tell him that he had been at the gates of Calais for the last year.

'Your master knew this well,' he went on. 'He should have come sooner, but he has allowed me to remain here and spend large sums of money on this venture. I am not ready to give way to his request now. If he and his army wish to pass this way he must find some other road, or he must come in and drive me out.'

The messengers returned to the King of France who, fuming with rage, saw that to attempt to oust Edward from the position in which he had ensconced himself would be certain defeat. How could they take that narrow bridge, defended as it was? It would be impossible. They would be mown down. It was suicide. And how otherwise approach the enemy?

There was only one course of action open to him, to go away and give up Calais.

He gave the order to be prepared to march at dawn. Before they left they would destroy their camp that it might not fall to the enemy.

When the citizens of Calais heard that their King had deserted them, when from the ramparts of the town they saw the flames of smoke of the burning tents, they knew the battle was lost.

It could only be a matter of hours before Calais was in the hands of the English.

Sir John de Vienne, the Governor of Calais, sent a messenger to Edward. Calais, he said, was ready to come to terms with the

King. The town should be surrendered to him if he would grant the lives of the garrison and the citizens.

When Edward received this message he burst into loud laughter.

'Go and tell your master that it is not for him to make terms,' he replied. 'Calais is mine for the taking.'

When the messenger had gone Edward's rage increased.

'They ask me this,' he cried. 'I have waited here for a very long time. I have expended much money on this siege. And now that it is over and they are surrendering as they should have done months ago, they talk of making terms with me! By God, I will show them that it is not for them to make terms. It is for them to obey orders. This is unconditional surrender.'

Philippa who was with him, replied that the men of Calais had defended their town as any citizen would. 'You would not, my lord, think highly of your own countryman who gave in immediately to the enemy.'

Edward growled: 'But to talk of terms! They will see.'

He sent for Sir Walter de Manny – one of his most trusted knights, and a native of Hainault who had come to England in the train of Philippa. He had proved himself completely loyal to both the King and the Queen and was a man of charm and courage, known for his chivalry and courtesy. Both the King and Queen were very fond of him.

'Well, Walter,' said Edward, 'at last Calais is ours. And the governor has had the insolence to send to me to make terms! Does that not make you smile? Yes, he would make *terms*. I am of a mind to put the whole town to the sword.'

De Manny was silent. He could see that he would have to speak with care. It was rarely that Edward allowed his temper to overrule his common sense; and de Manny knew that if he acted brutally now he would regret it later. Calais was the most important town in France strategically. It was in their hands and they must make the utmost use of it. This would not be done by putting its inhabitants to the sword.

'When I consider what taking this town has cost me . . . The months of waiting . . . building this town outside its walls . . . the constant stream of arms that has been poured into this venture . . . and then I am told *they* will consider terms.'

'A last defiant gesture, my lord, of men who have bravely defended their city through desperate months.'

'By God, Walter, you seem on their side.'

'My lord does not mean that, I know. But I cannot, nor could any man, do aught but respect them for their defence of the city which has cost you so dear. Lesser men would have given in long ago.'

'And saved me much expense.'

'And earned your scorn, my lord.'

Edward was silent. Walter de Manny was a wise man. He had often listened to him with profit.

'So . . .' he began, and waited.

De Manny said: 'A little mercy never did any leader any harm. They say that a touch of mercy indicates more than a touch of greatness.'

'By God, Walter, you would have me spare these people who have cost me so dear.'

'I would say set aside your wrath, my lord, and study what can best serve your cause.'

Edward was silent for a few seconds, then he said, 'Very well then, I will not put the town to the sword.'

De Manny's relief was obvious.

'But,' went on Edward, 'I will not allow these citizens to

imagine that they can defy me thus. Holding out for months! Costing me dear and when they give in, they expect to be treated as though they have been my good friends. No, I'll not have that, Walter. Now, you will go into the market place and there you will ask for six of their leading citizens. They shall come to me bare-headed, bare-footed, with ropes about their necks. They shall bring me the city's keys and then I shall hang them on their city's walls where they shall remain as a warning to all that it is unwise to stand against me.'

De Manny could see that it was no use trying to remonstrate with the King any further. That he had settled for six of the leading citizens instead of the whole town was a great concession. The King's temper was so uncertain as he contemplated what Calais had cost him, that it would be unwise to provoke it.

There was great consternation in the market place at Calais when Sir John de Vienne told the gathered crowd of Edward's demands.

'These six of our leading citizens,' he said, 'must go to the King of England in all humility, bare-footed, bare-headed, with ropes about their necks. They must take to him the keys of the city and after that they will be executed.'

There were groans of anguish in the market square but the richest of all the merchants, Eustache de St Pierre, immediately came forward. His son stood with him.

'Father,' he said, 'if you go, so shall I.'

Eustache tried to dissuade his son but the young man would not be persuaded and by that time four others had stepped forward.

'Six of us is a small price,' said the brave Eustache, 'when it could have been an entire town. If we do not offer ourselves all will be put to the sword. I have hope of grace and pardon from our Lord if I die to save my fellow citizens. I willingly give myself up to the mercy of the English King.'

The six men walked to the gates of the city taking with them the keys.

Sir Walter de Manny was waiting for them there.

Several of the women cried out to Sir Walter: 'My lord, save our men. Plead with the King for us.'

'That I will do,' answered Sir Walter.

Edward had arranged that there should be many witnesses of this scene and that it should be played to extract the utmost drama. He was attired in his splendid royal robes and a throne had been set up over which was a gold-fringed canopy.

Beside him were the Queen, the Black Prince and the ladies who had come in Isabella's train.

The six burghers, showing signs of their recent ordeal, gaunt with starvation, haggard with their suffering made a sad contrast to the splendour of the royal party.

They knelt before the King, Eustache de St Pierre proferring the keys of the city.

He spoke for the six men.

'Most gracious King,' he said, 'we are at the mercy of your absolute will and pleasure in order that we may save the rest of our people. They have suffered great distress and misery. I beg of you to take pity on us for the sake of your high nobleness.'

There was a deep silence among the spectators. There was hardly anyone there who was not moved by the sight of these men – the evidence of their suffering on their faces; the wretchedness of their appearance somehow lending them a dignity which the great King in all his finery could not match.

Edward frowned at them. He could not stop calculating what the siege of Calais had cost him. He thought of the

Scottish insurrection which might so easily have brought disaster to England. And it was Calais which had drained him of his money, taken his time and caused him such anxiety as he had rarely known throughout his reign.

No, he would not forgive Calais and these six richest and most influential of its burghers should die.

'Take them away,' he cried, 'and cut off their heads.'

De Manny murmured: 'My lord, show your clemency to these men. It will be good for your cause.'

'Be quiet, Master Walter,' muttered the King. 'It cannot be otherwise. Send for the headman . . . *now*.'

Philippa then rose from her chair and went down on her knees before the King.

'My lord,' she said, 'I have crossed the sea in some peril to come to you and I have asked no favours of you. But now I ask one. For the love of our Lady's Son and as proof of your love for me, have mercy on these six men.'

Edward looked at her intently; she began to weep silently and there was such unhappiness apparent in her attitude that he said gently: 'Rise, Philippa. I would that you were not here this day. This town of Calais has cost me dear and I would have it known that there shall be no mercy for those who flout me.'

'My lord, if you love me,' went on Philippa, 'you will grant me this. It is all I ask. Give me this and I shall be content having such sign of your love for me.'

'Do you need this sign, lady?'

She lifted her eyes to his and nodded.

He said: 'You entreat me in such way that you make it impossible for me to refuse. I say this against my will. Take these men. I give them to you.'

A great silence fell on the crowd as Philippa kissed the

King's hand. Then she rose to her feet and going to the six brave men of Calais she ordered that the ropes be taken from their necks.

She signed to one of the guards and told him to take them to her apartments, where clothes and food should be given to them. She would like to make them a present too for she greatly admired their courage. Let them have six nobles apiece and then they should be allowed to go through the gates of Calais to their homes.

Everyone who had witnessed these scenes outside the walls and those within who were soon to hear of it, would talk of it for as long as they lived. The people of Calais would tell their children of the day the six brave burghers who had left with ropes about their necks going as they believed to certain death, came walking through the gates free men – all due to the goodness of Queen Philippa and her dreaded husband's love for her.

Edward was not as displeased as he had appeared to be and was glad that the burghers had not been put to death. As soon as his rage had subsided he had begun to consider how he could best use his latest conquest.

It was certainly not going to be through cruelty.

Calais was worth everything it had cost him and he was determined that it should remain in his hands. The burghers, after his clemency, inclined towards him for Philip had now shown himself to them very unfavourably when he had failed to relieve them.

He immediately ordered that food should be sent into the town and the people fed. In fact so ravenously did they fall upon the provisions he supplied that some of them died through overeating after coming near to death by starvation. The burghers were ready to serve him now, for a King who showed mercy in conquest was a great King, it seemed to them.

Edward and Philippa rode through the town to fanfares of trumpets and the people came out to gaze on the lady whom they had come to revere.

Edward immediately set about making ready in case Philip should decide to attack the town in the hope of regaining it. He was pleased when a truce of nine months was arranged. So he garrisoned the town and confident that the people of Calais regarded him as a more reliable ruler than the French King, he sailed for England.

Chapter XVII

THE BLACK DEATH

O n their return to England Philippa gave birth once more. This time it was a boy whom they called William. Alas, it seemed an ill-fated name for the child died very soon after his birth.

Edward comforted Philippa and begged her to look to their strong and healthy children – Edward, Lionel, John and Edmund; and there were the dear girls – his beloved Isabella, Joanna, Mary and Margaret. They could not complain. It was true they had lost that other William and little Blanche, but God had blessed them in their children.

Philippa had to admit that this was true but while she delighted in her living children she could not stop mourning those whom she had lost.

Moreover there came a time when a queen must face the parting with her daughters. If Isabella had married Louis of Flanders she would have been not so very far away. But that had come to nothing and Philippa guessed that Edward was not displeased, and Isabella was only so because she thought that the manner in which Louis had decamped *after* he had seen her was a slur on her alluring attractions which her father had led her to believe were irresistible.

It was now Joanna's turn. Poor Joanna. If Philippa could be said to have favourites among her children Joanna was the best loved among the girls. She could not help doting on her magnificent first-born and she shared the general delight which amounted almost to reverence in the Black Prince, but it was Joanna who had the deepest love. She had never forgotten the terrible time the child had endured in Austria. Ever since Philippa had been trying to make up to her for that.

Now, as Edward pointed out, it was time that she married and although he hated to lose his daughter he was irritated by the prevarication of the Spaniards.

The delay was, the King suspected, brought about by Eleanora de Guzman, the mistress of the King of Spain. She was the most powerful woman at the Court for the King doted on her and she had already borne him three children. Her great hope was that the King's son Pedro – whom Edward had decided should be Joanna's husband – would either die or not have children so that one of her sons could inherit. It was for this reason that she was far from eager to see a marriage between Joanna and Pedro and she was contriving to delay matters.

But even the powerful Eleanora could not prevent indefinitely the marriage of the King's son.

The Joanna who prepared for her journey to Spain and marriage was different from the little girl who had gone to Austria. She was at this time in her fourteenth year and had known for some time that sooner or later she should have to leave home. She had seen Isabella return from Flanders and had heard the story of Louis's hasty departure. And here was Isabella back in London. So marriages were not to be considered definite until they actually took place. Anything

345

could happen to prevent them right at the last moment. She considered Isabella – only a week from taking her final vows!

In the meantime she must prepare herself for Spain.

Philippa was uneasy. She could imagine the intrigues of the Spanish court with the doting King and his mistress who wanted to see her son Henry of Trastamarre on the throne. She wondered how her Joanna would fare in such an atmosphere. Her children had lived a happy life which was rare in royal circles. She herself had enjoyed such a life in Hainault but how different Edward's childhood had been! Sometimes she wondered whether a pleasant and secure childhood helped a child to face the world.

Perhaps she had not done so badly; but then she had married the man whom she loved on sight and Edward was a remarkable man; he was a good father although inclined to spoil his daughters; he was a loving husband although at times his eyes strayed to other women. But he was anxious to be a faithful husband and she believed that he was.

But now for Joanna. She must prepare to leave for Spain and Philippa prayed every night for the child's happiness. She had heard uneasy rumours not only of the intrigues of Eleanora de Guzman but of signs of cruelty in young Pedro. It was said that he liked inflicting pain on animals and, if he could manage it, on his fellow human beings. Was it really true? One heard so much that was false. Oh yes, she prayed constantly for Joanna.

Joanna was resigned to the fact that she would soon be sailing. Isabella was a little jealous. With envy she fingered the robe of tissue of gold with matching mantle and sur-tunic which was for Joanna's wedding. Isabella liked all the attention and the fine clothes to be for herself.

'How fine you will look!' she cried caressing the gowns of

scarlet purple and velvet, the ermines and zones adorned with beautiful jewels. 'But,' she went on, 'I would rather be at home. I am glad I didn't marry into Flanders.'

'I would rather be home too,' said Joanna wistfully.

'You will be a Queen though – Queen of Castile. Think of that!'

But the thought did not give Joanna any great joy.

'I never thought Louis of Flanders was good enough for me,' went on Isabella. 'I'll swear that I shall have a king for a husband, one day.'

Joanna turned away and took up her embroidering. It gave her great comfort. As she stitched at it she revelled in the beautiful coloured silks and thought of the happy days she had had in the heart of her family.

In January she set out on her journey. The King, the Queen and her sister Isabella accompanied her from the Palace of Westminster as far as Mortlake. There they took a last farewell and both the King and Queen were overcome with their emotion. It seemed to the Queen that Isabella could always look after herself but Joanna was more vulnerable.

The Princess continued her journey across the country to Plymouth, the port from which she was to set sail.

There followed a stay of five weeks in the town, for the wind was such as to make the sea-crossing dangerous and it was the middle of March before Joanna and her entourage left England.

Seven days later she reached Bordeaux. It was necessary to remain there while negotiations went on between the Courts of Spain and England, for Edward was very suspicious of a Court which was under the spell of such an ambitious woman as Eleanora de Guzman. So eager was she to prevent a child being born who could oust her son that she was using every means she knew to delay the marriage. She was trying to persuade Alfonso to choose a different bride for his son. On the other hand the Queen of Castile, who was as eager to outwit her husband's mistress as the mistress was to put her own son on the throne, was anxious to bring about the union with England. Between the two Alfonso appeared to have no will of his own.

Edward was determined that Joanna should not go into Spain until everything was signed and sealed and there was no question of a marriage between his daughter and the heir to Castile being postponed or stopped altogether.

He had had one daughter jilted. He was not going to allow this to happen to another.

It was therefore necessary for Joanna to remain in Bordeaux until the King was perfectly satisfied that her marriage would take place.

The castle was set in very pleasant surroundings; from her windows Joanna could look out to wooded hills and vineyards and after the cold months in Plymouth and the sea-crossing she was not displeased to remain awhile in this pleasant spot. She would sit with her women while she worked with her needle and as she derived great pleasure from this occupation she was not unhappy.

If the negotiations took a year she would not mind. She was not by any means looking forward to continuing her journey.

So she and her women sat and talked and one day while they were at this pleasant pastime one of them said: 'I heard yesterday that a terrible disease is spreading across Europe. It started in Constantinople and is quickly coming to the sea ports.'

'There are always these stories,' said Joanna placidly.

'True my lady, but they did say that this is the most terrible that has ever been seen before.'

'Strange things happen in far away places,' said another.

'I like this blue silk,' said Joanna. 'But perhaps it is not quite the right shade. What think you?'

The ladies put their heads together and concerned themselves with the selection of blue silk.

It was not long before the whole world was talking in terror of the fearful pestilence which had passed by way of Armenia into Asia Minor to Egypt and North Africa; this had started in the east and as it passed from country to country it left behind a trail of horror and death.

People talked of it in hushed whispers and prayed that it would never come their way but each day brought accounts of death creeping nearer. It had reached Greece and Italy and was still creeping on.

It seemed that once a man or woman noticed the first symptoms – a discoloured swelling beneath the armpits – he or she was doomed and only a miracle could save them. Those who were afflicted were not left long in doubt. In a matter of hours more swellings would occur and the victims would cough blood, suffer from violent thirst before they mercifully fell into a coma after which death quickly followed. The only merciful aspect in this dreaded pestilence was the speed with which victims died. It had an unpleasant aftermath for no sooner was the sufferer dead than black patches would appear on the skin and the odour which emanated from the corpse would be suffocatingly obnoxious. This in itself would pass on the infection. Animals died from it; it was highly infectious and devastatingly contagious. And as it became increasingly difficult to dispose of the bodies, the disease spread with alarming rapidity. Once it came to a village or a town that place was doomed.

The plague was talked of all over Europe, for the fact that it had reached Greece and Italy sobered many people.

Edward assured Philippa that it could not come to England. The water would save them. He was flushed with victory at this time. He had Helvoetsluys and Crécy behind him and now Calais. He could afford to sit back and contemplate his successes.

His love of display did not diminish as he grew older. He wanted more Round Table tournaments, more jousting in which he could show himself as the champion of his people.

There was nothing he loved more than to sit under the royal canopy with his Queen and their children and watch the jousting. Better still he liked to take part in it, and to show himself as the champion.

How they cheered him. His people loved him. The way had not been difficult for him. He had followed a king who had earned the revulsion of his people and his reign was not so long ago so that many of them could remember how a country suffered through an unworthy King. Even his grandfather Edward the First had never been quite so popular. This vain trait in Edward which made him long for splendid show and entertainments appealed to his people for they shared in them; and to see their King looking exactly as they believed a king should look and to have him winning great victories over the French pleased them. They were content with their Edward.

At this time, he told Philippa he was going to create an order which he would bestow on only a few knights who were worthy of it. The idea had been in his mind since the victory of Crécy when certain of his subjects had distinguished themselves by their selfless service to their country.

He believed there should be some recognition for such people and he was brooding on the matter.

Meanwhile there must be more tournaments, more Court festivities, to remind the people that all was going well with their King and country. His victories in France needed celebrating and he had been so long before Calais he should show his people how pleased he was to be home among them. He wanted to see gallant knights and beautiful ladies dancing together.

The most beautiful of all the ladies at Court was Joan, known as the Fair Maid of Kent.

She was now nineteen years of age at the height of her beauty. She was more or less betrothed to William Earl of Salisbury but was very friendly with Sir Thomas Holland and the Prince of Wales was clearly not indifferent to her. The Black Prince was two years younger than Joan but it was noted that although he seemed friendly with her he would ignore her for long periods of time and this did not please the Court's leading beauty.

She was royal, her father having been the son of Edward the First, and although princes often had to marry into different countries to consolidate alliances, if the Black Prince had really wanted to marry his kinswoman it seemed hardly likely that Edward and Philippa — always indulgent where their children were concerned — would not have allowed the marriage to take place.

However there was no mention of it and the Black Prince, although he was clearly attracted by the beautiful Joan and often referred to her as 'Little Jeanette', did not show any sign of wishing to marry her. It was true he was only seventeen years of age but that was old enough to marry and rumour had it that he was not a virgin.

Joan was a clever girl as well as a beautiful one. She was greatly attracted by Thomas Holland who could offer her the least; she did not greatly care for Salisbury; and she liked the Prince of Wales. If the latter had suggested marriage she would have put aside the other two at once, for naturally she would have been delighted at the prospect of becoming the Queen of England in due course.

Everyone expected her to marry Salisbury as she had been contracted to him in her youth; but of course if the Prince of Wales wanted to marry her a dispensation could easily be acquired.

Courted as she was by the ardent Holland and Salisbury she was extremely put out by the indifferent conduct of the Prince. She was of a passionate nature and she quickly realised that she was not the sort to wait indefinitely in the hope of catching the big fish. She was a woman who would have to content herself with the lesser catch.

Thomas Holland had been with her in one of her moments of pique. He had declared his undying affection for her and embraced her in a most familiar manner to which it was quite obvious she was not averse. Indeed the dashing Thomas aroused in her emotions which for all her ambition she found it impossible to control.

It was unthinkable that a lady of her royalty should become his mistress so, having succumbed to him and found the experience very much to her liking, she had agreed to a secret marriage and when she came to Court to partake in the royal festivities she was in fact already married to Sir Thomas Holland.

Sir Thomas had been obliged to leave her soon after the ceremony to go to France and he was still there among those who were guarding Calais for the King.

Joan was therefore receiving the attentions of Salisbury and now and then catching the eye of the Prince of Wales who was so warm and friendly one day and the next seemed to have forgotten her existence.

The King had on several occasions asked her to sit beside him and it was becoming clear that he had great admiration for her. So had many others and she was used to admiration but she was certainly gratified to receive it from such a quarter. The possibility of becoming Queen of England had often occurred to Joan but it would not of course be through Edward the King. She was not prepared to be a royal mistress – not that it would have got so far with Edward. She had heard rumours about the Countess of Salisbury whom she had known very well – she had at one time resided with her because it had been planned that that very beautiful and most virtuous lady should be her mother-in-law – and that affair had come to nothing. Edward, thought Joan cynically, had been unwise to choose such a virtuous woman as the Countess, but of course Catharine de Montacute was an exceptionally beautiful creature. Old though, thought Joan complacently.

And the Queen had never been handsome. She was fresh-complexioned with a pleasant expression, that was all; and now constant child-bearing had spoilt her figure and she was really far too portly.

Joan revelled in the admiration of those about her and particularly that of the King and then there was of course

William the Earl of Salisbury who really believed she was still betrothed to him.

What a tangle her affairs had got into. She wondered what Salisbury would say if he knew that she and Thomas had already lived together.

Meanwhile she would snap her fingers at the future while she tried to captivate the Black Prince rather than his father. The Prince was the one who could put a crown on her head. But what about Thomas? She would arrange something when the time came. When the time came! What a strange man the Prince was. He did not seem as though he wanted to entangle himself in marriage – though as heir to the throne he must think of giving the country a future king.

Sometimes Joan felt furious with herself for having given way to Thomas. What she could lose by it! Oh, but she was clever. She would wriggle out of that if she needed to. How did one wriggle out of a marriage contract? There was such a thing as divorce and dispensation from the Pope. She was sure it could be managed. The real obstacle was the indifference of that laggardly lover the Black Prince.

Edward the King was in his element. The Round Tower which he had built at Windsor was the ideal place in which to hold his Round Table. He had had it built on an artificial mound surrounded by a deep fosse. The interior was approached by a flight of one hundred steps and there were more steps up to the battlements of the Keep. It was a most impressive sight and Edward was proud of it.

He allowed David of Scotland to join the revelry. David was his prisoner and would remain so until the enormous ransom Edward was demanding was paid. Edward had deliberately fixed it so highly because he knew that only while David was his prisoner could he be sure of peace in Scotland. However David was royal; he was his brother-in-law and a King. Edward wanted him to have all the amenities possible except complete freedom. David was at liberty to hunt and hawk in the forests but he was always surrounded by guards. He seemed to have become accustomed to being an exile from his country and as he lived in comfort he did not find this irksome. He had been in France for seven years, had reigned in Scotland for five and had at this time been for nearly two years the prisoner of Edward. He saw no sign of that captivity ending for he knew the money for his release could not be raised.

He did not bemoan his fate. He did not lack luxury. He was the guest one might say of the King of England and if he were allowed to partake in such festivities as these now proceeding at the Round Tower of Windsor, he would not complain too bitterly.

He enjoyed the jousting and the feasting, the dancing and the music.

Moreover he had several mistresses. He was a deeply sensuous man and the virtuous Joanna to whom they had married him was not cast in a mould to please him. Often he chose his women from the more lowly classes. He took great pleasure in them.

At the joust he met a woman to whom he felt immediately attracted. Her name was Katherine Mortimer; she was voluptuous, beautiful and experienced.

They were together through the days and nights of the tournament.

It had been a day of brilliant jousting. The King was in an excellent mood. He gave himself up completely to the banquet and the ball. He seemed to have forgotten that there was merely a lull in the fight for the crown of France; he gave no thought to the terrible pestilence which even as he and his guests danced crept nearer and nearer.

If Philippa thought of these things she tried not to show it. Edward so much enjoyed them and as she watched him indulging in his pleasure she was tender towards him as she was towards Isabella who sat with her parents, splendid in her glittering garments, so very pleased to be with them – which was good for Philippa had feared that a proud girl like Isabella might have taken her jilting to heart.

Of course there were occasional whispers about the King's roving eye. Philippa herself knew that he took a great delight in beautiful women. She had seen his eyes follow them and they seemed to take on a deeper blue as he did so. She knew of the Countess of Salisbury. Good Catharine de Montacute whose sound sense had brought the King back to his. Poor Catharine she was ailing, Philippa had heard; she never came to Court, nor had she since that affair which had been followed so soon by the death of her husband.

No doubt she had deemed it wise – and indeed so it had proved.

And now there was the willowy enchanting girl – Joan of Kent. Romantic because of her father's cruel murder and royal too, and the most beautiful girl at Court. It was small wonder that Edward should take pleasure in looking at her, for she was indeed an enchanting sight and would have been as outstanding in this assembly among the magnificently attired ladies if she had been clad as a goose girl.

Edward was dancing with her and suddenly there was consternation for lying on the floor at the feet of Joan of Kent was her garter.

There was a sudden titter throughout the hall. Joan flushed slightly. Joan was not the most modest of ladies and the assumption could not be dismissed that she had deliberately dropped the garter. Could it really be an invitation to the King?

Philippa thought: How foolish! As if she would do it that way if it were.

Edward had picked up the garter. He held it in his hands almost caressingly then he looked round the room and caught the expressions on the faces of many who were watching.

For a few seconds there was silence. Then the King attached the Garter to his own knee and in a loud ringing voice he said: 'Evil be to him who evil thinks.'

He took Joan's hand and the dance continued. When it was over he addressed the company and said:

'You have seen the garter and I shall now do honour to it. The garter is an old symbol of honour in the chivalry of our land. My great ancestor, Richard Coeur de Lion, ordered the bravest of his knights to wear it at the storming of Acre. Those knights excelled in valour and bravery and they became known as the Knights of the Blue Thong. It is a story which is handed down in the annals of chivalry. Now I shall name my new order the Order of the Garter and because it is an intimate article of apparel and I have seen such looks upon your faces which please me not, there shall be a motto writ on the garter and this shall be *"Honi soit qui mal y pense."* This honour shall be the highest in English knighthood and there shall be no more than twenty-five knights of the Garter excepting members of my family and illustrious foreigners.'

There was loud applause and the King was engrossed for days after deciding how the order should be presented and of what it should consist.

It was decided that the installations should take place in the Chapel at Windsor and that the badge of the Order should be a gold medallion representing St George and the Dragon suspended on a blue ribbon. The garter should be of dark blue velvet and worn on the left leg just below the knee. Chief of all was the inscription.

And the revelries of the Round Tower were remembered from then on not because of the champions of the joust or the great feasting that had ensued but because the Fair Maid of Kent had dropped her garter at the King's feet and so established the finest order of chivalry.

While the Court was revelling in its pleasure, tragedy was preparing to strike the Royal family.

The Princess Joanna was awaiting the summons to leave Bordeaux for Castile; she expected this every day and suffered a certain apprehension. She had already learned what it felt to be far away from home, to miss her family, to find that there was not the same warmth to be expected from others as there had been from her beloved parents.

Sometimes she heard her women whispering and she knew it was of her future husband. Every night she used to pray that she would not have to go to Castile. Something would happen as it had in Austria and she would be returned to her parents.

Marriage sometimes seemed to be elusive. Look what had happened to Isabella. She had been within a week of becoming a bride and her future husband had run away. There was a hope, of course, that some obstacle would prevent her own marriage. She had heard that there were people at the Court there who did not want her.

Perhaps this time next year I shall be back in Windsor, she thought wistfully.

She found great comfort in her needlework. How soothing it was to watch the silken pictures grow. She loved the soft colours and chose them with care. Her women liked to work with her and they talked as they worked.

They were all happy here in Bordeaux; the trees were so beautiful during the summer months and they had watched them bud and blossom. Joanna said that she would like to embroider a picture of the scene from the castle window so that when she looked at it, when she was an old woman, she would remember the time she had spent in this enchanting spot.

'One day,' she said, 'I shall look out of this window and see messengers arriving. They will bring commands from my father. Then I shall leave here and this period will be over . . .'

'You must not be sad, my lady,' replied one of her women. 'You will become a great lady.'

She did not answer. A shiver ran through her. If it had not been for her experiences in Austria she might have been hopeful. She thought of Isabella's going to her marriage. How excited she had been. But then she had been quite happy to return home.

A messenger had come to the castle. Joanna was aware of a certain activity below. Almost immediately one of the attendants appeared.

'My ladies, you must prepare to leave at once. The plague has come to Bordeaux.'

With a few of her women Joanna left the castle for the little village of Loremo.

It had been decided that villages were safer than towns and in any case Bordeaux would be a stricken city in less than a week.

The ladies were subdued. They thanked God for their escape. They tried to settle to their needlework but all the time they were thinking of the dreaded pestilence which people were beginning to call the Black Death because the victims were covered in big putrefying black spots which continued after their death.

It was not easy to work on these beautiful silks and not see the horrors of reality. People stricken with the disease died so quickly that those who remained were unable to bury them and they had to be thrown into pits. To come within sight of a person dead of the plague was the height of danger.

Thank God, said her women, that we had good warning and left Bordeaux.

But one day when Joanna sat over her embroidery a certain lassitude came over her. The brilliant blue of her silk turned dark; the tapestry receded and slipped from her hands.

Her women were bending over her. She heard the voices that seemed to come from far away.

'Our lady is unwell.'

Then the piercing cry: 'Oh, God in Heaven, it cannot be. Oh no . . . no . . . It must not be.'

They carried her to her bed. They stared at her in horror for there was blood on her lips and the black patches were beginning to form.

The plague had come to the village of Loremo and its first victim was the Princess Joanna.

Philippa was overcome with grief when the news reached her. She shut herself into her chamber that she might be alone with sorrow.

Her little daughter, her beloved Joanna who had always been so loving and affectionate . . . dead. She had been uneasy about her for she had heard whispers of the nature of the young man who was to be her husband and young though he was, she had heard people were beginning to speak of him as Pedro the Cruel. Joanna had suffered enough in her very early childhood when she had been sent to Austria. Poor Joanna, she seemed ill fated. Something told Philippa that the child would be better dead than the wife of Pedro the Cruel.

But perhaps she was merely trying to comfort herself.

Edward came to her and they mourned together. Edward loved his children as devotedly as she did and he had a special love for his girls. Joanna had never been quite such a favourite with him as Isabella but he had loved Joanna dearly and her death had shaken him deeply.

'We must remember that we have others, my love,' he told her. 'We have been singularly blessed in our family.'

She bowed her head. It was true. They had their family. She had been a fruitful wife to Edward and she was glad of that. Edward was thinking the same thing as he put his arm about her.

Dear Philippa who had been so unswervingly good to him. He loved her dearly but he was finding that his attention was being attracted more and more by younger women.

The constant child-bearing had made its mark on the Queen. She was becoming so plump that she was finding it less easy to move about. In the past she had been at his side whenever possible. Now there were occasions when she was unable to make long journeys.

He had always been a man of strong desires and they did not diminish because he was getting older and his good wife was no longer young. He loved Philippa; he was grateful for Philippa; he would have chosen no other if he could do that now. She was his dear wife and the mother of his children; but that did not prevent his attention straying to other women.

He believed in the sanctity of marriage; he wanted to be a faithful husband; but even though he was no longer young, he was as virile as ever. He was outstandingly good-looking; he was undoubtedly the leader of any gathering he happened to be in; his love of magnificence only added to his attractiveness; and of course there was the aura of royalty. It did not make it any easier for him to suppress his natural desires when it was clear that there would be little opposition from the objects of them.

He was gentle and tender with Philippa, the more so because of these faithless thoughts which were becoming more and more difficult to suppress.

But in a week or so after the news of Joanna's death there was little time or inclination to think of anything but the terrible affliction.

The Black Death had come to England. It first attacked in the west of the country on the coast of Dorset, brought by a sailor from the Continent. It spread rapidly and in a week had come as far as Bristol. It was only a matter of time before it reached London.

The capital provided the perfect conditions in which it could flourish. The overcrowded houses and streets, the filthy gutters infested by rats, were the best breeding ground possible.

There was no one to look after the sufferers. They were left to die and their foul-smelling corpses gave off such offensive odours that to come near them meant almost certain death.

People sought to escape from the crowded towns and the roads were full of men and children taking with them all they could carry on packhorses and donkeys. Some remained to do what they could and it was agreed that the bodies must be buried. Sir Walter de Manny then bought a piece of ground called Spittle Croft because it had belonged to the masters and brethren of St Bartholomew's Spittle. It consisted of about thirteen acres. Pits were dug here and the dead buried. Within a year it was rumoured that fifty thousand bodies lay there. It was enclosed by a high stone wall to shut in the pestilence which continued to rage through England.

It seemed to many that the end of man was in sight. 'This is God's revenge on mankind,' said the pious. Towns were deserted; hamlets lost every one of their inhabitants; ships floated aimlessly along the coast until a storm carried them off for ever; the reason was that every member of their crews had succumbed to the plague.

Frightened people looked round for scapegoats and as was customary in such cases on the Continent the Jews were blamed. It was said that they had poisoned the wells and springs with concoctions of their own distillation from spiders, owls and other such venomous animals. Many were tortured and as was to be expected in cases of extreme agony confessed to what was wanted.

Some more discerning people had discovered that it was the ships which carried the plague from one place to another because it always appeared first in the ports; but none realised that the carriers of the disease were the rats which were infested with vermin. In due course the traffic between countries was so slight because of the diminished world population that the plague began to disappear.

But the prosperity which had existed in the country was no more. There was no one to till the fields. Labourers were so scarce that they demanded higher wages. There would be inevitable famine and even though the population was decreased there would not be enough corn to meet its needs.

The belief that doom was staring them in the face had different effects on certain people. Some lived riotously indulging in sexual activities with an almost pious air because as they said it was necessary to be fruitful and replenish the earth as soon as possible. To Hungary and Germany came religious fanatics who called themselves the Brethren of the Cross. When they came to England they were known as the Flagellants. They declared that they would take upon themselves the sins of the people which had brought Divine vengeance on the world in the form of the plague. They marched through the streets in dark robes with red crosses on the front of them and on the black caps they wore. They carried scourges tied in knots with points of iron fixed on them. People flocked to hear them preach and to follow them. They were forbidden to have anything to do with women and if they did and were caught were sentenced to several lashes of the scourge.

Every day at an agreed hour they marched through the streets, when they threw off their robes so that the top half of their bodies were naked and they whipped each other as they went along. When they reached a certain spot they lay down one by one, each man before he lay giving the one who had lain before him a lash from his whip.

People watched them in awe, many joined them for it seemed to be a noble thing to take on the sins of the world. Some said that the plague was subsiding due to their efforts.

Edward, thankful that he and his family had escaped the pestilence – apart from Joanna – gave himself up to restoring the prosperity to the country.

He saw that it was impossible to pay the labourers the wages they were now demanding and the fields must be tilled; work must continue and because there were fewer people to perform these tasks it would be disastrous to the country if the high wages they were demanding were to be paid.

He acted promptly and brought in the Statute of Labourers.

In this it was laid out that:

'Because a great part of the people and especially workmen and servants have died of the pestilence, many, seeing the necessity of masters and great scarcity of servants will not serve unless they receive excessive wages and some are rather willing to live in idleness rather than labour to get their living; we, considering the grievous incommodities which a lack of ploughmen and such labourers has brought on us ordain:

'That every man and woman of our realm in England of what condition he be and within the age of three score years, not exercising any craft, be bounded to serve him which shall require him; and take only the wages which was accustomed to be given in such places . . .

'That saddlers, skinners, cordwainers, tailors, smiths, carpenters, masons, tilers, shipwrights and carters and all other workmen shall not take their labour above the same that was wont to be paid; and if any take more he shall be committed to gaol.

'That butchers, fishmongers, hostellers, brewers and other sellers of victuals shall be bound to sell the same for a reasonable price so that the sellers have moderate gains but not excessive.'

Gradually the country settled down to its normal routine. The greatly depleted population striving to make it the prosperous country it had been before the plague had struck.

Many children were born during the following months and this was taken as a sign that God's anger was appeased. The Flagellants swore that they were responsible and went about the streets beating themselves in ecstasy.

But with the plague fading away and so much work to be done, the people lost interest in the Brothers of the Cross.

They were now anxious to return to prosperity. They noticed that many women bore twins and more frequently than ever before some of them produced triplets.

'The bad times are over,' declared the people. 'God is smiling on us again.'

❈ Chapter XVIII ❈

THE PRIDE OF ISABELLA

The King was disturbed to receive a letter from his sister Joanna the Queen of Scotland. When he had last seen her he had been sixteen and she a child of seven. He had been very sorry for her, being sent off to marriage in Scotland which was by all accounts a dour and wild country.

He immediately went to Philippa to tell her of what Joanna proposed.

'She wants a safe conduct to England,' he said. 'You can guess what she seeks.'

Philippa nodded. 'A pardon for her husband. What will your answer be?'

'No,' replied Edward shortly. 'Soon I shall have to go into France again. It would be folly to give the Scots a rallying point in their King.'

'But you have no great opinion of David.'

'David!' the King laughed. 'Who would believe that laggard was the son of Robert the Bruce!'

He paused frowning. Who would believe that he was the son of his dissolute father? Great fathers sometimes had weak sons and weak fathers great sons. He was assured that the King who followed him would be a great one. The Black Prince, already the idol of the people, a man who had proved himself in war as a leader of men. I shall die happy, thought Edward. It was time the Prince married though.

Philippa said: 'Poor Joanna, I do not think she will ever be happy with him. It is common knowledge that he is a rake.'

'He seems to have settled down with Katherine Mortimer,' replied Edward.

'The woman lives with him, I believe. He is treated well as a prisoner.'

'He is a King and I would not deny him his paramour. No, I shall not listen to Joanna's pleas. It is better for her husband to remain in this happy captivity here than to return to Scotland and gather an army about him.'

'Do you think that is truly so?'

'I do, my love. But I cannot refuse Joanna a safe conduct.'

'Perhaps when she comes she will plead so earnestly . . .'

Edward shook his head and Philippa smiled. None could be more firm than Edward when he had made up his mind. She herself felt a great interest in the matter because it was when she was regent that David had been captured at Neville's Cross.

Edward changed the subject. 'It is time our son married. Why think you he delays so long?'

Philippa was thoughtful. She did not understand this son whom she adored perhaps more than anyone else, even Edward. Her Black Prince was a hero in every sense. His handsome looks, his valour, his prowess on the battlefield, were undeniable. People called him the victor of Crécy – and that had happened when he was little more than a boy. She had shivered when she heard how his father would not send anyone to his aid because he wanted young Edward to win glory that day. He might have been killed. But he had won his spurs indeed.

There was a strangeness about him, an aloofness. And why did he not marry? He was not without interest in women. In fact there had been a rumour that he had had a child by one of them. Why did he hesitate?

'He would seem to have no fancy for the state,' said Philippa, 'but it is true . . .'

'He has had a mistress or two,' said Edward. 'That may be, but now he is of an age to marry. I should like to see my grandson before too many years pass.'

'I believe he has a fondness for Joan of Kent. She is a beautiful girl . . . the most beautiful at Court some say . . . and she is royal.'

Edward did not meet the Queen's eye. He agreed that Joan of Kent was one of the most desirable girls at Court. Sometimes he wished he had not imposed so rigid a code on himself. Then he would have given way to his impulses. Other kings had done so and this little foible had been accepted. It was Philippa he was thinking of. He loved Philippa; he would not wish to hurt her in any way.

But Joan of Kent . . . what a beauty! Involuntarily he compared that willowy seductive shape, those exquisite bones, those languishing eyes, that smile which was almost an invitation, with Philippa. How fat she had grown! She wheezed as she walked and she could not move about without difficulty.

He always tried to see her as the fresh-faced girl she had been when he married her and had been so content with her. But of course she had always been homely.

'Joan of Kent,' he said. 'We could not say no to such a match. Why does he not ask her?'

'Perhaps you could speak to him.'

'Perhaps you should,' replied Edward.

Philippa agreed that she would do so, but it was not easy to talk to the Prince of such matters. He could evade the issue with the utmost of ease.

Edward thought of having the disturbing Joan as a daughter-in-law.

It would be disconcerting.

It was Philippa to whom the Scottish Queen turned for comfort. Philippa seemed to understand how desolate she was and how overawed by the English Court. Edward was kind as he had always been to her but he showed an uneasiness which she felt due to her presence in England.

It was a strange situation; his brother-in-law his captive and his own sister come to plead for his release. To a family man such as Edward it was a distressing situation and he believed it would have been better for all if Joanna had remained in Scotland.

When she asked earnestly for the release of her husband Edward was adamant. She must understand that if David were released it was very likely that the war would break out on the border once more. Edward could not allow that to happen. His country had been devastated by the pestilence – so was France for that matter; so was the whole of Europe, the whole of the world. This was no time to allow reckless men to make trouble.

Joanna saw this clearly, yet suggested to Philippa that there might be a treaty, one of the terms of which would be the release of her husband.

But Philippa was sure that Edward would never agree.

'In which case,' replied Joanna, 'I might stay here in England with my husband and share his prison.'

Philippa was embarrassed. How could she tell her sister-in-law that David already had a companion sharing his prison – the beautiful and brazen Katherine Mortimer?

She discussed this with Edward and they both agreed that no good could be served by letting Joanna know of this liaison between her husband and his mistress which was of such importance to him that he preferred – or so he said – to remain in England with her than return to Scotland and his Queen.

Of course if he were released there was no doubt that Katherine Mortimer would follow him to Scotland.

It was far better, reasoned Philippa, for Joanna to go back to Scotland believing that the King of England was firm in his resolution to keep her husband prisoner than to learn the true facts about her feckless faithless husband for whom it was clear she had a great deal of loyal affection.

So Joanna made her preparations to leave.

First she visited her father's tomb in Gloucester. She was sad thinking of his unhappy end and the tragedy of his and her own life. Mystery still surrounded events in Berkeley Castle but there were evil rumours about it and she dreamed of her father often and thought of him as he had been when she had been a child and forced into the Scottish marriage by her overbearing mother.

She did not possess many jewels but some she laid on the tomb of her father, thinking of him when he had been handsome and kind – though he had never spent much time with his children.

She prayed fervently for his soul and then she went to Castle Rising to see her mother.

Queen Isabella who had played such an important part in deposing her husband and had for a time ruled England with her lover Roger de Mortimer seemed to have accepted a life of tranquillity. She was still beautiful in spite of her years and was Lady Bountiful to the people of the neighbourhood. She lived well and seemed to have no qualms of conscience about the evil deeds which she had inspired.

It was hard to believe that this serene lady had been the instigator of that fearful murder in Berkeley Castle.

She received her daughter graciously and entertained her at the Castle in a royal manner. She talked with undisguised pleasure of the gifts she had received of wines and barrelled sturgeon which was her favourite food.

She was not the least interested in Joanna's troubles and scarcely mentioned her husband's imprisonment.

There was about her an aloofness, a strangeness even. Joanna heard that occasionally her mother lapsed into moods of near madness, but these were becoming less and less frequent.

The past seemed like a dream to Joanna; the present was tragedy and she dared not look into the future. Sadly she returned to Scotland.

❀ ❀ ❀

The Princess Isabella still smarted occasionally when she recalled the manner in which Louis of Flanders had jilted her and almost immediately married Margaret of Brabant.

The fact that he had felt so strongly as to plan an escape, which he had carried out with a few of his friends, really was insulting.

She had pretended not to care – and indeed she had had no great love for Louis – but the fact that she, the beloved daughter of the King on whom he doted more than on any other, had been jilted, was galling to her vanity.

She was a little annoyed too because of all the attention Joan of Kent demanded at Court. Joan was said to be the most beautiful girl at Court – out of Isabella's hearing, of course. She was royal too, which was irritating. She had many admirers and Isabella had noticed, too, that the King himself often allowed his eyes to rest on her.

Joan had created something of a scandal recently by admitting that she had secretly married Thomas Holland. That was when plans to marry her to the Earl of Salisbury were progressing too fast; and when it was discovered that she had actually lived with Holland as his wife, nothing could be done but to accept the marriage.

The Black Prince, who was quite clearly attracted by Joan, must have been deeply put out; but Isabella could understand Joan's impatience with him because although he was clearly fond of her he had made no effort to marry her.

Joan was sly; Joan was clever. Isabella believed that had Edward offered marriage she would have found some means of wriggling out of her union with Holland. Joan might be enamoured of that young man – so much so that she could not resist him – but her eyes would be on the crown which one day the Black Prince should inherit.

So there was too much talk of the Fair Maid of Kent, and not enough attention for the King's beautiful daughter.

It was a state of affairs which must not be allowed to continue.

Isabella had become interested in a young Gascon nobleman. This was Bernard Ezi, whose father – also Bernard – was Lord of Albret and he had come to England when Isabella's sister

Joanna's marriage was being arranged with Pedro of Castile. His son – Bernard the Younger – had accompanied him.

Young Bernard was very handsome, tall, charming and he and the Princess had become friends. In fact Bernard had fallen in love with Isabella.

Smarting from Louis's rejection Isabella was very happy to accept his attentions and she decided that here was someone who adored her, in great contrast to Louis of Flanders.

How delighted he would be if she agreed to marry him. Naturally he would not dare aspire so high but led on by her he declared his passion and told her that the greatest joy in his life would be to marry her.

Isabella said she would speak to her father before he did. This was by no means orthodox Court behaviour. Penniless foreigners did not come to Court and ask for the hands of princesses. Isabella snapped her fingers. She could get anything she wanted from her father, she boasted. Did not Bernard know that the King loved her dearly that he could deny her nothing.

Bernard did know this but he thought the King's indulgence to his daughter would not extend to marriage.

Isabella determined to prove him wrong.

She sought an opportunity to be alone with her father which was not difficult for Edward was growing fonder and fonder of her as he was becoming faintly critical of his wife. It was not that he did not love Philippa, but he did admire women with beautiful figures and Philippa's was becoming more and more unwieldy every week.

Isabella took his arm and drew him to a window-seat because, she said, she had something very important to tell him.

He was beaming with satisfaction, loving to share confidences with her.

'Oh my dear father,' she said, 'it is so wonderful to have you with me. How unhappy I was when I was in the Tower and you were in France. You wouldn't let me come with you . . .'

'I was afraid for your safety, my dear,' explained the King. 'You did come with me in the end remember, and then you were frightened when the French attacked our ships, were you not?'

She shook her head. 'You were close. I knew you would win.' She kissed his cheeks and he smiled fondly.

'You must have thought it is time for me to marry, my lord. And I fancy you do not urge it because you would hate to lose me. Confess it.'

'I confess,' said Edward,

'And you would be very pleased if I married someone who need not take me abroad so that we could all live happily in England.'

'That would be my wish, of course. Ah, if only it were possible.'

'It is, dear father, it is. And it is the only marriage I will consider. Do you think I should ever allow myself to be separated from you?'

'It will be a great sadness to me when the day comes . . . as I fear it must.'

'It shall not come,' she said. 'I have decided whom I will marry. Now father, dear father of mine, the one I shall love best in the whole of my life – husband or no – I will not be parted from you. That I swear. So it will be no foreign prince for me. It will be a man of such small estate that it matters not whether he go to his own country or stay in mine.'

375

'You are a dear sweet child. But alas you must grow up and marry some day.'

'That day will be soon, my lord. I have chosen Bernard Ezi.'

Edward was too astounded to speak and Isabella rushed on: 'I must marry him. No other will do. I know he has nothing . . . but you will give him estates here . . . near Windsor perhaps and I shall not lose you. That is my main concern.'

'My sweet child, this is impossible.'

'I have told Bernard that you will give your consent.'

'Nay, child. It will not do.'

Isabella's lips were firmly set. 'Yes, dear father, it will do. It must do. It is what I want.'

'Isabella, sweet daughter, you are young and this is passing infatuation for this young man. If you wish for a husband, I will find one worthy of you.'

'Someone who will take me away from you.' She stood up and stamped her foot. 'I will not go. I will never go. I shall marry Bernard or . . . *die*.'

'Now this is nonsense . . .'

'Indeed it is not. Dear father, you must agree to this, you must give your consent or I shall be the most unhappy woman in your kingdom. I must marry Bernard. Oh, dearest father, as you love me, say you will grant me this . . .'

He was wavering. He could never bear to disappoint her. He was a very sentimental father particularly where his daughters were concerned and the favourite of all the children was pretty Isabella.

He was thinking rapidly. The dear child is really serious. Well, consider this Bernard Ezi. What will he have? Albret! It is nothing. How could I possibly let my daughter marry a man of so little consequence? And yet I could raise him up. I could give him an earldom . . . And I should have her near me . . . I could make it so that they lived in England. I should see her often. Their children would be here with me . . . my own grandchildren.

She had thrown her arms about him; she was almost suffocating him with her embraces.

'You are the dearest kindest father in the world,' she declared.

And she knew that she had won.

The whole Court was astonished to learn that the King had agreed to his daughter's marriage with the son of a minor nobleman even though he was his father's heir. Philippa understood perfectly. Her wayward spoilt daughter had once more succeeded in getting what she wanted from her father. Well, if Isabella and Edward were happy that was enough for Philippa.

And Isabella did seem overwhelmed with happiness. She was determined to have the grandest wedding the Court had seen for a long time. She sent for the seamstresses and embroiderers for she had a passion for such decoration. She delighted in one garment especially. A mantle of silk which was edged with ermine and embroidered in silver and gold with birds, trees and animals. There were other gorgeous garments and Isabella insisted on trying everything on and parading before her mother and those sisters and brothers who were with the Court.

She persuaded her father to come to admire her and he sat, his arms folded, looking on with benign pleasure while his daughter walked about before him calling attention to the excellence of the embroidery and fine material of her clothes.

People had ceased to marvel at his fond indulgence of this daughter and to be surprised that the great King and warrior should become so involved in feminine fripperies.

He seemed quite pleased with the marriage and in fact he told Philippa that because his daughter was making such an insignificant marriage there was no need to supply her with the grand dowry which a prince or a king would have demanded.

In any case everything was worth while to see their daughter so happy.

The day for the celebrations of the nuptials was only a week away when Isabella came to her father and told him that she had decided not to marry after all.

Edward stared at her in amazement. Where was the happy bride of the last days? What had happened?

She flung herself into his arms and burst into tears. He sought to comfort her, asking for her reasons for this change of mind.

'Dear father, I do not know. I only know that I cannot marry Bernard. I don't want to marry anybody. I want to stay with you and be with you always. I cannot marry Bernard. Please understand.'

'My dear child, everything is arranged. The ceremony is shortly to take place.'

'I know, I know. But I cannot do it.'

The King was completely bewildered. But there was nothing to be done. The Princess was adamant.

The whole court was talking of the matter. Poor Bernard was heart-broken. He had been so deeply in love with the Princess and so enchanted with his great fortune in marrying the daughter of the King that to find himself deprived of love and honour when it seemed so nearly his sent him into the deepest melancholy.

Isabella kept her thoughts to herself. She was elated. She had done to Bernard what Louis had done to her. Her pride was vindicated. She was filled with a secret satisfaction and wondered whether she had intended all the time never to marry Bernard.

Perhaps. She had liked him very much. He was handsome, charming and she had so enjoyed stooping to his social level. He had always been so aware of the fact that she was a Princess and he a humble nobleman.

Now everyone was talking of her. They saw her in a different light from the poor jilted princess.

Moreover she was going to remain close to her father, for whatever arrangements had been made she would have had at some time to go with her husband to his estates in Gascony.

It was a piquant situation which she enjoyed thoroughly. It was particularly gratifying when Bernard declared he was weary of the world, retired to a monastery to become a cordelier monk and gave up his inheritance to a younger brother.

Chapter XIX

POITIERS

One of the effects of the Black Death was to make it impossible for hostilities to continue between France and England and Edward's dream of taking the French crown had to be postponed for a while.

Philip of France, now an old man, had remarried and his bride was Blanche of Navarre, a girl of nineteen, but a few months after the wedding Philip died and his son Jean became King.

Jean wanted to put an end to Edward's claims which he considered absurd and when an opportunity occurred which would allow someone else to help fight his battles he seized on it.

Jean realised that England's advantage was in her superior sea power which had grown considerably after the battle of Helvoetsluys and he believed that if he could cripple that power, ultimate victory over the English would be in sight.

Alfonso of Castile, father to that Pedro the Cruel who would have been Joanna's husband had she not died of the plague, had himself been a victim of the terrible scourge so Pedro was now King of Castile. However Pedro had had an elder brother who had died but had left a son and this son,

Charles de la Cerda, maintained that he had a prior claim to the throne of Castile. Charles appealed to Jean of France for help to gain his rights and Jean implied that if he would take action against the English and show himself to be indeed the friend of France, then Jean might consider helping him to gain the crown of Castile.

Charles therefore began gathering together his ships with the object of invading England. Edward was immediately alert to the danger. So many of his sailors had died; work in the shipyards had almost stopped, and the country desperately needed peace to become prosperous again.

He fervently hoped that the Spanish fleet would not be large, for if it were he would not be able to match it. True he had beaten the French at Helvoetsluys with far fewer ships than the enemy had had. He could doubtless do it again; but he was not bent on war. How typical of Jean of France to get others to fight his battles for him!

There was nothing to be done but set out for the coast and muster as many vessels as he could. Consequently he, with the Queen and his family, set out for Canterbury.

The Black Prince, excited as he always was at the prospect of a battle, rode with his young brother, ten-year-old John of Gaunt. The Prince was very fond of this brother and when young John asked if he might be with him during the battle the Prince rashly promised that he should. The Queen, her daughters and her ladies, were to stay in Canterbury and pray for victory.

Philippa was uneasy. She hated the thought of battle and as usual suffered greatly when her family was so engaged. She would pray fervently for victory, of course, and she well knew that as the Queen of England she must expect her husband and

381

her elder son to go to war; but she was horrified when she heard that the Black Prince was taking little John with him. She protested. 'He is only a child,' she cried. 'No, Edward, I will not have it. John must remain here in Canterbury with me.'

The Black Prince laughed aloud. 'Why, my lady, the boy has to learn how to go into battle some day.'

'Some day,' said Philippa, 'but not now when he is so young.'

Young John looked stormy. He turned to his brother and cried: 'But you promised. Edward you promised me . . .'

Edward ruffled his brother's hair and said: 'Don't fret, boy. You are coming with me. Our lady mother will see that it is necessary. You would not have him a weakling, my lady?'

'He is ten years old . . .'

John drew himself up to his full height and frowned at her. The Black Prince laughed.

'I will tell you what we will do. We will ask our father. He will tell us whether or not you are old enough to come.' He bent towards his brother. 'I'll promise you he will say you are to go. He was fighting battles himself at an early age. Besides, I shall be with you. You'll not stray from my side. Swear to it.'

'I swear,' said John.

The King gave the verdict that the boy was old enough and Philippa knew herself beaten.

Her task would be to remain behind, to pray for them, to fret for them and she would not know peace until they came back to her.

From Sandwich the King set sail in his best loved ship, *Cog Thomas*. The Black Prince sailed in another ship and with him was young John of Gaunt.

They cruised along the coast looking for the Spanish fleet.

The weather was warm and misty for it was August and as there was no sign of the enemy the King sat on deck listening to his minstrels playing to him. Men were stationed at every look-out in case the Spanish should attempt to creep up on them unawares.

The prospect of battle now, as always, stimulated the King and, dressed in a black coat and black beaver hat which set off his fairness ideally, he looked young and handsome.

Suddenly from the castle on the mast there was a shout of: 'I spy Spaniards!'

The King was on his feet.

'Sound the trumpets,' he cried. 'Call every man to his duty. The hour is come.'

Hastily armour was donned and by this time the Spaniards were very close. Exhilarated because he was fighting against great odds, Edward led his fleet into the attack. They rammed the Spanish and when close enough boarded their ships. Edward was going to beat these Spaniards; he was going to drive them off the sea. He knew it. His son knew it too. They were of a kind.

The Spaniards were heaving lumps of iron on the English ships in an endeavour to sink them – and sometimes succeeding. But Edward was always to the fore shouting encouragement, teaching his men how to fight, reminding them that he was invincible.

Cog Thomas went down, but only after Edward had captured the ship which was attacking him, boarded it and taken command of it. The same thing had happened to the Black Prince who had made sure that his young brother was safe beside him.

It was a great day – a great battle. Edward was exultant. To win a battle was always exciting but when it was done against desperate odds then it was the most exhilarating adventure in the world.

Fourteen Spanish ships had been sunk while very few English had suffered the same fate and what was left of the Spanish fleet limped back to the French coast while Edward sailed triumphantly to that of England.

It was a moment of great joy for Philippa when they had all returned to her residence.

'Praise be to God!' she cried.

'It was a great victory,' Edward told her.

'See,' mocked the Black Prince, 'I have brought your little John safely home to you.'

John ran to her and began telling her how the wicked Spaniards had sunk their ship and even *Cog Thomas*. 'But we sank more of theirs,' he cried excitedly.

'And I can tell you, Madam,' said the Black Prince, 'your son acquitted himself well.'

Philippa could only rejoice that they had come safely back to her.

The battle was called *Les Espagnols sur Mer* and because of the great victory Edward began to be called the King of the Seas.

He was pleased with the way things had gone. It was a great defeat for the French and they would realise it.

He said there should be feasting to celebrate it and Philippa agreed with him. She could not help wondering though what would have happened if the fight had gone against them; and the stories of how the King's ship and that of the Black Prince had been sunk almost under them made her shiver with apprehension.

None could have been more aware than Edward of the need for peace. With a depleted population and the terrible loss which the pestilence had inflicted on his country, he must have time to build up its strength. This could not be done in a few years; but it did seem as though God repented of his vengeance – for it was generally agreed that the plague had been visited on them through Divine wrath – because in the years following children were born at a great rate and many women had twins and there were far more cases of triplets than had been noticed ever before.

The people wanted peace; so, fervently, did Edward. He admitted this to his Parliament and it was agreed to send the Archbishop of Canterbury and the Duke of Lancaster to France to negotiate.

Jean of France also realised the need for peace, but he had made up his mind that he was going to quash the English claim to the French crown once and for all. So he prevaricated and declared that the matter must be laid before the Pope. During this time Edward was obliged to maintain an army for he could not be sure whether or not the French would decide to strike; and so the months passed.

Philippa had become pregnant once more and on a cold January day gave birth to a son at Woodstock. She called him Thomas and there were lavish celebrations in spite of the need to equip an army.

The rejoicing was short lived for spies came from France to tell Edward that the French King was swearing to drive the English out of France and that he was mustering a large army for this purpose.

Edward lost no time in planning his campaign. The Black Prince was to take his own army to Bordeaux and attack from there; he, Edward, accompanied by his sons, Lionel and John, would set out for Calais.

Once again Philippa must watch her loved ones go into danger. Beyond anything she wanted peace and she often wondered what her life would have been like if Robert d'Artois had not goaded Edward into claiming the French crown. That that claim should have come through the Dowager Queen Isabella whose coming to England had changed the country's history, fitted neatly into the pattern of events. Had a different bride been chosen for Edward II the whole face of English history might have been different. But how could one say 'If' in this way? Was not that how life was made up?

All the same, as a woman, a wife and a mother she knew in her heart that whatever conquests were made in France they would not be worth the anguish and the suffering which would be the price paid for them.

No sooner had Edward reached Calais than the Scots decided to strike on the Border, clearly believing that with Edward and the Black Prince out of the country they had a good chance of victory.

Messengers were sent at full speed to Edward to tell him that the Scots had laid siege to Berwick.

His fury was great.

'I swear by God,' he said, 'that I shall sleep in no town more than one night before I have reached the border between England and perfidious Scotland.'

He sent word to his son.

'I leave you to conduct this campaign in France. I know that I can rely on you to succeed.'

True to his word he rested nowhere longer than was necessary. In a short time he had relieved Berwick.

❀ ❀ ❀

The King of France chuckled with delight when he heard that Edward had been forced to go to Scotland. He talked of his good allies the Scots for it was not the first time they had been of use to him, and any who were enemies of England were friends of his.

'This time,' he declared, 'I shall crush them once and for all time.'

For the King of England Jean had always had a mingled awe, admiration and hatred. His father had spoken of him with the utmost respect. He had once said that if Edward the Third had been like his father this mad matter of the English claim to the succession would have been settled long ago and England beaten to her knees, a province of France. But fate had given England this other Edward. He was like his grandfather. There was a certain mystique about such leaders. Men followed them and gave of their best without reward, having nothing in their minds but to serve. Such men were invincible unless faced with others of their kind. Jean hoped that he was such a one; but in his secret heart he had his doubts.

So it was good news that the Scottish action had taken Edward back to England and it was only his son they had to face. It was true that the Black Prince was earning a reputation to match that of his father. It had been attached to him after Crécy, though he might so easily have been killed or taken prisoner there. What a triumph that would have been. But fate had been kind to him and he had lived to win a great victory and the English had beaten the French, and what made it so much more galling was the fact that they had done so with fewer men. It must not happen again.

Jean was always eager to know what Edward was doing. When Edward had instituted the Order of the Garter he had imitated him by forming a brotherhood called Our Lady of the Noble Star. To this he admitted five hundred knights who must take the oath never to yield to the enemy more than four acres of ground and to die in battle rather than retreat.

He believed that now was his great chance. The Black Prince was marching through the country, ravaging it as he went and finding it an easy conquest. He took up his position outside Poitiers and there awaited the arrival of the English army. There the decisive battle should take place.

Jean was certain of success. He had to face the Prince – not the legend which was Edward the Third. He had forty thousand men – a far greater number than the English could possibly put into the field. Almost the whole of the nobility of France was with him and there were twenty-six dukes and counts. His four sons marched with him; his youngest Philip was only twelve years old and he had commanded the boy not to stray from his side, for this boy was his favourite among all his children and he loved him dearly.

There was some consternation in the English camp when it was realised what a great disparity there was in the numbers of the opposing armies. Even the Prince felt an inward qualm. Not that he would show it. As he said to his close friend and constant companion, Sir John Chandos, who was now at his side: 'Battles are often decided before they begin. The last thing that must handicap our men is fear of greater numbers.'

'And you, my lord?'

'The difference is great,' said the Prince. 'But I must show my father that I am worthy to be his son.'

'You have done that again and again.'

'And shall continue to do so. I shall talk to the men before battle. I shall tell them that it is the English way to win a battle when the opposing numbers exceed their own. If they had thought of defeat they cannot do so now. Regard the might of the French. It means certain victory for us. Remember Crécy, Helvoetsluys, Les Espagnols sur Mer. It is an English tradition. Face great odds . . . and win.'

Chandos nodded.

'It is good to remind them of that.'

But at the same time Sir John had seen the doubts in the Prince's eyes.

'If a truce was offered . . .' began Sir John.

'If I could make it with honour, well, my friend, I should consider it. Should I not be a fool to ignore it?'

That was enough for Sir John. The Prince was uneasy about the size of the French army.

In his tent the King of France talked to young Philip. 'What say you, my boy, shall we take the Black Prince prisoner or shall we slay him on the field?'

'Let us take him prisoner,' cried the boy. 'We shall have more sport that way.'

'You are a bright fellow,' said the King placing a hand on his son's shoulder. 'It would be a real feather in our caps if we took that one to Paris with us, eh?'

'May I ride beside you when you do, my lord?'

'You shall be there, I promise you.'

The boy looked at his father with shining eyes; he believed him to be the greatest man that ever lived. There was no doubt in young Philip's mind that they would ride back to Paris with the Black Prince.

They went together into the royal tent, a glorious affair of vermilion samite as became the King of France. In the tent a table had been set up and over this had been hung the Oriflamme of France.

They feasted sumptuously while they discussed the action which should be taken.

It was different in the English camp. There was no feasting there. It was impossible to forage for food for the French surrounded them. And what were ten thousand men against forty? The Prince could not forget that the superiority in numbers meant that the French King could split his army into four and each one would be the size of the entire English force.

'When the battle is won we shall feast,' said the Prince.

But first that which with every passing hour seemed to be more and more like a miracle must come to pass.

Meanwhile in the town of Poitiers the Cardinal Talleiran de Périgord called together certain of his clergy and declared that he was going to do everything he could to stop the battle. The town might well be laid waste if it took place and the surrounding country would be devastated. God had recently shown his displeasure by inflicting the pestilence upon them. Now God was beginning to smile on them but if this war continued the fair land of France would be laid waste and that was something it could not afford having already faced one enemy in the dreadful scourge.

There was great support for this and as a result the Cardinal came riding to the French King.

Jean received him with mixed feelings. He wanted desperately to beat the English but even equipped as he was he had his doubts of achieving this. He feared those English archers who had devastated the French army at Crécy, and, although at first he thrust aside the Cardinal's suggestions, at length he agreed to wait and see what terms could be arranged.

The Cardinal then went to the Black Prince and talked to him.

The Prince listened and while he did so he was thinking quickly. He was outnumbered. Any student of military matters would say that the victory for the French was inevitable. As a great general he knew that if he could avert this battle with honour he must do so.

'Sire,' pleaded the Cardinal, 'have pity on those fine men who this day will die on this field if the battle should go forth. You know that the King of France has a great army which outnumbers yours four to one.'

'I know it well, good and gentle Father,' said the Prince. 'But our quarrel is just. My father, King Edward, is the lawful King of France and should possess this land. Yet I would not have it said that good youth was slain through my pride. I cannot though settle this matter without the King, my father. But I will give my men respite and if my honour and that of my army be saved I am ready to listen to any reasonable terms.'

'You say well, fair son,' replied the Cardinal. 'I shall do my best to bring about peace.'

The Cardinal went back to the French camp and as a result a day's truce was declared while negotiations took place.

A delegation of English headed by the Prince, and the Earls of Warwick and Suffolk went into the French King's camp. Jean and Edward regarded each other steadily. Jean had seen the determination in the Prince's eyes which made him uneasy. Here was another of those leaders. Why had God not sent another Edward the Second? If that had been the case this war could be finished now and for ever.

What would the Prince offer for his side of the bargain? asked the Cardinal.

391

The Prince said that he would dismiss all his prisoners free of ransom, give up the towns and castles he had taken during the campaign and agree to peace for seven years.

Jean pondered this. It seemed reasonable enough. He looked around at those of his nobles who were attending the council. He saw disgust in many of their faces. Here we are, they were telling him, with four times the men that the English have. Victory is in our hands. This is not the time to parley with them. This is the time to go in and annihilate them.

'I demand the surrender of the Prince into my hands with a hundred of his leading knights,' said the King.

The Prince laughed aloud. So Jean had no intention of making a truce. Edward would have thought him a fool if he had, with an army four times the size of his enemy's.

'Your countrymen think highly of you, my lord Prince,' said the King. 'Methinks it would not be long before they raised your ransom.'

'What sort of knight do you think I am!' cried the Prince hotly. 'I will rather die sword in hand than be guilty of deeds so opposed to mine honour and the glory of England. Englishmen shall never pay ransom of mine.'

The Earl of Warwick unable to suppress his indignation cried out. 'You French have no intention of making a truce. Why should you? You have four times more men than we have. We care not for that. Here is the field and the place. Let each do his best and may God defend the right.'

The Prince smiled with approval. The conference was over and the battle of Poitiers would soon be fought.

At sunrise on that fateful day the nineteenth of September 1356 the Prince was astir. He must be prepared for a dawn attack. He was going to need every bit of his military skill on this day. Oddly enough he felt exhilarated by the fact that his army was so small. He had talked to his men during the night, visiting them after dark, inspiring them, telling them that so it had been at Crécy and as one Englishman was worth five French they had the great chance of victory. Every one of them would give of his best. If he would do that then they could not fail to win.

'By God,' he cried to Chandos, 'we are going to win this field. I feel it. I want messengers ready to go to my father when the day is won. There must be rejoicing in England, Chandos, for I intend to make this not only a victory over the French but a decisive one.'

'God be with you, Edward.'

'And you will be beside me, my good friend.'

'Until the death.'

'Do not talk of death, John. Better say throughout life and when you and I are greybeards we shall talk of this day and laugh together because at one time we felt a qualm of uncertainty. Now to work. Our archers will win the day as they did at Crécy. There is no army on earth that can withstand good English bowmen. Our men know their posts. They will be protected behind hedges, along narrow lanes and among the vineyards and these will be lined with our good archers. Let us to work.' Activity began.

How fiercely the battle raged and how often it seemed inevitable that the overpowering forces must decide the day.

There was one who never faltered, who was always there in the forefront of the battle, recognizable by his black armour. The legend! The Black Prince who could not be beaten.

Always beside him was his good friend Sir John Chandos and where the Prince was there must be hope.

The archers, as at Crécy, played a decisive part, and nowhere in the world were there archers to compare with the English; but all through the morning the battle swayed and there came a time when the archers had no more arrows. Even then they would not give in; they picked up stones and threw them at the enemy. It appeared then to many Englishmen that the battle was lost but not for one moment would the Black Prince concede this.

One knight, seeing the shining armour of the French column advancing upon them, cried out: 'We poor devils of English are done for. This is the end.'

The Prince shouted loudly so that all could hear: 'You lie most damnably. It is blasphemy to say that I can be conquered alive.'

When he appeared men's spirits rose. He was the Black Prince. He was invincible. It was impossible to believe that he could be anything but the victor.

Shouting orders from the small hillock in which he had stationed himself, his black armour like a talisman to them all, he was their inspiration. He was invincible – then so were they, his men. There was not a man who would have dared turn and seek shelter for himself. There was not one who would not have preferred to die rather than live with the eternal shame of not fighting beside the Black Prince that day.

That they were weary, that they were spent, was clear. That the French had suffered heavy losses was true too. But there were so many of them. How long, they were asking themselves, could they hold out?

The King of France was sorely tried. He was in the thick of the battle, for he was as determined as the Black Prince to win this day. It seemed incredible that the battle should have endured so long. It should have been won long ago. Four to one, he kept thinking. And even then . . . it is so long.

Young Philip was beside him, remembering his injunctions. 'You must not leave my side,' the King had said. Philip did not want to. He was not afraid. He knew that men were falling about him; he knew that the day was not going as his father had planned. He was aware that had the King known that there would be such disorder he would have sent his son to a place of safety.

Philip did not want to be in a safe place. He wanted to be beside his father. This was a terrible baptism of war but he was with his father and his father must win.

The King was on foot now. His men were surrounding him, rallying to his side. But the English were crowding in on him. Young Philip stared in horror as he saw one of the knights collapse to the ground covered in blood.

They were coming to his father. One by one those who had rallied to him were falling.

'Look to the right, Father,' he cried. 'Father, to the left. To the right. To the left . . .'

They were all round him now.

Philip heard the shout of 'Surrender.'

Surrender! His father! It was unthinkable.

He opened his mouth to tell them that they were speaking to the King of France. But he hesitated. That would not be wise. They were his father's enemies.

Philip saw the golden lilies fall to the ground. He saw the blood on them and that seemed to him symbolic. His fears were all for his father – that great man who in his eyes was godlike. He had never seen his father before except at the centre of some ceremony treated with respect; no one – not even his children – ever forgot that he was the King of France.

The crowd parted and a man was pressing forward. He recognised the King and realised what a prize this would be to take to the Black Prince.

'Stand aside,' he commanded those soldiers who were mauling the King's armour. Then to the King: 'Sire, surrender yourself.'

'Surrender!' cried the King. 'To whom should I surrender myself? Where is the Prince of Wales? I would speak with him.'

'Sire, if you will surrender yourself to me I will take you to him.'

'Who are you, pray? You are a Frenchman.'

'I am Denis de Morbeque, a knight of Artois. But I serve the King of England because I have lost my possessions in France.'

This conversation had conveyed to those watching that the prisoner was the King of France and all wanted to claim the honour of having taken him. One of them seized Philip who struggled madly and crying out: 'Let me go, you rogues. How dare you lay hands on the royal son of France.'

'He is a bold little fellow, this one,' said the soldiers.

'Harm him not,' ordered Denis de Morbeque. 'Come, Sire, I will conduct you to the Prince of Wales.'

The crowd surrounded the captives and the Black Prince on seeing the commotion and fearing that it might mean mutiny sent two of his knights to find out what was afoot. When the knights heard that the captive was the King of France they forced the crowd back and came to the Black Prince with the prisoners.

The Prince could scarcely believe his good fortune. It was indeed the King of France. Then the day was won. Poitiers was a name that would be mentioned with Crécy. A great victory was his.

He almost loved the King of France in that moment. He took off his helmet and going to meet Jean bowed low to him.

'Sweet lord,' he said, 'this is God's doing and I have played but small part in it. We must render thanks to Him beseeching Him earnestly that he will grant us glory and pardon us this victory.'

Then he gave orders that wines should be brought to refresh his honoured guest and he himself undid the lacings of the French King's armour.

'Fair cousin,' said Jean quietly, 'have done. Let us look the truth in the face. This is the most bitter day of my life. I am your prisoner.'

'Nay, cousin,' answered the Prince, 'you are my honoured guest.'

Edward had returned from Scotland and was in Westminster. He knew nothing of what was happening in France and his first realization came when messengers arrived at the palace.

It was a moment he knew he would never forget as long as he lived for when he realised whence the messengers came his heart was filled with apprehension. One could never be sure whether such messengers brought good or bad news. He had been uneasy for he had heard that the French were amassing and he knew how heavily their armies would outnumber those of his son.

These messengers though had not the appearance of men of doom.

No, they were smiling broadly.

'My lord,' said one, as though rehearsing a speech, 'the Prince of Wales has sent a gift to you. He trusts it will give you pleasure.'

'A gift! My son! He is well then?'

'Well and in high spirits, my lord.'

'A victory,' thought the King. 'It must be a victory.'

Two messengers were bowing before him. Between them they carried something which they handed to Edward.

He stared at it. It was a coroneted helmet such as could only belong to a King.

The French King's helmet. It could mean only one thing.

' 'Tis so, my lord,' cried the messengers. 'The King of France is the prisoner of the Black Prince. The victory of Poitiers was complete. The war must be over now.'

Edward felt his emotions ready to overwhelm him. 'My son! My son,' was all he said.

Then he recovered himself. 'You could not have brought me better news. You shall be rewarded for this. This is a great day for England. She will have reason to bless the Black Prince.'

He went immediately to Philippa and laid the coroneted helmet in her hands.

'Your son's work, my lady,' he said. 'Our noble son. There is not a prouder man in England this day.'

'The French King's helmet!' cried Philippa. 'Then the fighting is over.'

'A great victory. He won his spurs at Crécy, and praise God at Poitiers he has crowned himself with glory. England has reason to rejoice this day.'

'This will mean peace,' said Philippa. 'Our boys will come home. I trust this is an end to this war.'

Edward was smiling triumphantly, but Philippa thought: There will never be an end to war. Not while there are crowns to gain and hold.

But it was good news. She must not spoil the pleasure of it by thinking melancholy thoughts.

'The whole country must rejoice,' cried the King. 'There shall be feasting and bonfires. And you and I, my dear Queen, must prepare ourselves to receive the conquering hero with his royal prisoner.'

❊ ❊ ❊

The Black Prince had no intention of hurrying home. He wanted to savour his victory. He must entertain his prisoner royally so that it should not be said that English hospitality fell short of French.

This gave him an opportunity of indulging his love of extravagance which he had inherited from his father. His armies needed relaxation too. They had fought valiantly at Poitiers and deserved some rewards. All through that winter he had remained in Bordeaux and it was April before he decided to travel across country to take ship to Sandwich.

England was waiting for the conquerors and on the way to Canterbury where they spent the night, people came out of their houses to cheer the Prince. From Canterbury to Rochester and Rochester to Dartford the triumphant cavalcade made its way – and then to London.

The King could not restrain his impatience and arranged to be hunting in the forest close to the route.

The Prince was not surprised when riding out of the woods came the royal party headed by the King.

With great ceremony the Kings met each other.

'Welcome to England, my lord of France,' cried Edward.

Jean received the greeting with dignity and Edward told him that he was his most honoured guest and if he would care to join the hunt he was at liberty to do so.

The King of France declined and the King and his party rode with the procession to London.

It was a great occasion for the capital. It was not often that a captive monarch was brought to their town. It was all very well to treat him like a guest, but everyone knew that the King of France was the prisoner of the King of England.

The houses had been hung with banners and tapestry; the fountains ran with wine, and there was free beer in barrels for any who preferred it. In one street a golden cage had been fixed and in this was a beautiful girl who threw silver and gold filigree flowers over the Prince and the King as they rode by.

'Long live the Black Prince!' was the constant cry. 'God bless the victor of Poitiers.'

The King glowed with pleasure and pride and rejoiced that he had not been at Poitiers to steal any of the glory which belonged to his son. He was proud and happy to have given his people such a man.

What a King he will make, he thought. England is sure of prosperity under him. Thank God for him.

It was typical of the Black Prince that he had chosen for himself a somewhat insignificant black palfrey. He liked to remind people that he was the Black Prince and the blackness of his armour contrasted with the shining glory of his deeds. Now the King of France came on a magnificent showy white horse while his captor rode in some humility. Such contrasts appealed to him and in truth they called attention to his greatness.

They came to Westminster Hall where Philippa waited to

greet them. All the royal children who were in England were with her, and a great banquet had been prepared to welcome the King of France, but Philippa wanted most to see her eldest son.

At last he stood before her. Her boy, her first-born, the best loved of all her children.

'My lady,' he said, taking her hand and kissing it.

'God's blessing on you,' she replied.

She greeted the King of France warmly. She was sorry for him. It must be a very sad time for him, made even more so by the wild rejoicing he had seen in the streets. England's triumph could only be his failure. But this must be an end to the senseless war.

At the banquet the King insisted that Jean should sit on his right hand; and beside the King of France was his son Philip, whose looks were sullen because he knew that what he had believed impossible had happened.

Edward himself seemed a little insensitive to the feelings of his captive and seemed to expect him to join in the revelry which was asking too much.

Lavish dishes were served and there were those which it was believed would please the King of France.

Jean ate little and Edward at last said reproachfully: 'Come, my lord, cast off your melancholy. You are our guests. Sing with us and be merry.'

Jean looked steadily into Edward's face and replied tersely: 'How shall we sing the Lord's songs in a strange land?'

Philippa smiled at the King sadly and said: 'It is a difficult time for you, my lord. I doubt not that it will come to an end ere long.'

At this moment the cupbearer came with wine and served Edward.

At that moment young Philip who had been looking on sprang to his feet and delivered a sharp blow across the cupbearer's face.

There was an astonished silence at the table. Then the boy cried out: 'How dare you serve any before the King of France?'

All eyes were now on Edward. What would his reaction be. The boy, his face flushed, his eyes flashing, stared back at Edward. Everyone was expecting that such an insult to the King's cupbearer might provoke the notorious Plantagenet temper, but it was not so.

Edward laughed and said: 'You are indeed Philip le Hardi.'

Philip the Bold! The boy was from that day called by this name and it stayed so throughout his life.

The King of France could see that Edward was determined to treat him with the utmost courtesy. He was given the Savoy Palace for his residence; he might hunt and hawk when he pleased.

In fact he could lead a life of luxury. The only condition being that he remained the prisoner of the King of England.

🌸 Chapter XX 🌸

MURDER IN MELROSE

With his great enemy captive in England Edward no longer need fear the Scots and as a result, he decreed that David the Bruce should return to his kingdom.

David's wife Joanna was delighted. Now they would be able to live happily together, she believed. It was what she had always hoped for. Their married life had been ill-fated from the start; they had never had a chance of any domestic happiness, and when she had been at the English Court and seen the devotion of Edward and Philippa and their family she had longed for a similar felicity. Fate had been against them. Life in the Château Gaillard had been so artificial and David had seemed indifferent to his destiny while he was in France, but she had always believed that if he could return to the land of his fathers he would change. That he had not when after seven years in France he returned to Scotland she chose to forget. There had always been trouble and those five years together in Scotland had been far from pleasant, but when he had been taken prisoner by the English and there had been another long separation she had allowed herself to dream that they had been happy together. It was eleven years since he had gone to England.

We are older now, she promised herself. We are wiser and we shall learn to understand each other.

The meeting was an emotional one for her. He was still very handsome and he behaved as though he were as delighted to be with her as she was with him, and for a few weeks she was very happy; then she began to see less of him because he explained he was busy with state affairs.

The truth was she bored him. She reminded him of her sister-in-law and he had often wondered how Edward could turn a blind eye to all the beautiful women at his Court and remain the faithful husband of plump and homely Philippa.

Joanna was not plump; she was handsome enough in a gentle way but he did not care for gentle women. He liked a certain coarseness, a bawdiness . . . he liked a woman like Katherine Mortimer.

Where was Katherine now? Missing him doubtless as he missed her. She had sworn she would not let him go. She would make plans to follow him, she had said, and it would not surprise him if one day she arrived in Scotland.

And then what of Madame Joanna?

An idea occurred to him. He could not wait to put it into practice. He made sure that Joanna noticed how preoccupied and uneasy he was and when she asked what troubled him he admitted that certain matters lay heavily on his mind.

'It's the treaty with your brother,' he told her. 'There is bound to be trouble over it. God knows I want peace but Edward will impose hard terms for that.'

'I think he is eager for peace in Scotland.'

'Doubtless, but on his own terms, and it may well be that

some of our Scottish lairds will not take kindly to what he suggests. Edward has always been hard on me. I believe he did not approve of our marriage in the first place.'

Joanna was silent. It was true Edward had not liked the marriage. He had avoided being present at the ceremonies. He had thought she was too young; and later of course she had sensed that he disapproved of David.

'Of course he is devoted to *you*,' went on David. 'He loves well his female relations. They say his daughters can persuade him to anything. It may well be so with his sister.'

'Edward has always been very kind to me.'

'I know it. He always spoke so warmly of you. Now if it were you who had to deal with him instead of me . . .'

'You know, David, that I would do anything . . . anything for peace between our two countries.'

'Would you? No, it is asking too much. Besides I could not lose you now we have just come together.'

'You mean . . . Go to England . . . *I* negotiate with my brother!'

'The thought entered my mind. It would mean peace . . . a long long truce between our countries. That is what Scotland needs.'

She was thoughtful. 'I will go to England if you wish it, David.'

'I wish it for Scotland but not for myself.'

'We must think of Scotland before ourselves.'

'It need not be for long. Oh Joanna, you could complete this business in a week. Edward would indulge you . . . listen to you. What a happy fate for Scotland to have the sister of the King of England for its Queen.'

'The sooner I go the better.'

'The sooner you go the sooner you will be back.'

'I will leave at once,' she said. 'And I promise you I will do all in my power to help this country.'

Before the end of the week she had set out.

It was just in time, David delightedly told himself, for what he had prophesied had come to pass. Katherine Mortimer had arrived at the palace.

How they laughed together! How they revelled in being together! Making up for lost time, David called it.

He did not care what those about him thought or said. Katherine was back with him, and there was no woman who could satisfy him as she did.

They were together night and day and none of the knights or ministers could see him alone.

What will happen, they asked each other, when the Queen returns? David did not concern himself with that question. Katherine was installed as royal mistress, the woman on whom the King doted, who was beside him at all hours and without whose advice he never acted.

David was quite content to live in the ecstatic present.

❀ ❀ ❀

Edward received his sister kindly and listened attentively to her pleas that he should not treat the Scots too harshly.

He had not been exactly lenient and was demanding a ransom for David's return and was also presenting him with a bill for his expenses during the time he had been in England.

This was no small sum and Joanna pointed out that she did not see how the Scots could meet it.

When she pleaded with him Edward was deeply touched. She was a good and faithful wife to David who did not deserve such a wife. Both he and Philippa had been deeply shocked by David's behaviour when he was in England and Edward had discovered that Katherine Mortimer had gone north and was certain that she would now be in Scotland.

His pity for his sister – in which Philippa joined – made him determined to help her all he could so he took pleasure in modifying his terms which pleased her very much for she felt that her journey to England had indeed been worth while.

'You should stay with us a while,' Philippa said. 'It has been a long and tedious journey. You must not plan to leave so soon.'

'I love to be with you,' replied Joanna. 'You have both been so kind to me. But I long to get back and tell David what I have been able to achieve.'

Edward then laid no obstacles in her way and very soon she was on her way to Scotland.

'Poor girl,' said Edward to Philippa, 'I trust she may not find what I fear she may when she gets there.'

Crossing the Border Joanna felt happy. She had come to love the dour land of her adoption. The mountains enchanted her; she had grown accustomed to the climate which was so much harsher than that of the south. If her marriage had not been so beset with disasters she could have been very happy with her husband.

David had charm; he was undeniably handsome; she knew that women admired him. She had noticed their looks in the crowds when they rode out. In Château Gaillard there had been women . . . But she preferred not to think of that. He had been such a boy then, an unhappy boy, driven from his own country. What could one expect?

It would all be different now . . . so different.

She reached Edinburgh and rode into the castle. She had thought David would be there to meet her.

In her chamber they had lighted a fire for her. She would be cold after her journey. They knew that she felt the cold.

Her women helped her dress. It was a strange homecoming.

She wanted to ask where the King was, but that would call attention to the strangeness. She thought her women were trying to tell her something.

When she prompted them they looked embarrassed and feeling uneasy she left her apartments and went to those of the King. From them came sounds of laughter — a woman's laughter. Yes, and that was David's voice.

One of the guards stepped before her. 'My lady . . .'

She looked at him questioningly. Something was wrong, she knew. She stepped past him and opened the door.

David was there; he was seated on his chair and at his feet on a stool sat a woman, with dark hair falling loose about her bare shoulders over which her gown had slipped down.

'David!' she began.

He did not look round.

'It is the Queen returned from her mission,' he said.

The woman did not look either. She merely laughed.

'What does this mean?' cried Joanna, her heart sinking, her mind telling her what she knew full well. This was the meaning of her attendants' embarrassed looks, the seeking to detain her from coming to her husband's apartments.

'What does what mean?' asked David languidly.

She had come forward and faced them now. She saw the table on which was food and wine. One of the goblets was overturned and the wine trickled over the table.

'Who is this woman?'

The woman rose and dropped a curtsey which was full of mockery.

'Katherine Mortimer my lady at your service – and the King's,' she said.

'And who . . . ?'

'You might say the King's friend,' was the answer.

Joanna stepped back, her face flushed.

'I . . . I think I understand,' she said, and walked from the room.

Neither of them moved. She heard them laughing as she went out of the room.

Back in her own apartment she dismissed her women.

It cannot be true, she said to herself. But she knew it was. This was worse than Château Gaillard. There it had been furtive, petty infidelities, which he had made half-hearted attempts to keep from her. This was blatant insult.

She had deceived herself, of course. He would never change. He was weak; he was licentious, a profligate. What hope was there for their marriage? What hope for Scotland? She had been deceived throughout her life. She was foolish; everyone must be laughing at her. They would have known what he was; and she, the one who had thought herself closest to him, was the one who saw least.

The Countess of Carrick was asking to come in.

She was a member of the Bruce family and had been a good friend to Joanna through her troubles. Now she looked at her with great sympathy.

'You have discovered then,' she said now. 'Oh my poor Joanna!'

'Who is the woman?'

'A low creature whom he met in England. She shared his prison with him.'

'He has been faithful to her for a long time,' said Joanna bitterly.

'She followed him to Scotland. She has been openly with him since you went away.'

'I shall not endure it.'

'What shall you do? He's the King. He will act as he pleases.'

'What do the people think?'

'They are ashamed for him. They speak so highly of you. They do not like it – but he does not care.'

'I cannot stay here and suffer these insults to continue,' said Joanna. 'I shall go to England. I will send a messenger at once to ask my brother's permission to stay at his Court.'

'It is the best thing,' said the Countess. 'I will come with you. I do not care to stay here and see a member of my family behave in this way . . . even though he is the King. I wonder what his father would think of him if he were living today.'

'If he were,' said Joanna mirthlessly, 'David would not be King of Scotland.'

'Aye and Scotland a happier country than it is under the son of Robert the Bruce.'

'I shall prepare to leave at once,' said Joanna, 'for I am determined I shall not stay here to be insulted.'

'We will leave tomorrow and make our way south. I am prepared because I knew what you would find and what you would feel.'

'Thank you, Annabella. It is good to have friends. Now, let us make our preparations to leave.'

Edward and Philippa greeted Joanna with a warm welcome. Edward was furious that his sister should have been treated so and said that a residence should be found for her and she should have an income so that she could be completely independent of her husband.

Meanwhile David, learning of his wife's departure and knowing full well the reason for it, was greatly disconcerted. When he rode out the people were sullen and silent; now and then he heard voices raised against him. The Earl of Mar and several of the lords showed clearly their disapproval of his actions which had led to Joanna's departure and the Earl pointed out the effect this was going to have on the King of England. The terms Edward had imposed were harsh enough but there was always a possibility that they might be modified. What hope was there of getting Edward to agree to this leniency when his sister had been grossly insulted?

Edward was a stern enemy; he was also a family man, and always most angry if any harm came to those close to him.

Distracted, David was ready to do what he could to remedy the situation except one thing. He would not give up Katherine Mortimer. When the Earl of Mar suggested she be sent back to England he was adamant and declared he would stand out against them all rather than lose Katherine.

The Earl could see that he could well lose his kingdom through that woman and a kingdom without a king could lead to all sorts of trouble. His advice – and this was supported by most of the lords and counsellors – was that David should go at once to England and beg his wife to return with him.

'It may be,' said the Earl, out of the King's hearing, 'that if he is separated from Katherine Mortimer for a while he might escape from her wiles. It is a chance.'

'Go to England!' cried David. 'Beg Joanna to return. That I will not do.'

'My lord, you must do this. The Queen is a peace-loving, gentle lady. When she sees what her absence means to Scotland she will return to you. You need not go in too supplicating a manner. You can save that for when you are alone with the Queen. It is known throughout the land that we cannot meet the next instalment of your ransom, so let it be thought that you come to the King to beg him to give you time to raise the money. It is a plausible reason. But the main object is of course to bring the Queen back.'

David was at last persuaded and he set out with a party of eighty horse headed by the Earl of Mar.

It was too much to expect Edward to receive him at Court and he took up his quarters at the priory of Holborn, from where he sent a message to Joanna begging her most humbly to come to the priory to see him.

She came and found him in a very different mood from when she had last seen him. He looked at her apologetically.

'My dear Joanna,' he said, 'I fear I was the worse for wine when we were last together. I want to ask your forgiveness.'

She was silent.

He took her hand which she allowed to remain limply in his.

He began to exert his charm, to try to win her confidence. He did not understand Joanna. She was gentle and she hated conflict; she was prepared to endure a good deal in the cause of duty; but she was not weak. And she would never be deceived by him again. He made the mistake of confusing gentleness with weakness. He had to learn that when a woman of Joanna's nature had made up her mind she could show a firmness of which he could never be capable.

'You may spare your efforts,' she said coolly. 'You want me to come and stay here while you are here because of the effect it will create. I will do so. But do not think there shall be the slightest degree of intimacy between us. I will be with you at ceremonies and that is all. I will help plead the cause of Scotland with the King my brother but I no longer regard myself as wife to you and never shall.'

This seemed victory to David. She would live under the same roof. It would only be a matter of time he was sure before he cajoled her into returning to Scotland with him. And when there she would perforce accept the presence of Katherine. It would not be the first time that a queen had had to agree to live side by side with her husband's mistress.

Joanna was true to her word. She joined her husband and went with him to Edward to plead for alleviation of the Scottish debt.

Philippa understood the situation and applauded Joanna's tact and wisdom.

'With your help,' Joanna told her, 'I shall stay here. I know that I have your support and that of Edward. I shall never go back to him again.'

Philippa placed a hand over that of her sister-in-law, saying warmly: 'You will always be welcome here.' She was deeply sorry for Joanna and was sure that had she been in her position she would have behaved in the same way. How fortunate she had been in her married life. For that very reason she wanted to show her thankfulness by helping Joanna all she could.

Edward agreed that the payment of the instalment should be postponed and made it clear that this concession was granted for the sake of his sister who had pleaded so earnestly for it. They discussed a peace treaty and it was agreed that

Scottish youths should be allowed to work in English universities.

When this business had been completed, there was no reason why David should remain in England and he prepared to return to his own country.

He had quite expected that Joanna would accompany him and for the first time it was brought home to him that he did not understand his wife.

She faced him squarely. 'You may rest assured that I shall never return to Scotland. I have decided to stay here with my family who love and respect me.'

In vain did he protest. She was determined.

He rode back with his grim-faced nobles across the Border. The real object of the mission had failed. Joanna had left him; and the people were not pleased with his treatment of his Queen.

He was growing very unpopular and if it had not been for memories of his father Robert the Bruce they might have risen against him.

Katherine Mortimer was waiting for him and when he was with her he forgot everything else.

In Castle Rising the Dowager Queen Isabella lay very ill. She was sixty-three years of age and it was nearly twenty-eight years since her lover Roger de Mortimer had been snatched from her side and barbarously executed. He had been her life; the only person she had ever loved and when she had lost him she had declined into temporary madness. As she had grown older these bouts had grown less frequent and during the last ten years there had scarcely been any.

She had changed a great deal. She had become the Lady Bountiful of Castle Rising, known for her good works. But older people who remembered the havoc she had caused and the murder of her husband Edward the Second, which was said to be the most cruel ever known, whispered that a lifetime of good works could never expiate her sins.

She had grown serene, forgetful of that in the past which she did not want to remember.

Lying in her bed she dozed and when she awakened her thoughts were happy ones. She thought of all the good works she had done and caused to be done. Twenty-eight years was a long time. She was loved and respected here in Castle Rising. It was only now and then that people remembered, and when all was considered she had deprived the country of an unworthy king and given it a great one. Surely that was justifiable.

She had enjoyed hearing news from outside the castle. How her son Edward was revered wherever he went; how he was claiming the French crown because she his mother had been a daughter of a King of France; how he and his plump wife had produced that hero, the Black Prince. Surely it was not such a bad life? What had happened in Berkeley Castle had been long forgotten. Surely she could die in peace.

Edward came to see her. How handsome he was, how kingly!

He knelt by her bed and taking her hand held it firmly in his. 'Dear son,' she said, 'you fulfilled all my dreams for you.'

He bowed his head. He could not pretend to love her. Perhaps he had long ago when they had been in France and Hainault together and he first met Philippa. In those days he had looked to her and Mortimer and had been their tool. Well, he had been only a boy and they had ruled through him. Then he had discovered the truth about them — their adulterous relationship and worse still their relentless ambition. It might have been because of his mother that he had been a faithful husband and devoted father. He had determined that he would not resemble his parents in any way.

But all that was in the past. She was dying now.

He wondered if she knew it.

She did, because she said: 'I am dying, Edward. Promise me that I shall be buried in the Grey Friars of Newgate.'

'It shall be,' said Edward, for none could deny a dying wish. But the Grey Friars in Newgate was where the mangled body of Mortimer lay. So she remembered her lover still and would be laid beside him.

She went on: 'And your father's heart must be with me. I want it laid upon my breast. Will you do this for me, Edward?'

Edward swore he would.

Her wishes were carried out and little was said of her burial. She herself was a figure of the past. Few remembered her story so there were not many to marvel that she should wish to have the heart of the husband whom she and Mortimer had caused to be murdered buried with her.

The King of Scotland refused to be depressed by what he called his wife's desertion.

'Let her stay with her noble brother,' he cried. 'At least I do not have to support her.'

Katherine consoled him and he was relying more and more upon her. In vain did those who wished him well implore him to use discretion. He snapped his fingers at them and the conduct of the lovers grew more and more blatant.

Katherine showed her contempt for those lords who were cool to her. She contrived that they could not even speak to the King unless it was in her presence. Having flamboyant tastes she adorned herself in the royal jewels and was a glittering figure beside the King wherever he went.

In the streets the people muttered against her. They called her the wanton harlot, the King's whore, but Katherine merely laughed at them and made David laugh with her. Sometimes he felt a little uneasy but Katherine always made fun of his moods. She could excite him and soothe him and he told himself he could not live without her.

Anyone but David would have seen that he could not continue in this way, but he was blind to everything but the satisfaction he derived from his mistress's company.

They were riding together near Melrose one day with a small party of friends.

David was a short distance ahead of Katherine when suddenly he heard a cry of agony and turning sharply he saw her fall from her horse.

Those who were riding with him were some little way behind. They did nothing when a man broke into their ranks and ran into the forest. Then to his horror David saw that Katherine was covered in blood and that a knife was protruding from her side.

He knelt beside her calling her name. She looked at him with glazed eyes and then he knew that she could not see him; she would never see anything else again.

So Katherine, the King's mistress, had been murdered and David was beside himself with grief which could only be assuaged by violent revenge. He wanted the man who had done this deed. He wanted him brought before him. He wanted him tortured. Oh, it should be a long and lingering death.

Enquiries were made and it was discovered that the murderer was a peasant called Richard de Hulle.

'Bring him to me,' cried David. The thought of what he would do to this man was all that could pacify him. Only to see him writhing in misery while his life was prolonged that he might suffer again and again could give him any comfort.

But Richard de Hulle was never brought to justice. He had too many friends in high places. In fact he had worked for men who paid him well and promised him protection because they saw that the only way to save Scotland and her King from complete disaster was to dispose of that woman. So David was forced to live without his beloved Katherine. On the advice of his ministers he asked Joanna to return. Katherine was dead. He would be a good husband to Joanna now.

But Joanna had heard that before. She was firm. 'I am happy,' was her reply, 'to remain in my native country, where I enjoy the love of those whom I can trust. I shall never return to Scotland.'

Chapter XXI

THE MARRIAGE OF THE BLACK PRINCE

The Princess Isabella declared that she had made up her mind not to marry and her father, indulgent as ever, seemed content that this should be so. She was twenty-seven years old and so it seemed that she really meant what she said. She had vindicated herself by cruelly jilting Bernard Ezi and she liked to hear the story repeated of how broken-heartedly he had given up everything in life. Then she could forget how Louis of Flanders had insulted her.

If she ever thought of Louis it was to congratulate herself on her escape, for his marriage with Margaret of Brabant had been far from felicitous. Margaret had died horribly and there were rumours that it was her husband's doing. The story was that while he was away from Court Margaret had discovered that a particularly beautiful peasant girl had been his mistress and was to bear his child. In a fury of jealousy Margaret had had the girl seized, her nose and lips were cut off and she was imprisoned in a damp cell and left to die which she very quickly did. When Louis returned and sought his beautiful mistress and was told what had happened he was overcome by such fury that he put his wife into a dungeon similar to the one in which she had imprisoned his mistress. There was no window in this dungeon, only a hole through which bread and water were pushed daily. Either she was still there or she had died. Louis it seemed had no intention of setting her free.

'Of course he is mad,' said Isabella. And that seemed a good enough reason for jilting her.

Why should she, the beloved daughter of the King, whom everyone knew he loved more than anyone else in the world, want to exchange her comfortable existence for marriage.

Then take the case of her sister Joanna who had died of the plague near Bordeaux. Some said that she had met a happier fate than she could possibly have done had she married Pedro of Castile, who had already earned the name of Pedro the Cruel. He had neglected his wife and when she had died it was said he had poisoned her. He undoubtedly poisoned his father's mistress Eleanor de Guzman and there were many others whom he had killed by extremely cruel methods.

No! Who would marry and take such chances?

The Princess Isabella was very happy in the state she had chosen – and so was her father. How often had he said to her that he was content to keep her near him.

Her sisters Mary and Margaret did not share her views. Moreover their father knew that he could not allow all his daughters to remain unmarried. Margaret was enamoured of John Hastings, Earl of Pembroke. John's father had died when he was a year old and he had become a ward of the King. Consequently he had been brought up in the royal nursery and from an early age he and Margaret had always shared secrets and taken a great delight in each other's company.

'When I grow up,' Margaret had said, 'I am going to marry John Hastings.'

Isabella had laughed. 'He is not good enough for a princess,' she had told her haughtily.

'John is good enough for anybody,' Margaret had retorted. 'Even you,' she had added rather maliciously for Isabella's over-weening vanity was often commented on among her sisters.

Isabella replied that if he was not good enough for Margaret he certainly was not for her elder sister. But it was never wise to indulge in arguments with Margaret for Margaret could always get the better of anyone in that field. She was admittedly the cleverest of them all and she and John Hastings used to get together over their books and nothing could draw them away from them. At this time a young man who was a page in the household of Margaret's brother, Lionel Duke of Clarence, had caught their attention. His name was Geoffrey Chaucer and he was very interested in literature, a subject which intrigued Margaret. She had written poetry herself and she and John had read certain things written by this Geoffrey.

Isabella could not concern herself with a mere page so she knew very little about the young man but she did wonder what would be the outcome of Margaret's infatuation with John Hastings. Mary was betrothed to another John, the Earl de Montfort, who had a claim to the Duchy of Brittany. His position at this time was not very secure and it was for this reason that there had been a delay in the marriage for Mary who was two years older than Margaret was of a marriageable age.

Isabella thought that if *she* had wanted to marry the Earl of Pembroke she would have done so. It would not have taken her very long to wring her father's consent from him. Of course Margaret was not Isabella and everyone knew that the King could deny his eldest daughter nothing at all.

But Margaret was well aware of her father's fondness for his children and even if Isabella was his favourite he dearly loved them all and particularly his girls.

She chose her moment well. For it was necessary to approach him when he was in the right mood, and as he was always glad and ready to see his daughters she had no difficulty in talking to him alone.

She took his hand and kissed it; then raised her eyes wistfully to his. She told him how she and John had always been inseparable in the nursery, how their interests were the same, how they wanted to be together for the rest of their lives.

'Pembroke,' said Edward rather teasingly, 'not a very grand title for one of my daughters.'

'It is the one I would rather have than any other.'

'Bah, you are a love sick child.'

'I am not a child, Father. I do know what I want, and that is to marry John and to live in England so that I may never be separated from you and my mother.'

It was inevitable. His eyes were glazed with affection. These dear girls of his! He could no longer bear to lose them than they could him.

He was a foolish old man, a doting father. Men would marvel at his weakness. But how could he refuse her?

She was smothered with kisses. It was a moment such as he loved.

'Now,' he said, 'you must go to your mother and tell her what you have decided. *I* have had no say in the matter.'

'Dearest dearest Father,' cried Margaret sincerely, 'it is you who decide everything for us. If I did not know that you were happy with this I could not be either.'

'It shall be a grand wedding, eh. I will show you that your father is not beyond dancing a measure with his daughter.'

Philippa was delighted because she knew it was what Margaret wanted and she recognised that this, the cleverest of her children, needed a husband who was of her own kind. Margaret would be near her all her life and that was what she wanted. All her children should marry for love as she herself had. When she thought of the fate of poor sad Joanna of Scotland she rejoiced in her own marriage. Then there was her own daughter Joanna who had died it seemed fortunately of the plague. It was horrible to contemplate that a daughter of hers was better off dead than married to a monster – and one whom her parents had chosen for her.

She said to Edward: 'I want to see them all make happy marriages. That is all I ask.'

'You are a sentimental creature,' said Edward, and she smiled at him. He knew what she meant. None could be more sentimental than he was . . . but only where his family was concerned.

So Margaret was married and the King gave her a coronet mainly of pearls which he said was suitable on account of her name.

It seemed that marriages were in the air because a few months later her brother John of Gaunt was married to Blanche of Lancaster. John was nineteen years old, the most forceful of all the brothers next to the Black Prince. There were many speculations about the latter for he showed no sign of wanting to marry. Some said that he had wanted Joan of Kent about whom there had been a scandal when it was discovered that she had been living with Thomas Holland. And since she had left England for the Continent as the wife of another man the Prince had lost interest in matrimony. None was sure though, for he confided in no one, not even John Chandos.

The Black Prince's life seemed to be dedicated to war and he was with every year taking on the mantle of his father. The same aura of invincibility which had been the First Edward's and which now surrounded his father was without doubt inherited by him too; and what was so gratifying was that the father and son were in complete accord with each other. Brilliant warrior that he was the Prince never sought to usurp his father's power and although he was in every way preparing himself to be King he showed himself in no way eager to inherit the crown before that time when it should come naturally to him. Apart from the fact that he declined to marry and give the country an heir, he was the perfect prince.

As David of Scotland was showing himself completely unworthy to wear the crown of Scotland and it seemed unlikely that there would be any trouble from that quarter, and as the truce with France had come to an end it seemed that the time was ripe to begin another invasion in the hope of gaining complete victory and possession of what Edward regarded as his rights.

He left England and once more Philippa was filled with misgiving. However Edward did not engage in battle because the Dauphin Charles refused to meet him and before he could be forced to do so a strange event occurred which appeared to be both to Edward and his army a sign of supernatural interference.

It was Easter time and the weather had turned suddenly so cold that many of the English soldiers died because of it, collapsing and falling from their horses while riding. Nothing like it had ever been known.

It was the Monday after Easter Day when the storm broke. It came upon them suddenly; the air was full of darkness at midday and the hail rained down on the army. Then the sky was rent with such sound and fury as none of them had ever known before. Lightning streaked across the sky to be followed by utter darkness and the violent sound of the thunder.

Many of the soldiers believed that the world was coming to an end; many of the horses and men were struck by the lightning, and hailstones the size of eggs began to shower down on them.

This appeared without doubt to be a sign of divine anger and why should God visit his fury on Edward's army? There was one answer to that and it was that God did not like the claim to the French crown and he was not going to allow the King of England's efforts to be successful.

Edward was dismayed. Six thousand of his finest horses had been killed by lightning. One thousand of his men had suffered the same plight. The soldiers had turned to him expecting him to act.

But what could even the greatest soldier in the world do against the acts of God?

Edward saw only one way. He leaped from his horse and bare-headed with the hail beating down on him and the hideous lightning illuminating his face cried out: 'Oh God, take away this storm. If I have incurred your wrath I will make amends. Let my army survive this day and I will make reasonable terms with the King of France. I will release him from bondage. I give my word on this.'

There was silence all about him. He lifted his eyes to the sky and it seemed that the lightning was less fierce, that the thunder was growing more distant.

The storm was passing. His vow remained, and it was not as a promise given to another King. This one he had made to God and he must keep it.

When he told his men that they were returning to England without delay there was a great shout of joy. Every man among them had had enough of war and the sign that God was not with them would have undermined any feeling they might have had for it.

Edward was fully aware of this. That was why he knew that he must abandon the fight.

Philippa received him with the utmost joy and King Jean was informed that he was to be released on payment of a smaller ransom. Edward stressed though that his sons would be requested to come to England as hostages until the sum was paid.

Jean left for France conducted there by the Black Prince and the Duke of Lancaster; and Philippa, delighted with this outcome of affairs in France, settled comfortably to enjoy having her family with her and for the moment at least out of imminent danger.

Joan of Kent had returned to Court, a widow. Her husband, Thomas Holland, had just died in Normandy where he had been on the King's service, so there was nothing for Joan to do but return with her children to England.

Her arrival coincided with that of the Prince of Wales who had just returned from France whither he had been escorting King Jean.

The Prince appeared very pleased to see his cousin again. She was no longer young being thirty-three years old and the mother of three children but as soon as she returned to England he sent a silver beaker to remind her of him; and with it was a note welcoming his Cousin Jeanette back to England.

Joan was equally pleased to see him. She had found Thomas Holland a satisfactory husband and had been physically attracted to him but in her youth her secret ambition had been to marry the Prince of Wales.

It seemed strange to her that he had never married for she was sure some pressure to do so must have been brought on him. But Edward and Philippa had ever – contrary to royal custom – concerned themselves with the happiness of their children. And doubtless Edward had been firm in his inclination not to marry. Moreover there were other sons so the matter was not as pressing as it would otherwise have been.

Joan had no intention of remaining a widow and having married a man considered to be far beneath her socially she was now determined to pick the highest in the land. She had always been wily and if she was slightly less beautiful than she had been in her youth she made up for that by an increased astuteness.

She contrived to put herself in the Prince's path and as he made no effort to evade her they were together often. He was two years younger than she was and to her dismay he seemed to have made up his mind that he would never marry. She was hurt and angry when he talked to her of the possibility of her doing so.

'Oh, I shall not marry again,' she answered and added untruthfully, 'I have no wish to.'

'Holland is so recently dead,' replied the Prince. 'You will change your mind later, I swear it.'

'You do not know me, cousin,' she answered.

427

'Dear Jeanette, there are few I know better. We have grown up together.'

That was the trouble, she thought. He saw her as his cousin, the companion of nursery days. He was such a strange man. It was true that no one could understand what he really felt.

Still she was going to show him. He was not indifferent to women and clearly he liked her company. She was handsome enough still to be known as the Fair Maid of Kent. If she had grown a little plump it was becomingly so. She had always been the most beautiful woman at Court and refused to believe that she had moved in the slightest degree from that position.

Matters came to a head when Sir Bernard de Brocas, a very worthy and wealthy knight of Gascony, asked the King's permission to marry her.

The King talked over the matter with the Prince because he knew of the friendliness between his son and Joan.

'A good match,' said the King. 'Sir Bernard has served me well and I should like to reward him. The marriage would be a great one for him. She will bring him the family estates and I shall feel that I have rewarded him for his good service.'

The Prince nodded. As the only surviving member of her family the Kent title and estates had come to her. She was indeed a great heiress.

'Of course,' said the Prince, 'she is a widow and will doubtless wish to have her say.'

'We may trust Joan for that,' replied Edward. 'But it shall be known that I am agreeable to the match and it is only for her to agree to it. Perhaps, my son, you would speak to her and tell her my wishes.'

The Prince said he would do so and at the earliest opportunity sought out Joan.

He asked if he might speak to her in private.

Her heart was beginning to beat so wildly that she wondered if he would be aware of her excitement. Was this the moment? Had he at last made up his mind?

'You are a widow, Jeanette,' he said, 'rich and by no means old. My father thinks you should marry again.'

She dared not look at him but she said quietly: 'And you, Cousin. What think you?'

'Yes,' he replied. 'I think you should.'

She closed her eyes. Her dream was coming true. He was going to suggest marriage. Princess of Wales, Queen in the not too far future.

'As a matter of fact there has been an offer for you.'

'An . . . offer!'

'Sir Bernard de Brocas loves you dearly. He has spoken to the King.'

She stared at him blankly, angrily.

'And the King,' she said shortly, 'what says he?'

'He says that he would wish to reward Sir Bernard and this would be a way of doing so.'

'So . . . I am to be a . . . reward!'

'You are an excellent match, Cousin.'

'My family's estates, yes. A good reward for a faithful servant.'

'And you are very beautiful, Cousin.'

'I had not thought you had noticed.'

'You know full well how much I admire you.'

'You have never deemed it fitting to tell me so.'

'Why should I tell you what you know already?'

'The answer is that I should have liked to hear it.'

'Well then, 'tis so, Cousin. I repeat you are a beautiful

woman and a rich one. But I do not believe it is your estates alone that he considers. What is your answer?'

'What would you have me do?' she asked almost plaintively.

'I would have you consider the offer.'

'Then let me tell you this,' she said. 'I shall never marry again.'

He was surprised. 'You do not mean that,' he protested. 'You are too young . . . too beautiful to remain unmarried. I know that you have had many suitors.'

'None that I would take,' she said. 'I hope the King does not plan to force me into this.'

'Indeed he would not. He would only advise you.'

She turned to him and lifting her beautiful eyes to his cried: '*You* advise me.'

He took her hand and held it fast. 'Sir Bernard de Brocas is a very worthy knight,' he said.

'Stop it!' she cried. 'Don't say it. I will not listen.' Then she sat on a stool and covered her face with her hands.

He stared down at her in amazement; then he knelt down beside her and drew her hands away from her face. Her eyes were feverish with excitement.

'Dearest Jeanette, what is wrong with you? You must know that de Brocas is one of the most chivalrous knights in my father's service.'

'I will never marry him . . . as long as I live. I cannot because . . .'

'You are in love with someone else!' cried the Prince.

She did not deny it. She cried out: 'You tell me Bernard de Brocas is a chivalrous knight. I am in love with the most chivalrous knight in the world. How can you ask me to take something less.'

430

'Then perhaps . . .'

She shook her head. 'Nay,' she said. 'I cannot marry this man so I shall take no other.'

'He has made you unhappy . . . this knight. That does not seem to me a chivalrous act.'

She smiled wanly. 'Nay, he knows not the extent of my love for him. It has ever been so and he unaware of it.'

'Tell me his name.'

'You know it well.'

He stood up and she rose and stood beside him.

'I could never bring myself to tell you,' she said.

'Jeanette,' he said, 'you *shall* tell me. I must know. I want to do everything I can to make you happy.'

She laughed. 'Oh, Edward, surely you know. Is it not clear? Who is the most chivalrous knight in the world? Who was the companion of my childhood? Whom did I love always? Surely you know.'

He looked at her incredulously.

'The Black Prince,' she said. 'There has never been one to compare with him nor ever shall be and as I will take only the best I shall remain unmarried all the rest of my life.'

He continued to stare at her and the joy suddenly showed in his face. She had made up his mind for him. Jeanette! Of course it was Jeanette. The most beautiful woman at Court. She was the one he had been waiting for.

He kissed her hands fervently.

'So all the time . . . I was the one . . .'

'*All* the time,' she said fervently. 'Since I was small and you were small . . . Even then it was only you.'

'Yet you married Holland.'

'Because I despaired. I would not take Salisbury whom I

431

disliked. I thought it was no use waiting for you. There now, I have betrayed myself and you will despise me.'

'I vow to God,' said the Prince earnestly, 'that I will not take any to be my wife but you – my dearest cousin, my Jeanette.'

She was triumphant. Why had she not done this before? It was so easy. This strange man whose thoughts were so wrapped up in military glory had only needed a woman to make up his mind for him.

She was alert to danger. What would the King and Queen say to the proposed match? Before she had married Thomas Holland they would have agreed to it; but she was no longer a favourite of the Queen. Philippa had not approved of the somewhat shady match with Holland when Joan had disclosed that she had already lived with him as his wife while pretending she was going to marry Salisbury. Moreover Philippa had noticed the King's eyes on the beauty. There was that incident of the garter. Philippa would not want her eldest son to marry a scheming woman. And the King. How could he feel about accepting as his daughter-in-law a woman whom he had once desired – for Joan knew well enough that he had and because he was the King she had given him several promising glances knowing full well that the high moral code he set upon himself would prevent their relationship straying beyond the boundary of flirtation.

They would both regard her as something of an adventuress and that was not the woman they would want as future Queen of England.

They would want someone like Philippa – stern, always aware of her duty.

And how determined was Edward? A short while ago he had been ready to offer her to Bernard de Brocas.

'My dearest Edward,' she said quickly. 'I am bewildered by my happiness. So precious are you to me, for I have waited all these years never believing that my dreams would be fulfilled, that now I am afraid.'

'You must never be afraid of anything with me beside you.'

'I am afraid they will try to stop our marriage.'

'Nay, they never would.'

'To please me, Edward. Do not tell anyone yet . . . not until we have made our plans. Not until we can go to the King and tell him that we are set for marriage, that the plans are made and there can be no delay.'

To humour her, he agreed.

When Edward and Philippa heard that the Black Prince was going to marry Joan of Kent they were dismayed.

'A widow!' cried the King. 'A woman older than yourself.'

'By two years,' replied the Prince, 'and I am not too old to beget sons, nor is she.'

'The relationship is very close,' put in Philippa.

'I have already sent to Rome for a dispensation,' answered the Prince. 'There will be no difficulty in acquiring it, I am sure.'

Philippa was thinking: Will he be happy with her? It had really been disgraceful the manner in which she had pretended to be unmarried when all the time she had lived with Holland. Philippa would have liked her son to marry a gentle young virgin, someone who looked up to him and adored him – not an experienced woman, older than himself, full of wiles and who had already borne three children.

As for the King he thought: She will be a disturbing

daughter-in-law . . . She made him uneasy. There was flaunting sexuality about her, a quality which bothered him in women even more so than in the past. Philippa had aged more quickly than he had and she was so fat that she could not move about without difficulty. As he was getting older temptation came more often. No, he did not want a woman like Joan of Kent in the family.

But both of them saw that the Black Prince, after holding back for so long, was now all eagerness and was going to conduct his marriage like a military campaign. It was clear that nothing was going to deter him. He was no longer a boy and it appeared that he must have been waiting for his cousin as before he had shown clearly his lack of desire to marry and settle down.

Edward and Philippa discussed the matter together and they both agreed that they must accept the marriage.

News came from Rome that the dispensation was granted and would be sent to England. However, the Prince and Joan decided that they could not wait for it.

They were married in the Chapel at Windsor. The King was not present. Somehow he could not bring himself to see his son marry a woman who aroused such desires in himself. He felt too uneasy and it was better for him to stay away.

Joan guessed the real reason but she was content to let it be believed that the King was not entirely pleased with the marriage. What care I for that! she thought. Poor old Edward! He looked magnificent still, of course, but he was ageing a little. There was a good deal of white in the once golden hair. He was a little jealous of his son for having chosen such a voluptuous bride. She knew it, and she could understand it. Pious old Philippa was scarcely a siren these days.

They left Court soon after the ceremony for one of the Prince's residences in Berkhamstead and as the King had granted his son all his dominions in Aquitaine and Gascony, the newly married pair left England and in a short time had set up a splendid Court which was sometimes in Aquitaine but more often in Bordeaux.

The whole family rejoiced when in due course, Joan gave birth to a son. He was called Edward, which seemed appropriate as he was in direct line to the throne.

☸ Chapter XXII ☸

ISABELLA AND DE COUCY

B
efore the birth of the Black Prince's son, a tragedy
had struck the family and it was one from which
Philippa never recovered.

Now that her sons were moving away from her which was
inevitable she was more and more in the company of her
daughters. Isabella was like a queen in her own right and gave
herself more airs than ever Philippa had. Philippa knew that
the King was largely responsible for the behaviour of this
overbearing daughter but the older he grew the more dotingly
fond he became.

Margaret was married and was the Countess of Pembroke
but she was too young to live with her husband and remained
in her mother's care.

Mary was older and wished to marry the Duke of Brittany
to whom she had long been betrothed. Edward had however
delayed the marriage because of the uncertainty of the
bridegroom's position; but now, as the young people were
eager for the match, he decided that it should take place.

So now both her daughters were married. The only one who
was not was Isabella and she was twelve years older than Mary.

Isabella it seemed would remain unmarried but she and Philippa had never been as close as the others; and Philippa knew that she must resign herself to parting with her daughters in due course.

She did not realise how soon and how tragically.

She had noticed for some weeks that Margaret seemed lethargic. She slept a great deal even during the day and seemed unable to rouse herself.

One morning Philippa's women came to her in some distress and said that Margaret's attendants were dismayed as they could not arouse her. Philippa, who had known for some time that there was something wrong with her daughter, went uneasily to her apartments where she found Margaret lying on her bed looking very tired.

'What is it, my dearest?' asked Philippa. 'Are you feeling ill?'

'Only tired, my lady. Very tired.'

'Come, let me help you dress.'

Philippa tried to lift her daughter but Margaret fell back on to her pillows.

'I beg you, dear Mother, let me stay as I am. I cannot get up. I am so very tired.'

In dismay Philippa sent for the doctors. They did not know what ailed Margaret but as the day passed she sank into a deep sleep.

'Let her rest,' said the doctors. 'Then she may recover from her exhaustion.'

But Margaret did not recover. Quietly she slipped away from life.

Philippa was stunned. She had thought her daughter had been merely tired. It was not possible that she could be dead.

But she was. It was some disease which had never before been heard of; and it seemed it was fatal.

Philippa wept and shut herself away. If Margaret had been ailing she could have been prepared. But she had been so happy. She had loved her young husband dearly and he her. Poor boy. He was heart-broken; he came to Philippa and sobbed at her feet. She did her best to comfort him but it was useless.

It seemed as though the hand of God was against her for a few weeks after Margaret's death Mary was struck with the same disease.

This time they were prepared for it and when the drowsiness attacked a second daughter Philippa and Edward had every physician of standing to come to their daughter.

It was no use. No one had any idea what the mysterious illness was and there was nothing to be done but watch the young girl's strength slowly ebb away.

In a few weeks Mary was dead.

Philippa, completely stricken, seemed to have lost interest in life.

There was deep mourning throughout the Court and the two young husbands vowed they would never marry again.

Philippa tried to assuage her misery by having a fine tomb erected in the monastery of Abingdon and there the bodies of her two daughters were laid side by side.

Isabella was now the only living daughter. She was treated with the greatest respect and indulgence but she began to feel that she was missing a great deal in life. It was her own wish that she had remained unmarried for she had as shamelessly jilted Bernard Ezi as Louis of Flanders had jilted her.

She could congratulate herself on her escape from Louis but she had decided that perhaps she should marry after all.

When the King of France had returned to his country escorted by Edward, Isabella had been a member of the party and among the company was the Lord de Coucy who distinguished himself by his extraordinary good looks and success in the jousts; he could sing and dance most elegantly and Isabella thought he was the handsomest man she had ever seen. He was seven years younger than she was but that did not prevent an attachment springing up between them.

It was for this reason that Isabella decided that she would abandon her vow to remain unmarried and take Ingelram, Lord de Coucy as her husband.

The fact that he was merely a French nobleman did not deter her. She knew that he hesitated to suggest marriage because she was the daughter of the King of England but she quickly let him know that if she decided to marry the King would never let anything stand in the way of her happiness.

De Coucy was a little sceptical of this which only made Isabella all the more determined to marry him.

When she broached the subject with her father he was taken aback. 'My dearest Isabella,' he cried, 'I thought you were reconciled to the single state.'

'So was I, my lord. But now I have met Ingelram. Is he not the most handsome man you ever saw?'

'I have seen others who appeal to me more.'

'No one has the grace of Ingelram. In any case, I love him, Father, and I want to marry him. I know you want to see me happy and you will not prevent my being so.' She slipped her arm through his. 'I shall not be far away. I should see you often. Dearest Father, I cannot miss all that other women

439

have. I want children. I want to marry now, before it is too late.'

As she had known Edward would not hold out against her for long. He did say: 'I trust there will be no hasty cancellation of this if I allow you to go ahead.'

'Nay, I swear it. I want to marry Ingelram. I long for the day.'

'So be it,' said the King.

So the marriage took place and the thirty-three year old bride really did seem in love with her twenty-seven year old bridegroom.

In due course the pair left for the Château de Coucy where Isabella lived in a state almost as royal as that which she had enjoyed in her father's Court.

Isabella was more deeply in love with her young husband than ever and to their delight in less than a year after the marriage she gave birth to a daughter. She called her Mary after her dead sister and said they must take the child to England for the King would never rest until he had had a glimpse of his granddaughter.

When they arrived in England Edward was overjoyed and delighted that his beloved Isabella was happy in her marriage. He admitted that he was glad that she had a husband although it had taken her from him.

'You will always be very dear to me, Father,' she told him. 'Nothing else I had could change that.'

Revelling in their company, arranging elaborate feasts and jousts for their entertainment, Edward was happy. She noticed that he was showing his age, though not as much as her mother was.

Poor Philippa scarcely left her chair now. It must be a great hardship for her not to be able to accompany the King on his journeys.

Edward said to his daughter one day: 'I have a plan for keeping you here. I am going to make your husband an English peer.'

Isabella laughed aloud with triumph.

'I see,' she said. 'You will give him estates and in honour bound he will have to stay in England to look after them.'

It would mean, admitted Edward, that he would have to spend a great deal of time in this country.

'It seems an excellent plan,' said Isabella demurely.

Thus the Lord de Coucy became the Earl of Bedford, and Edward bestowed on him the Order of the Garter.

They had an ample income and estates in England but on the King's request they resided mainly at the Court.

'This is a happy outcome,' said Edward to Philippa. 'Our daughter has acquired a husband but we have not lost our daughter.'

❀ Chapter XXIII ❀

THE PASSING OF PHILIPPA

Philippa was finding it increasingly difficult to hide her infirmities from those about her. She suffered from internal pains and was a victim of dropsy which made her limbs swell to such an extent that she found it very difficult to leave her chair. If she moved it was with the help of her women and this caused her great distress.

Edward was a year older than she was but he seemed much younger. He was active still and appeared to have lost very little of his early vigour.

Philippa knew that he had a great affection for her but the days of their youth when they had been enough for each other had passed.

There was a sly woman who had come to Court as one of her bedchamber women. Philippa feared this woman. She was sure there was evil in her.

Alice Perrers was not exactly handsome and studying her closely Philippa could not understand exactly why she should have aroused the King's interest. Perhaps it was a latent sexuality in her which was not obvious but Philippa had begun to suspect. She had seen looks which passed between her attendants and she noticed that they were brusque with Alice who did not seem to mind in the least. There was a secret brooding air about her as though she were biding her time.

The truth was that the King had at last succumbed to temptation.

He had noticed Alice Perrers as soon as he saw her and she had clearly been aware of his interest.

Alice was not of noble birth. Edward was not sure how she had wormed her way into the royal household but he made no effort to find out. She was a woman to grant favour for favour so it may have been that she had acquired her position through some well placed person at Court. Edward decided not to go into that. Suffice it that Alice was there.

She had caught his eye on her and had smiled invitingly. Other women had before, of course, and he had never strayed from Philippa, but Philippa was now a sick woman. He was as fond of her as he ever was, but he was virile and a King and Philippa could no longer help him to turn from temptation.

For some time he wrestled with his conscience. After a life of fidelity to his marriage vows it was not easy to break faith. But Alice was different from the others. She was determined. One night she came and slipped into his bed and there was nothing he could do short of turning her out and that was the last thing he wished.

After that night Alice was his mistress and nothing would stop his keeping her so. It had been a wild experience, different from anything he had known before and it left him dazed, bewildered and – said some of his courtiers – bewitched.

However, it had happened at last. The King had a mistress. And a low-born one at that. 'She will not last long,' prophesied those about him. They did not know Alice.

Having set one foot on the road to debauchery Edward could not stop himself going further. It was as though he had to make up for the lost years. There were times when he was overcome by remorse but then Alice would appear and laugh at his conscience. He was the King, was he not; and should not kings do as they wished?

He tried to explain to her the deep affection that existed between himself and the Queen. Alice thought that was all very well and that the Queen would understand. After all she was too old and infirm to be a wife to him.

'She is younger than I,' Edward reminded her.

'Ah, but you, my King, are immortal.'

Sometimes he tried to understand what this lure was. Alice was not as beautiful as the Countess of Salisbury had been; she was certainly not like Joan the Fair Maid of Kent. But there was something so irresistible about her, something so sensuous, so matching his own nature which he realised he had held in check all these years that he could not leave her.

His children were scattered about the country and some abroad. It was no longer as it had been when they had been young and in the nursery and a continual source of interest between himself and Philippa. Philippa sick and heavy with that disfiguring and painful dropsy no longer had anything to offer him. In fact he eluded her – chiefly because to be with her aroused his conscience to such an extent that he began to despise himself.

His only consolation was in Alice, and Alice had plenty of comfort to give him.

She did not make too great a display of his generosity towards her. She was secretly a little in awe of the Queen. There was a quiet power about Philippa and Alice knew it would be unwise to rouse that to action. The King had a great regard for his wife; Alice knew better than he did how often Philippa was there in their bedchamber – a shadowing restraint, a curber of joys. Oh yes, the spirit of Philippa would always be with him . . . until she died.

And that Philippa could not be long for this world was growing more and more obvious every day.

Philippa knew that her end was near. She lay in her bed so heavy now with her dropsical complaint that it was exhausting to move.

It had been a life well spent, a happy life and she cherished still the memory of her first meeting with Edward at her father's Court. Theirs surely had been one of the happiest royal marriages ever known. Until now. She would not think of that brazen woman who crept about with secrets in her eyes. It was a pity she knew of her. But it was so obvious and she could not help it. She had always been aware that Edward was a man of strong passions. One of his nature naturally would be. She knew there had been temptations. She had heard whispers of the beautiful Countess of Salisbury and he had cast many a yearning glance on that minx Joan of Kent; but never had he given way to temptation. Until now. She must not take it hardly. He was a man and she had become a poor creature, too sick for anything but to lie in her bed and wait for the end, to look back over the past. She had much happiness to reflect on and she could be proud of the family she had raised.

Edward the first-born, the best loved, was now a father of two children, Edward and Richard, and seemed content with his life in Bordeaux with Joan of Kent. Perhaps Joan had loved him all the time. It was strange that he had not spoken for her when it would have been fitting for him to. Neither she nor Edward would have raised any objection to a match when they were young. Isabella was at last happily married. Poor Joanna had not had much of a life; and her two Williams and little Blanche would never be forgotten even though they had lived such a short time. Then there were tall and good-natured Lionel, bold John of Gaunt, Edmund and Thomas. She tried not to think of Mary and Margaret; she had never got over their deaths.

Her beloved children – all living their own lives which did not really concern her. Edward was pleased with the children they had had. She had nothing to reproach herself with on that score.

And now the end was fast approaching.

One morning she awoke in her apartments in Windsor Castle and knew it was close, so she sent a messenger to the King asking that he come to her bedchamber without delay. And when he came in all speed and saw how ill she was he was overcome with grief and his conscience smote him more strongly then ever before.

She smiled at him lovingly.

'Edward,' she said, 'this is the end.'

He knelt by the bed and taking her hand kissed it. He kept his head lowered for he could not bear to look at her.

'It must not be,' he murmured.

'Dear husband,' she said, 'dear lord and King, we cannot go against God's will. He has decided that my time has come and we must perforce accept this. Our union has been long and you have given me so much happiness.'

Edward could scarcely bear to listen. He kept thinking of

Alice Perrers and he reproached himself bitterly. Why did I not wait? Why did I do this to Philippa? For she knows . . . everybody knows. This shame has come upon me.

'My lord,' said Philippa, 'I beg you fulfil my engagements as I have entered them in my will. I have named those of my ladies who should receive some benefit.'

'Everything you wish shall be granted, my beloved Queen.'

'Edward when your times comes will you lie beside me in my tomb and shall it be in the cloisters of Westminster?'

'It shall be done,' said Edward.

'Then let us thank God for the happy years. For the children He has given us . . .'

'I thank God for all this,' said Edward, 'and I beg him now not to take you from me.'

He was vowing to God: Only let her live and I will never see Alice again; but even at that moment he knew the allure of Alice would be too strong for him. He was overcome by misery which was heavy with remorse.

If only I had waited! he thought. If only she had never known!

She had closed her eyes.

It was the end. The long association with his Queen was over and he felt lost and bewildered. His son Edmund who was at the bedside with him laid a hand on his father's arm.

'My lord,' he said, 'come away. She has left us for ever.'

Edward wrestled with his conscience. She did not know. I was always so careful. She would never have guessed what was happening.

He kept seeing her as the rosy-faced girl she had been when they had first married. Then he had been sure that he would never want anyone else as long as he lived.

But she never knew, he promised himself. She believed to the end that she was the only one.

But when he read her will and saw her bequests to the women of the bedchamber, he noticed at once that there was one name missing. That of Alice Perrers.

Chapter XXIV

THE LADY OF THE SUN AND
THE OLD MAN

W ith the death of Philippa the influence of Alice Perrers over the King began to increase. His conscience no longer worried him and he became more and more besotted. He was never parted from her; he became her slave; she only had to express a wish and he wanted to grant it. It was said of her that she was very skilled in the ways of love and that this gave her special powers over an ageing man who had kept his passions in check until this time.

Alice was greedy for riches. She loved jewels and could never have enough of them; moreover she was shrewd and in view of the King's age she knew her reign could not be of long duration; therefore she was determined to make the most of it while it lasted.

She sought about for means of making herself the richest woman in the country. There were plenty of tricks she could play. Edward was ready to bestow lands on her and these she accepted eagerly, but it was not enough for her rapacious needs. She made use of the custom of guardianship which meant that when rich parents died leaving heirs under age some member of the Court took charge of them. To be allotted a rich heir was a great concession, for a good income from the estate came with the heir. Alice had already three boys under her care, as it was said, which was very lucrative.

It was amusing that she who had been a woman of no importance should have become the most important in the land. She grew bolder and bolder as she became more and more sure of her power and even joined the King during council meetings and sat beside him giving advice to which he listened with something like awe; she had formed a habit of going to Westminster Hall and taking her place beside the judge that she might tell him what verdict to give. And that verdict would depend on whether the accused had rewarded her in a manner she considered suitable to bring about his acquittal.

She was seen wearing the late Queen's jewels when she sat with the King at banquets. She had a passion for jewels and her gowns were ablaze with them, and the fur trimming on each gown was a fortune in itself. Edward could not have chosen a woman more unlike Philippa and just as the people had loved their Queen, their feeling for the woman they called The Harlot carried the same intensity but in the opposite direction.

Alice Perrers' name was spoken with venom in the streets of London and she was notorious throughout the country.

The death of Philippa had undoubtedly brought a great change to the country. She and Edward had stood as pillars of strength and virtue. Edward could scarcely be called that now. Instead of the great warrior the upright noble knight he had been, he had become a doddering old man who could not keep his hands – even in public – from caressing a brazen strumpet. Deeply the people mourned the passing of the Queen. When she had been alive they had been aware of her virtue but they had failed to recognise her strength.

Yes there was change. Once it had seemed that the war with France was coming to a victorious end when the King of France had been made captive and honourable peace terms had been arranged.

The Black Prince – idol of the people – had scored successes on the Continent where he had remained with his devoted wife; he had two sons, Edward and Richard, and everything had seemed set fair for prosperity.

Then came disturbing news. The Black Prince was suffering from ill health. He was attacked by intermittent fever which often meant that he must take to his bed for long periods.

Moreover a fresh wave of patriotism had come to France. King Jean was dead and his son Charles had come to the throne. He was determined to win back what had been lost in his father's day and Frenchmen were remembering to whom they owed allegiance. The Black Prince realising what was happening was forced to send for reinforcements. There were attacks on Aquitaine which he managed to defend but while he was engaged in that quarter trouble was breaking out elsewhere.

Joan would have been completely happy had it not been for the constant absences of her husband and the fact that she was worried about his health. Her eldest son Edward on whom her husband doted, had been in poor health too. Joan longed to return to England and Court life there. If she could only do that and her husband be restored to health she would be content. But she began to see that one of these wishes if granted would mean that the other could not be for he could only return to England if his health failed and if he were well and strong he would be forced to stay in France.

She was too realistic to hope for complete contentment. She loved the Black Prince devotedly. He was the national hero; the most chivalrous knight in the world and he was the heir to a throne. He would make her a Queen and the mother of a King. She felt that the hideous murder of her father was vindicated.

But the anxiety about the Black Prince's health continued; and when he heard that his greatest friend John Chandos had been killed he was plunged into melancholy which brought on another bout of the fever.

Joan herself nursed him and when he had recovered a little broached the subject of their return to England.

'It is no use going on in this way,' she said. 'These attacks are becoming more and more frequent. Someone else must take over your duties.'

'Who?' asked the Prince.

'The most likely seems your brother, John of Gaunt.'

'A very ambitious man, my brother John.'

'All sons of kings are ambitious, particularly younger ones.'

'John is the cleverest of them all.'

'And if he came to take your place he would take credit for all your victories, I doubt not,' said Joan tartly. 'Even so your health is more important to me than your glory.'

The Prince smiled at her fierceness. 'You have been a good wife to me, Joan,' he said.

She kissed him lightly. 'There was much time to be made up,' she answered lightly. 'You shillied and shallied and could not be brought to marry me until I forced you to it.'

He agreed it was so.

'Then you see,' she told him, 'I am able to manage our affairs far better than you can.'

He was too tired to argue; he could feel the fever rising within him.

These wretched wars! thought Joan. What a curse they were! She remembered Philippa's attitude to them and how right she was. The difference in them was that Philippa would have kept her irritation with them to herself. Joan was not like that.

The affair at Limoges had upset Edward more than he would admit. It was a mistake, Joan knew, to become involved in the Castilian war. Pedro was hated by his subjects; many said he had no right to the throne which he had taken from his elder brother's son, Charles de la Cerda. His half-brother Henry of Trastamara who was the illegitimate son of Pedro's father and his mistress Eleanor de Guzman now sought to take the crown and when Pedro had sent appeals to the Black Prince he had answered them.

A great mistake, reiterated Joan. It had given the French the chance they needed.

And now with the death of the much loved Chandos and the fever returning . . . it was time there was change.

Joan sent for the doctors and questioned them.

What were these fevers from which her husband suffered and would they increase as time passed?

The answer was that the disease had been contracted through the Prince's way of life – camping in damp places and foreign countries; and the nature of the disease was that it must inevitably grow worse as time passed.

'I want you to insist that he returns to England,' said Joan firmly.

The doctors agreed with her that a rest away from camps and long days in the saddle would be beneficial to the Prince.

Brought low by fever, mourning the death of his friend Chandos, realising that his victories in France were slipping from English hands, he allowed Joan to make the arrangements for their departure.

He knew he was very sick. He had nightmares and the siege of Limoges figured largely in these. The town had been in English hands and had been treacherously given to the French by Jean de Cros, the Bishop of Limoges, whom he had counted his friend. What a rage he had been in then! Unable to mount his horse he was carried on a litter. He had sworn that he would take Limoges and woe betide the betrayer when he did.

Nor had he spared himself though the fever almost maddened him. The town was taken and the carnage was terrible. He himself ordered that it should be so. There should be no mercy, he had declared. Every living thing should be slaughtered. He had ridden through the town in a heavy four-wheeled cart because he was too ill to sit on a horse. There was blood everywhere, corpses in heaps in every street; hot with fever he surveyed the slaughter. He felt defeated by circumstances which were too overwhelming to control.

The defaulting Bishop who had surrendered the town to the French was dragged before him. 'I'll have his head,' he cried.

It was his brother, John of Gaunt, who begged him to consider that the Bishop was a man of the Church. True he had given the town to the French but it could have been to save slaughter. Edward must remember that the Church would be displeased and they could not afford to offend the Church.

By this time the Prince's anger was spent. The hot blood which sent him crazy with the need for blood-letting had passed; he was shivering with the ague and longed for the quiet of his bed.

'Take the Bishop,' he said to his brother. 'Do what you will.'

And he was carried back to Joan.

Do what you will. Yes, John would do what he would. John was an ambitious man who bitterly resented not having been born the eldest.

But I have two sons, mused the Prince. My little Edward to follow me and if aught should befall him there is also Richard.

So back to the peace of his home where he must continue to dream of Limoges – a blot on his shield of glory. He had once been a great Prince who did not need to resort to the killing of women and babies to prove his strength.

Joan and the doctors said: 'You must go to England. You must rest awhile.'

At first he protested but he knew they were right. A warrior did not go into battle in a litter; he did not ride through a captured city in a four-wheeled cart.

So the preparations went on. As soon as this bout had subsided they would set out.

One morning just as the loading of the ships was nearing completion, Joan came to him in a state of great consternation. Young Edward was ill.

The doctors were not sure what ailed him but they were deeply concerned about the child's condition.

It proved to be not without cause. Within a few days little Edward was dead.

This was the greatest blow of all.

Limoges, the rising of French power, the loss of that of England, the death of Chandos . . . and now little Edward.

Joan was overcome by grief. This young Edward had been her pride; she had looked far ahead into the distant future and seen him mounting a throne. A long long time yet she had promised herself, but it would be one day.

And now . . . he was gone.

But she was a woman of energetic ambition. She had after a long wait achieved marriage with the Prince of Wales. She had lost their beloved son. But there could be more, she promised herself. They already had little Richard. He was not quite four years old, a tall fair-haired boy with the Plantagenet looks.

The little boy known as Richard of Bordeaux because of his birthplace was now in direct line to the throne.

How changed was the Court. How everyone missed the presence of Queen Philippa which they had not noticed while she had been there.

In her place ruled the brazen hussy, sitting in the Queen's chair, wearing the Queen's jewels, wrapped in the royal mantle edged with ermine and supported in this by the King.

And most changed of all the King himself. No longer alert, no longer concerned with his country's welfare, wanting only the comfort his strumpet could offer and letting everyone know it.

The Prince took in the situation at once. The King had changed. His mind had weakened; he had suffered some illness. This could not be the great commanding figure who had guided the country for more than thirty years.

The King received his son warmly, condoled with him on the death of young Edward and received his grandson Richard with affection.

But there was an absent-mindedness about him; and the Black Prince refused to meet Alice Perrers.

It soon became clear that if he persisted in this attitude he would not be welcome at Court.

He took the first opportunity of speaking to his sister Isabella who had been closer to the King than any of them.

Isabella was bewildered. It was no use trying to make their father see what he was doing. He was completely bewitched by the woman.

'All through my life I have only had to ask to see him and I was allowed to,' she explained. 'But if that woman says I should not come to him, I am not allowed to.'

'It must pass,' said the Prince.

'There is no sign of it. She grows more and more outrageous but still he keeps her with him. He cares only for her. I believe he is growing feeble-minded.'

'It would seem so,' said the Prince. 'I shall not stay here nor will Joan to be treated thus by a woman of that kind. You will return to France doubtless.'

Isabella was silent. Those about her often said that she had become a changed woman since her marriage. The imperious Princess had strangely become a somewhat meek wife. The fact was that her youthful husband was less enamoured of her than she was of him, and he was quite content to leave her in England while he went to France. He was reluctant to take up arms against the French King and on the other hand he could scarcely do so against his father and brothers-in-law. The handsome Lord de Coucy was less pleased with his marriage than he had first thought he would be. The tragedy for Isabella was that each day she grew more and more in love with her husband.

457

This had had the effect of subduing her and of bringing a certain humility into her nature which had never been there before. She was devoted to her daughters and now that her father was less determined to please her she was discovering a greater affection for him than it had seemed she could be capable of.

'It grieves me,' she told her brother, 'to see him thus. There have been times when I have thought of leaving the Court but somehow I feel I must stay. He needs one of us with him and I am the only daughter left and was always his favourite. No, Edward, I shall stay here at Court and I have even gone so far as to make myself agreeable to Alice Perrers. I cannot tell you what joy that gives our father. Moreover it gives me an opportunity to keep my eye on him — and help him escape from the enchantment . . . bewitchment or whatever it is.'

Edward was surprised that Isabella could become unselfish but he was too ill to concern himself with anything but his own needs. Moreover Joan was at hand to hurry him off to their home in Berkhamstead and there she set about nursing him and comforting him for the terrible losses he had sustained on the deaths of Chandos and young Edward.

The reign of Alice Perrers showed no sign of coming to an end. The King grew more and more besotted. Alice had given birth to a little girl whom she called Jane and although the hatred of the people was intensified with the passing of the time, she kept a firm hold on her power.

Edward gave great jousts in her honour and at these she would sit beside him far more sumptuously gowned than Philippa had ever been.

The King was showing his age and many people thought that his end was near. Until the death of Philippa he had looked younger than he actually was and had had more vigour than men half his age, but the life he was living with Alice was beginning to show its effects. Alice herself wondered how long it could last for her.

If he died that would be the end of her glory and as she remarked to a certain somewhat impoverished knight who had taken her fancy: A woman must take care of the future.

Alice was doing that very well. As soon as her eyes alighted on a jewel she had the urge to make it hers. She took great delight in finding new ways of enriching herself and she was doing very well. But she had to think of the future.

The man on whom her fancy had fixed itself was William de Windsor. He was not of high noble birth nor was he possessed of great wealth; but could she have expected some noble knight to marry her? Of course she could not. Her marriage would have to be secret for if it were known that she were married she would immediately be accused of adultery – and so would the King. They would have the meddling prelates talking of excommunicating them – and that was something even drooling old Edward would have to take seriously.

William de Windsor was nothing loth. He saw a far more brilliant future with Alice than he could hope for without her. Besides she was a woman of wide sexual knowledge which promised to bring some excitement into his colourless life.

So they were married . . . in the utmost secrecy and when Alice gave birth to another daughter it was easy to pass young Joan off as the King's.

It was an amusing life and riches flowed into Alice's pockets.

The King's devotion did not diminish and the older he grew the more he was her slave.

He would give a great joust at Smithfield in her honour. She should be the Lady of the Sun. She would be there as a Queen and all should do honour to her. She would ride from the Tower of London to Cheapside and her garments would come from the royal wardrobes.

It was a great day for Alice. There she rode at the head of the cavalcade in a russet and white gown edged with ermine and decorated with gold thread. From under her leather cap her beautiful dark hair flowed about her shoulders; her great dark eyes bright with excitement beamed on the crowd who could only stare in wonder and awe at this low-born woman who had captured the heart of a great King.

England was in a sorry state and the French took advantage of it. The Black Prince was growing weaker every day. There had been no more children born to him and Joan and the heir to the throne was the young boy Richard of Bordeaux.

John of Gaunt had returned to England and almost all the English conquests in France were now in the hands of the French. The wily John showed friendship to Alice Perrers in order to curry favour with his father and consequently was acting as Regent in the government of the country.

Isabella's husband had left her in England and showed no signs of returning to her. She was sad and remained at Court although she knew that to keep close to her father she must placate Alice.

Lionel had died in Italy; Edmund and Thomas showed no particular talents; and the great and heroic deeds of the King's earlier years seemed to have been in vain.

The Black Prince followed events with growing melancholy. Although on his return to England his fever had abated a little the attacks returned and they were becoming more frequent. He was filled with misgiving when he watched his little son Richard. What would become of him? he wondered. How long could the King last? His health was deteriorating rapidly; and what of himself? How long could he continue? He knew that the disease he had contracted would kill him in time. It seemed inevitable that this little Richard would be King before he came of age. John of Gaunt longed for the crown. He was clever and cunning. How would this innocent boy fare against him?

'Give me strength to live until my son is of age to rule,' he prayed. 'Give me time to teach him what he must know.'

In the meantime there was the old King ruled by a loose woman who had no sense of honour and whose one idea was to amass as much wealth as she could. The people were restive. How long would they accept the state of affairs into which the country was falling?

If only the King would be as he once was – strong, just! None could deny that Edward had been one of the greatest kings England had known before this senility had overtaken him. If only Philippa had lived. Ah yes, if only Philippa had lived! If only the Black Prince, hero of Crécy and Poitiers, had his strength.

It was almost impossible to believe how England could have been brought so low through a chain of some unexpected circumstances. The death of the Queen; the domination of Alice Perrers over a King who had slipped from greatness to senility; a fever-stricken Prince of Wales; a scheming John of Gaunt; and an heir to the throne who was little more than a baby.

The Prince had emerged from the fever and was feeling a little better when William of Wykeham, Bishop of Winchester came to Berkhamstead in some haste and excitement. William of Wykeham had always been a friend of the Black Prince and with him had deplored the way in which England was declining.

He immediately told the Prince the reason for his visit.

'I think, my lord,' he said, 'that we now have what we need to break this association between the King and the strumpet. I have discovered that she is married and therefore commits adultery.'

The Prince was excited. 'Is this indeed so? Can it be proved? The matter should be laid before the Parliament.'

'Indeed it shall be, my lord. The woman's adultery shall be considered and with it the evil practices of bribery and corruption which she has brought about. This gives us an opportunity.'

'Let us make good use of it,' replied the Prince.

He felt better. There was a chance. The King would have to give up Alice Perrers. The thought of it made him feel well again. He was going to get up from his bed. He was going to be the strong man again. His father, rid of that woman, would return to his old way of life. Who knew he might have many years before him and after him would come the Black Prince and years and years ahead when Richard was a man taught wisdom by those of experience the crown should be placed on his head and England be prosperous again.

The Parliament assembled. Its members were ready to go against the wishes of their King and the people rejoiced for they, like the Black Prince, believed that this Parliament could bring about a return to the old sane ways. They called the Parliament the Good Parliament. It was supported by their idol the Black Prince and it would work against John of Gaunt whom they disliked and moreover it would bring to light the evil practices of Alice Perrers.

The Parliament lived up to the people's expectations. Alice was summoned to appear. She was accused of practising nefariously in the courts of law, of meddling in other matters and of having seduced the King through black magic.

Alice displayed an insolence which did her little good and the result was that she was dismissed from Court and threatened with excommunication if she returned.

The King was desolate. A delegation headed by the Bishop of Winchester called on him and told him that Alice had married William de Windsor and therefore he and she were committing adultery.

'I refuse to believe it,' he cried in anguish. 'She has never married anyone.'

They proved that she had recently done so, and he was overcome with grief.

'She is also guilty of fraud and theft,' he was told.

'She has done nothing without my consent.'

'My lord, even so she is guilty.'

There was not a man present who was not amazed at the state to which this once great King was reduced. A few years ago which one of them would have dared stand before him and tell him what he must do?

Now he listened meekly. He said: 'I beg of you deal with her gently.'

Great Edward left them and went to his bedchamber and wept.

❧ ❧ ❧

When the Black Prince heard that Alice was dismissed from Court he was delighted.

He knew that throughout the country people were looking to him. They knew that it was his support and his strength which had given the Good Parliament the courage to defy the King and send Alice from Court. But what everyone was marvelling at was that Edward should have allowed it.

He must indeed be a sick man.

During the weeks that followed the Prince's health deteriorated rapidly.

He sent for his little son Richard, a boy of nine, handsome, bright, alert. God preserve him, he prayed. If only he were a little older! If only his brother Edward had lived!

What could he say to Richard? How could he instil into that young head the importance of the destiny which lay ahead of him.

He asked that the King should come to him for he was too sick to go to him.

Edward came and sat by his son's bedside. His grief was intense.

This son of his, this noble knight, could he be this sick and wasted man! How could God be so cruel to him! He remembered when this son had been born to him and Philippa and their great delight in him and when he grew to manhood it had seemed that all their dreams had been fulfilled in him.

Crécy. Such a boy he had been. 'Let the boy win his spurs,' he had said; and how he had won them! How the people had loved him! He had been their perfect knight, the symbol of chivalry; people had bowed their heads in reverence at the mention of the name of the Black Prince.

'Oh my son, my son,' sobbed the King. 'Can this really be the end? It must not be. You will recover. You will be strong again. I need you, Edward. The country needs you.'

The Prince shook his head. 'I am dying, Father. I know it well. I grieve to leave you . . . and England. There are three wishes I have to ask of you. Confirm those gifts which I have bestowed, pay my debts from my estate and above all protect my son from his enemies. He is young yet . . . only a boy. I fear for him, Father.'

'You will live to reign after me, my son and I am not dead yet.'

'Oh Father, you must live, you must not go . . . not yet . . . not yet . . .'

The King promised that he would do all his son asked of him and went sorrowing away.

Joan knew that the end was near and there was nothing she could do to prevent it. She had nursed her husband through his illness and for a long time she knew that she must be prepared for the end.

All that was left to her now was her boy. A great responsibility rested with her for when his father died that boy would be the heir to the throne.

There would be those who would try to depose him. It was always so when a boy became King.

She prayed for strength and she knew it would be granted her.

In the meantime she did all she could to keep her husband alive.

There came that day when the Black Prince sent for the Bishop of Bangor and his family gathered about his bed.

He prayed for forgiveness of those he had wronged and that

God would pardon him his sins. As he died his eyes were on the stricken face of the little boy Richard who could not then understand what the future held for him.

The King was overcome with grief. He gave orders that his son should be buried with great ceremony in Canterbury Cathedral and his surcoat, helmet, shield and gauntlets hung over his tomb that none might forget that the greatest of all warriors lay there.

With the death of the Black Prince Edward dismissed the Good Parliament. John of Gaunt was in the ascendancy and appeared to have complete power over his father.

With the latter's connivance Edward recalled Alice who came back with the utmost exuberance.

The people were enraged but in view of the King's obviously failing health they did not insist on taking Alice from him.

She certainly pleased the King and he was almost happy with her because she could make him forget that the prosperity of the country which he had taken such pains and a lifetime of endeavour and attention to duty to build up was crumbling. She would not let him remember that he was leaving a restless kingdom to a young boy who had no experience of ruling. He shut his eyes to the ambitions of John of Gaunt and sank into a state of euphoria.

Alice was back. Alice had comfort to offer. She would not accept the fact that he had a short time to live.

'Nonsense,' she cried. 'You are not dying. You and I are going to ride out together to the hunt. I have a new falcon. I am going to show him to you. You must hurry and get well so that we can ride together.'

So eagerly did she talk, so loudly did she laugh that he believed her.

'Alice, my love, we shall ride out together. Shall we have another joust at Smithfield? I shall never forget you riding as the Queen of the Sun. You are Queen of the Day and Queen of the Night, my Alice. There was never anyone like you.'

Sometimes he was drowsy dreaming of the past. He would have Alice beside him, her vibrant looks contrasting sadly with his ageing ones. But with her he felt young again. He was convinced that they would ride into the forest and there would be a joust and he would carry her favour on his helmet. He would be the champion of them all again as he had been in the past.

He was so feeble that he must as yet stay in his bed. Few people came near him. That did not matter while he had Alice.

'We shall have a tournament,' she said, 'as soon as you are able to get up. And that will be soon.'

'Will it, Alice? Do you think it will?'

'I know so. I must have a gown which shall be studded with pearls, and furred with ermine. I shall need a zone of emeralds and rubies to go with it. Shall I order it to be made?'

'Do so,' he answered. 'Do so.'

She kissed him fervently. 'You are the best man in the world,' she told him.

Her zone was to be made at all speed. She was well aware that there must be no delays. She knew even as she talked of hawking and hunting and the lavish jousts, that time was running out.

The whole Court knew it. It was no longer necessary to show respect for the King. How could they when it meant getting past the strumpet as they called her.

She ordered the immediate servants to do her bidding; they brought food which he was too weak to eat.

Shrewdly Alice watched. It would not be long now.

There came the morning when he lay still unable to speak and death had set its mark clearly on his brow.

He would never speak to her again. He would never smile at her.

She knew that in his mind he was far away.

He was with Philippa of Hainault, the first time he had seen her, a rosy-cheeked buxom girl standing in the great hall with her sisters. He had known she was the one and she had known it too. He remembered her bursting into tears when he had said good-bye . . . there before the assembled Court. It was then that he had loved her and determined to marry her.

They had been happy together – an ideal marriage it had been. Fruitful, happy and he had known she was the best woman in the world.

Only once had she failed him . . . by dying. And then everything had gone wrong.

The light was fading and darkness was enveloping him. He was going to Philippa now . . .

Something touched his hands he believed, but he was not sure. He was too tired to look.

It was Alice quickly taking the rings from his fingers. The time had come for her to leave.

There was only one priest at his bedside. He was holding the cross before his eyes.

'Jesu miserere . . .' murmured Edward.

This was the passing of Great Edward. He was buried as he had commanded he should be in Westminster Abbey close to the body of Philippa.

🏵 Bibliography 🏵

Aubrey, William Hickman Smith, *National and Domestic History of England*

Bain, Joseph *The Edwards in Scotland*

Barnes, Joshua *History of Edward III and the Black Prince*

Bryant, Arthur *The Medieval Foundation*

Cammidge, John *The Black Prince, An Historical Pageant*

Costain, Thomas *The Pageant of England 1272–1377 The Three Edwards*

Davis, H. W. C. *England Under the Angevins*

Green, John Richard *History of England*

Green, Mary Anne Everett *Lives of the Princesses of England from the Norman Conquest*

Guizot, M. *History of France* Translated by Robert Black

Hardy, B. C. *Philippa of Hainault and Her Times*

Hume, David *History of England from the Invasion of Julius Caesar to the Revolution*

Johnson, Paul *Life and Times of Edward III*

Longman, William *The Life and Times of Edward III History of Edward III*

Mackinnon, James *History of Edward III*

Norgate, Kate *England Under the Angevin Kings*

Stenton, D. M. *English Society in the Middle Ages*

Stephen, Sir Leslie and Lee, Sir Sidney *The Dictionary of National Biography*

Strickland, Agnes *Lives of the Queens of England*

Wade, John *British History*

Warburton, Rev W. *Edward III*